Praise for Carolyne Aarsen's **novels**

"Carolyne Aarsen writes with tender empathy and a true understanding of the struggles her characters endure in *A Family-Style Christmas*."
—*RT Book Reviews*

"A warmhearted story of great sorrow and the healing and hope for the future God can supply."
—*RT Book Reviews* on *The Rancher's Return*

"In this heartfelt story, Aarsen reminds us that life's challenges can be met and overcome by trusting in one's faith."
—*RT Book Reviews* on *The Cowboy's Lady*

"An emotional story."
—*RT Book Reviews* on *The Baby Promise*

CAROLYNE AARSEN

A Family-Style Christmas
&
A Mother at Heart

HARLEQUIN® LOVE INSPIRED®CLASSICS

LOVE INSPIRED BOOKS

Recycling programs for this product may not exist in your area.

ISBN-13: 978-0-373-20863-0

A Family-Style Christmas & A Mother at Heart

Copyright © 2017 by Harlequin Books S.A.

The publisher acknowledges the copyright holder of the individual works as follows:

A Family-Style Christmas
Copyright © 2000 by Carolyne Aarsen

A Mother at Heart
Copyright © 2000 by Carolyne Aarsen

www.Harlequin.com

Printed in U.S.A.

CONTENTS

A FAMILY-STYLE CHRISTMAS   7

A MOTHER AT HEART   213

Carolyne Aarsen and her husband, Richard, live on a small ranch in northern Alberta, where they have raised four children and numerous foster children and are still raising cattle. Carolyne crafts her stories in an office with a large west-facing window, through which she can watch the changing seasons while struggling to make her words obey. Visit her website at carolyneaarsen.com.

Books by Carolyne Aarsen

Love Inspired

Cowboys of Cedar Ridge

Courting the Cowboy
Second-Chance Cowboy

Big Sky Cowboys

Wrangling the Cowboy's Heart
Trusting the Cowboy
The Cowboy's Christmas Baby

Lone Star Cowboy League

A Family for the Soldier

Refuge Ranch

Her Cowboy Hero
Reunited with the Cowboy
The Cowboy's Homecoming

Hearts of Hartley Creek

A Father's Promise
Unexpected Father
A Father in the Making

Visit the Author Profile page at Harlequin.com for more titles.

A FAMILY-STYLE CHRISTMAS

As a mother comforts her child,
so I will comfort you.
—*Isaiah* 66:13

This book is dedicated to all foster parents, official and unofficial. May God give you the strength and love you need.

I owe a big thank-you to Anne Canadeo, who has been an encouraging and inspiring editor on my first four books. I also want to thank my new editor, Ann Leslie Tuttle, for her enthusiastic help on this series.

Besides the fact that my sister-in-law and good friend are both nurses, I make no claim to being an expert on nursing care. I had help in that department from Corinne Aarsen, Diane Wierenga and Ruth McNulty. Thank you as well to Steve Kondics, Hera Angelo and Heather Toporowsky.

Prologue

"This is a fire-sale price, Simon, and you know it."

Simon Steele slipped his hands in the pockets of his leather jacket and lifted one shoulder in a shrug, negating the earnest comment from the real estate agent.

"Maybe," he drawled. "We both know the bank wants to dump this property, Blaine. Badly. The building needs major renovations to attract decent renters or owners." His quick glance took in the stained carpets and marked walls of the lobby before slanting the real estate agent a meaningful look and a smirk. "I'm prepared to offer thirty thousand less than the asking price. Firm." He ignored his partner, Oscar Delaney, who stood behind Blaine, shaking his head.

To his credit Blaine Nowicki never batted an eye. "Of course, I'll have to speak to my client on that and get back to you…"

"Phone them now and let's get this deal done," Simon interrupted, glancing at his watch. He didn't feel like playing out this fish any longer. He and Oscar had done their homework. They knew the situation at the bank and how long this particular apartment block had been on the market.

Long enough that Blaine's clients were willing to settle more quickly than he'd intimated.

"Simon, you're enough of a dealer to know that can't be done this quickly." Blaine fiddled with his tie as he favored Simon with an overly familiar smile that set Simon's teeth on edge. "This is a prime piece of property and worth far more than you're offering."

Simon held Blaine's determined gaze, his own features devoid of emotion. He lifted his hands, still in the pockets of his coat, signaling surrender. "Then, I'm history." He angled his chin in his partner's direction, "Let's go, Oscar. We've got a ferry to catch."

He turned and started walking away, measuring his tread so he looked like he was going quickly, yet giving Blaine enough time to protest before Simon hit the front doors of the lobby.

Oscar caught up to him, glancing sidelong at his partner with a frown. Simon gave him a warning shake of his head, then slowed fractionally as they approached the double doors.

For a moment he wondered if he had underestimated Blaine as he pulled his hand out of his pocket to grab the brass bar when...

"Wait," Blaine called out.

Simon allowed himself a moment of triumph, threw his partner an I-told-you-so glance, then forced the smirk off his face. When he turned to face Blaine, he was all business again.

"I'll call them right now," Blaine said, his cell phone in hand, his jacket flying open as he rushed over. "See what I can do for you." He punched in the numbers, frowning intently. Simon lifted his eyebrows at Oscar, who grinned back.

In ten minutes the papers were signed and Oscar and Simon were standing outside the building they had just purchased.

"I hope you know what you're doing," Oscar said as they stood outside on the pavement, shivering in the damp that had rolled in.

Simon looked back at the five-story apartment block behind them. The first-story walls were pitted and marked, covered with graffiti. A few of the sliding glass doors were boarded up, but the rest of the building was sound.

"When you get back from vacation, we'll get some quotes on renovations," Simon said, pulling his keys out of his pocket. "It's got a decent location. I'm sure once we get this thing fixed up, it will be full." He turned, squinting across the bay toward the hills of Vancouver Island now shrouded by the drizzle that had descended. He swung the keys around his finger. "It has a great view."

"When it's not raining," Oscar said, pulling his glasses off to clean them.

Simon grinned at his partner. "You sure you don't want to head south to the sun instead of camping with your wife's relatives? Why don't you come where I'm headed?"

"Right," Oscar said drily, replacing his glasses. "I can see us already. Two overgrown teenagers on motorbikes heading down to the Baja." He pulled his coat closer, giving another shiver, moisture beading up on his dark blond hair. "Someone's got to be the mature, responsible one in this partnership."

Simon pulled a face. "Please, no bad language," he said with a laugh.

Oscar looked back at the apartment block. "You know, one of these days you should buy yourself a house instead of old apartment blocks and new businesses." He looked back at Simon, his expression serious.

"And start a family. Why not?" Simon flipped his keys once more, his tone sardonic. "One of those nice cozy groups of people you see on television commercials selling long-distance phone plans."

"Being on your own is no picnic," Oscar said as they headed toward a nearly deserted parking lot.

Simon stopped beside his bike and zipped up his leather coat with a decisive movement. "It's a whole lot easier than trying to work around other people's needs."

"Mr. Free Spirit personified," said Oscar with a rueful shake of his head. "One of these days you're going to get too old to keep running. Then you'll be panting and wheezing, wishing you had taken my advice and bought a nice house, found a nice girl and settled down."

"There is no such thing as a nice girl."

"Oh, c'mon. You just don't know where to look."

Simon pulled his helmet off his motorbike and dropped it on his head. "I suppose I could head out to your church. Scope out the girls there."

"Wouldn't hurt you to go once in a while anyhow." Oscar shivered again. "I gotta go. I've got a few things to do at the office before Angela and I leave town. She told her folks we'd be there before supper."

"See what I mean?" Simon said, buckling up his helmet. "Family means schedule, expectations. Watch the clock. Stifling routine."

Oscar just looked at him, and Simon felt a flicker of reproach in his partner's gaze.

"Family means people who care, too, Simon," Oscar said quietly. Simon looked away, snapping the top snap of his jacket, pulling on his gloves.

"Can't speak from personal experience on that," he said, forcing a light tone into his voice. He looked up at Oscar and shrugged the comment away. "I'll see you in a couple of weeks."

"Take care of yourself," Oscar said, hesitating as if he would have liked to say more. Then he got in his vehicle and left.

Simon watched him go, his shoulders lifting in a sigh. He and Oscar had been partners for three years now. Oscar was a discreet sort of guy. He didn't pry, didn't ask a lot of questions and didn't intrude on Simon's personal life. Which was just what Simon wanted in a partner.

Simon liked things to be businesslike and at an arm's length distance from him. It made things a lot easier that way. The less people knew about you, the less of a hold they had over you. Strict access to information, he reminded himself as he pulled his leather pants over his now-damp jeans. That's what made his and Oscar's partnership work so well. Oscar only knew what he needed to know about Simon that pertained to how their partnership worked and vice versa.

Starting his bike, Simon turned onto the Island Highway and settled into a safe speed. He still had lots of time and would probably beat Oscar to the ferry.

As he drove his mind went back to his conversation with Oscar. He wished Oscar would lay off the broad hints about settling down. It was like an obsession with him.

Three years ago he and Oscar had met in a bar, had formed their loosely based partnership on the basis of a shared interest in the stock market and real estate.

Then Oscar got married, got religion and was now the sickeningly proud father of a little girl. Like a reformed smoker he was on Simon's case to follow suit.

Something Simon had no intention of doing. Oscar might look happy now, but people always let you down. That much Simon knew from personal experience.

And the many foster homes he'd been in after his mother had given him and his brother up for adoption when he was four. As far as he knew he had no other family. For a brief while, they'd had a loving father, Tom Steele—a widower who adopted them. When he'd died, he and Jake were moved, then moved again and finally split up.

Now Simon had no one.

He cut in front of a car and wove through the traffic, pushing the memories back into the recesses of his mind where they belonged. Living in the past did nothing for the present. And for the present, he was doing quite well, thank you very much. He and Oscar had a good business going. They made enough money that they could both take vacations when it suited them. And he could do pretty much as he pleased.

Yes, Simon thought as he gave the throttle another twist, he was doing very well indeed.

Chapter One

Heartbreak must be a regular occurrence here, Caitlin Severn thought, ignoring the elegantly dressed people in the hotel lobby who were politely ignoring her. She would have liked to walk through the lobby with her head up, but she couldn't. Her eyes prickled with unshed tears, and her nose was starting to run. It always did when she cried. She gave her eyes a careful wipe, and walked down the few steps toward the entrance.

When she got there, she stopped.

Perfect, she thought, staring out at the moisture dripping down the glass door. Her life was becoming more like a bad movie script with each passing moment. This unexpected drizzle was a dramatic touch. All she was missing was a soaring soundtrack.

She hugged herself, glancing over her shoulder as if hoping that by doing so, Charles would come running up to her, pleading with her to change her mind. But he didn't.

The world carried on. Clichéd, but true. Nothing had stopped just because her own world had been rearranged.

Just ten minutes ago she had broken up with Charles

Frost. Again. When Charles had made this date, he'd said he had some special news. They'd been dating for three years, and she foolishly thought he was going to propose. Instead he told her about his promotion and subsequent move to Los Angeles.

In the moment when he lifted his glass of wine to her to toast his success, Caitlin was faced with something she knew she'd been avoiding.

Charles's career would always come before her.

Caitlin knew that this was not how she wanted to live her life.

So with a few succinct words, she broke up with him.

Caitlin took a step closer to the front doors and was grateful to see a row of cabs. With a last glance over her shoulder, she stepped out into the early-evening drizzle.

She walked down the sidewalk, her high heels clicking on the wet pavement, moisture beading up on the fine fabric of the short, fitted dress she had chosen so carefully for this date and the "important news" Charles had to tell her.

Important to him, she thought with another sniff.

She hailed the first cab, then got in. She gave him quick directions to her home, then sat back, shivering with a combination of cold and reaction, thankful she had an escape.

As the driver pulled away from the front of the restaurant, she felt the first sob climb up her throat. She covered her mouth with her fist, but the hoarse cry slipped past her clenched hand into the quiet confines of the cab. One more got past her guard before Caitlin regained control. The cabbie didn't even look back.

She wouldn't cry, she thought as she defiantly swiped at her cheeks.

But Caitlin knew it was more than her breakup with Charles she grieved.

She watched out the window vaguely noting the buildings flowing by. She had lived in Nanaimo in Vancouver Island all her life and had never moved. It seemed as if her life had flowed along the same lines for the past twenty-eight years.

Twenty-eight and single again. Tonight, after their supper, she and Charles were to have gone to stay with his parents at their cabin on Pender Island for ten days.

And now...

Caitlin sighed. She wished she could skip the next few days and head back to work right away. The comforting steadiness of her work at the hospital would have taken her through the week, would have helped her get over the pain she felt. Now she didn't even have that.

Thankfully the driver was silent. The tires of the cab hissed over the wet pavement as a lethargy came over her. Reaction, she thought remembering all too easily the sight of Charles's impassive face as she delivered her ultimatum.

He just didn't care.

The entire evening stretched ahead of her, and she didn't feel like going home. She knew what would be waiting there. Her dear parents sitting in their usual chairs, drinking tea. Her sister Rachel would be curled up with her husband, Jonathon, on the couch, reading while soft music played on the stereo. Rachel, who had just told their parents she was expecting.

Caitlin had been jealous.

Caitlin shook her head at that thought. She was unable to put her finger precisely on why. It had much to do with the malaise she felt before she broke up with

Charles. That her life was following the same path without any variation. She had the job she had trained for. She loved her work. But she still wanted someone in her life. Someone who needed her. She wanted to start her own family.

A blast from a motorcycle passing them made her jump. It zoomed ahead, then slowed as the cab caught up. Puzzled, she watched, wondering what the motorcycle driver was doing. She found out as soon as the cab came up beside him again. In the bright streetlights, she saw the driver look sideways and, with a cheeky grin, wink at her.

Caitlin only stared back as he kept pace, still looking at her. He didn't look like anyone she would know. His well-shaped mouth had an insolent twist to it, his eyes shaded by his helmet seemed to laugh at her. Not her type.

Then he tossed a wave in her direction and with a twist of his wrist and a flick of his foot, was off again.

Caitlin shook her head at his audacity, watching as he wove expertly around the cab and the vehicle slightly ahead of them. Then a car swerved unexpectedly.

She heard a sickening *thud* as the car hit the biker. The bike wove once, then dropped, spinning in one direction while the driver shot off in another.

The cabdriver slammed on the brakes and swerved to miss the driver.

"Stop," yelled Caitlin, leaning over the seat. "I'm a nurse. Stop."

The cabbie screeched to a halt twenty feet away from the driver, who now lay in a crumpled heap on the side of the road.

The car that caused the accident slowed, then sped away.

Caitlin's breath left her in a swoosh, her hands shaking as she fumbled for the catch on the door. Finally she pushed it open and shot out of the cab. She ran to the driver who was moaning softly.

"Thank you Lord," she breathed at the sound. He was still alive.

Ignoring the expensive hose bought for this, her special night, the drizzle dripping down her neck, she dropped onto the wet pavement.

The cabbie came up behind her. "I called an ambulance, and the police," he said.

"Get me something to cover him with," she called out, as she automatically did her own assessment of the situation, drawing on her limited experience with emergencies. The man had a pulse, was breathing, albeit shallowly, and blood from a head injury ran in an ugly rivulet down his forehead. His leg was twisted at a grotesque angle. His leather coat was ripped.

Possible broken femur and spine injury, Caitlin thought, noting the angle of his leg. He's in big trouble. She knelt close to keep him from moving, her finger on his pulse as she counted and prayed.

The cabdriver came back with an overcoat. "This is the best I could do. I got a first-aid kit, too."

Caitlin opened the kit as he spread the coat over the prone man. Right about now she regretted not having had more emergency training. In her ward at the hospital, she only got the patients from the operating room or emergency. All the critical care had been done by either paramedics or emergency room nurses.

Caitlin willed the ambulance to come, praying as she dug through the kit for a bandage to stop the bleeding from the most serious cut on his head. Her sore knees trembled with tension, she almost shivered in the damp weather, but she was afraid to shift position.

The man at her feet moaned, tried to roll over but was stopped by Caitlin's knees. He cried out, and his eyes flew open, staring straight up at Caitlin. "Hey, angel, you found me," he murmured, then his face twisted in pain.

Caitlin felt relief sluice through her in an icy wave even as she steeled herself against the sounds of his pain. Thankfully he was conscious. That meant no major head injury other than the cut on his temple. She carefully laid the pad on his head wound, applying pressure. "Can you feel your hands, your feet?"

"Yeah." She could tell that even that one word was an effort. "Feel too much."

"What's your name?"

"Doesn't matter..." He bit his lip. "Please stay."

"Are you allergic to anything?"

"No." He blinked, looking up at her, then arched his back and cried out again, grabbing her hand.

Caitlin winced at his strength. "Can you tell me where it hurts the most?"

"Everywhere." His words were slurred, and Caitlin feared he would lose consciousness after all.

"What's your name?" she repeated.

"You're a pain," he mumbled, still clinging to her hand. "Everything's a pain." He squeezed her hand, hard, moaning. "Who are you, angel?"

"I'm Caitlin. Tell me your name. Stay with me."

But though his hand clung tightly, he wouldn't answer.

"Please, Lord, keep him with us," she prayed aloud. "Keep him safe, help him. Please send that ambulance, now."

She watched him as she prayed. His eyes were shut, his lashes lying in dark spikes against his high cheekbones. His hair hung over his forehead, some of the strands caught in the trickle of blood from the wound on his forehead, curling in the damp.

He looked to be in his late twenties, well built, she reasoned from the weight of his body against her legs, the breadth of his shoulders. It made his vulnerability all the more heart-wrenching. Caitlin wanted to check his pulse, but his hand still held hers in a death grip.

"Can I do anything?" The cabdriver hovered over her.

Caitlin glanced over her shoulder, feeling utterly helpless.

"Pray the ambulance comes quickly," she said, shivering with reaction. The wind had picked up, chilling her.

In her peripheral vision she saw a few people coming out of their houses, some offering help. Someone even dropped a coat across her shoulders.

The victim's hand still clutched hers. Thankfully the flow of blood from his forehead eased, and Caitlin could put her finger on his pulse. It was weak, but then his grip loosened and his pulse slowed. Her prayers became more urgent as his eyes remained closed and beneath her trembling fingers she felt his life ebb away.

"Please, Lord, don't let him go. He's so young," she whispered, watching him. Nothing.

His breathing slowed.

Caitlin lifted his hand, clasped it against hers, her other hand still on his nonexistent pulse. *Please don't take him.*

Then, suddenly, his pulse returned, his hand tightened on hers.

His eyes fluttered open.

"You're still praying," he gasped.

"Yes, I am," Caitlin replied, relief turning her bones to rubber. He was still with her, he was still alive. "Thank you, Lord," she breathed.

She knew it wasn't over yet. His broken femur and the accompanying loss of blood were life threatening.

But she was reassured by the solid answer she received—a touch of God's hand on the situation.

"You're wasting your time praying," he said, his teeth clenched against the pain.

"No, I'm not," Caitlin whispered, shaky with reaction.

Then came the welcome wail of an ambulance's sirens and its blue and red lights, flashing through the gathering dusk.

"What happened?" A paramedic ran up to Caitlin while the driver jumped out and pulled the stretcher out of the back.

"Motorcycle accident." As relief weakened her legs, she forced herself to stay calm, to be the professional nurse she was, relating what she had seen of the accident and how she'd treated his injuries. The police could deal with the driver of the car. She was more concerned about her patient. As the older of the paramedics immediately positioned himself at the victim's head, stabilizing it, she said, "I'm a nurse so tell me what to do."

"Just step back for now, ma'am."

She quickly got up and out of the way, her knees aching. She drew the stranger's coat around her, shivering against the chill wind.

The paramedic at the victim's head had his knees on either side, stabilizing him as he checked his breathing, the pulse at his throat. "Give me O2, ten liters, nonrebreather," he called out to his partner as he lifted the victim's eyelids.

"He's conscious. Superficial head injury," the young paramedic said as he started an IV.

"I need a C collar, large."

"Spine seems okay, no internal injuries so far. Fracture of right femur. Both arms, okay. Possible sprain."

"Got the fracture stabilized."

"Let's get him on the board."

The older paramedic at his head looked up at Caitlin. "We'll need your help, now, ma'am."

She nodded, and positioned herself. "Watch for that fracture," she couldn't help saying.

"On three." They rolled him onto the board, the paramedic still holding his head. With quick, efficient movements they had the victim strapped in, stabilizing him. Someone handed her her purse while she watched. The paramedics placed foam on either side of his head, taped the foam in, strapped the spine board on the stretcher and slid him into the ambulance, headfirst. It was all done with a calm efficiency that drew Caitlin along, comforting her. Routine she understood. What she didn't understand was her reluctance to let this man go.

"I'm coming," Caitlin decided suddenly. She handed the coat to someone and scooted into the ambulance before it sped away.

Caitlin's head ached in the overly bright lights of the ambulance's interior as she braced herself against the movement. She sat down on the long bench beside the stretcher. Vaguely she heard the driver on the radio, "Patch me into the hospital…"

Caitlin felt as if her breath still had to catch up to her.

The older paramedic switched the oxygen to a fixture in the wall of the ambulance.

"What can I do?" she asked, reaction setting in. She was a nurse, and she needed to be busy.

"Here's a blood pressure cuff and stethoscope. Get me a set of vitals." He smiled at her as he handed her the equipment. "I'm Stan."

"I'm Caitlin." She unrolled the cuff and stuck the stethoscope in her ears.

"Hey, guy, you with me?" Stan asked the victim while he did a head-to-toe check again, opening the patient's leather jacket and his shirt to check his chest and stomach. "What's his name?" he asked Caitlin, as he worked.

"I don't know," Caitlin looked up at Stan, then down at the patient. His face was hidden by the oxygen mask, his eyes shut. His skin had a waxy pallor that concerned her.

The driver called back, "Is he awake?"

"Yes, but poor response. He's a little shocky," said Stan, as he steadied himself in the moving ambulance.

"Vitals are BP 118 on 76, pulse 116, respirations 24," Caitlin told him, pulling the stethoscope out of her ears.

Stan nodded as he pressed on the patient's sternum. The ambulance swayed around a corner and then with a short wail of sirens, came to a stop.

"Let's go, Caitlin," Stan said as he pulled a blanket over the patient. The door swung open, and Caitlin grabbed the coat and purse, exiting with the stretcher into a murmur of voices.

She strode alongside the stretcher as they entered the warmth and light of the hospital, watching the unknown man. His eyes flickered open, looked wildly around.

Caitlin lightly touched his face and he homed in on her. He blinked, and through the oxygen mask she saw his lips move. He lifted his hand toward her, then with a grimace of pain, faded away again.

Stan gave the triage nurse and doctor a quick rundown of what he knew and what they had done.

"Put him in the trauma room," she said and Caitlin stood back while they wheeled the stranger down the hall and away from her.

It was over, but she still couldn't walk away.

Caitlin felt the noise and heat press in on her aching head. For a brief moment, she felt all alone in a room full of people caught up in their own pains and sorrows.

She found an empty chair and sat on the edge, bunching her purse on her lap. Unbelievably the delicate shawl was still wound around her shoulder but her nylons sported a large hole in one knee, she noted with a disoriented feeling.

As an orthopedic nurse she rarely saw death. When she did, it was in a hospital setting where there was immediate help. Routine. What she had seen tonight was raw and powerful—a potent reminder of how fragile life was.

She heard a measured tread and looked up as the paramedic named Stan stood in front of her.

"Caitlin, you okay?"

"Yeah, I'm fine." She smiled weakly up at him, surprised he remembered her name. "How is he?"

"They've got him stabilized. They're going to get him into OR right away. He's been asking for you by name. Do you know him?"

"No. I gave my name when I was trying to find out about him." Caitlin frowned, surprised this man who must be in a tremendous amount of pain would remember her. "Can I see him?"

"He's headed for the operation room. But if you wait, you might catch a glimpse of him as he's wheeled by."

Caitlin got up, her knees still trembling. She followed Stan down the hallway, her shoes clicking loudly on the floor. "Just wait here," he said. "I've got to go now. Take care, Caitlin."

Nodding, Caitlin waited until the curtain on the cubicle was pushed aside and the stretcher wheeled out.

Caitlin caught up to the stretcher, walking quickly alongside it.

"Are you Caitlin?" the nurse pushing the stretcher asked.

"Yes," Caitlin replied quietly, looking down at the stranger, his face still obscured by the oxygen mask. His eyes were open, focused intently on her, his hair still matted with blood. Caitlin couldn't stop staring at him. His high cheekbones and full mouth gave his features a fascinating appeal.

He reached out for her and once again, Caitlin caught his hand. "You'll be okay," she said as they hurried down the hallway. "I'll be praying for you. You're in good hands."

"I am now," he said, his voice muffled by the oxygen mask, his hand squeezing hers.

Chapter Two

This is ridiculous, Caitlin thought as she strode down the hallway to her own unit. You don't know anything about that motorcycle victim. He's not your concern. For the past two hours she had wandered around the emergency department, then gone for coffee. It was now nine thirty, and she'd decided to see this through to the end and go up to the ward where the unknown man would be taken after surgery.

It was the best way she knew of avoiding home and facing the questions of her family when she showed up there. It seemed the only logical thing to do.

Sort of logical, she thought, ignoring her self-doubts over this impulsive, un-Caitlin-like behavior.

She approached the desk of the ward she had been working at since she graduated from nursing school. It was as familiar to her as her own street.

And so was the face of the nurse at the desk.

"Hey, Caitlin, what are you doing here?" Danielle asked, leaning her elbows on the desk, fully prepared to chat. "Thought you and Charles had a date?"

"We did. I cut it short." She knew she had taken a

chance coming up here instead of going home. Danielle Jones and Caitlin had been friends since nursing school. Danielle knew all Caitlin's secrets. But coming to her ward seemed the less painful of two evils. "You busy?"

"Steady. Got a guy coming up from OR in a while. Motorcycle accident."

Caitlin felt a guilty flush climb up her cheeks. "I know," she said. "I saw it happen."

Danielle frowned, shaking her head. "That must have been horrible. That why you cut your date with Charles short?" She glanced over Caitlin's dress. "By the way you look gorgeous, sweetie. That bronze dress sets off your blond hair just perfectly."

"Thanks," Caitlin said, ignoring her first question. She walked around the desk, glancing at the assignment board. "Mrs. Johnson's been discharged over the weekend?"

"She had a miraculous recovery when her reluctant daughter said she would come to the house to help." Danielle picked up a pen, made a few more notes on a chart, then looked back up at Caitlin. "So, how is the very handsome Charles Frost?"

Caitlin felt a pain clutch her chest at the mention of her boyfriend's name. Ex-boyfriend she reminded herself. "He got a promotion," she murmured, flipping through some papers on the desk, deliberately avoiding the reality of what she had done.

"Wow, you must be pleased."

"As punch." Caitlin stopped her pointless fiddling.

"You don't sound pleased." Danielle tapped the pen on the desk. "Sit down. I've got time."

Caitlin was just about to say no, but Danielle looked concerned and she needed a sympathetic ear. Who better than her best friend? So she sat down, unwinding her shawl from her neck.

Danielle reached over and laid a gentle hand on her friend's shoulder. "What's wrong, Caitlin?"

She opted for the direct approach and told her the day's events.

"I broke up with Charles tonight," she said, her tone deliberate.

"What?"

"He said he had good news." Caitlin plowed on, ignoring Danielle's expression of utter surprise. "Unfortunately like an optimistic idiot, I thought he meant…" her voice trailed off as she took a quick breath, embarrassed.

"He was going to propose." Danielle finished off the sentence.

"I should have known," Caitlin said angrily, crushing the scarf on her lap. She loosed it, carefully smoothing it out again, glancing up at her friend. "The past few months we've been drifting apart, but I kept hoping things would change for both of us," she said with a wry laugh.

"Well, then, it's a good thing you broke up with him. If I find out in a couple of dates this isn't the kind of guy I want to spend the rest of my life with, *phwwt…*" Danielle made a dismissive gesture with one hand. "Out he goes. Companionship I can get from my friends and pets. Hanging on is a waste of time."

And how much time hadn't she wasted, Caitlin thought, considering the three years of dating Charles.

"I thought Charles and I were headed in that direction, but I guessed wrong." Caitlin shook her head, winding the scarf around her hands. "Can you believe I was that dumb?" She clenched her fists, shaking her head.

"Well, at the risk of sounding like a cliché, I'm sure you'll get over it. I mean Charles is a nice guy, he's good-looking, he's ambitious, but..." Danielle lifted her hands as if in surrender. "I just don't sense a real spark between you two."

Caitlin said nothing at that, knowing that, as usual, her friend had put her finger directly on Caitlin's own malaise concerning the relationship.

Before she could formulate an answer, the recovery room called to say they were sending up the accident victim.

Caitlin glanced at the clock. There was no avoiding it, she had to go home sooner or later. "Well, I'm history," she said, winding the scarf around her shoulders and picking up her purse.

"I should make sure the room is ready for our new admission," Danielle conceded, getting up. "Will I see you before you fly down to visit your sister Evelyn and her new baby?"

Caitlin nodded, wondering how she'd fill the ten days before she left for Portland. "Yeah. I'll need something to do besides sit and watch my mother eagerly knitting baby booties. Rachel's expecting, too!"

Danielle touched her arm as if sensing Caitlin's yearning for her own family. "You want me to call a cab?"

"I'll get one myself. Thanks." Caitlin smiled at her friend. Danielle gave her a quick hug and then left.

Caitlin sighed lightly, and turned to go. But when the elevator door swooshed open, a stretcher was wheeled into the ward. The motorcyclist.

Caitlin stopped beside the stretcher, taking another look at the patient lying there. A fine net held his hair back, exposing his strong features. A dressing covered the gash on his forehead.

The patient moaned once, his eyes fluttered open and homed in on hers. He blinked, tried to lift his head and then closed his eyes again.

But once again his hand reached out toward her and once again, Caitlin took a step closer and took it in hers. He squeezed it lightly. "Angel," he whispered, the word coming out in a sigh. "Don't go."

And Caitlin knew she was staying.

Someone was talking to him. The words came slowly, echoing down a long, dark corridor. Simon tried to catch them but he couldn't move, couldn't focus on what the voice said.

More words and sounds coming closer, sharper. Then, finally, "He's coming around." The words pierced the haze of darkness holding him captive.

"Can you hear me?" the voice continued.

Why was it so much work to talk, to do something as simple as lift his eyelids?

He struggled and as awareness dawned so did the pain. It pressed down on him, heavy, overwhelming, taking over his slowly awakening senses.

He moaned, the sound forced out of him by the extent of an agony he couldn't pinpoint. Where was he?

He tried to focus, to comprehend. It was so much work. A face swam into his vision and he strained to see it better. He blinked hard, willing his eyes to function.

Finally the blurred edges coalesced. He recognized his angel of mercy, her soft green eyes like a refreshing drink.

He called out as he closed his eyes, fighting a fresh

wave of pain. Cool fingers slipped through his. With another effort, he clung to her as if to a lifeline.

More movement as he felt himself being lifted, then a surge of pain.

He dug his head back into the pillow as he rode it out. It slowly eased, but he kept his eyes shut as he breathed through the last bit.

"Where are you?" he panted. "Angel."

"I'm here." She touched his face lightly. "Just try to rest now," she said, fussing over the blanket, tucking it around his chest. She straightened, pulled up a chair and sat down beside him.

He felt himself drifting off again. He didn't want to go, didn't like the feeling but couldn't stop it.

Unaware of how much time had passed, he felt himself drifting, heard voices far away.

Then increasing agony pulled him up into awareness. He fought it, preferring the blessed relief of the darkness, the not knowing to the perception of deep aching overlaid with sharp pain.

"Hi, there." A soft voice beside him made him turn his head toward the gentle sound. "How are you doing?"

He forced his eyes open and there she was again. The face he'd been seeing since this all started. Every time he opened his eyes, she was there.

A name drifted out of another part of his memory, attaching itself to her serene beauty. Caitlin.

"It hurts," was all he could say when he wanted to say so much more. *Who are you? Why are you always here?*

"Do you want something for the pain?" she asked, leaning forward. Her hand was a light touch on his forehead, a connection with reality.

"Please," he gasped. Anything to escape this agony,

he thought at the same time resenting his vulnerability. He closed his eyes, searching for some bit of memory to explain what had happened to him. The only thing he could remember was seeing her again and again.

Then he felt that same gentling hand at the back of his neck. "Here," she said quietly. "Open your mouth." He obeyed and she placed something on his tongue. He opened his eyes again, seeking hers as she held a cup of tepid water to his lips. He swallowed, thankful for the moisture, then lay back, watching as she set the cup on the table and sat down again.

"What's your name?" she asked, leaning forward, taking his hand in hers.

"Why do you want to know?" he mumbled, pain pressing his eyes closed.

"So I know who I'm praying for," she said quietly, squeezing his hand lightly.

"Waste of time," he said.

"Please. I want to know who you are."

Light from the hallway, muted by the curtain around him shone on her delicate features. What was she doing here and why did she want to know his name?

The questions grew fuzzy, his need to find answers receding as the pill took effect.

She squeezed his hand again. "Don't drift off on me without telling me your name."

He sensed she wasn't going to stop. He didn't like the frustration that edged her voice and decided, reluctantly, to grant her request. "My name is Simon."

That made her smile and he was glad.

"Thanks for being here," he said, squeezing her hand back. Then blessed unconsciousness brought him ease.

Again, he was unaware of the passage of time, aware

only that each time he came up from the darkness, she was there, offering what comfort she could.

Once he woke to find her sleeping, her head pillowed on the bed, her face buried in her arms. The room was dark. He felt unaccountably bereft, alone. He didn't want to disturb her, but felt an urgent need to connect, to touch.

Her hair lay in tangled disarray close to his hand. He reached out and touched it, marveling at its softness, wondering again who she was and why she had stayed with him.

But his mind didn't have much room for wondering. It was taken up by a throbbing ache in his legs, arms, chest.

"Caitlin," he whispered, then he drifted off again.

Chapter Three

Caitlin didn't want to think what she was doing here. One o'clock in the morning was no time to figure out where else to go.

A moan from the bed made her turn. She'd only meant to catch a few winks when she laid her head on the bed, but had, instead, slept a couple of hours. She got up, the floor cool under her feet.

"Caitlin." Simon's voice was a harsh whisper. "My throat's sore."

It still gave her a start to hear him speak her name. She turned to see him looking at her, his eyes glinting in the refracted light coming from outside. For a moment she held his gaze, wondering again why she stayed, why he seemed to want her with him.

With a shake of her head she dismissed the thoughts. Walking to his side, she poured him some water, lifted his head and let him take a drink. He swallowed with difficulty and then laid his head back. "Your throat is sore from a tube that gets put down your throat during surgery," she explained. "Your chest will be sore, too."

"What happened to me?"

Caitlin relived the shock of the accident. She had been so close to it all.

"Caitlin?" he asked again. "Tell me."

"You were in a motorbike accident. You've sustained some very serious injuries."

"How serious?" he asked, closing his eyes and drawing in a breath.

"You've a fractured femur, a bruised pelvis and bruises that I'm sure you're beginning to feel."

"How did it happen?"

"I didn't see all of it. A car hit you, and your bike went down on top of you." She took a slow, deep breath, seeing the accident again. She'd explained what happened to other patients many times before, but never had the picture of the events been so indelibly printed in her mind. Never had she seen a cocky smile replaced by a grimace of pain, a man full of self-confidence in one moment, thrown like a rag doll across the pavement in the next. She wondered if she would ever forget it.

"You helped me."

Caitlin laughed a short laugh. "I did very little."

"You stopped." He turned his head, his hand reaching out to her. Caitlin wanted to pretend she didn't see it. Wanted to break the tenuous connection they had developed by her being by his side. One look at his eyes narrowed with pain, the lines along his full mouth and she couldn't stop herself from placing her hand in his. "You're here now," he said, his voice hoarse as he tightly grasped her hand. "Why?"

Because I don't know where else to go right now? Because, unlike my ex-boyfriend, you needed me?

But as she looked at him, she knew it was more.

Caitlin kept her replies to herself and only squeezed his hand a little harder. "Doesn't matter. Just try to rest."

He took a slow breath, his eyes drifting shut. "Stay with me a little longer, Caitlin?"

"I'll be here," she said softly. "Now, don't talk anymore."

He lifted one corner of his mouth. A careful smile. Then she felt his fingers loosen their grip on hers but not enough to let go.

With a sigh, she pulled the chair up closer and tried to get some more sleep.

Caitlin woke a few hours later, blinking in the brightness of the room. The curtains behind her only muted the morning light pouring in over her shoulder.

Her one arm was asleep, her hand still anchored in Simon's. Carefully, she pulled it free. His fingers fluttered a moment as if seeking hers, and Caitlin thought he would waken.

But he slept on, his breathing heavy.

Caitlin stretched her hand in front of her, wincing at the harsh prickling. She yawned and pulled a face at the stale taste in her mouth.

She got up, grabbing the arm of the chair as her one leg gave way under her. She had slept in an awkward position, her arms on the bed.

Sometime in the night she had kicked off her shoes. She saw one beside the chair, the other had been pushed under the bed.

Her stomach was empty, a grim reminder of her missed supper last night. Her neck was stiff, her shoulders sore and her mouth felt fuzzy.

Last night she had been angry and her impetuous

decision to come here wasn't made with a rational mind and now she was paying for it.

She bit back a sigh as the events of last night came back with the cold clarity that accompanies the sharp light of morning.

Charles and she had broken up, and this time she knew it was for good. She knew she didn't want to go back to the half limbo that had been their relationship the past while.

Caitlin glanced at Simon. His face was drawn, his hair was caked with blood at the temple. The sight of him reaching out to her, pleading for her to stay had struck the very spot Charles had wounded with his lack of caring. This man, this total stranger, made her feel needed, and after last night it was what drew her toward him.

But now, it was morning. The night was over and she had to get home and…

Caitlin bit her lip, thinking of telling her parents and her sister. Her family who all thought the world of Charles and who wanted so badly for Charles and Caitlin to come to a stronger commitment. Her family to whom finding someone and marrying was the natural progression of events. Her older sister was married and had just had her third child. Her younger sister was married and expecting her first. Even her unreliable brother was married, living off in the East who knew where.

But he's married, Caitlin thought wryly. And I'm not.

She glanced again at the man on the bed. He'd had a restless night and Danielle was thankful for Caitlin's presence. They had two more admissions and were running off their feet.

After her brief nap she'd given him his pain medication, adjusted his leg, keeping it elevated to avoid blood clots. She tried to talk to him when he was lucid, tried to ask him questions about his relatives, his family. They would need to be notified. But he'd said nothing.

There had to be someone who would need to know about him, she figured. Parents, brother, sister. Maybe a girlfriend?

"What do you care?" Caitlin admonished herself, reaching down and pulling her other shoe out from under the bed. "You won't be back here." She slipped her shoes on, thinking of her much anticipated vacation.

"And what are you going to do about that?" she asked herself, stretching once again.

She glanced at her watch, groaning at the time. Six o'clock in the morning. Her parents would still be sleeping, and she badly wanted to change.

"Hi, there."

Caitlin turned at the sound of the sleep-roughened voice. Simon was watching her, and she wondered how long he had been awake, listening to her babble to herself.

"Hi, yourself," she said, crossing her arms across her stomach as she walked to the side of the bed. He looked pale, his eyes still dull with pain. "How are you doing?"

"Horrible. I feel like I've been hit by a train." He tried to lick his lips. "My mouth feels like I've been on an all-nighter."

"In a way, you have," Caitlin replied. "Want some ice water?"

"Sounds wonderful," his voice drifted off on the last syllable and Caitlin guessed he was in pain again.

"Do you want some painkillers with that?"

"I don't know," he whispered, his teeth clenched. "I hate the way they make me feel."

"I'm sure it can't be worse than the way that plate in your leg makes you feel?"

"What?" Simon blinked, tried to raise his head and then fell back with a grimace. "What are you talking about?"

"Drink first," she ordered, raising his head and placing the cup against his lips.

He took a long drink and then lay back. "Now tell me," he demanded.

"Do you remember what I told you about the accident?"

He nodded.

"They had to fix the fracture with a metal plate and screws. The surgeon will be doing his rounds later on and he can tell you exactly what he did to your leg."

"Where's my bike?"

"That I can't tell you. We'll be in contact with the police later on. They can let us know where it is and how badly it was damaged."

"What about the other guy?"

"The one who hit you?"

Simon only nodded, his eyes shut again.

"It was hit-and-run. Like I said, I saw it, but didn't get a clear view of the license plate. I'll have to tell the police what I know, and I'm sorry I can't tell you more."

Simon opened his eyes, zeroing in on her. "Why did you stay with me all night?"

Caitlin pulled back, feeling the impact of his direct gaze. She still wasn't able to analyze why she had done it. "I saw the accident. I came with you in the ambulance. I stayed because the night staff was running off their feet…"

"Thanks," he whispered, his perfectly shaped mouth curving up in a smile. He closed his eyes again and was gone.

Caitlin drew in a shaky breath, trying to dispel the odd feeling his smile gave her. A feeling much different from any that Charles's smiles had created.

Rebound, she reminded herself with disgust. That and the ego-building feeling of being wanted by a man she knew had an earthy appeal most women would notice.

"So you can't leave earlier for Evelyn's place, what else are you going to do?" Rachel bent over and picked up a rock, angling her hand. With a flick of her wrist she tossed it out, and it skipped across the quiet water of Piper's Lagoon.

"I don't know. I sure don't feel like hanging around Nanaimo for ten days, but I don't have the energy to make other plans." Caitlin shoved her hands deeper into the pockets of her jean jacket, her feet scuffing through the shale and rock of the beach, retracing steps they had taken so often in their youth.

Caitlin needed to get out and away from her mother's sympathetic glances, her sorrowing looks. Her mother really liked Charles and had so hoped he would some-day be her son-in-law.

Well those hopes were dashed as surely as the shells she was even now crunching under her feet.

"Maybe you should go away. Take a trip with all that money you've got saved up."

"I don't know where I'd want to go. And I don't feel like traveling alone."

"Yeah, I know what you mean." Rachel slipped her arm around her sister's waist. "I just don't like seeing you like this, so lost and forlorn."

"I'm not forlorn," Caitlin said with a note of disgust in her voice. "I'm probably more ticked than anything. Going back to him and then breaking up with him." Caitlin stopped at a driftwood log and lowered herself to the sand, leaning against the log. The September air was quiet, unusually still. A white gull wheeled above them, sending out a shrill, haunting cry. The afternoon sun shimmered on the water. It was as if the entire world had slowed down.

"You look tired."

Caitlin shrugged. She had told her family about spending the night at the hospital, but not why. Sitting at Simon's bedside seemed quixotic in the harsh light of the day. She came home just before her family came back from church, giving her time to shower and change. It also gave her time for personal devotions, and a chance to question God about the events of the past twenty-four hours.

"What about going back to work?" Rachel sat down beside her, sifting her hands through the coarse sand, tilting her face to the sun.

"I would dearly love to, but unfortunately it's not an option." Caitlin settled farther down on the log, squinting against the sun to the mountains of the mainland beyond. Mountains as familiar as the wallpaper of her own bedroom. She and Rachel spent hours here. It was a short bike ride from their parents' home. In the summer they swam here, on cooler days they walked along the beach, exploring, planning, dreaming. "All the shifts are planned out. Much as I'd love to get back to work, I'd throw a huge monkey wrench in the whole business if I tried to get back into it right now." She pushed her hand into the sun-warmed sand, reaching down to the cooler layer below.

"Well, you have to make some plans."

Caitlin wrinkled her nose and laid her head back against the log, letting the sun warm her face. "I don't have to make any plans. I've spent three years working around Charles's schedule, and I think the next week and a half will be a good opportunity for me to figure out my own life."

"Have you ever thought about moving out of Mom and Dad's house?"

Caitlin squinted across the bay again, looking but not seeing. Right now she didn't want to make any decision more strenuous than whether she should get up and keep walking or stay leaning against this log while her behind got slowly colder. "I should," she said. "It's just too easy at home. Mom takes care of me, and I don't have to think about anything."

"Well, someday you'll find somebody. Someone you can care for." Rachel reached over and stroked her shoulder, trying to comfort Caitlin.

"I suppose I will," Caitlin said, stifling a sigh. She didn't know if she wanted to invest her emotions in another relationship. It seemed a lot of work for little reward. She pushed herself up, brushing the cool, damp sand off her pants and giving her sister a hand, pulled her up. "I guess I'll just have to wait for someone to come and sweep me off my feet."

"Charles will regret this, you know."

Caitlin pursed her lips, nodding absently at her sister's confident proclamation.

"I think he was just taking you for granted. He's probably just afraid of commitment."

"He seems pretty committed to his job," Caitlin said drily. "And if he can't give me that same kind of commitment, then I'm really wasting my time."

"Maybe breaking up with him will show him that you're serious. It will be a wake-up call for him." Rachel smiled at her sister in encouragement. "You just wait. He'll be calling you by the end of the week, begging you to come back."

"We've done this break-up-and-begging thing before. I wouldn't take him, Rachel," Caitlin said firmly, her hands bunched in the pockets of her jean jacket.

"What?" Rachel punched her sister on the shoulder. "Of course you would. Charles is such a great guy."

Caitlin looked down at some shells, kicking them up and watching them fall. "He may be great, but I don't know if I've had any passionate feelings for him." She angled a questioning glance at her sister. "Surely that should be part of a relationship."

"I still can't believe you're saying this."

"I can. Amazing what a few different events can do to change your perspective on life."

"Like what?"

Caitlin stopped and turned to face her sister. "Yesterday you told me you were expecting. Yesterday I saw a man almost get killed. I realized how precious life is and how much of mine I've wasted waiting to see if Charles could squeeze me into his agenda."

"What?" Rachel said, frowning. "What do you mean

about a man getting killed? You never said anything about that."

Caitlin held her sister's puzzled gaze and then turned away, walking a little quicker. "It happened after I broke up with Charles. Some guy on a motorbike." His name is Simon, her inner voice taunted her. You stayed with him, all night. He's more than "some guy." "It was pretty traumatic and it shook me up," she continued, ignoring the insidious thoughts. "He was afraid and wanted me to stay with him. So I did. That's why I was home so late."

"Wow, Caity. That was nice of you."

Caitlin was reassured by the tone of her sister's voice, by her use of an innocuous word like *nice*. It told her that what she had done was kindness, nothing more. It had nothing to do with emptiness and being needed. Nothing to do with eyes that demanded and a mouth that promised.

Chapter Four

"You didn't tell me Eva was working evenings." Caitlin pulled a face at the time sheet in front of her. Danielle had called her earlier in the day to offer her the shift for a nurse who'd wanted to take the week off but hadn't been able to because of Caitlin's pending vacation with Charles.

Danielle gave her friend a light punch on the shoulder. "Beggars can't be choosers, my dear. If it's any comfort, I'll be in the last two days of the rotation. We can gossip together." A light blinked on above the doorway across from the nurse's station and Danielle looked up with a frown. "There goes that Simon again," she grumbled. "Had that student nurse, Tina, all in a dither this morning."

"Do you want me to go?" Caitlin offered.

"Sure. Just don't let him get to you!" warned her friend.

Caitlin only smiled. "I think I'm okay in that department," she said as she walked into his room. She knew she wouldn't be succumbing to any male charms for a while.

"Took you long enough," Simon grumbled as she walked to the foot of his bed. As he glanced at her he frowned, then his hazel eyes brightened "Well, hi there, angel," he said, a slow smile curving his lips, his gravelly voice softening. "You came back to see me."

Caitlin could see how this man could get a young woman flustered. With just a smile, a shifting of his features, he changed from harsh to appealing. "I just came on the ward to see when I'm working again," she said, walking over to his side. "Danielle's busy. Did you want some water?" She poured him a cup.

"You work here?" He shifted as he reached for the cup, his smile disappearing in a grimace of pain.

"Yes, I do. I'm on vacation now, though, but I'll be back tomorrow."

"Really?" He tried to smile again, but he squeezed his eyes shut and took a few slow breaths, fighting the agony Caitlin knew he must be suffering.

"Do you want a painkiller?" she asked quietly, taking the cup out of his trembling hands.

He shook his head once, quickly. "No," he gasped, "I'm okay."

Caitlin watched him battling the pain, his head pressed back against the pillow, his fists clenched at his sides.

"You don't have to suffer like this," she said, touching his shoulder lightly. "You don't have to be so tough."

Simon took a few more quick breaths, then slowly exhaled, his eyes opening. "Maybe not," he said with a sigh. "I hate feeling out of control."

"Better than feeling like that motorbike landed on you all over again," Caitlin said drily, setting the cup down on the table.

"Maybe," he whispered, beads of sweat glistening on his forehead.

"When's the last time you had something?" she asked, folding her arms across her chest.

"I don't know."

"I'm going to check."

He opened his eyes. "You coming back?"

Caitlin paused. His brusque question held a faint note of entreaty at odds with his character. Their eyes met, held, and for a heartbeat Caitlin felt the same emotion he had created in her the night of his accident.

He needed her.

Caitlin forced herself to look away, to break the tenuous connection.

Don't be ridiculous she reprimanded herself as she walked out of the room and over to the desk. He's just doing what comes naturally. Flirting.

"So, what did the old bear want now?" Danielle asked, looking up from her paperwork.

"When was the last time he had a painkiller?"

Danielle reached over and pulled up Simon's chart, shaking her head. "If you want to give him something, I wish you luck. He won't take anything unless he's just about dead from pain. I've been tempted to slip him something in his IV." She flipped through the papers. "Here. About five hours ago. He's got to be hurting now."

"He is."

Danielle nodded. "Dr. Hall changed the order this morning. He's got him on a stronger medication. I'll get him something. Maybe between the two of us we can get it in him." Danielle left and Caitlin walked back to the room.

Simon lay still, his arms at his sides, his eyes closed.

"Is that you, angel?" he asked, his voice quiet.

"It's Caitlin, not angel."

He carefully opened his eyes, zeroing in on her immediately. "When I first saw you, I thought you were an angel, then you saved my life."

"I didn't save your life, either," Caitlin said matter-of-factly.

"I felt myself slipping away, going down into darkness, I knew I was going…" He stopped, took a deep breath at the effort of talking. "But you pulled me back." He smiled wanly at her. "How did you do it?"

Caitlin held his gaze. "I prayed."

"Sure."

"Your heartbeat was weakening, almost nonexistent," she replied, ignoring the sarcasm in his voice. "I was praying and then it came back. Simple as that."

Simon shook his head, closing his eyes again. "I don't believe you." He took another breath and Caitlin could tell from the lines around his mouth he was really hurting.

Danielle came in the room with a med cup. "Here we are," she said, handing it to Caitlin. "See if you can get that in him." She looked back at Simon. "I couldn't connect with Oscar, Simon. Do you want me to try again?"

"No," he replied tightly. "He's camping. I forgot."

"I'm going on a break now, Caitlin. I'll be back in about twenty minutes to check his dressings."

Danielle left and Caitlin set the small paper cup on the bedside table. "Are you going to take this?"

Simon opened his eyes again. "What are you going to do if I don't?" he said, forcing a wry smile. "Pray again?"

"That, and put something in your IV, or give you a needle. Either of those will really knock you out." Caitlin picked up the med cup and his glass of water. "This is a better alternative."

"Isn't that against my human rights?"

"Hospitals are not a democracy," she said, shaking her head at his obtuseness.

"Total dictatorship," he said with a short laugh. He reached up and took the cup. He tipped the pill into his mouth and then grimaced. "This place sounds like my old foster home."

He handed Caitlin the paper cup and lay back again. His comment about foster homes piqued Caitlin's curiosity. "You know, I never did find out your last name," she said, pulling up a chair.

"Read my chart," he said obliquely. He glanced sidelong at Caitlin. "You settling in for a heart-to-heart chat?"

"Hardly," Caitlin said. "Just making sure you didn't put that pill under your tongue so you can spit it out later. If I sit here long enough, it will dissolve."

"Do you want me to open my mouth so you can check?"

"That will be fine." She watched him a moment, knowing she should leave, but curiously unwilling to.

"So, where are you from?" she asked, leaning back in the chair, lightly tapping her fingers on the armrests.

Simon looked away, his hazel eyes, narrowing. "Does it matter? Knowing that won't change anything." He sounded testy, angry.

Caitlin stopped tapping and tilted her head to one side, studying him. "It makes you more of an individual. Tells me something about you."

Simon curved his mouth into a smile but it lacked the warmth and appeal of the smile he favored her with a few moments ago. "I'm from nowhere, and I don't have a family." The statement was made without emotion, without any attempt to garner pity from the listener.

"What about Oscar Delaney?"

"He's my partner."

"You also said something about a foster home…"

Simon glanced sidelong at Caitlin, his eyes hard. "I think you better go now," he said firmly.

Caitlin held his gaze until he looked away. He was breathing quickly, fighting the agony she knew must be coursing through his body, confusing him and making him short-tempered. She got up and carefully pushed the chair back against the wall under the window, feeling slightly frustrated herself and wondering why she should care. "Do you want me to pull the curtains?" she asked, reverting to her role as a nurse and professional.

He shook his head, his eyes drifting shut again. Caitlin waited a moment, watching as his mouth relaxed, the frown eased from his forehead. The medication was kicking in, she thought. He looked more peaceful now, and Caitlin couldn't deny his appeal. Wavy hair that fell over his forehead, hiding the cut, high cheekbones, a mouth that could curl up in disdain and yet, now that he was asleep, show a softness she knew he wouldn't want to show.

She was still surprised that no one had come to see him, that no one missed him.

Then again, she wondered why she should care. In spite of his good looks, he was a patient. She was a nurse.

"But I need this information, Mr. Steele." The young nurse looked down at the clipboard she was carrying.

Simon looked up at the woman hovering at his bedside, wishing she would go. He hadn't slept much last night, his leg was throbbing, his arm and the top of his leg felt as if they were on fire, and he was tired of feeling woozy from the medication he was on. And now he had an ambitious nurse standing by his bed pumping him for information. He still hadn't been able to connect with Oscar and he was feeling hemmed in and testy.

"I want you to leave me alone. You've got all the information you need to have. My insurance number, legal name, allergies and previous medical history, as far as I know."

"But we need an emergency contact number and…"

"Look, sweetheart, I already went through an emergency without a contact number. I think you'll do okay without it now." He glared at her and this time she took a step backward, her pen still hovering over the clipboard she was carrying.

"The police need to talk to you about pressing charges." She bit her lip, running her finger nervously along one side of the clipboard.

"I'm not pressing charges. I don't care about the bike. It can be replaced. If they say they want to talk to me, tell them that I'm in a coma, okay?" He stopped, as a fresh wave of pain washed over him.

"But, sir, that would be lying."

Simon took a breath, his anger too easily coming to the surface. "Just go," he snapped. He closed his eyes. For four days he had been in constant pain. Each time he thought it was getting better, the physiotherapist came and got him moving around and the agony would start all over again.

He felt the fuzziness of the painkiller slowly overtaking him and he fought it even as he welcomed it. Out of control, he thought, I hate being out of control. He drifted along for timeless moments. Then...

"Hello, Simon. How are you doing?"

That voice, he thought, forcing his eyes open.

Caitlin stood beside the bed, a stethoscope clipped around her neck. Her hair was pulled back away from her face enhancing the delicate line of her chin, her narrow nose, eyebrows that winged upward from soft green eyes. He wished he didn't hurt so much. He wished he had the strength to reach up, pull her close to him and kiss that gently curving mouth.

But all he could do was lie immobile with metal and screws holding his leg together and some kind of wrap covering it. A cripple. It wasn't fair, he thought.

She unrolled a blood pressure cuff and gently raised his good arm, slipping it around. Her hands were cool, her touch careful.

"Hi yourself, angel," he said slowly. "You working now?"

"Yes. I'll be taking care of you for the next twelve hours." She pressurized the cuff and she slipped the stethoscope in her ears.

"Sounds like a wonderful twelve hours."

She only set the stethoscope on his arm and listened. When she was done, she pulled the cuff off, rolled it up and tucked it behind the fixture on the wall. She was all aloof efficiency and order and it bugged Simon more than he liked to admit.

When her soft hands lifted his wrist to take his pulse, he held his breath, knowing that the other nurses counted his respirations while they thought he wasn't looking. She dropped his wrist and pulled the stethoscope out of her ears.

Didn't even notice, he thought feeling childishly disappointed.

She pulled a pen and pad out of her pocket and made a few quick notes. "Let's see, blood pressure normal, pulse strong, respirations—" Caitlin stopped and glanced sidelong at Simon "—normal, now."

He grinned back at her. "I guess you know all the tricks," he said.

"I'd say you need to get out more when someone your age needs to resort to tricks to get extra attention," she said, her voice dry.

"I got yours, didn't I?"

Caitlin looked up at him. "What you *got* was a nurse doing her job."

"And being so aloof is also part of your job?" Simon groused. He didn't like hearing that professional tone of voice. Not from a woman who looked like an angel with her wings clipped. "You weren't like that before."

"I wasn't working before," she said briskly. She picked up the machine that took his temperature and clipped a new earpiece on. "Turn your head to the side, please."

"Whatever happened to good old thermometers?" he asked as she inserted it in his ear.

It beeped and she took it out. "Good old thermometers aren't as quick or reliable." She marked something down and slipped the notepad in her pocket. "Of course, it was a great way to keep the patient quiet," she said with a quick lift of her eyebrows at him.

He smiled at that. She returned it with one of her own that made Simon catch his breath.

"How have you been feeling?" she said, her voice lowering, taking on a softer tone.

She had switched from efficient nurse to the caring woman who had stayed with him a whole night. He couldn't stop his response to her warmth and concern. "It's bad," he said simply.

"I know," she said softly. "But you fight the pain and the medication stops you from doing that. You may feel out of it, but you need to let your body rest so you can heal."

"I can't get out of here soon enough."

Caitlin shook her head. "I wouldn't rush it. You won't be walking when you do and you'll need therapy and home care. You'll probably be walking with the help of a walker, then crutches, then a cane. A broken femur is a huge injury and takes a long time to heal."

Simon nodded, not wanting to hear what she had to say or the vulnerability it represented.

"Where is home?" she asked suddenly.

"I've just got an apartment along the bay in Vancouver, on the mainland." Hardly home. More like a home base.

"You're going to need some help the first couple of weeks. Is there anyone who can come or will you have to hire a nurse?" She looked down at him, her one eyebrow lifted questioningly, but Simon didn't want to bite. She didn't need to know there was no one he could ask. He didn't want to be reminded of his lack of family—reminded that he had lost touch with anyone who had ever meant anything to him. It made his life less complicated. He had never needed anyone. Oscar's words came back to haunt him. They were frighteningly appropriate.

She waited a moment, then with a gentle sigh, turned his IV stand around and read some figures off it. He knew that once she was done recording all the numbers that nurses seemed so awfully fond of, she would be gone until later on this evening when she would check his dressings. Perversely he didn't want her to go.

"Why do I need help?" he asked, reluctantly acknowledging her previous comment.

"Because you're not going to be able to move around very easily. You'll need help with bathing and moving around. You'll still be in pain…"

"I'll figure something out."

Caitlin looked down at him. "What about your work?"

"I work for myself. Have for years."

"Is that why you are so tough and independent?"

Simon heard the slight note of censure in her voice and bristled. "I've had to learn from early on to take care of myself, find my own way."

"Well, for now you're in our capable hands."

"And are you going to hold me in those capable hands?" he asked with a wink.

"See you later, Mr. Steele." And with that she turned and left.

Chapter Five

Caitlin pushed her chair back from the computer and stretched. She had trouble falling asleep yesterday after working her first night shift. It always happened. So she was feeling a little woozy. All the patients were asleep.

Except one. Simon.

She had to check his dressings. Now was as good a time as any. She had put it off for a while, hoping one of the other nurses on the team would, but they all seemed to avoid him.

Caitlin had avoided him, too. She was uncomfortable around him.

She walked into the room. The patient just recently admitted was asleep. His name was Shane. Football injury. Same temperament as Simon, just a little younger.

"Hey, company. Sit down, talk to me," Simon said as she walked around the curtain dividing him and Shane.

"Sorry. Can't oblige." She checked his IV while she spoke, adjusting the flow. She turned back to him and lifted his bedsheet, folding it back to check his incision. Caitlin frowned as she rolled back the wrap that held the dressings in place. She bent over to take a closer look at the incision. It was redder than it should be.

"Does this hurt?"

"C'mon, Caitlin, it always hurts." He reached up and laid a warm hand on her arm, his finger moving up and down her arm in a caressing motion.

She felt her heart flutter at his touch and glanced sidelong at him. His eyes were crinkled up at the corners, and she didn't like the way he was smiling at her. It looked polished, purposeful, fake.

She took his hand and laid it back on the bed, angry at her own reaction. Simon was an accomplished flirt. She would do well to remember that.

"Does it hurt more than usual?" she asked, touching the skin lightly, forcing her mind back to her job. She frowned. His skin felt unusually warm.

"I don't know," he said. "Like I said, it always hurts." He placed his hand on his chest and sighed. "Just like my heart."

"Give it a rest, Mr. Steele," she said, now truly ticked with him. He was bored and she was overreacting.

She frowned and lowered the sheet, then walked around the bed to his other side. "Let me see your arm, please."

"My goodness, aren't you all efficiency tonight?" he said, his voice suddenly testy.

Caitlin glanced at him, then away. He had been alternately flirtatious and cranky ever since she had come on duty this evening. Guys usually were ornery after a few days of being confined to bed, but Simon had been getting worse each hour she worked. It didn't help that his sleep had been interrupted when they brought the new admission into his room. Things were always busy the first hour after a patient came up from surgery, and Simon had been irritable at the constant comings and goings.

She carefully peeled back the tape, unable to avoid pulling the hairs sprinkled over his forearm.

He sucked in his breath at the pain. "That hurts, angel."

"Sorry," she murmured automatically, quickly pulling back the rest of the dressing.

He took a deep breath and then another, slowly relaxing. "That apology didn't sound too sincere, Caitlin," he said quietly.

"Probably not," she said evenly, determined not to let him get under her skin.

Simon laughed at that. Their eyes met and held, and Caitlin again felt her heart give a little kick. And again, she berated herself for her reaction. He was demanding and confusing, turning his charm on and off at will, yet she couldn't seem to reason her way past her reaction to him.

Because each time she saw him, what she remembered most was the feel of his hand clutching hers, the entreaty in his eyes, his vulnerability.

She looked down at what she was doing, forcing her mind back to the task at hand. She frowned. "Is your arm feeling itchy yet?"

"Do I have that to look forward to, as well?"

Caitlin shrugged. "If it's itchy, that's a sign that it's healing."

"Well, it's not."

"I'll change this for now."

"Why are you frowning?" Simon caught her hand in his, tugging on it.

"I'm a little concerned about infection," she said, pulling on her hand. But Simon was a lot stronger now than he was at first, and he wouldn't let go.

"You're a good nurse, Caitlin," he said with a wry grin.

"It's my job. Now let go of my hand so I can do it."

"Nurse means 'to take care of,'" he said, his voice lowering. He ran his thumb over the knuckles of her hand, his eyes on hers. "I want you to stay and talk to me, take care of me."

Caitlin wanted to be angry with him, wanted to dislike what he was doing. She wanted to pull away, but his hand was warm, his gaze compelling.

"Just talk," he said softly, tugging on her hand. "I'm lonely."

Caitlin forced herself to look away, reluctantly pulling her hand free. What was wrong with her? She knew virtually nothing about this man and here she was, at his bedside, holding on to his hand. Again.

"I've got to get some clean dressings," she said, turning away. "I'll be right back."

"I'll be waiting."

Caitlin grimaced at how that sounded. "I didn't mean it like that," she muttered to herself as she marched to the supply room. Once there she stopped a moment, frustrated. She, a professional nurse who prided herself on her objectivity, had let a patient get to her.

She shook her head as if to dispel the feelings she had experienced in the room a few moments ago. She straightened her shoulders, and wheeled the dressing cart back to his room.

He lay looking out the darkened window to the night outside. Most patients liked to have the curtains shut during the evening, but Simon always had his open. The light above his bed illuminated his reflection in the large sheet of glass.

But as Caitlin paused at the foot of his bed, she

seemed to sense that he was looking beyond his reflection in the window, beyond the lights of Nanaimo that spread out below him. He seemed to be in another place and for a moment, she wanted to know where.

She sighed, exasperated with herself. Wasn't it just twenty seconds ago that she prayed for detachment?

She walked between him and the window, pushing the cart to the side of his bed.

Caitlin usually liked to explain what she was doing to patients, just in case they had any concerns. This time, however, she worked in silence, careful not to hurt Simon any more than she had to.

When she was done, she tidied up and turned to leave.

"Do you have family, Caitlin?" Simon asked suddenly.

Caitlin paused, curious as to why he would ask. "Yes. I have two sisters and one brother."

"Do they live around here?"

"No. My brother lives in Toronto, my older sister in Portland, Oregon, and my younger sister and her husband live in Vancouver."

"They're all married and you're not?"

It was more of a statement than a question, but it still sounded mocking to her. And it sounded exactly like her mother.

"That happens sometimes," she said drily.

Fortunately even he sensed that he had gone too far.

"What about parents?"

Caitlin smiled, wondering if he was joking. "Parents usually come with the package."

"No, they don't." His voice was quiet and when Simon turned to look at her, his eyes were devoid of expression.

"I remember you said something about a foster home the first time I talked to you. Were you there all your life?"

Simon laughed shortly, then turned his head again, not answering her question. Caitlin waited a moment wondering if he would say anything more. When he didn't, she left, puzzled as to why he had even asked her the questions.

You're a fool, Simon Steele, or whoever you are. Don't get to know her, don't ask her questions. She's just a nurse, not an angel. When she stopped to help you, she was just doing what she was trained to.

Including staying the whole night with you?

Simon closed his eyes, willing away the picture of Caitlin, her mouth relaxed, her hair spread out on her arms that night she slept at the foot of the hospital bed. So beautiful, so peaceful. He didn't want to wonder why she had stayed the night, why she wasn't married. He had almost asked her if she had a boyfriend. As if that should matter to him.

Forget her, Simon, he reminded himself, she's not your type.

Of course, he didn't know anymore what his type was. He used to be attracted to more obvious women—the ones who knew how to play the game. The ones he could date a few times, then forget to call. The ones who didn't require commitment. The ones who didn't get close.

But the past few years he'd grown weary of the games, the empty talk. He was tired of the emptiness of the relationships in his life.

When the nurses asked about next of kin, he almost mentioned his older brother Jake. Then he stopped himself. The last time he'd spoken with Jake was from a pay phone. Simon had run away from his last foster home and wanted Jake to join him in his search for their biological mother. Jake had refused. When Simon had told him that he had to choose between Jake's current foster parents or him, Jake had chosen the Prins family.

Simon told Jake that he'd never hear from him again. He didn't need Jake. He didn't need anybody. He would make it on his own.

And he had.

His fortunes went up and down, but he never cared. It was a game and one he was good at because it only required luck, some intuition and a lot of nerve.

And he'd done well. But as his bank account grew, his own dissatisfaction increased proportionately. He had indulged in the toys—a few fancy cars, a sailboat, his motorbike. He lived out of hotels, indulging and pampering himself. He bought what he wanted when he wanted, but as soon as he owned what he wanted he lost interest.

So he'd finally bought a condo in Vancouver, hoping that establishing some kind of home base would give him whatever it was that eluded him. Happiness, contentment. He wasn't sure. He only knew that the old restlessness that sent him out on the road as a young man had captured him again. He had promised himself once he'd settled down, once he'd made it, he'd contact Jake. But as each year passed it got harder. His pride kept him back. And his shame. For he knew that his life was still not what it should be and he didn't need to be reminded.

Now he lay in a hospital bed in a city that was supposed to be only a quick side trip, wishing he could get on with his life.

Tired of his own thoughts, he blew out his breath and pushed the call button again. He didn't care if Caitlin got angry with him, he was hurting and bored. Not a good combination.

She came after a few minutes, appearing at his bedside to turn off his pager. She turned to him, her arms crossed over her stomach. "What can I do for you?"

Simon had to give her a lot of credit. He knew she was ticked but you couldn't tell from her voice. He didn't know exactly how he knew. He just did. "That's not really a nurse's uniform is it?" he asked taking another look at her aqua pantsuit topped with a sweater in a paler shade.

"I'm sure you didn't summon me to discuss fashion," she said quietly. She glanced at his IV and walked to the foot of his bed. "Do you want me to lower the bed for you. You really should be sleeping."

"I'm tired of sleeping, of being drugged and lying here."

"Good. That means you're getting better." She flashed him a quick smile and bent over to crank the head of his bed down anyhow.

"Don't. Please." He didn't know where the "please" came from. It wasn't like him to beg.

She straightened. "You really need to sleep, Simon."

Her voice was no-nonsense and firm but hearing her say his name gave him a jolt. "I can't. I'm bored, and everything still hurts. I feel like a child."

"Do you want something to read?"

"I've read all the magazines already."

"What about books?"

Simon looked away, frowning, trying to remember the last book he read. "Maybe," he said with a shrug.

"We've got some Westerns, which might appeal to

a modern-day cowboy like you, some science fiction, mysteries, thrillers—the usual cross section."

"I don't like fiction. Why don't you just sit and talk to me?"

Caitlin shook her head and walked over to the side of his bed, leaning against the metal radiator that ran along the wall below the window. "You are probably my most persistent patient. It's one o'clock in the morning, you really need to sleep."

"So you said." He smiled at her and folded his hands on his chest. She looked like she was willing to stay awhile, which suited him just fine. "How long have you been working here?"

"Five years."

He raised his eyebrows at that. "That long?"

"What do you mean?"

"I don't think I held a job down longer than a year."

"What did you do?"

Simon hesitated, lifting his thumbs and inspecting them. "This and that."

"Sounds fishy," Caitlin said, dropping her head to one side, as if inspecting him.

"Not really." He frowned at her. "Did you grow up here?"

She nodded, her head still angled slightly sideways. "My parents own a house close to the ferry terminal. I've lived there all my life."

"Tire swing, tree house, big porch?"

"Yes, actually." She smiled and once again Simon felt a peculiar tightness in his chest and once again he wondered why she had this effect on him. "My dad built us a tree house and Mom helped us furnish it."

"Us being the brother and sisters?" He couldn't help

the sardonic tone in his voice. "Sounds very cozy and small-town America."

Caitlin shrugged. "It was, until I pushed Tony off the ladder because he and his friends were chasing me. He ended up with a broken leg, and I ended up being banished from the tree house for a month."

"But you nursed him back to health, and that's how you discovered you wanted to be a nurse?"

"Right," Caitlin said with a short laugh. "Tony wouldn't let me within five feet of him, then or now. We weren't close then. Unfortunately we still aren't."

Simon heard the plaintive note in her voice and couldn't stop himself from asking, "Why not?"

"My brother has made some pretty poor choices in his life that we've had a hard time living with."

"That sounds 'Caitlinese' for he messed up."

Caitlin tilted her shoulder up in a light shrug. "I guess that was full of euphemisms." She held his gaze as if weighing his reaction. "Tony got involved with a gang when he was young. They ran wild, and he ran with them. He married one of the girls, moved to Toronto and we haven't heard from him since."

"The black sheep of the cozy family."

"Why do you say that with such sarcasm?"

Simon didn't reply, not sure himself. He had spent most of his life disdaining family, so it just came naturally. No one had challenged him on that before.

"Our family is close, but we're not an unusual group of people," Caitlin continued, pushing herself away from the radiator. "Stable American families are more common than television, newspapers and movies would have us believe."

"And you probably pray before every meal, too."

Caitlin drew in a slow breath, as if weighing her answer. "As a matter of fact we do. We read the Bible regularly, and we struggle each day to live out our faith in all the things we do and say. Tony gets mentioned in just about every prayer that gets uttered either aloud or in quiet."

Caitlin spoke quietly, but Simon easily heard the sincerity in her words. They intruded upon a part of his life he thought he had safely pushed aside. He tried to hold her steady gaze, to keep his eyes on her soft green ones, reaching for the sarcasm he knew would push her away from the place she had ventured too close to.

"Nice to know I'm in such good company."

"What do you mean?"

He winked at her, but it lacked conviction on his part. "You prayed for me, too," he said sarcastically. "Do you still pray for me?"

She held his eyes captive, her expression serious. "Yes I do, Simon." Her voice was quiet, her words simple, yet what she said shook him to the core. "Do you need anything else?"

He watched her a moment, noting the change in her expression at his tone and suddenly disliking it more than he thought he would, but knowing he had to take this through to the end. "I still need something to read."

She reached behind her and pulled open the drawer of his bedside table. She pulled out a Bible and laid it gently beside his hand. "You said you didn't like reading fiction, this might be just the thing."

And with that she left.

Chapter Six

"Cup of tea, honey?"

"That sounds wonderful." Caitlin yawned, shooed the cat off the wooden chair and sat down at the kitchen table. She finger-combed her hair, still damp from her shower as she looked around the brightly lit room, smiling.

Watching her mother move unhurriedly around the kitchen gave her a sense of order and continuity. As long as she could remember, her mother made her tea when she woke up whether it was in the morning for a regular day of school or work or in midafternoon when she started working shifts.

Her mother set a steaming mug in front of her. Caitlin wrapped her hands around it, stifling another yawn.

"And how was work?" her mother asked, sitting down at the table close to Caitlin, holding her own cup.

"Busy." She spooned sugar into her tea. "Where's Rachel?"

"She and Jonathon packed a picnic and headed up to Denman Island. They were hoping to check out the market there." Her mother took a careful sip of tea and brushed a lock of graying hair out of her face. "You could have gone with them if you hadn't decided to work."

Caitlin shrugged, ignoring her mother's heavy hint and the guilt that came with it. Spending time with her sister should be more important than working but it wasn't.

Her mother had tried to convince her she needed time at home to catch her breath. She didn't understand Caitlin's desire to get busy, to work in an effort to push aside what had happened, to get on with her life.

"I got a phone call last night." Her mother's soft voice broke the silence.

"From…" Caitlin prompted, her heart fluttering at the intensity of her mother's gaze.

"Charles."

I knew she was going to say that, Caitlin thought. "What did he want?" she asked, putting down her cup.

"He said he still had your suitcase and was hoping to drop it off."

Caitlin had forgotten about the arrangements she and Charles had made for their holiday. A day before their fateful date she had brought her clothes to his parents' place. They were to bring it to the cabin so that Caitlin and Charles could leave directly for Pender Island after supper.

"What did you tell him?"

Jean Severn pulled in her lips, looking down at her cup of tea. "I told him when you would be awake, but he said he would bring it to the hospital once he was done work."

"Why didn't you tell him to just bring it here?" Caitlin didn't want to see him again.

Jean looked up with an encouraging smile. "I thought he might want to talk to you. Maybe he wants to get back together…"

"Don't even say it, mother," Caitlin said, raising her hand in warning. "He's moving to LA. He doesn't want to commit himself. We've been through this before."

Caitlin knew her mother had loved Charles and had such high hopes for the two of them. That those hopes had been dashed was more of a disappointment to her than it had been to Caitlin.

"How many evening shifts are you going to be working?" her mother asked, wisely changing the subject.

"I've already done three, so I'll be working two more."

"Too bad your tickets to Portland are booked already, otherwise you could leave earlier."

Caitlin shrugged. "Doesn't matter. Maybe I'll head up-island myself. Hit Hornby Island for a while, go up to Miracle Beach."

"You don't sound very enthusiastic about that," her mother said intuitively.

"You're right. I'm just thinking aloud." Caitlin pulled one leg up on the chair, hugging it. "I'm just feeling a little mixed up right now. Maybe I kept dating Charles because I thought if I let him go, who else would I have?" Caitlin rubbed her chin on her worn jeans, feeling distinctly melancholy. "I think we were just a convenience to each other."

"You and Charles were never a passionate couple, Caity, but you were never a passionate person. You've always liked things orderly and neat. I never had to nag you to clean up your room like I did your siblings."

"You make me sound boring."

Jean leaned over and ran her hand over Caitlin's cheek. "You are anything but boring, Caitlin. You have a caring, steady nature and a solid faith I know many people envy."

I still sound boring, Caitlin thought. Nice, but boring. But she smiled at her mother, secure in the love that surrounded her. "And you're a good mom." She leaned her head against her mother's shoulder. "I feel like I'm still in high school, coming home and dumping on you."

Jean stroked Caitlin's hair, rubbing her chin over Caitlin's head. "I am glad you can. I pray you will find some direction in your life. I know that God isn't…"

"…through with me yet," Caitlin interrupted, finishing the familiar saying with a smile. She straightened and gave her mother a quick kiss. "Let's see, what else could you tell me. I'm still young and there's lots of other fish in the sea. There's not a pot so crooked that a lid doesn't fit on it." There were many more homilies her mother often used and all had to do with finding someone in her life. Marriage, the ultimate goal.

Jean shook her head and tousled her daughter's hair. "That's enough, you pest. You had better head upstairs and get dressed if you want to get to work on time."

Caitlin stood up, looking down on her mother. Much as she teased her mother about her truisms, she also knew that there was a lot of truth in those simple phrases. Truth and love dispensed in equal measure.

She smiled, and bending over, dropped a kiss on her mother's forehead. "I love you, Mom. I hope you know that."

"Yes, I do." Jean Severn smiled up at her daughter. "You're a wonderful daughter and a wonderful person. That hasn't changed."

* * *

"And how have our model patients been doing?" Caitlin walked into the hospital room and stopped by Shane's table. Schoolbooks, papers and cards covered it. He was hunched over a handheld computer game, ignoring her.

"Hey, you little twerp," Simon said from the bed beside him, "Caitlin asked you a question."

Shane looked up at that, his eyes opening wide when he saw Caitlin. He laid down the game, the frown on his face fading away to be replaced by a sheepish grin. "Sorry," he said, pushing himself to a sitting position. "I didn't know it was you." He looked up at her again, smiling.

"That's okay," Caitlin said, puzzled at the change.

Yesterday he had been snappy. Now he seemed eager to please.

"You working tonight?" he asked, pulling the table closer. He laughed shortly. "Of course you are," he said without giving her a chance to reply. "That's why you're here. Sorry."

Caitlin could see he was embarrassed and resisted the urge to smile. "I'm just checking up on everyone. Usual beginning-of-the-shift stuff."

"Well, thanks."

"I noticed you had a bunch of visitors today."

Shane nodded, relaxing enough to sit back. "Friends from school, some of the teammates."

"The day nurse told me your girlfriend came," Caitlin prompted, smiling now.

"Well, she's just a friend. We're sort of seeing each other, but not really."

"I wish my girlfriends treated me like that," Simon

interjected from his side of the room. Caitlin turned to him with a frown, and he only winked at her. "She was hanging on him like a bad suit."

Shane looked down at his computer game. "Well, she'll dump me quick enough, when she finds out I can't play football anymore," he muttered.

"Oh, she'll stick around for a while," Simon disagreed, his voice holding that world-weary tone that set Caitlin's teeth on edge. "As long as you've got money, you'll be okay."

"Thanks for your input, Simon." Caitlin's voice took on a fake sweetness as she turned to him. "I'll talk to you later." And with that she pulled the curtain between them. It was a flimsy barrier, he could still hear everything she said to Shane, but it gave the idea of privacy. Hopefully Simon would take the hint.

"Do you think she went out with you just because you are a football player?" Caitlin asked, lowering her voice.

"Maybe." Shane lifted one shoulder in a negligent shrug. "But that doesn't matter anymore." He looked up and tried out a smile that aimed for the same casual familiarity that Simon had mastered to perfection. But Shane's missed the mark. Obviously not as experienced, Caitlin thought.

"I'm sure the fact that you won't play football doesn't matter as much to her as it does to you," she said, her voice taking on a brisk, reassuring tone. "And who knows. Once you get mobile, you might be surprised what you can do yet." She left, fighting the urge to smile.

"You're looking mighty cheerful," Simon said as she came around the curtain.

Caitlin shook her head as she glanced at him. "And you seem pretty good compared to what your chart says. Your temperature is up a bit, and you look flushed."

"I'm fine." Simon winked at her, then tried to push himself up with his hands. He sucked in a quick breath through clenched teeth, his eyes shut. He lay still for a moment, then was about to try again.

"Don't, Simon." Caitlin laid a warning hand on his shoulder. "Here, I'll put another pillow behind your back, then you don't have to move."

He nodded weakly, showing to Caitlin how deep his agony really was. She got a pillow from the foot of his bed and carefully inserted it behind him. He was breathing with slow, controlled breaths, riding out the pain. He lay back against the pillow which allowed him to sit up a little higher. "Thanks, angel," he said, pulling in another slow, deep breath, as he smiled up at her.

Her heart softened as their eyes met. While she had thankfully never had to endure what many of her patients had, experience had given her an idea of how they felt. Seeing a man of Simon's age and strength made so weak and helpless always wounded her deeply.

He slowly settled back, relaxing now. "Are you going to stick around awhile? My girlfriend didn't come today."

Caitlin felt a slight jolt of disappointment. So, he had a girlfriend after all. "Does she know you're here?" she asked, trying to sound nonchalant.

Simon angled a grin up at her. "She doesn't even know I exist. I don't have a girlfriend."

"Oh. I see." Caitlin didn't see, though. She didn't see why that should matter to her. She didn't see why she should care. But she did.

"But Shane over there does have a girlfriend, even though he doesn't want you to think so." He waggled a finger. "Come here," he whispered. "I've got to tell you something."

Puzzled, she stepped closer to the bed, bending down slightly.

"You're too far away," he whispered.

Caitlin bent nearer, disconcerted to feel Simon's hand on her neck, pulling her down.

"I think that boy likes you."

Caitlin heard his words, but even more than that, she felt his warm breath feather her hair, felt her own breath slow at his touch. She pulled abruptly away, her heart pushing against her chest. "Don't be absurd," she said, quickly trying to cover up her reaction to him. What was wrong with her?

"I'm not absurd." Simon smiled up at her, his mouth curved in a mischievous smile that showed her quite clearly what kind of a man he really was. "And you know what? I have a crush on you, too." He cocked his head, raising his eyebrows suggestively and Caitlin turned away, disgusted with him and even more, herself. In spite of what she knew about him, his smile still gave her a slight jolt.

"I'll check on you later," was all she said.

She made the rest of her rounds. The next two patients she saw were a good balance to Simon and his innuendoes and leading comments. He was a study in frustration. It seemed each time he showed his vulnerability, he had to counteract that with some ridiculous behavior.

Caitlin continued her rounds, checking her patients' vitals. When she stopped to check on Shane again, his parents had him laughing so she left him alone for now. The curtain was drawn between his and Simon's beds and when she stopped on Simon's side, it was to find him with the head of his bed elevated as he stared at the curtain dividing the room. He seemed to be listening to the chatter going on beside him. If Caitlin didn't know him better, she would say his expression was almost wistful.

Her earlier pique with him had dissipated in the routine of her work. Once again she found herself watching him, wondering who he really was and where he really came from, why no one visited him or phoned. Not even the elusive Oscar.

He turned his head and caught her looking. He gave her a bold wink and sly grin which completely broke the very temporary mood.

"You still love me, angel?"

I give up on this man, Caitlin thought. She walked to his side, clipping the stethoscope in her ears. "How are you feeling?" she asked as she put on the blood pressure cuff.

He held her gaze a moment, then looked away. "Not great," he said succinctly.

His face was still flushed, and she laid her hand on his forehead. It was warm.

"Have you been feeling shaky, or trembly at all?"

"Not really." He picked up the book he had been reading and closed it. "Can you put this back on the table?"

Caitlin took the book, surprised to see that it was the Bible. She glanced at Simon, but he was looking sidelong at the curtain again, listening to the voices beyond so she laid it beside the bed.

He laid his head back and sighed, his eyes squeezed shut. Caitlin was concerned. By now she knew Simon well enough to realize he wouldn't tell her if he was dying.

She took his temperature.

"Still good. Only .04 above normal. Must be something else," she murmured, making a note on his chart.

"How often do you hear from your brother in Toronto?" Simon asked. "The black sheep."

Caitlin felt taken aback, surprised that he remembered, wondering why he brought it up. "My parents haven't heard from him in four years. We don't know where he lives anymore."

"And what would you do if he showed up on your doorstep?" Simon opened his eyes, holding hers with a steady gaze.

"Let him in. Feed him and then give him a smack for making us worry about him."

"Would you forgive him for making you worry?"

"Of course."

Simon quirked an eyebrow up at her, his expression slightly cynical. "You say that so easily. C'mon," he urged. "Try to imagine him coming back, then tell me you'd just let him in."

Caitlin looked past Simon, lost herself for a moment in memories and wishes. "You're right. I said that quite easily. I think it would be hard. But in spite of never being close, he's still my brother." Caitlin looked back at Simon. "That will never change no matter how I wish it. My mother and father love him dearly. For their sake as much as my own I would probably forgive him. I believe God has forgiven me a whole lot more."

"Sort of like the parable of the debtors."

"Which one do you mean?"

"You know. The one where the king forgave a man a huge debt and then the man turns around and sends one of his debtors to prison for an even smaller debt."

"That would be the one," she said, surprised that he knew it. "How did you know that?"

"My adoptive father used to read the Bible to us pretty regularly." Simon shrugged as if uncomfortable admitting even that much.

"I'm glad to hear that." She smiled, pleased to find out that he had some faith training in his life. It made him more approachable somehow. "I'll be back in half an hour, and I'll check your temperature again. I'm a little concerned about how you're feeling."

She looked down at him, still holding the thermometer. His hazel eyes held hers and she couldn't look away. She felt as if she were drifting toward him, falling, losing herself in his mesmerizing gaze.

"Caitlin." His voice was quiet, barely above a whisper and the sound of it speaking her name created a subtle intimacy.

She couldn't look away, didn't want to.

She was standing close to him, and when he reached up to touch her, to gently run his fingers along her elbow, she couldn't stop him.

"What are you doing to me?" he murmured, stroking her upper arm with light movements of his fingers, his eyes warm, soft, holding hers. "You save my life, you stay with me, you take care of me, you've even got me reading the Bible, something I haven't done in years." He laughed lightly, his fingers encircling her arm with a warmth that quickened her pulse. He gave her a light shake, as if in reprimand. "What are you really, Caitlin? An angel?"

Caitlin swallowed, trying to find her breath. "I'm just a nurse," she replied, her own voice tense with suppressed emotion.

The words, spoken aloud, were a palpable reminder of where she was and who she was. "Just a nurse," she repeated again. Shaken, she pulled away and without looking back, left.

She managed to make it to the desk, sat down behind its high wall and dropped her face into her hands. What was happening to her? She who prided herself on her professionalism, her detachment, her ability to calmly assess a situation was getting drawn into something that was moving out of her control.

She was falling for a patient.

All through her training warnings against precisely that had been drilled into each nurse. The dangers of the enforced intimacy of the patient-nurse relationship. The helplessness of a patient creating a false romanticism. Bored patients who whiled away their time trying to get nurses to pay attention to them.

Simon was all the warnings she had ever heard, all the warnings she had ever given other student nurses, wrapped up in one dangerous package. And she was falling for him.

Blowing out a sigh, she pulled her hands over her face, resting her fingers against her mouth. She had been crazy to come back to work so soon after breaking up with Charles. She thought it would help. But she was emotionally vulnerable and Simon was bored and carelessly handsome.

A bad combination all the way around.

Chapter Seven

Simon closed his eyes, wishing sleep would drift over his mind, pulling with it the thoughts that wouldn't stop. But sleep was the one thing he couldn't accomplish through force of will.

At the bed beside him, Shane's parents were saying goodbye. The quiet sound of their voices created an unexpected sorrow he disliked.

All evening people had come and gone through this room, and the only people who stopped by his bed were Caitlin and the cleaning lady. He wasn't a maudlin sort. Ever since he and his brother Jake had been split up he knew that to need people was to give them an edge over you. And once they had an edge over you, they were in charge.

The solution was easy. Keep relationships light and superficial and don't let anyone get close. He had accomplished both quite well.

But that meant Simon now lay, alone, in a hospital bed and no one knew or cared.

Snap out of it Simon, he reprimanded himself. You

want it this way. You don't want anyone intruding on your life with their expectations, telling you what to do.

He heard the scrape of chairs beside him, heard Shane's mother murmur, "Make sure you get enough rest, honey."

"Don't go racing down the hall," his sister added with an attempt at humor.

"Like I could," Shane replied but his voice didn't have the petulant whine of a few days ago.

"We'll come by again tomorrow," Shane's father said. Simon didn't want to look, but did anyhow. He saw the faint shadow of someone bending over the head of the bed, then another and another.

"Love you, Shane," the mother whispered.

"Love you, too, Mom," he whispered back.

Simon turned his head back to the window. Wasn't that cute, he thought. Mom and Dad and sister kissing Shane goodbye. He didn't think anyone did that anymore. He didn't think anyone did that, ever.

He closed his eyes, but he couldn't erase the image. He wondered what it would have been like, at Shane's age, to have lived with adults who touched in kindness instead of in anger. Parents who cared, who loved, who surrounded you in times of need.

Once in his life he had been surrounded with love. The love of his adoptive father, Tom Steele. Once he had been tucked in and kissed good-night by his adoptive father. But that was in another age, another life.

"Do you want me to turn off your light?"

Caitlin's soft voice gave him a start. He opened his eyes, to see her standing beside his bed.

"No," he replied, unable to keep his eyes off her. "I can't sleep."

"You have to. You haven't been able to sleep for a couple of nights now." Caitlin frowned, looking concerned as she stepped closer. She fussed with his sheet, folded his blanket back—little maternal things that touched on a hidden sorrow, reinforcing the mood brought on by Shane's family.

Her hair was loose this evening, framing her delicate features. Her eyes looked brighter, her cheeks pinker and her lips shone.

"You really are beautiful," he couldn't help but say.

Caitlin's cheeks grew even pinker. She was blushing, he thought with a measure of wonder. Without thinking, he reached out and took her hand.

Maybe it was the loneliness, maybe it was the sappy mood he had worked himself into, but when he felt her delicate fingers in his, he couldn't stop himself. He lifted her hand to his face and pressed a kiss in her palm.

And what was even more amazing, she let him. He felt her fingers curve around his cheek, brushing it lightly, then she slowly pulled her hand back.

"How are you feeling?" she asked, sounding breathless.

Like I should be standing up, with my arms around you, kissing you, he thought, sucking in a deep breath. "I'll be okay," was all he could say. He really had to get out of here. This woman was starting to get to him.

Caitlin laid the back of her hand on his forehead and frowned. "You're not feverish, thank the Lord."

"Why thank him?" he said, trying for his usual flippant attitude, the one he knew she hated. Anything to avert his reaction to her gentle touch. "He didn't have anything to do with this."

Caitlin only smiled. "I think He did."

"You been praying again?"

"Yes."

"I told you not to do that." Her talk of prayer always made him uncomfortable. Just like reading the Bible had. It reminded him of living with Tom Steele and Jake.

"Well, I did it anyhow."

"Like I said before, you're wasting your time. I'm just a blip in your life, sweet Caitlin." Simon could tell from the look on her face he had hurt her, which was what he intended to do.

Then why did it bother him, he wondered. "So what do you want from me now?"

She was supposed to say "Nothing" and then leave. She was supposed to stop tormenting him with her sincerity, her concern, her talk of prayers. Instead she pulled a chair close and sat down beside him in spite of how he had just talked to her.

"Simon, isn't there anyone we can call, anyone who we should tell about your accident?"

"There's no one else."

"You had said something about a foster home…"

"I've been in a bunch of them, Caitlin." Simon turned to face her, unable to keep the bitterness out of his voice. "I ran away from just about every one of them. They don't care. The very nature of foster homes is temporary."

"Why did you run away?"

Simon held her soft gaze, a gentle pain building in his chest and warnings ringing in his head. But he was lonely and in pain, and Caitlin was here. She'd be out of his life in a week anyhow so he took a chance and told her the truth. "Because it was easier than letting someone get close," he said finally. "At least that's what the counselors always said."

"You've been to counseling?"

"Seeing a counselor doesn't make me crazy, you know."

"Don't be so defensive," she chided, lightly shaking her head. "Seeing a counselor is a sign of strength, not weakness."

Simon felt himself relax at what she said, felt that peculiar tension that always gripped him when she was around, loosen. "I saw some when I was in foster care, and I went a bunch of times in the past few years."

"So how old were you when you ended up on your own?"

"Sixteen."

"Wouldn't you have been in care until you were eighteen?"

Simon shrugged. "If I had followed the rules, yes. But I took off from the treatment foster home they put me."

"Where did you go from there?"

"I ended up hitching a ride with a bunch of tree planters. They told me about the good money they made and I joined them."

"And then…" she prompted, smiling in encouragement.

"Then I moved from one job to another. I made good money tree planting, worked on the rigs offshore, saved my money and invested it."

"So what do you do now?"

"This and that. I play the stock market, own some property. Oscar takes care of the details." He caught her gaze and smiled. "I've done well for myself. I've got a lot of money. I can do pretty much what I please." Simon stopped himself. He sounded as if he were trying to impress her and maybe in a way he was. He had gotten where he was by virtue of his own hard work, his own luck and making his own choices. "I've been luckier in the second part of my life than the first."

"Until now," she said, her mouth curving up.

He swallowed, her smile winding around his heart, warming and softening it as he held her eyes with his own. She didn't look away and slowly all else drifted away, meaningless, unknown. His past, his need for independence all seemed to disappear. There was only him and Caitlin. It seemed too right to reach out, to feather his fingers against her soft cheek. She turned her face oh-so-slightly, her eyes drifting shut as her hand came up to hold his hand close to her face.

They stayed thus, the tenuous connection holding them, creating a fragile bond. Then a cart rattled past the door and Caitlin abruptly dropped her hand. Simon could see her stiffening, straightening, pulling back.

"I have to go," she said quietly, getting up. She pressed her hand to her cheeks, as if to cool them. She looked away, biting her lip, then turned to him. "I'm sorry, Simon, this shouldn't have happened."

How could she say such a thing? That was traditionally his line. "Why not?"

She faced him, her eyes now clouded with sorrow. "I'm a nurse, that's why not. This was a mistake. It's unethical and wrong."

Her words were like repeated douses of cold water. His feelings for her had been confusing ever since the first moment he saw her, but he would never have called them unethical and wrong.

Because for him, for the first time in his life, what he felt for a woman was pure and decent.

"You better go, then," he said, his voice tight.

She did.

Stop it, Caitlin rebuked herself. Stop thinking about him. She bent over the sink in the ladies' room, splashing cold water on her face, the shock of it clearing her mind. She did it again, and again and again until her cheeks were numb and her fingers stiff.

She dried her face and hands, pausing a moment to look at herself in the mirror again. A wide-eyed, frightened face stared back at her. Her lips looked as if they had been kissed. Puzzled, she lifted a finger to her mouth, wondering what it would be like to have Simon's lips on hers, to feel his strong arms hold her close.

Please help me, Lord, she prayed. *I can't have this happen. It's wrong and it doesn't make sense. Please help me stay objective. Help me remember I'm a nurse, a professional who doesn't fall in love with her patients.*

She closed her eyes, took a breath as she felt a peace come over her. *I want to take care of Simon, Lord, but I want to do it the right way. Help me keep my focus. Show me what I should do.* And as she laid it in God's hands she was reminded that she didn't go through life on her own strength. She waited a minute, regaining her composure, then, when she felt her control return, she left.

The ward was quiet when she returned to her desk. It was only nine o'clock, and she had an hour of charting ahead of her. Danielle was on her break and Valerie, one of the other nurses, was just returning to the desk when Caitlin sat down. Thankfully she didn't indulge in any chitchat and Caitlin could get to her work.

Routine, that's what she needed, she thought, pulling out Shane's chart. She clicked the pen when the *ping* of the elevator made her look up. Who would be coming on the ward this time of the night?

The doors of the elevator slid open, and Charles stepped out.

Caitlin felt as if the cold water she had recently splashed on her face shot through her veins. Her throat went dry, and her hands went still.

He stopped just outside the elevator, looking around, his expression puzzled. He saw her then and with a hesitant smile, walked over to where she sat.

"Hello, Caitlin," he said, his deep voice familiar. He came to a stop in front of the high desk, his face and shoulders visible above it. He wore a black topcoat over a navy suit, setting off his blond hair and blue eyes. He was handsome in a clean-cut way.

She only nodded at him, fully aware of the curious stares of Valerie beside her.

"Do you have a few minutes?" he asked quietly.

"I'm kind of busy right now," she replied. She didn't want to spend any more time with him and she was afraid to leave the familiar territory of her desk.

"I brought back your suitcase," he said, lifting it slightly so she could see it above the high wall she sat behind.

"Just set it down where you're standing. Thanks." She was surprised how easy it was to keep her tone impersonal.

Charles disappeared as he set it down. When he

straightened, he rested his elbows on the desk, leaning closer to her. He glanced sidelong at the nurse sitting beside Caitlin, then back. "How have you been?" he asked, his voice lowering.

"I'll just be in the supply room, Caitlin." Valerie pushed her chair back.

Caitlin wanted her to stay. She didn't want to be alone with Charles, not after what just happened in Simon's room. She felt as if her life were spiraling out of control, and the last thing she needed was to face Charles, the man who had started it.

But she said nothing. Charles smiled his thanks, then when Valerie was gone, turned back to Caitlin.

"Can we go for coffee, or something?"

"No. I just got off my break." Which I spent beside the bed of a patient, with Simon, she thought guiltily busying herself with some papers.

"I need to talk to you." Charles's voice held an intensity she had never heard before. She looked up to see his eyes staring down at her, his mouth unsmiling. For the first time she noticed how drawn and tired he looked. Very un-Charles-like.

"What do we have to talk about?" she asked, pulling back from the force of his gaze, unable to stop the touch of sympathy she felt.

"Us. What happened last week. What's going to happen in the future."

"We don't have a future, Charles. I don't know now if we ever did." Caitlin felt intimidated by him towering over her and stood up.

"I made a huge mistake that night. You caught me by surprise."

Caitlin couldn't believe how obtuse he could be.

"We've been dating, Charles. Wondering where our relationship is going is hardly a surprise. Moving to Los Angeles, now, *that* was a surprise."

Charles pulled his hand over his face, looking away from her. "I know that, Caitlin. I know all that. It's just that…"

"You've been busy with your career, and I've been busy with mine," she finished for him, crossing her arms over her waist as if in defense. Charles was still attractive, familiar in a comfortable way. But she also knew she never cared for him the way she should have. "We've broken up before for the same reasons."

"That's true, Caitlin, but you know—" he looked back at her, leaning even closer "—I got the promotion I had been wanting for years. Now I have it and I don't have you. I don't know if I came out ahead."

"Are you saying you miss me?"

He sighed as he rubbed his forehead with one finger. "I'm saying I want to try again. I know I haven't always been as attentive as I should and I'm hoping we could find a new footing for our relationship."

Caitlin heard him and knew that beneath the vague words, he still cared for her. He looked up, his expression pained and it hurt her to see him like this.

"I'd like to try again, Caitlin. I know we have a good relationship, we share a common faith, we have the same interests. Please."

"And what about Los Angeles?"

Charles bit his lip. "I'm still going."

Caitlin nodded. "Come, I'll walk with you to the elevator." They were silent until they came to the shining doors. Caitlin turned to him, unable to prevent herself from comparing him to Simon.

"I know it won't work, Charles," she said softly, lifting one shoulder in a negligent shrug. "This isn't the first time we've had to analyze the relationship. Nor is it the first time we've broken up." She softened her words with a smile. "But this time it's for good. Goodbye, Charles," was all she said.

He stared at her a moment, then turned and left.

Caitlin pressed her hand against her chest, but her heart beat steady and sure, her breathing was regular, pulse moderate. Her old boyfriend had stopped by to see her, had asked her for another chance and she didn't really feel any different.

No passion here, she thought with a vague disappointment, remembering what both her mother and sister had said about her. Maybe it was a genetic disorder. Maybe rapture and thrills were not part and parcel of her relationships.

"That your boyfriend?" Valerie asked, finally daring to make an appearance. "He's a honey."

Caitlin sat down, staring sightlessly at the notes pinned on the board in front of her, easily recalling Charles's blue eyes, blond hair styled to perfection. "I suppose," she said vaguely, picking up her pen again.

"What do you mean, you suppose. He's got the good looks of a male model."

Caitlin only shrugged. She knew that when she and Charles first went out, she was attracted to his looks, but over time his face simply became familiar, as did his personality.

Now, he wanted her back and she knew she couldn't be with a man whose touch did nothing to her.

Nothing compared to what happened when Simon had placed his hand on her cheek just minutes ago.

Caitlin bit her lip at the memory. Tried to eradicate pictures of Simon's face, his eyes, the memory of how he had made her feel with that simple touch, wondering why only thoughts of him could do more to her heart than actually seeing Charles did.

Simon stared ahead, listening to voices outside his room. Sound carried so well in this hospital. He often heard the nurses chatting, not realizing how well he could often understand what they were saying.

He had heard the nurses talking about what a difficult patient he was, usually in exasperated tones. He heard them talk about what they were going to be doing when they got off work. He could recognize Danielle's rough voice, Tina's shrill one. Knew that a nurse named Valerie was working tonight and that she thought Caitlin's boyfriend was attractive.

You're a fool, Simon, he berated himself. You should have known that someone like her would have a boyfriend.

He remembered the sound of the guy's voice as he talked with Caitlin. Simon only heard snatches of the conversation but enough to know they had planned a date.

He didn't know why he should care. Caitlin was merely a distraction. He was bored and out of sorts and what he felt toward her was gratitude, nothing more.

He shifted his weight, riding out the pain that accompanied the movement. This morning the physiotherapist had him up on crutches, putting what he called "feather" weight on his leg. He had felt dizzy, but it passed. When Caitlin had said he would be discharged in a couple of weeks, he hadn't believed her, but each day he progressed a little further and he knew it would come.

He was looking forward to leaving. He needed to get out of this room, away from this hospital. In the past few days he had spent too much time thinking about things he had managed to avoid.

Jake, his mother, the lack of family in his life.

Caitlin.

He remembered too vividly the softness of her cheek, how her fingers felt against his. He liked the sound of her voice and too often, when he was bored and lonely, yearned to hear her talking to him.

He found himself wishing she worked the day shift so he could see her more, then thankful she worked the night shift when it was quieter and she could spend some time with him.

He had spent half of today trying to reason his way past how he felt about her, wondering what he meant to her.

He pushed himself over with his elbow, ignoring the pain that accompanied the movement and wishing he could forget Caitlin Severn.

Tonight he had touched her, she had touched him. He had discovered feelings he never knew he possessed. A tenderness of emotion, a caring that passed beyond a physical attraction.

He needed her and even as the thought had bothered him, it gave him a peculiar ache that wasn't unwelcome.

Then after being told that the pure and tender emotions he felt for her were unethical, he found out she had a boyfriend.

He had to quit thinking, that's what he had to do. He never spent this much time sitting around. He was far more accustomed to spending his day on the phone, reading reports, investigating hot leads, analyzing data, running around until it was time to either find a date, or go to bed.

One of the day nurses had brought him a book, an action-adventure thriller. He figured he may as well read it now. It would be just what he needed to get his mind off a nurse who prayed, for goodness sakes.

He heard Shane snoring quietly and without thinking, rolled over to turn on his light. The quick movement sent shattering pain down his leg. He waited until it eased, then reached farther to take the book he had been reading off his night table.

He opened it, turned a few pages to find his spot. The words flowed past his eyes, black lines and circles on paper that were supposed to take him away from this hospital, push aside the thoughts that circled in his mind, tormenting him and teasing him.

His mind returned back to his brother, wondering once again where he was, what he was doing. Wondering if Jake regretted not leaving with him that day Simon had called him from a pay phone.

Simon wondered about his mother and where she was, if she was even still alive.

He turned back a page, trying again to read words he had just finished. Concentrating, he managed to pull himself into the story; then he heard Caitlin's voice, and his heart missed its next beat.

He glared past the curtain to the open door.

"Simon, do you need anything?" Caitlin stopped at the foot of his bed, her hands resting on the rail. Her smile was hesitant, appealing, and Simon reminded himself of what she had said only a few moments ago. He reminded himself of the boyfriend. Time to retreat.

He forced himself to look back down at the book. "Nothing you can give me, sweetie."

"I'll be in later to check your dressings. The day nurse was concerned about some discharge."

"Can't someone else do it?" he asked, forcing a disinterested tone into his voice. He looked up and curled his lip into a smile. "I wouldn't mind seeing that Valerie again. She's kind of cute."

"I'll tell her you said so," she said, her voice quiet, her face registering no emotion.

"You do that, Caity honey." He winked at her and setting his book down, leaned back, clasping his hands behind his head in what he hoped was a nonchalant pose. Lifting his arm like that made it throb but he refused to let that show. "Or is thinking she's cute, *unethical*." He put a hard emphasis on the last word, hoping it would create some kind of reaction.

"You can think whatever you want, Mr. Steele." Caitlin showed neither by action nor expression that what he said struck home, but as she turned and left, Simon instinctively knew he had hurt her.

It was what he had wanted to do, wasn't it?

Then why did it bother him so much?

Chapter Eight

"Rachel, when you first met Jonathon, what did you feel?" Caitlin asked as she sat on the couch, sipping the hot chocolate her sister had brought her. Caitlin had come home from work, tired and confused. She needed to talk. Thankfully Rachel had been waiting for her.

Rachel smiled, her expression turning dreamy. "Like all the air had been squeezed out of my chest."

Caitlin felt a twinge of jealousy at the emotion in her sister's voice, the breathy sigh at the end. "And when you see him now," she continued, "what do you feel?"

"You know, we can be sitting together in a room and he can look up at me and I can still feel the same thrill."

"Well, I never felt that way with Charles." And I have with Simon.

"Never?"

Caitlin slowly shook her head, setting her cup down on the table in front of her. "Nope. Never."

"A relationship is more than thrills, you know," Rachel said, leaning forward to lay a consoling hand on her sister's arm. "And like I said before, this sure doesn't sound like the Caitlin I know."

"I don't know, Rachel." She pulled her legs under her, laying her head along the back of the couch. "Sometimes when I'm praying, I feel a thrill. When I feel especially close to God, it makes my heart beat faster. I don't think it's unrealistic to expect the same feelings from a relationship with a man."

Rachel held her gaze, then nodded knowingly. "I see what you mean."

Caitlin looked past her sister, remembering another man's touch, the glow of his eyes.

His swaggering attitude.

The clock's resonant *bong* chimed off the hour and Caitlin reluctantly got up, yawning. "I've got to go to bed."

"How many more shifts are you working?"

Caitlin stretched her shoulders back, working a kink out of her neck. "One more night and then I'll be around for a few days. After that it's off to Portland to spend time with Evelyn and Scott."

"Jonathon and I will be here until Monday. We can do something together then."

"Sure." Caitlin bent over and dropped a kiss on her younger sister's head. "I'll see you tomorrow."

She trudged upstairs to the bathroom and had a shower, indulging in a long soak, hoping the hot water would chase away thoughts of mocking eyes, a cocky grin.

A man who could set her heart beating with just a lift of his mouth, the angle of his head. Something her boyfriend of three years couldn't quite manage.

Caitlin closed the door to her bedroom, walked over to the bed and fell backward on it with a *twang* of the bedsprings. She pressed her hands against her face, trying to find equilibrium, a place where she didn't have to do all this thinking and wondering.

Simon.

How easily his face slipped into her mind. His deep-set eyes, the way his hair fell over his forehead, framing his face, the curve of his lips. He had a beautiful mouth.

Too bad he misuses it so often.

Ah, the sharp voice of her own reason, pulling her back to reality. Simon was, as he had said, a blip. He was confusion and frustration and mixed-up emotions all tied in with the reordering of Caitlin's own life. He was a textbook case of the problems encountered with the enforced intimacy between patient and nurse. He was totally out of her league. She knew precious little about him. He didn't share her faith, in fact he often mocked it. He was overbearing and…

And vulnerable and handsome and fascinating in a deep, heart-clenching way that Charles never was.

She knew so little about Simon, his past. The little bits and pieces he threw her were just vague hints. He spoke of a brother, foster parents, an adoptive father, but no mother, no other family. So casually he spoke of his inability to let people get close, as if it were merely a fact of life, not something to deal with.

She got up, and slipped into bed. Yawning, she reached over and picked up her Bible from the night-stand and opened it to the passage she'd been reading. Ecclesiastes. She started reading it a few weeks ago, taking comfort in what she saw as a basic realism, an almost world-weary take on life that suited her own mood.

It put her own problems in perspective and reading it reminded her of something she knew since she was young. She had one basic mandate in life. To love and serve God. Everything else, as the writer said, "was meaningless, chasing after the wind."

But when she got to verse eight of chapter four, she stopped.

Her finger traced the words and as she reread them, they filled her with an eerie sadness. "There was a man all alone; he had neither son nor brother. There was no end to his toil, yet his eyes were not content with his wealth. 'For whom am I toiling,' he asked, 'and why am I depriving myself of enjoyment?'"

She placed her fingers on the words, thinking immediately of Simon. How proud he was of his success, that he had done it all on his own. Yet she sensed a sorrow and a loneliness that his money hadn't been able to assuage.

He had no one who missed him, no one who cared enough to visit, to phone or call or send a card or letter.

He was all alone. Like the writer of Ecclesiastes said, he had neither son nor brother. He had money, but no one who mattered to him.

She closed her eyes, laying her head back as she lifted her heart in prayer for him. It was the one time she could think of him and not feel guilty, when she prayed for him.

"Just go slowly now," the physiotherapist urged Simon, "and we'll do this once more."

He nodded, easing his weight to his injured leg. He breathed through the pain.

"Good, you're doing just great," he encouraged, standing close to Simon to support him.

"I'm doing nothing, Trevor," Simon grunted, gripping the crutches.

"Considering you had major surgery to the largest bone in your body almost a week ago, you're doing a lot." Trevor Walton nodded, watching Simon's leg. "Okay, back onto the bed and we'll work on your other exercises. Tomorrow we'll get you down to the gym for some mat work. Arm over my shoulder now," he instructed, as he easily got Simon onto the bed.

Simon allowed Trevor to help him, much as it galled him. Helplessness was a foreign concept to him. It was something he had fought his whole life. The helplessness of being moved around, of being shifted from home to home. He had vowed he would never be in a situation where he wasn't in control again.

And here he was. In many ways more reliant than he had been as a child. He was completely dependent on people bringing him his food, on helping him in and out of bed. He hadn't been outside for days now and in order to accomplish that, he would have to ask someone.

All day people came in, did something, then left. His bedding got changed, his dressings checked. The day shift was always busy, though some of the nurses would take time out to chat with him.

He laughed with them, told them jokes, talked about inane things but none of them caught his fancy enough that it mattered whether they stopped and visited or not.

But it seemed he spent his entire day waiting for the night shift to come on. Waiting for Caitlin to stop by, hoping she had time to talk.

You're nuts, he chastised himself, trying to get comfortable again. Tonight is her last night and then she's finished.

The thought stopped him momentarily. He didn't want to think he might never see her again.

Nor did he want to acknowledge how important she had become to him. He made it a rule with the women he met to keep things at a superficial level. Once he sensed they wanted more, he would leave. But Caitlin had worked herself into his consciousness, into his very being. He wanted to find out more about her, to spend more time with her.

It was her eyes, he figured. Eyes that watched him, watched over him during that first night, eyes that could soften with caring. His heart fluttered as he remembered touching her face yesterday, how she had turned her head into his hand.

When she had called what was building between them unethical, it made him angry. It was the first time in his life he recalled wishing he was a better person. It was the first time in his life that a woman challenged him to do just that.

She's got a boyfriend, idiot. He forced himself to remember that, to recall the date he heard them arrange last night. Caitlin belonged to someone else.

Yet if she did, why did she allow Simon to touch her? Why did he feel so right with her? Why had she stayed?

Well, after your little performance last night she won't be spending much time with you tonight, he reminded himself, recalling how he had made that ridiculous comment about wanting Valerie to check his dressings.

Simon picked up the action-adventure book he'd begun, forcing his mind back to the story and away from a woman who made him more confused than anyone before.

He read the same page about four times before putting the book down.

Still bored. Bored and confused and his head was busy with thoughts he couldn't seem to still.

Glancing sidelong, he saw the Bible again.

Why not? he thought, reaching for it. He had read it a couple of times since he came here. This time he flipped past the first books of the Old Testament and stopped at Isaiah, not really sure why. He skipped the first part with its woes and imprecations of doom for Israel.

Then he saw it. *Comfort, comfort ye my people.* Isaiah 40. The words spoke to a part of him he hadn't wanted to bring out in a long time. Comfort. Who had ever offered him that before? Counselors spoke of owning the problem, of acknowledging his part in what happened in his life, of taking charge and being in control. Foster parents spoke of letting down his guard and allowing people to care.

But other than his adoptive father none of them had offered the comfort he had just read about.

The words were familiar in an old way, he thought, tracing them with his finger. "The voice of one crying in the desert, prepare the way for the Lord." He vaguely remembered hearing them at a church service with candles.

Christmas, he realized as the memory returned. Christmas with Jake and Tom Steele, the widower who'd adopted them. The picture of the three of them sitting in a church pew slipped unbidden into his mind, the soft glow of candlelight as the minister spoke the words of Isaiah 40. The words of promise, of peace, of rest.

Allowing even that small memory to come back created a sharp surge of pain. Simon swallowed, closing his eyes. Weakness, he thought. Dependence.

Loss.

He almost threw the book aside, but forced his eyes open, forced himself to get past the pain. He was alone out of choice. Simon pushed his memories aside and read on, determined to get past this.

He got to verse 28 and read, "Do you not know? Have you not heard? The Lord is the everlasting God, the Creator of the ends of the earth. He will not grow tired or weary, and His understanding no one can fathom. He gives strength to the weary and increases the power of the weak. Even youths grow tired and weary, and young men stumble and fall, but those who hope in the Lord will renew their strength. They will soar on wings like eagles; they will run and not grow weary, they will walk and not be faint."

Simon read the words, his heart constricting. He had stumbled and fallen in so many ways. Reading the verses vaguely familiar to him made him look backward to memories he thought he had safely stored away, and by doing so, he compared them to his current life. The decisions he'd made that were so far from the ones he'd been raised to make.

I had no choice, he said to himself. I had to learn to take care of myself. No one else would.

He willed the memories away, laying down the Bible. Mentally he cursed the disability that kept him here in this hospital. He needed to get out, to leave, to keep himself busy.

He needed to outrun the thoughts that plagued him, reminded him of a different life and values.

He didn't want to look at himself anymore. Because when he did, he saw himself through Caitlin's eyes and he didn't like what he saw.

As Caitlin walked up the steps to the ward, she wished she could suppress the sense of expectation that lifted her steps. Much as she liked to deny it, deep within her, she knew it was because of Simon.

His behavior yesterday should have put her off, should have made her realize what kind of guy he was. So why did thoughts of him still make her heart flip?

I'm really going nuts, she thought pushing open the

door to the ward. Thank goodness she would be leaving in a few days. She needed to get away, see other places. Balance out the strangeness of her attraction to a patient compared to the lack of emotion she felt around Charles.

Thank goodness it was her last day of work here. Once today was over, Simon would be part of her history.

"Hi, girl," Danielle already sat at the desk. "How was yesterday?"

Val piped up from behind the desk, "Her boyfriend stopped by. What a babe."

Danielle gave Caitlin an appraising look. "What did Mr. Frost want?"

Caitlin shrugged, pulling her purse off her shoulder. "To take me out."

"And…" Danielle said.

Thankfully the charge nurse from the previous shift had come to the desk, ending the conversation.

Caitlin checked on a new admission. Vitals had just been done so she would be okay for a while. With a flutter of trepidation, she stepped into Shane and Simon's room. The crowd around Shane's bed was noisy and boisterous. She only recognized Shane's older brother, Matthew, out of the group of mostly teenagers.

"You'll have to keep it down, a bit, I'm afraid," Caitlin warned the group with a smile. "There are other patients in this room."

"We can do that," Matthew said with a wink. The girl beside him noticed and turned to give Caitlin an appraising stare that wasn't really friendly. He added, "If there's anything else I can do for you…" He was cut off by an elbow planted in his midsection.

"Give it up, Matt," Shane joked, glancing quickly at Caitlin. "She's got a boyfriend."

Caitlin didn't bother to correct him.

She gave them an inane smile and then stepped around the curtain to face Simon, suppressing a silly schoolgirl flutter at the thought of facing him again.

The light was off above his empty bed, the sheets thrown back.

Her heart stopped, then started again as she noticed a figure by the window, leaning on a pair of crutches.

I never realized he was so tall, she thought. He stood sideways to her. Even in the subdued light from Shane's bed, it wasn't hard to make out his broad shoulders, long legs. He had thrown a hospital-issue dressing gown over his pajamas but even hunched over the crutches, he had a commanding presence.

"Hi, there," she said, unable to think of anything else to say. "How did you get out of bed?"

"Determination," he said, still looking out the window. "What can I do for you?" His voice held the same mocking indifference she had come to associate with him.

"I just came by to see how you're doing. The usual shift-change stuff." She clasped her hands in front of her and lifted them in his direction. "According to Trevor's report, you've been working quite hard today. You should have waited until someone could help you out of bed," she said carefully, striving to keep her voice neutral.

"I had to try myself. I figure the further I progress, the sooner I'm out of here."

It was what she had thought as well, but hearing him articulate it gave it a sense of finality.

"I'll be by later to check on you and help you back into bed. Don't overdo it, okay?"

"You don't have to worry about me, Caitlin," he said

quietly, still looking out the window. "I'm sure you don't when you're out of this building."

If only you knew, Caitlin thought. But she wisely said nothing and left.

The evening moved along with painful slowness. Once visiting hours were over a quiet settled onto the ward. Danielle managed to convince Simon to sit in a chair.

Caitlin had checked on the patients after all the visitors had left. Some were sleeping, some were reading.

Simon now sat in his chair, reading, as well.

Caitlin walked closer, her pulse quickening as he looked up at her.

"You should let me help you back into bed," she said, trying to keep her voice steady.

"I've spent too much time in that bed already," he said, looking down again at the book on his lap. With a start Caitlin recognized the Bible from his bedside table.

She wanted to say something, to acknowledge what he read but she felt suddenly tongue-tied and self-conscious.

But he didn't seem to be so afflicted. "So what is it about this book?" he asked, turning a page and looking up at her. "Why am I reading it so much?"

Caitlin took a casual step nearer, encouraged by his questions, the change in his attitude. She wished she could figure him out. "What are you reading?"

Simon looked up with a wry grin. "Isaiah."

"Why did you choose that book?" she asked, surprised. Most people looking for encouragement chose the Psalms.

Simon gave a careful shrug. "I've been going through a bunch of them. Did some of the Psalms, but this fit."

"Fit what?"

"My life." He ran one finger along the gilt edge of

the pages, a frown pulling his dark eyebrows together in a scowl. "You know, the wayward, stubborn people."

"But Isaiah holds out hope, as well," Caitlin said. "That was the whole purpose of all of the prophets. To point toward the hope of the Messiah, the hope of reconciliation with God."

"The only reconciliation I do is at year end." Simon tilted his head up to her, still frowning. "Did you learn everything you know from Sunday school?"

"Amongst other things." Caitlin recalled the different Bible studies and classes she had attended. "I didn't always enjoy them, but now that I'm older I appreciate the tremendous heritage and wealth of Bible knowledge I've been given by my parents and teachers."

"I went when I was younger," Simon said. "Used to like it."

"Used to…" Caitlin prompted. Simon gave out so little of his past, every bit he handed out made him more real, more accessible.

"Just used to," he said with finality, closing the Bible. Caitlin heard the weariness in his voice.

She knew he would say nothing more tonight so she reverted back to her own job. "According to the physiotherapist, you spent the requisite amount of time sitting. You don't want to overdo it."

"I'll be okay." He shifted his weight and grimaced. "If you don't mind, I'd really like to be alone," he said without looking up. He was pushing her away again, she realized with dismay. He had shown her too much.

"Buzz someone when you want to get back into bed," she said softly, hesitating a moment yet. But Simon said nothing and she left.

Chapter Nine

As Caitlin looked over the inventory in the supply room, she couldn't keep the picture of Simon as he sat in his chair reading the Bible out of her mind. She wondered if he gained any comfort from it, if it made him think. What was he seeking there?

She knew he wouldn't ask. She knew Simon well enough by now to know that, to him, asking was a sign of weakness.

When she was done, she glanced at her watch. This was crazy. It didn't matter anymore what he wanted to prove, she had to get him back into bed.

As she passed the desk, she dropped the inventory sheet off and kept walking to Simon's room.

His light was still on and as she came around the curtain dividing the two beds it was to see him staring out the window. The Bible no longer lay on his lap.

He turned his head when she came in and this time, instead of indifference, she saw sorrow.

"How are you doing, Simon?" she asked, her voice quiet.

"I'd like to get back into bed now."

"I'll call Danielle to help."

"No. I got out by myself. I could probably get back in by myself…" his words drifted off and Caitlin wondered what he was going to say. But he kept silent.

"But you're tired now."

He simply nodded and Caitlin took it for acquiescence. "Just put your arm around my shoulder and lean on me when you stand up." Caitlin approached the chair, bending at her knees to take up a position right beside him. Simon laid his arm across her shoulder. "Lean on me and on three we'll stand up." She counted and Simon slowly got up as she straightened. She put her other arm around him, trying to ignore the strength of his muscles and the warmth of his torso through his pajamas, the thin hospital gown. "Now take a few short steps backward to your bed."

Simon didn't move and Caitlin looked up at him, puzzled.

His dark eyes glittered down at her and as she watched, he shifted his weight to his good leg, turning to face her.

"What are you doing?" she asked, her voice suddenly breathless as, for the first time since she met him, she looked up at him. She had to tilt her head back to do so.

"Something I've been wondering about for too long." His other arm came around her waist to hold her close to him and then, as Caitlin watched, mesmerized, he lowered his head. In a last, futile effort to keep her sanity, she kept her eyes open when his mouth touched hers. Then as his lips moved softly, gently, she felt her eyes drift closed, all coherent thought fled. There was only him, and the strength and warmth of his arms, his mouth on hers.

He was the first to draw away, resting his forehead against hers as he drew in a ragged breath. "What are you doing to me, angel?"

Caitlin felt as if all her breath had slowly been pressed out of her chest. She tried to take a breath, tried to force herself to move, but all she wanted was to be held by Simon, to stay in this place where time had ceased to exist, where she was no longer a nurse and he no longer a patient.

"I used to know what I wanted," he said, his breath teasing her hair as he touched his lips to her temple. "I thought I didn't need anything. Now you've got me all mixed up, reading the Bible, finding out what a scoundrel I really am…" He kissed her hair, a light touch of his mouth.

Caitlin heard his words, felt a surge of hope at his doubts. But her practical nature took over and she carefully drew back. "You have to let me go, Simon," she whispered.

His chest lifted in a sigh and he pressed her head in the lee of his neck. "No. I don't want to."

"Please, Simon." She didn't dare shift her weight for fear he'd fall. She wished she had asked Danielle to help.

He raised his head, as he let one arm drop to his side. The other still lay heavily across her shoulder. For a moment they stood, facing each other, unasked questions keeping her from taking that small step closer to him to lessen the distance.

Why did you do that? What do I mean to you? What am I doing? The questions tripped over themselves with no answer coming.

He was all wrong for her. He was a dangerous unknown, a lost, lonely soul.

"Caitlin, what's wrong?"

"Nothing's wrong," she lied, ignoring the tripping of her heart, the breath that refused to return to her lungs. She resisted the urge to run away, to flee.

He shook his head as he reached for her, sliding one rough finger down her cheek. "How do you manage to turn your emotions off so quickly?" he asked, tilting his head to one side to look at her.

"Simon, please. It's late, and you need to get back into bed."

"I'm safer there, aren't I, Caitlin? I can't reach you there."

She didn't want to listen, to know he was partially right. She didn't want to admit that he frightened her.

"Once I'm lying down you're in charge," he continued. "You can keep me at a distance. You can fool yourself into thinking just like I've tried to do that what's happening between us will simply go away once you leave this hospital and you can go back to Charles." As he took a step nearer he swayed slightly and Caitlin instinctively reached out to catch him.

Once again his arms were around her. Once again his mouth sought hers. As they met, he stifled her cry of protest. He held her tight against him, his arms strong, protective, his mouth insistent. He pulled away, a grin lifting the corner of his mouth. His expression was triumphant.

She didn't like the look on his face and forced his arms down. "Stop it, now. I don't care what you think, I don't care how you see me. This is wrong, and you can't make it right just by force of your will." She didn't want to look at him, didn't want to acknowledge the emotional hold he had over her. "What's happening between us is nothing new. Once you're gone, you'll forget all about me and the same will happen to me."

"And you can go back to Charles?" he said with a sneer.

Caitlin's heart flipped but she forced herself to concentrate, to remind herself that he was her patient, that she had a job to do. "My personal life is none of your concern." She drew in a slow breath as she prayed for equilibrium, for strength, for wisdom. "And now, I'm going to ask you once again to let me help you back into bed."

Simon stayed where he was, as if measuring her strength, then with a shrug, turned.

"Wait a minute, Simon," she warned.

But he moved too quickly. He didn't get his injured leg around soon enough to bear the weight. He threw out his arms just as Caitlin rushed forward.

Simon let out a harsh, loud cry as his leg twisted. She caught him, but his momentum combined with his weight was too much for her to hold up.

Caitlin managed to turn him so that he fell on top of her instead of the floor. She felt her breath leave her as they landed with a crash.

Stars and electrical impulses shot through her head, followed by a jolt of pain. Above her, Simon cried out again and she could do nothing. He was a dead weight.

She heard the squeak of rubber-soled shoes as thankfully, someone rushed into the room.

"What happened?" Caitlin heard Danielle's voice and then Simon was carefully rolled off of her.

"He moved too quickly," Caitlin said, her voice groggy with pain. "Then he fell. I couldn't stop him."

"Simon, Simon, can you hear me?" Danielle was crouched over Simon's inert body, checking him over.

"Where's Caitlin?" he called out, his eyes shut against the agony Caitlin knew must be coursing through his body. "Is she okay?"

"I'm okay," she said. She could get up, but her head was spinning and she couldn't seem to focus on what was happening.

"What about you, Simon? How's your leg?"

"Hurts," he whispered tightly.

Another nurse, Eva, came running into the room as Caitlin slowly got to her feet.

"Page the resident, Dr. Foth. Get him down here stat," Danielle said.

Eva ran out of the room leaving Caitlin and Danielle with Simon.

Simon's cries cut through Caitlin. Sweat broke out on his forehead, and he was clenching his teeth.

"He's going to need an X-ray," Danielle said, holding Simon's head. Caitlin only nodded, her head spinning.

Thankfully they didn't have long to wait. Dr. Foth came immediately, Eva right behind him pushing a gurney. Dr. Foth checked him over and ordered him to be taken immediately to X-ray.

"We need to make sure there's been no damage to that plate." He shook his head as he got up.

Hating her ineffectiveness, Caitlin managed to work her way around to the other side of the gurney, pushing it closer to Danielle, Dr. Foth and Eva. As they carefully lifted Simon on it, he cried out again, a harsh sound in the usual quiet of the night.

He lay panting, his eyes closed, his hands clenching the sheets at his sides. Each breath came out on a whimper that tore at her heart. Head spinning, Caitlin had to force herself to focus, to concentrate as she stepped closer to him. She had to touch him, to let him know she was there.

"Angel," he breathed, when he opened his eyes and saw her. "I hurt you."

"No. Just relax now." Talking was an effort but she needed to reassure him, to ease his own suffering. *Please, Lord, let his leg be all right. Please don't let anything serious have happened to him*, she prayed, touching his arm, connecting with him.

She felt Eva take her arm and resisted. She didn't want to leave until she knew he was okay.

"Danielle and the doctor will take him down," Eva said, gently drawing her away from Simon's side. "You should get checked over, too. You don't look too good."

"I'm okay," she lied, straightening and walking slowly out of the room.

I hope they take good care of him, Caitlin thought as she watched the elevator doors slide behind them.

She blinked slowly, swaying as the lights above her seemed to dim. Then the desk in front of her tilted, spun then receded down a long black corridor.

"Are you sure you should be up and about?" Rachel asked from the bottom of the stairs.

"I'm okay," Caitlin protested, her head pounding ferociously with each step. "I'm sick of lying around."

"Here, let me help you." Rachel held out her arm.

"I'll be okay," Caitlin said, ignoring her sister's help. She misjudged the last step, and the jolt of hitting the floor too hard sent pain slicing behind her eyes.

"Don't be so stubborn, Caitlin. What if all your patients acted like you do?"

I already have one who does, Caitlin thought. She realized her folly and leaned on her sister's arm, grateful for the help.

"We're just going to start lunch." Rachel brought her down the hallway to the kitchen.

Caitlin's mother got up. "Oh, honey. You should still be in bed."

"I'm fine Mom. It's just a concussion."

It wasn't "just" a concussion and Caitlin knew that. She had experienced a loss of consciousness. After being checked over by a neurologist she was ordered home to bed. After lying around for a day, she knew exactly why Simon had been so irritable. In fact, she gave him a lot of credit for not being even worse than he was.

Her mother pulled out a chair for her. "Sit down then and have something to eat. You're so pale."

Caitlin obediently sat down, allowed her mother a moment of fussing as she met her father's eyes. He smiled at her over his glasses, but his expression was concerned.

"Let's have a moment of prayer," he said as they all bowed their heads.

Caitlin heard her father's familiar voice as he prayed, his tone familiar, as if he were addressing a well-respected friend. She heard the words of his prayer as he asked for a blessing on the food, a blessing on each of their children, healing for Caitlin, strength for Jonathon and Rachel, and Evelyn and Scott in Portland. He didn't mention Tony by name this time, but each family member present echoed his unspoken words. Before raising her head at the end of his prayer, Caitlin sent up her own prayer for Simon, that he didn't suffer any major injury from his fall.

Her own head still throbbed, but it was a bearable pain. She knew that by tomorrow it would be gone.

"I made some chicken soup, Caitlin. I know it's your favorite." Jean handed her a bowl of steaming broth, with thick egg noodles and chunks of chicken floating in it.

"Smells and looks delicious." Caitlin smiled her thanks up at her mother as she took the bowl.

Soon everyone was eating, the conversation desultory.

"So, what exactly happened to you, Caitlin?" Rachel asked, turning to her sister.

"I was helping a patient into bed and we fell," Caitlin said simply.

"And how's the patient?"

"I don't know. I was hoping to phone the hospital once I felt a little better."

"I always told you, one day you'd fall for a patient," her father teased.

Caitlin couldn't stop the blush that warmed her neck and crept up her cheeks.

After lunch, the rest of the day slipped by. Caitlin napped, tried to watch television and tried not to think about Simon.

She and Rachel sat out in the backyard for a while, but the rain and wind soon sent them back inside again. They ended up in Caitlin's room, sorting through old pictures. Rachel wanted to make up a photo album for her future child.

"Oh, look. This is a cute one of the two of us." Rachel leaned sideways, tilting a photograph of Caitlin and Rachel dressed in identical bathing suits. "This was taken at Long Beach, over twenty years ago."

Caitlin obediently looked and smiled. She couldn't get excited about pictures from the past when her future seemed to loom ahead of her uncertain and vague.

She didn't know in which neat compartment of her life to put Simon. He was unsuitable in so many ways. His past was a question, and he didn't care about the future. He seemed to be searching, yet wouldn't admit that to anyone.

He didn't profess to believe in or hold the same values she did, yet she sensed that he had been raised with them. He read the Bible, yet didn't want to talk about it.

She recalled the look of confusion and yearning on his face yesterday as he sat in the chair, the Bible on his lap. He looked defenseless and once again she was drawn to him.

"...one of the only times I saw you really angry."

Caitlin blinked, pulling herself back to the here and now. She glanced sidelong at Rachel, wondering if her sister had noticed her lapse.

Rachel was looking directly at her. "I don't think it's the concussion that put that dreamy look on your face, Caitlin." She set the box of old pictures aside and turned to sit cross-legged on the bed, facing Caitlin. "What's been happening at work, Caitlin? You didn't say much the other night when I waited up for you, but I could tell something's been going on."

Caitlin frowned, pretending not to understand. She had spoken to Danielle about Simon, but only in the vaguest terms. She wouldn't get away with that with her sister, but at the same time she wasn't sure she wanted to pull out and examine such new and fresh feelings. Feelings that were confusing and frightening.

"You've met someone, haven't you?" Rachel said quietly, leaning her elbows on her knees.

Caitlin leaned back against the headboard. "Yes," she replied softly. "Yes, I have."

"And..." Rachel prompted.

"And what?"

"Does he make your heart do those painfully slow flips when you see him? When your eyes meet, does it feel like you might never breathe again? Does he give you that thrill you've been looking for?"

Caitlin could only nod, feeling that very sensation right now. "Yes, he does," she said, thinking of Simon's dark hazel eyes that could tease and challenge at one time and yet show glimpses of vulnerability and need.

"Who is he? Do I know him?" Rachel leaned forward, grabbing her sister's hands. "How come you never mentioned him before? Is he the reason you broke up with Charles?"

Caitlin met her sister's excited gaze and debated the wisdom of telling her. It would make something that she thought of as nebulous, real and the thought frightened her.

"No, you don't know him," Caitlin said, adding with a short laugh, "I barely know him."

"What do you mean?"

Caitlin pulled her hands free from her sister's, folding her arms across her chest. "He's a patient in the hospital."

Rachel's one eyebrow shot up and she tilted her head sideways as if inspecting a person who had mysteriously taken the place of her sister. "A patient?" she asked, incredulous.

"You don't have to act as if it's evil, for goodness sakes. Happens often," Caitlin replied, a defensive tone creeping into her voice.

"I know that. But I remember how you used to talk about the nurses it happened to..." Rachel's voice trailed off. "You used to get so angry at them."

"Well, maybe the Lord figured I needed some humbling," Caitlin said, her shoulders lifting in a sigh. "Believe me, I've fought it myself. I don't even know if what I'm feeling is really what I'm feeling, or if it's just rebound. The circumstances are a little extenuating. I was at the scene of the accident where he was injured."

"The one that you talked about? The motorcycle accident?"

Caitlin nodded. "He was in really rough shape. Broke his femur, a very major and life-threatening injury. I was at the scene, my hand on his pulse. I could feel him slowly drifting away. I'm sure he was dying, Rachel. Right in front of my eyes. I started praying and then his pulse came back. I still get the shivers when I think about it. He claims I saved his life. He wouldn't let me go, kept asking for me in spite of the pain he was in." Caitlin drew in a steadying breath, holding her sister's surprised gaze.

Rachel puffed up her cheeks and slowly released her breath. "Wow, Caity. That's quite dramatic."

"I know. I'm wondering if that's part of the problem."

"What's his name?"

Caitlin let out a short laugh. "It's Simon. From the precious little he's told me, he was raised in a variety of foster homes. He ran away from the last one at age sixteen."

"If I didn't know you as well as I do, I would say that what you feel for him is a type of misplaced mothering syndrome. But you're not the type, Caity." Rachel traced the pattern on the quilt, looking down. "It sounds like he's had a pretty rough life..." Rachel's voice trailed off and Caitlin could hear the unspoken question in it.

"I'm not going to marry him, for goodness sakes." Caitlin said. "I don't know what's happening between us, if anything." She lifted her hands in a helpless gesture. "I have to admit he's very appealing and he makes me feel..."

"Weak in the knees."

Caitlin laughed shortly. "Yeah. Pretty much. I suppose it's just a physical thing, yet sometimes there's more. I've caught him reading the Bible, but one of the first things he told me was that praying was a waste of time."

"Cynical, then."

"Big-time." Caitlin frowned. "Yet, I see in him a searching. He as much as said he won't let people close."

"How does he feel about you?"

"I wish I knew. He claims something is happening between us and at the same time he pushes me away."

"Defense mechanism." Rachel rested her elbows on her knees, her chin on her hands. "He sounds the complete opposite of Charles, maybe it's like you said—a type of rebound thing."

Caitlin shook her head, then winced. "But you know what? When I saw Charles again, I realized there was something missing. More than just how Simon makes me feel..." She paused, thinking of Simon, remembering her last evening with him, how his arms felt around her, his mouth on hers, remembering him reading the Bible, his questions. She and Charles had always made assumptions about their faith. They never spoke much of it. But Simon's questions showed her a man who, in spite of his own bravado, still wasn't afraid to show his own weakness.

She didn't know Charles's weaknesses, she thought.

"You're going dreamy again, sis," Rachel waved a hand in front of Caitlin's face. "Suitable or not suitable, you've got it bad."

Caitlin blinked. "Maybe I do," she said, sighing lightly. "I just know that for the first time in my life, I *don't* know what to do." Caitlin closed her eyes, her head throbbing. "Maybe it's just this concussion that's got me all confused." But even as she said that, Caitlin knew it wasn't true. Simon had her befuddled long before this.

"Caitlin, you have never known any other boyfriend but Charles. This Simon guy sounds like trouble, yet when you talk about him I see a hint of that passion you were talking about. I think you care for him and I don't think that's so wrong. Don't worry about it, Caitlin. Pray about it. God will work His perfect and pleasing will, whatever that may be." Rachel gave her sister a hug.

Caitlin returned the hug, comforted by what her sister said, realizing that no matter how many times she heard the phrase, it was true.

"And I'll expect a progress report when we come back for Mom's birthday," Rachel said with a wink.

Chapter Ten

It was just like before. Dim sounds. Snatches of conversation. Unknown. Unable to understand.

Simon struggled to open his eyes, his head pounding but he couldn't focus.

"Caitlin," he called out involuntarily, then stopped himself. Why did he always want her? What made him call out for her?

"It's okay, Simon," he heard. But it wasn't Caitlin. He tried to turn his head in the direction of the voice, tried to focus.

"Who are you?" he croaked. "What's wrong with me?"

"Danielle. I'm the evening nurse. You've got a bad case of the flu. Do you want a drink?"

"No. Where's Caitlin?" he couldn't help asking.

"She's not working."

As her words registered, a sudden panic pressed down on him. "She's supposed to come. She said she'd stay."

"Lie still or you'll be in trouble again."

"No, I can't..." Part of his mind registered his incoherence, yet he couldn't stop the agitation that gripped him. His thoughts spun around his head. He couldn't pin them down, couldn't catch them. All he knew was that he wanted Caitlin beside him. He wanted to tell her…to tell her…

He closed his eyes as a wave of vertigo washed away the words. He drifted away, his eyes burning, his leg on fire.

Time was nothing. There was no way to measure what was happening. Nothing made any sense.

He thought he saw Jake standing beside the bed but Jake didn't know he was here, did he? He tried to reach out for him, but his brother slowly disappeared. He heard voices, laughing, mocking. Sounds amplified and confusion reigned.

He was afraid, alone, wandering through darkness, pushing aside hands that held, that pulled on him, trying to find a brother who was always out of his reach. How could Jake turn his back on him? How could he so easily forget him? Everyone had forgotten him. Everyone.

My son, pay attention… You are my son… This is my beloved son…my son, give me your heart…

Words slipped through his delirium. Words from a father to a son. Words he realized came from the Bible.

He didn't want to remember them. He wasn't anyone's son, but the words echoed, words of love.

Such a weak word, *love*. So overused and overrated.

He didn't want to think about love. Didn't want to think about being a son, having a father, a brother. He wished he could stop his thoughts, he wished he could control them. Hearing voices happened to crazy people.

"He's been like this for most of today."

More voices, but these came from outside. Real voices.

"He's really spiked a temp." Caitlin's voice. He was sure of it. He tried to open his eyes but the light was too harsh. "Infection?" he heard her ask.

"No. Blood work shows nothing. It's that flu that's been going around."

"I'll stay with him. You can go back to work."

Then through the heat and confusion he felt a cool touch on his forehead, a click as the light above his bed was turned down a notch. He didn't know if he imagined the gentle touch of lips on his cheek.

"Simon, I'm here."

He felt a soft peace drift over him at the sound of her voice. "Angel," he whispered thankfully. He could finally open his eyes without a sharp pain from the light hitting him behind his eyes.

And there she was. Leaning above him, her hair framing her face, as she gently smoothed his own hair back from his forehead. "You came," he said.

She nodded, as she let her hand linger on his cheek. He smiled back at her and tried to lick his lips. They were dry and cracked.

"I'll get you a drink," she said, straightening. He heard the clatter of ice and water being poured into a plastic cup, then her hand was behind his head again and she was helping him to drink.

The water was cool, soothing. When he was done, he looked up at her, remembering with a sudden clarity what he had done the last time they saw each other. He remembered that he had hurt her then.

"Caitlin, I'm sorry." He forced the words past his own resistance. He wanted to touch her, to connect with her, but it seemed each time he did it wrong. "I'm sorry I hurt you. I'm sorry I kissed you…" He tried to find the right words to do something he wasn't very good at. Apologizing.

"No, Simon, don't say that." She sat down beside him, the chair pulled up close.

"Are you going to stay with me?"

She nodded, laughing shortly. "Yes, it seems that is to be my fate. Holding your hand through your various crises."

He smiled weakly, then closed his eyes again. Unorganized thoughts were coming back, spinning around, sucking him down.

"Caitlin," he whispered.

"What, Simon?"

"Pray for me."

"I always do," she replied. "Now just rest. I'm here."

And that knowledge made it easier for him to sleep.

The dreams came anyhow. Unbidden and unorganized—a jumble of memories and people from his past and present melding, accusing. Verses from Bible passages he read condemned him, his lifestyle. In his dreams he tried to run away, to leave the voices behind him, but they always found him, circling, attacking. He tried to beat them off but couldn't. There were too many—old girlfriends that he walked away from without a second glance, foster parents he left with a shrug, people he had ignored. Jake. His brother, his only brother.

They all hovered and tormented…

"'Comfort, comfort my people, says your God.'"

There were those words again. Simon strained toward them, reaching out. Caitlin was reading, her voice an anchor, the words soothing. "'Speak tenderly to Jerusalem, and proclaim to her that her hard service has been completed, that her sin has been paid for, that she has received from the Lord's hand double for all her sins.'"

Simon heard the words of assurance, the same words he had read only a few days ago. They gently brushed away the confusion.

Paid for, Caitlin had read. Hard service completed, sin paid for. It sounded too easy.

Simon opened his eyes. The first thing he saw was Caitlin's bent head. She was still reading aloud, her voice resonant with conviction. She glanced up as she turned a page and met his gaze with her own.

"Hi," she said with a hesitant smile. "You were so restless, I thought I would read for you." She held up the Bible. "You had a bookmark in this section. Isaiah 55."

Simon felt a blessed moment of coherence. "Yeah," he said with a short laugh. "Thought it was appropriate, considering where I've been."

Caitlin lowered the Bible to her lap. "And where was that?"

Simon heard the concern in her voice and once again wondered at this woman. Wondered why she willingly spent time with him in spite of what he had said and done to her.

"If you don't want to talk about it, I understand."

He shook his head and smiled. "No. I want to." He drew in a slow breath. "I've been all over and nowhere."

"Where did you start from?"

"Foster home."

"What about before that?"

Simon was quiet, remembering Tom Steele, his adoptive home and the vague memories he had of a mother before that. He had tried to keep the memories alive but over time they had faded into the dim picture of a smile, dark hair and the faint smell of bread baking. It was all he had left of her, and it was all he had left of Tom Steele, the only father he ever knew. Memories.

"My mother gave me and my brother up when I was four years old. I don't remember much of her."

Caitlin leaned closer. "Do you know why she gave you up?"

"No." His head ached again and he felt a burning pain in his leg. "I wanted to go looking for her but Jake didn't."

"Jake is your brother?"

Simon nodded, turning his head to look back at the ceiling. "We used to visit each other after we got split up. He ended up in a great place."

"And you got split because of your running away?" Caitlin sounded surprised.

"Well, I was the bad boy and Jake was the good boy. Special Services wanted to give him a chance separate from me." He felt the ache behind his eyes and a peculiar pressure building in his chest. "But Jake didn't want to leave. Didn't want to come with me. He made the right choice, I think."

"Where is he now?"

"I don't know." Simon drew in a long breath, surprised at the emotions those few words brought out. Sorrow, regret, pain. In his weakened state he couldn't fight them. Had no defenses to draw from. "When he wouldn't leave with me," he continued, "I told him he'd never hear from me again. And he hasn't."

"Would you want to see him again?"

Simon shrugged, but the movement sent a wave of dizziness over him. "I don't know," he said, suddenly weary. "It's been so long. I don't feel I have the right." He closed his eyes and felt Caitlin lightly lay her cool hand on his forehead.

"You're burning up," she murmured. "I'll see if I can get you something."

She walked out of the room, a shadow in the half light and Simon felt bereft.

How had she done it? he wondered. How had this woman managed to so completely take hold of him, invade his thoughts and dreams, make him talk about things he had long buried and tried to forget? Remind him of where he had come from and make him wonder where he was going?

He needed her and didn't want to need her.

Simon forced that thought aside. He couldn't allow those emotions to take over his life, determining what he would do. He had been too long on his own, too long independent. He couldn't afford to lean on anyone, to be weak. Caitlin had the potential to destroy everything he had worked so hard to build. He reminded himself that she was a temporary part of his life. She told him over and over again. She was a Christian, far removed from him. She had a boyfriend. A family—something he knew nothing about.

So why did he feel this way about her? Confused, frustrated. Seeking.

Comfort, comfort my people. Those words again, he thought, clinging to them, remembering that God promised that sins would be paid for. He remembered vague snatches of Sunday school songs, words of promise and hope, but also of responsibility.

He had to confess, to show his need to God, to recognize his part in what had been happening in his life. He had to open himself up, look at what he had done.

He didn't know if he could.

His thoughts circled again and when Caitlin returned he was tired and confused.

"Here," she said, lifting his head again. "Take this."

He obediently swallowed the pill she gave him and lay back. She placed a damp cloth on his forehead and he felt immediate relief.

"That feels good," he murmured. "Thanks."

"You want to sleep?"

"No. Just talk to me." He was tired, but he feared the confusion of his dreams. He wanted to hear her voice, to keep the connection between them, however fragile.

"About..." she prompted.

"Tell me about you."

"I already have," she replied quietly. "You know most everything about me."

Simon turned his head, his eyes blinking slowly. "No, I don't. I don't know your favorite color, what you like to do when you're not holding my hand, what you order in a restaurant?"

"I like the color blue, I read books in my spare time and I always order chicken." She fussed with his sheets, her fingers lingering on his shoulder. "Now rest."

Simon laughed shortly. "That was supposed to be the start of a longer conversation." His head ached and his body felt as if it were slowly being pulled in different directions. He should be sleeping, but he had Caitlin all to himself. She wasn't going to rush off to be with another patient, she wasn't here as a nurse, but as a visitor.

He didn't want to speculate on the reasons she was

at his side. He was thankful for her presence and for the moment he just wanted to enjoy having her undivided attention.

"I could ask you a few questions," she said.

"You already have."

"These will be simpler. Your favorite color."

"Brown."

"Favorite food."

"French fries."

"Hobbies?"

Simon paused. "I don't know. I keep pretty busy with my work."

"Which is?"

"Work. Just work."

"Sounds fishy, Simon." Caitlin leaned back, crossing her arms, her I-mean-business pose.

"I don't know what else to say," he replied defensively. "I'm self-employed. I buy and sell stocks and businesses and real estate. I have a couple of fast-food franchises, a soft-drink franchise. I manage my own funds…" He stopped, looking at her, trying to read her expression, feeling as if he had to justify what he did. "It's not your usual nine-to-five, pack-a-lunch job. I worked enough for other people, spent enough of my life trying to rise up to other people's expectations and failing…" He stopped again, realizing he had said more than he had wanted to.

"Do you mean the foster homes you lived in?"

Simon said nothing, as a band of sorrow squeezed his heart into a tight knot.

"You said your mother gave you up when you were four," Caitlin persisted.

"You said easy questions," Simon said, trying to smile.

"Sorry." She leaned forward. "I can't help it. I want to know more about you. More than you're telling me."

Simon met her eyes and once again felt as if he were falling. He closed his eyes and took a few deep breaths. "When my mom gave us up, we were brought to a foster home. The man was an older man. A widower. We were only supposed to be there temporarily, while we waited for an adoptive home. It took a little longer than social services thought it would. He got attached and adopted us. He took care of us until we turned twelve. Then we were moved."

"How come?"

Simon clutched the bedsheet as he stared sightlessly up at the ceiling tiles. "It wasn't because of our father. Tom Steele was a good man. He took us to church, taught us about God. He took us to hockey games, came to parent-teacher interviews. Did all the right things." Simon stopped, untangled his hand from the sheet and closed his eyes.

"What happened?"

Caitlin wouldn't let up, he thought. Her soft-spoken questions slowly kept him going back to places he had thought he had long abandoned.

He drew in a deep breath, swallowing. Sixteen years had passed and dredging up this memory still hurt.

"He died." He ignored Caitlin's cry of dismay. "And Jake and I were moved." He waited a moment, letting the pain pass. "Jake seemed to take it better than me. I couldn't take it at all. So I ran away. I said it was to find my mother. The home they moved us to couldn't handle it so social services moved us again. I kept running. And we were moved again." He stopped.

"What happened at that time?" she said, her voice quietly persistent.

"Jake went to stay on a farm in the country and I ended up in a treatment foster home. But I kept running."

"Why?"

The question was simple enough but it required so much. He didn't want to analyze his past. It was over. There was nothing he could do about it. But against his rational judgment, he wanted her to know all about him. Wanted her to see what his life was like. That way, if she stayed then it meant…it meant…

"I'm sorry," she said quietly. "I'm getting nosy."

"No," he replied, looking back up at the ceiling. "That's okay." He went back through his memories, digging up old emotions, realizing he was laying himself bare for her. But he didn't want to analyze, to defend, to hold back. He wanted her to know. "I hated everyone for a long time. I hated my mother for giving us up. I hated Tom Steele for dying and leaving us. I never knew what to do with the emotions. The first home we were moved to was a good place, but I never gave it a chance. I didn't want to. I figured the only way I would be in charge was if I was the first one to leave. The family kept coming after me and finally they couldn't handle it anymore. So Jake and I got moved. And the same thing happened. Finally we were split up. Jake hated me for a while. I hated him. He ended up in a good place, and I ended up in a sterner home. So I kept running. I suppose by that time it was just a habit, a way of avoiding life."

"And where is Jake now?"

Simon shrugged. "I don't know. Once kids in foster care turn eighteen, they're on their own. I figured he left there, too!"

"Have you ever tried to contact him?"

"No."

"Why not?"

Simon felt it again. Regret, hurt pride. "I don't know if he'd want to hear from me."

"But he's your brother."

Simon shook his head slowly. "Family doesn't work the same for me as it does for you. We've been apart longer than we've been together. He's got his own life. He doesn't need me."

Simon stopped, reaching up to touch his forehead.

Caitlin got up right away, took the now warm cloth off his forehead and replaced it with another. She gently smoothed it against his head, her fingers lingering at his temple, stroking his damp hair back. He saw pity on her face.

He caught her hand, squeezing it hard. "Don't do that, Caitlin," he said, his voice low. "Don't feel sorry for me."

She only smiled, turning her hand in his to curve around his fingers.

"That's not what I want from you."

"That's not what I feel for you," she whispered.

Caitlin's eyes met his, held, and Simon felt his breath leave his chest.

Then she bent forward, touching her lips to his cheek. Her mouth lingered a moment, then she raised her head, clutching his hand.

"What am I going to do with you, Simon?" she asked.

He didn't answer, only held her gaze with his own, yearning and fighting at the same time. He felt a fear grip him at the feelings she evoked in him, the vulnerability she was creating. But he knew that for now, he needed her. "Just stay here, okay?"

She nodded and gently touched his eyelids. "Go to sleep now," she said, her voice quiet, weary.

He kept his eyes closed and clutched her hand as he slowly slipped away into a dreamless sleep.

Caitlin yawned and stretched her arms in front of her.

The light above Simon's bed reflected off the ceiling, creating a soft glow, a soft intimacy.

Beyond the drawn curtain, the bed was empty. Shane had left this morning.

Déjà vu all over again, Caitlin thought remembering another evening, sitting at Simon's bedside. Except this time she was dressed more for the part with sensible shoes and pants. This time she came out of choice.

And this time she couldn't keep her eyes off Simon's face, couldn't keep herself from touching him, connecting with him however she could. In sleep he looked defenseless, his features relaxed, the parenthetical frown between his eyebrows eased. His mouth lost its cynical twist, softened and curved into a gentle smile.

Caitlin tried to reason out her attraction to him, hoping that by doing so she could deal with it and maybe, understand it.

Simon wasn't as handsome as Charles, she thought, her eyes traveling over his face. He didn't have the classical profile or the even features. If she was to be honest, his nose was a little large, his eyes deep set, yet as she looked at him she felt a yearning, a need to touch him, to comfort him. Thinking of his eyes made her heart give a silly jump. Thinking of his kiss made her jittery.

All the things Charles had never made her feel.

Caitlin knew it wasn't enough to build a relationship on. As she and Rachel had discussed, maybe it was merely rebound. Maybe once she was in Portland she would discover that it was Charles she really wanted.

If dating for the rest of your life is what you want, she thought wryly. And that was the harsh reality of going out with Charles. That and moving to LA.

What kind of relationship did we have? she wondered, leaning back in the chair. *We dated for three years. I'm apart from him a couple of weeks and I easily forget him.*

She slouched down in the chair, opening the Bible. As she flipped through the pages she stopped to read a few Psalms, then turned to Isaiah, still puzzled as to why Simon had chosen this particular book. She turned to the passage she had read to him just a few moments ago, remembering how it had settled him.

He was seeking, she knew that. How close he was, well, that appeared to be another question. Simon didn't answer them very readily.

Help me to understand what I should be feeling, Lord, she prayed. *I want to serve You, I want to do what is pleasing in Your sight. I want to be a faithful child of Yours and I know that any future partner must also be Your child. Otherwise it just doesn't work.*

She knew what happened to relationships where one was a Christian and the other not. She had seen evidence of it over and over again. Even in her own family. She wasn't going to make the same mistake her brother had.

Simon moaned softly and laying the Bible down, Caitlin got up. The cloth she removed from his forehead was warm, attesting to the fever that racked him. She took it to the bathroom sink, soaked it in cold water and when she came back, he was awake. Barely.

He smiled at her, his eyes blinking slowly. "Dear Caitlin," he whispered as she laid the cool cloth carefully on his forehead again.

He watched her as she carefully wiped away the excess water that ran in a rivulet down the side of his head. She tried to ignore him, tried not to answer the gentle summons of his gaze.

But she couldn't. As their eyes met, she felt her heart lift. Then he smiled once again, and drifted back off to sleep.

Caitlin watched him a moment, then shaking her head, sat down in the chair again.

Chapter Eleven

"Simon." The soft voice slowly pierced his sleep, a warm hand held his shoulder. Caitlin, Simon thought.

"Hi," he said, focusing on her face. "You're here."

Caitlin nodded pulling her hand away from him. "How are you feeling?"

"Much better." He blinked and looked around, testing his vision. "A lot better."

"Your fever is down." She straightened his blankets, her hand lingering on his arm. "You slept pretty deep."

"Sorry, I would have preferred to talk to you." He didn't know how long he slept, but even if it was only an hour, he felt as if it was too long. "What's on the agenda for the rest of the day?"

Caitlin looked away, pulling her bottom lip between her teeth. "Not a whole lot."

Simon grinned. "Then I have you to myself."

"Not really. I have to leave this afternoon."

"For home?"

"No." She straightened, turning away from him. "I've got to catch a plane in three hours. I'm going to Portland to stay with my sister for a week. She had a baby by caesarean a couple of weeks ago, and I promised her a long time ago I would come and help her. By the time I'm back you'll be discharged."

"You're leaving," he said flatly.

Caitlin turned to him, but didn't look at him. "I already have the ticket."

"Of course. Of course you have to go. I understand." And he did. He knew the rules. Never let anyone get close, never share anything with someone. He had made them his mantra. And in the past few weeks he had broken each one of them, on his own. If his heart hurt, if he felt a roiling anger beginning, it was his own fault. Well, that was how it went. But now he had one more thing to do.

"Help me sit up," he said shortly.

"But you've been sick."

"I said, help me up, Caitlin."

He could see hurt on her face at the anger in his voice, but he ignored it. He had to start relearning the lessons life had taught him.

She raised the bed slowly and an attack of vertigo gripped him. He rode it out, focusing on the wall above Caitlin's head, forcing himself not to look at her, not to meet her puzzled gaze.

He carefully pivoted himself, swinging his legs over the edge of the bed until he was sitting up without support.

"Simon, what are you doing?" She hurried to his side, her hand automatically catching his shoulder.

"I want to stand up."

"No. You can't."

"The doctor said the plate was fine, didn't he?"

"Yes."

"Well, then. I was standing before I got sick. Help me stand up now." She only stared. "Now," he barked.

She jumped, then he could see her straighten, could almost hear each vertebra snap into place. Now she was angry, as well.

All the better, he thought. It would make everything much easier.

She helped him up and he was surprised to find that his leg didn't hurt nearly as much as it had before. He was healing, just as everyone had promised him.

Caitlin supported him with her arm. His lay across her shoulder. It was just a matter of turning slightly, slipping his other arm around her waist and he had her.

"If you're leaving me, I can't let you go without saying goodbye, can I?" He looked down at her soft green eyes, the delicate line of her cheekbone sweeping down to a narrow jaw. He memorized the curve of her mouth, the faint hollow of her cheeks, each detail of her beautiful, beautiful face. He didn't want to forget her.

She wanted to fight him, he could feel her tense in his arms, but he also knew she didn't dare. Not after what happened the last time. Ignoring the flare of panic in her eyes, he lowered his head, capturing her mouth with his.

She resisted at first, her arms stiffly at her sides, then, as he murmured her name against her lips, as he drew her closer to him, he could feel her soften, feel her arms slip around him, then, hold him close.

His heart tripped, his breath felt trapped in a chest that grew tighter the longer their kiss went on. What he had started in anger, changed with her soft response. When she whispered his name, when her hand reached up to caress his cheek, to hold his head, he felt a melting around his heart and a pain that pierced with a gentle sweetness. Almost he spoke the words, almost he bared his soul.

But he couldn't.

She was leaving and so was he. It wasn't meant to be.

Caitlin sat on the edge of her bed, staring down at the phone in her hand. Jonathon her brother-in-law had just called her here at Evelyn and Scott's house in Portland. By using his connections in the Royal Canadian Mounted Police, Jonathon had found Jake Steele.

Now Caitlin had the number she had to call and she didn't know if she dared.

It was the best time. The house was quiet. Evelyn and Scott were already in bed, as were the children.

With the time difference, it would only be nine o'clock where Jake lived.

She couldn't stop the restless pounding of her heart, the trembling of her fingers. Was she doing the right thing? Did she have a right to intrude on Simon's life? Simon—who didn't need anyone?

But she thought of her own brother and knew that if something had happened to him, she would want to know. She thought of Simon lying on his hospital bed, staring with longing at Shane's family. She knew in spite of what he had done to her, she had to make this call for him.

Caitlin took another breath, sent up a prayer for wisdom, courage and the right words, and punched in the numbers. The phone rang in her ear, and she felt her heart skip. Another ring. A third.

Disappointment and relief vied for attention. She was going to let it ring one more, no, maybe two more times then she would hang up.

And then what?

Caitlin rubbed her hand over her jeans, waited and

was just about to lower the phone to push the button to end the call when…

"Hello?"

Her heart jumped and she was momentarily speechless.

"Hello?" the voice repeated.

"Hello, Mr. Steele," Caitlin replied breathlessly, frantically searching for the right words. What if Jonathon was wrong? What if this wasn't who he thought it was?

Well, then, you make a fool of yourself in front of a stranger you will probably never talk to again, she reassured herself. "My name is Caitlin Severn," she continued struggling to catch her breath. This was ridiculous. She was acting as if she had never made a phone call to a complete stranger before. *A complete stranger who happens to be the brother of a man who you are fascinated and possibly in love with.* "I'm a nurse at Nanaimo General Hospital. I'm calling about a patient I took care of, who I believe is your brother. Simon Steele."

Silence. Utter, heavy and complete silence.

Wrong number, Caitlin thought stifling a hysterical laugh.

"What happened to him?"

Well, it was the right number after all, she thought. "Before you get too concerned," she continued, forcing herself to breathe, to remain calm, "I want to tell you that he's fine now, Mr. Steele. He was in a bad motorcycle accident. Broke his right femur. I was at the accident when it happened and I worked in the ward he was on." She forced herself to stop, to keep from babbling nervously on.

"How do you know he's my brother?"

Because right now, you sound exactly like him,

thought Caitlin, hearing the defensive tone enter Jake Steele's voice. This was harder than she thought. "He gave me your first and last name and told me you were his twin. I didn't think there were more than one Jake Steele born on February 16."

"Did he ask you to call me?"

Caitlin bit her lip. "Actually, no."

"Then why are you calling?"

Caitlin fiddled with the edge of her sweatshirt, folding it back and forth as she tried to find the right way to explain her reasoning. From the sounds of things, Jake didn't appear to be any happier to hear about Simon than she presumed Simon would be to hear about his brother.

It disturbed her. "I'm calling because I care for your brother…" The words sounded lame and she knew it. She had been gone from Nanaimo for only four days, and each morning she woke up with a heaviness pressing down on her heart. She had resisted the urge to phone the hospital every day to see how Simon was, reasoning it was better this way. Better for who became less clear each day she was away. She had hoped and prayed that being with her sister and her family would bring clarity to her thoughts. Instead, she felt more confused than before.

She didn't just care for Simon. She loved him.

Caitlin forced her thoughts back to the present, to the phone in her hands and the muted anger of the man on the other end of the line. "Simon sustained very serious injuries and is currently in the hospital in Nanaimo. He's been there for about two weeks. He talked about you and the homes you've been in."

Jake was silent and Caitlin could almost feel the antagonism over the phone. Whatever it was she had expected from this phone call, it wasn't these clipped questions and curt replies.

Somehow she had foolishly thought he would be eager and happy to hear from his long-lost brother. She thought he would be thankful that she took the time to track him down.

"So, why did you think I needed to know this?"

Caitlin straightened, her own anger coming to the fore. "Your brother has been through a lot of pain and has been struggling in many ways, physically as well as spiritually. I called you because in the entire time he was in the hospital, your brother never received one visitor, or one phone call. He is all alone…"

"The fact that my brother doesn't have anyone doesn't surprise me," Jake said, his voice even, almost harsh. "Simon has never needed anyone, never cared for anyone except himself."

Caitlin almost gasped at the coldness of Jake's reply. "I can't believe you're talking like this," Caitlin replied, now thoroughly angry. "He's your brother. Doesn't that relationship mean anything to you?"

"Simon hasn't been a part of my life for a long time now, out of his own choice. If he wants to talk to me, I would imagine he could get hold of me."

Caitlin knew the truth of that, but also knew that Simon, for whatever reason, wouldn't do that. "I don't know Simon as well as I would like to," she said, "but I do know that he is seeking and that he is unsure of what he's looking for."

Jake was quiet and Caitlin knew she had touched something in him.

Please, Lord, help me find the right words, she prayed as she spoke. "He is your family. I have a brother who I haven't seen for a long time, out of his choice. I know that if something happened to him, I would want to know and I would want to see him again, to be a family again."

"I don't think it's your place to lecture me on family reunions, Miss…" He paused and for a moment Caitlin was tempted to simply hang up and put the Steeles and their brokenness behind her. But she thought of Simon clutching her hand, his eyes full of sorrow and pain he couldn't express and she knew she had to fight for him.

"Severn. Caitlin Severn," she reminded him, clutching the phone, forcing herself to stay calm.

"Well, Miss Severn. I suppose it would be incumbent on me to ask where he is right now."

Incumbent? Oh, brother, Caitlin thought, he sounded just like Charles. *Please, Lord, if ever I needed to keep a clear head and a soft tongue it's now. Help me. Help this coldhearted man who I don't even know to understand how important this is.*

"Right now he's in the orthopedic ward of the Nanaimo General Hospital," Caitlin said, forcing her voice to a more even tone. "He's due to be discharged in less than a week, so if you want to see him, I would suggest you go as soon as possible."

"Well, I thank you for your time and persistence, Miss Severn. Unfortunately I'm in the middle of my busiest season. It's been a late harvest and I won't be able to get away for at least another month."

"Please, Jake. I'm not asking for myself. I'm asking for you and Simon. I don't know if you're married…"

"Not currently," he replied curtly and Caitlin sensed there was a whole other story behind those two clipped words, but she kept on.

"Then you and Simon are all each of you have. I would like you to see this as a gift from the Lord. A gift not given lightly." *There was a man all alone. He had neither friend nor brother.* The words from Ecclesiastes came back to her and in that moment she realized they might just as easily apply to Jake. "I believe that you and Simon are meant to find each other. You're his brother. You can't change that."

Silence again. But Caitlin waited, forcing herself not to try to fill it, to let what she said sink in as she prayed and prayed.

"Like I said, I won't be able to get away for a while, but I will make the effort. I'd like to thank you for your call…"

Which was a neat way of sounding thankful without really being thankful, Caitlin thought. She didn't know if she liked him.

"Are you currently working on the ward?"

"No. I'm staying with my sister in Portland. If you want more information, you can call the hospital. But you are more than welcome to call me, as well." Without waiting for him to ask, she gave him her sister's number as well as the number of the hospital. More silence as she prayed that he wrote them down.

She took a breath and forced herself to continue. "I don't know exactly what happened to you after you and Simon were split," she said. "Simon said that you went to a good home. However, I do know that you and he were raised together in a Christian home. I believe the Lord has brought me to you, and I want you to know that I'll be praying for both of you."

She could almost feel a melting, a relenting coming across the line.

"Thanks," he said, his voice quiet. "And thanks for

taking the time to call." Then a *click* sounded in her ear and she knew he had hung up.

Caitlin laid the phone on the bedside table, then dropped backward on the bed, her hands trembling, her heart racing. She covered her face with her hands as she prayed.

Please, Lord, let Jake go. Let them become brothers again. Reconcile them to each other.

Because it didn't sound as if either of them was too eager to meet again.

"Has Simon Steele been discharged yet?"

Caitlin looked up from her desk with a start at the mention of Simon's name.

"I'm pretty sure this is his coat," the orderly in front of her said, holding up a leather jacket. "It's been hanging around emerg for a while now. One of the nurses who was on duty when he came in just came back from vacation. Said he was up here."

"He was discharged over a week ago. But we can see that it gets to him."

"There were some keys in the pocket and a few other things," the orderly said, handing her a plastic bag holding the personal effects that must have come out of the jacket. "There were a pair of leather chaps, but they got cut to ribbons and had been tossed."

"I'll see that this gets to him," Caitlin said, taking the jacket with a smile.

As the orderly left, Caitlin walked into the office behind the front desk, setting the coat on an empty table. She couldn't stop a foolish trill of her heart at the sight of Simon's coat. She reached out, touching it with a forefinger, tracing the rip in one arm of the coat, the marks left behind when he had gone skidding across the pavement.

She closed her eyes at the memory of him, lying so helpless on the side of the road. His life had been completely rearranged by that one event.

Unfortunately, so had hers.

Caitlin thought her visit to her sister in Portland would have given her back a sense of equilibrium. Instead she'd spent most of her days wondering how Simon was and if Jake had contacted him.

She wondered if he even gave her a second thought. She knew she should forget him, but couldn't. Now, seeing his jacket seemed to bring all the memories she had slowly filed away, flooding back.

She lifted up the bag and, ignoring the voice of caution, opened it up. Inside were a set of keys, as the orderly had said, a folded-up piece of paper, a receipt for a restaurant in Vancouver, and some change. Curious, she unfolded the piece of paper.

But it told her no more about Simon than did the other impersonal effects. It was merely a listing of numbers, some scratched out and a few calculations. On the other side was an address and the name of an apartment block with a phone number underneath it.

Frustrated, Caitlin put the things back in the bag and the bag in the pocket of the coat. It shouldn't matter to her what happened to it, but she knew it did.

"What've you got there?" Eva, one of the other floor nurses, walked into the office and laid a folder on the desk.

"It's Simon Steele's jacket," Caitlin said, forcing an impersonal tone in her voice.

"I imagine that will have to get sent back to him."

"Probably." Caitlin shrugged, leaving the room. For a foolish moment she had thought of bringing it back to him herself, of testing the newness of her emotions away from the hospital.

She was crazy she thought, forcing her mind back to her job. But it was difficult. While she was in Portland her sister commented on how listless she seemed.

She *had* been listless and she had tried to pray and reason her way out of it. But ever since Simon had kissed her, she had felt as if her entire world had been flipped end over end. She, who so dearly liked order and control.

Before Charles she had dated precious few men. Too busy getting her degree. Then she wanted to work and then she started dating Charles.

But not even Charles had managed to get her in such a dither, she thought, doodling on the calendar in front of her. She wanted to see Simon again, she didn't want to see him again. All too well she remembered their last time together, the touch of his mouth on hers, his arms around her. She remembered the sorrow in his eyes.

She was sick and tired of her own dithering. In her own lectures to student nurses she talked about patient-nurse intimacy and how it seldom lasted beyond the walls of the hospital. She just didn't know if she wanted to test it out.

Chapter Twelve

"Here's figures on those funds we were talking about before I left on vacation." Oscar dropped a file folder on the desk beside Simon. "I don't know why you're in such a rush on them."

"I want to catch them before they go up," Simon said, clicking on the "save" icon. He leaned back in his chair, wincing as a twinge of pain shot through his leg.

"How's the leg?" Oscar asked, sitting down in an office chair beside the desk Simon had set up in one empty corner of his condo.

Oscar had balked at moving their office to Simon's home. Simon had merely stated that it worked easier for both of them. He liked being able to work out of his living quarters. Besides, it gave him another tax write-off. Now he was glad they had done it.

"Some days are better than others."

Oscar shook his head. "I still can't believe you didn't try a little harder to get ahold of me. I would have cut my vacation short, you know that."

"You were camping. How in the world was I supposed to find you."

"The Mounties could have found me."

"It wasn't important." Simon dismissed his comment by grabbing the file folder. "Tell me a little more about these funds."

Oscar's sigh told him Oscar wasn't pleased, but they knew each other well enough to know that he would go along with whatever Simon chose to tell him.

"I've checked out the funds, and it looks like they've bottomed out and should pick up in the next couple of days. European funds are a better bet than Asian these days." Oscar tipped back his chair, his hands locked behind his head.

"Sounds okay. Hear anymore from the contractor on that apartment block in Nanaimo?"

"He gave me a quote. I'm shopping around for a better one yet, but it comes in where it should."

Simon pulled a face. "Don't get too picky. We'll do okay, even with the higher quote."

"We'll do more than okay. The cash flow looks pretty healthy." Oscar glanced around the bare apartment. "I bet we make enough money you could even buy some decent furniture," he said, his tone heavily sarcastic.

Simon looked around and shrugged. "I don't know if I feel like furnishing an apartment. I might sell it."

The condo was large, spacious and sunny. Everything the real estate agent said it would be. But Simon had little inclination to make it a home. It was just like the boat, the trips, all the other toys. Once he had it, it didn't do what he had hoped it would.

He had bought a large leather couch and matching chair at the same time he'd bought the condo. A wall unit stood holding only a stereo and some of the books Simon had collected over the years. He hadn't collected enough possessions over the years to fill such a large space.

Oscar leaned ahead, his elbows resting on his knees. "Would you feel more like fixing up, say—" he hesitated, his hands spreading out "—a Victorian house on five acres, north of Nanaimo, facing the mainland?"

Simon leaned back, making a steeple of his hands. "And why would I want to do that?"

"Because it's a good deal." Oscar held up his hand, ticking off the virtues. "The buyer needs to sell it, and because I think you're ready to buy a house instead of sharing halls and elevators with complete strangers. You need a place to bring a girlfriend."

"I don't know about the last," Simon said, forcing aside thoughts of an angel with soft blond hair and sea green eyes. Caitlin was out of the question, out of the picture, and he was out of his mind to be even thinking about her. She represented obligations and commitment.

Family.

He got up, pushing aside his own thoughts.

"It's a great deal even from a business standpoint," Oscar continued, leaning back with a creak in the old office chair Simon had bought for his apartment. "And since your accident, I sense you've gone through some soul-searching, some change-of-heart-type stuff. You might even be ready to, dare I say it—" Oscar lowered his voice, his eyes wide, and did a quick drumroll on his knees "—settle down."

"Wishful thinking on your part, Oscar," Simon said shortly. Oscar was too intuitive by half.

"After I met Angela, I would walk around with this dazed look on my face, just like you are now. Someone would be talking to me, and I wouldn't even hear them. Just like you were a few moments ago."

"You won't quit, will you?" Simon said irritably.

"Nope." Oscar rocked back and forth, and Simon resisted the urge to snap at him to sit still.

He was like that more often these days. Irritable and easily angered. Peace eluded him. Before his accident, life had flowed along quite well, but not anymore.

Now all he could think of was Caitlin and the words she had read to him out of the Bible. The passage that offered comfort and at the same time required more of him than he was prepared to give.

All he could think of was how he destroyed the fragile bond building between them with a kiss born out of anger.

A kiss that changed to need and want and a desire to protect and nurture.

"I've got the information you wanted on that company that's going public," Simon said, forcing his mind back to business, back to the safe and predictable. "They're in my bedroom, if you want to get them."

"Okay. Change the subject. I can do this," Oscar said with a laugh, getting up.

The sudden chime of the doorbell broke the quiet.

"Shall I get it?" Oscar asked.

"No. That's okay. The papers are in a folder beside the bed," Simon replied over his shoulder as he walked to the door, wondering who it could be. The home-care nurse stopped by only weekly now and she had come yesterday. He wasn't expecting anyone else to come.

He worked his way slowly across the living room and then to the hallway. This condo was way too big, he thought, trying not to hurry.

Finally he reached the door and opened it.

"Delivery for Simon Steele." A ponytailed delivery boy held out a form for Simon, who signed it. "Do you want me to bring it in for you?" the boy asked, noticing Simon's cane.

"Sure. Just set it on the table there."

Whistling, the boy brought in a package, then sauntered out, closing the door on a very curious Simon.

It was from the Nanaimo General Hospital.

For a weird and wonderful moment he thought it might be something from Caitlin but when he opened it, surprised to see his fingers trembling, he pulled out his jacket.

"What was that?" Oscar walked into the room, frowning at the box on the table.

"My jacket. From the hospital."

"You dropped something." Oscar bent over and picked up a piece of paper, handing it to Simon.

Simon took it, read it and swallowed. It was a note from Caitlin, asking how he was, hoping that all was well with him. Signed with her name. Underneath that, in smaller letters she wrote that she was praying for him.

"What's up, Simon? You look like you've been told your biggest stocks just tanked." Oscar tilted his head, as if to get a better look at his partner. "You okay?"

"Yeah." Simon took a deep breath, rereading the note as if trying to find something else, some hint of her feelings in it.

"Who's it from?"

"Caitlin," he said without thinking.

"Newest girlfriend?" Oscar asked with a grin. "Is that how she got your coat?"

"No. She works at the hospital. She was my nurse."

"Is she why my tough wheeler-dealer partner is looking as mushy as a cooked marshmallow?"

"Never mind, Oscar," Simon snapped, dropping the letter in the box.

"Ooh. Touchy, too."

"I wasn't mushy."

"Maybe *mushy* was the wrong word. Maybe *wistful* would be better." Oscar sighed dramatically, placing a hand over his heart.

Simon ignored him, putting the coat back on the table. "Can we get back to work?"

"Sure." Oscar grinned as he walked back to the desk. He dropped into a chair. "Caitlin," he said with a tinge of sarcasm and a wink. "I like that name. She's obviously a very organized and caring person. Sending you your coat like that."

"Drop it, Oscar."

Oscar held his partner's gaze, his expression suddenly serious. "I don't know if I will. I've never seen you this flustered, ever. You're cranky on the one hand and on the other, you seem to take things easier. Like I said, I catch you staring off into space. Definitely twitterpated."

Simon sighed, realizing Oscar wasn't going to let this one go. "Okay. I like Caitlin. You happy now?"

"Nope. Not until I know what you're going to do about it."

"Nothing. Zilch. Nada."

"Which begs the question, why not?"

"Beg all you want. She's off-limits," Simon said, rubbing his leg. It ached again, which meant he should probably lie down. But he didn't want to do that, either. "Did you want to go over those funds?"

"No. I want to check out that Victorian house on the island for you, and I want to see you phone the lady who has you all tied up in knots and ask her out."

Simon sighed, plowing his hand through his hair in frustration. "By all means, check out the house. Maybe you can move there yourself," he said, thoroughly exasperated with his partner.

"Nah. Angela always gets sick on the ferry. You're more flexible than I am anyhow. Doesn't matter where you live. But I'll check it out for you." Oscar pointed at Simon, winking at him.

"Then do it now. Anything to get you off my back."

"You know, I think I will." Oscar bounded off the chair with a grin and shoved the papers into his briefcase. "Catch ya later, pardner," he said with a smile as he headed out the door.

Simon glared at it as his partner left, feeling pushed and hemmed in by the people in his life. Oscar would never have dared talk to him as he did a few weeks ago. Simon wouldn't have let him.

But as Oscar had said, things had changed. Simon was tired of the loneliness and emptiness of his life. He had allowed Oscar to get closer.

Had allowed Caitlin to get closer still. The downside was the vulnerability, the obligations.

Obligations and the promise of a pair of green eyes that haunted him at every turn.

And the sooner he got that out of his system, the better.

Simon pocketed his car keys, moved the flowers over to his other arm and sighed deeply. A quick glance at his watch showed him that he could figure on the shift change to be happening in about fifteen minutes.

He gave the arrangement a critical once-over. Looked innocuous enough. Carnations and lilies and a few roses.

A very proper thank-you-type bouquet, he figured, no strings attached. It was the least he could do after being such a miserable patient.

He sucked in another deep, cleansing breath, blew it out again, straightened his new leather jacket and then forced himself to move. The December air was chilly, even for the island, and he hoped the flowers would be protected enough until he got to the hospital.

Once inside, he felt a slight moment of panic. What if Caitlin wasn't working at all?

Well, then, so be it, he thought sauntering down the hallway toward the ward, trying to recapture the laissez-faire attitude that had taken him through other situations with other women. The kind of attitude that gave him a measure of protection.

But his cavalier attitude seemed to dissipate as quickly as frost in the sun when he rounded the corner to the ward and came near the desk. He wiped one palm on his jeans, the other hand still holding the flowers. No one was there.

He looked hopefully around, wondering where everyone was, resisting the urge to just drop off the flowers and go. Then he heard the sound of voices in the room opposite. My old room, he thought, turning.

Danielle walked out laughing. She turned her head and stopped dead in her tracks.

"What are you doing?" Another nurse came up behind her, gave Danielle a light shove and then stopped herself.

"Hi," Simon said, shifting the flowers uselessly to the other hand. He couldn't stop the thrum of his heart at the sight of Caitlin. She wore her hair up today, emphasizing the delicate line of her jaw. Her face was flushed, her eyes bright. She licked her lips once, her hands clasped in front of her and gave him a curt nod.

"Thought I'd drop these off for you ladies," he said, holding up the flowers. "A thank-you for all you did."

Danielle gave Caitlin a nudge, who stepped slowly forward. "Nice to see you again, Simon," Caitlin said softly, taking the flowers. She walked around the desk and set the basket on the ledge, pulling the plastic off. With her eyes still on the flowers, she bent over, sniffing them. "They're beautiful. I'm sure everyone will appreciate them. Thank you."

Her voice was quiet, well modulated, unemotional. Simon wondered if he had done this all wrong.

He shoved his hands in his back pockets and shifted his weight to his good leg. "You're welcome," he said, casting about for something witty and urbane to say. It would have been easy a couple of months ago, but much had happened to him since then.

"How's the leg?" Danielle asked, breaking the silence.

"Good," Simon replied, glancing at her, his eyes returning to Caitlin who still fussed with the flowers. "It hurts once in a while, but even that's getting better."

"And work? How's that going? Still dabbling in the stock market? Got any good tips for some poor lowly nurses? Any inside information?"

Simon forced his attention back to Danielle. "All I

can tell you is that helium is up," he said, grasping for something, anything that would make Caitlin look up from those infernal flowers and at him.

Caitlin's head came up at his poor attempt at humor, a grin teasing the corner of her mouth. "I suppose diapers remain unchanged," she returned quickly.

Simon felt the tension that held him slowly release and he smiled back at her. "How are you doing, Caitlin?" he asked quietly.

"I think I should get the report ready for the new shift," Danielle said to anyone who cared to listen, then left, leaving Caitlin and Simon looking at each other.

"I'm fine," she said, looking away again. "Been busy on the ward."

"You'll be done in a few minutes?" He asked it as a question even though he knew what the answer would be.

She nodded, glancing sidelong at the clock on the wall. "Ten minutes to be precise."

"You want to go for a cup of coffee?"

She looked up at that, smiling again. "Sure. Sounds good. I have to do a report for the new shift coming on and then I'm done."

"I'll wait for you by the entrance," he said. She nodded her assent and he turned and left, unable to stop his grin.

Pacing around the entrance took up about five minutes. Synchronizing his watch so that it was on time with the clock in the entryway took another sixty seconds. Running his hands over his hair filled fifteen seconds.

Shaking his head at his own behavior, he found an empty chair, picked up a magazine and tried to read about landscaping a summer home. He turned the page to an article about the advantages of shrubs in a back-yard.

He thought again about the Victorian that Oscar said he was going to look at. A home. Was he nuts? What did he know about homes and families? Nothing. He had never given himself enough time to figure out how they worked.

Then what are you doing waiting for Caitlin Severn to show up?

He threw the magazine down and instead kept himself busy watching the people, his legs stretched out in front of him, feet crossed at the ankles. You're not pro-posing to the woman. You're just asking her out for a cup of coffee, he told himself. You've done it hundreds of times before with dozens of other women.

But none of the other women had shown him what Caitlin had shown him. None of them had encouraged him to return to his faith in God, had nurtured a sense of shame and need.

Chapter Thirteen

Caitlin walked down the hall, her steps brisk, efficient. She caught sight of him, then slowed, one hand coming up to smooth her hair.

Simon got up slowly, ignoring the slight pain in his leg.

She wore a yellow anorak and blue jeans. Her hair was loose and at the sight, he smiled. She looked more approachable now. Less a nurse, more a woman.

"Hi," she said, stopping in front of him.

Did he imagine that breathless note in her voice? Was it wishful thinking on his part?

"Hi, yourself." He pulled his car keys out of his pocket, jingling them a minute, just looking at her. "Any place special you want to go to?"

"There's a nice spot past the mall heading up-island," she said, fiddling with her purse straps.

"I've got my car in the parking lot. Do you want a ride with me?"

"Sure."

"Then let's go." They walked in silence out of the hospital, to his car. He unlocked the door for her, watching as Caitlin ducked her head and got in. He walked around the front of the car, his eyes still on her and got in on his side.

He drew in a steady breath as he buckled up and turned the key in the ignition. Caitlin sat back against the headrest, watching him as he backed out of the hospital parking lot and turned onto the road.

"This is a lot different than your motorbike," she said, looking around the interior. "Are you turning over a new leaf?"

"More like starting another book," he said quietly. "The motorbike had to go."

"That sounds profound. How is your leg?"

"Good." Simon drew in a deep breath, smiling. "Really good." He glanced sidelong at her. "And how was your visit with your sister, the one in Portland?"

"Nice. Evelyn and her husband have a lovely little baby girl."

Silence.

Well that exhausted those topics of conversation, he thought.

They drove on for a while, both quiet. Simon never had trouble talking to a woman before, but Caitlin made him uneasy, nervous.

Caitlin glanced at Simon while he gave the waitress their order. His hair was longer than before, hiding the small scar she knew was on his forehead. His eyes held the same glint, his mouth curved up in the same impudent grin. He looked far more at ease than she felt.

His street clothes emphasized his masculinity and at the same time created a distance. This was a Simon unfamiliar to her. Strong, in charge and independent.

When she had seen him standing by the desk, she felt as if all the breath had been squeezed out of her chest.

She fiddled with her spoon and, just for something to do, put some sugar in her coffee, stirring it slowly. She could feel Simon's eyes on her but didn't know what to say.

"Isn't this where we are supposed to make intelligent conversation?" he asked suddenly. "You ask me a question, I ask you a question…" He let the comment fade as he smiled at her.

"And the purpose is?"

"Getting to know each other in a neutral setting." Simon set his cup down. "The hospital was definitely your territory. This is just a restaurant. Neutral ground."

Caitlin looked down at her own cup, hardly daring to hope that he wanted the same thing she did. Something had started between them, something she didn't know if she dared explore.

He was right about territory. They had met on the unequal footing of patient and nurse. She had seen his vulnerability. However, he had also voluntarily opened himself up to her in a way no other man had. She had seen him searching for God and that, in itself, touched her deeply.

"I'll start with a question for you, seein's how you're not saying anything," Simon said, pushing his cup and saucer around on the table, a hint of a smile teasing the corner of his mouth. "What new and exciting things have happened in your life? How's the boyfriend?"

Caitlin frowned. "Boyfriend?"

"Yeah. The guy who came to the ward that night. Charles." Simon spun his cup in the saucer, holding her gaze.

"He's not my boyfriend. I broke up with him a while ago."

Simon stopped the spinning, his hand resting on the rim of the cup. "What did you say?"

"I said Charles is not my boyfriend."

Simon sat back, a smile curving his beautiful mouth. "Really."

"I broke up with him the night you had your accident." Caitlin swallowed as she saw the glint in his eyes and knew that in that moment something had shifted, changed. "He came to the ward hoping to get back together with me. I told him again that it was over." She looked down remembering all too vividly the reasons she knew she would never go back to Charles Frost. Remembering Simon's gentle touch and the not-so-gentle kisses of a mouth that now curved up in a smile.

She felt her cheeks warm at the memory and quickly took a sip of coffee to cover up her embarrassment.

"I see," Simon said quietly.

Silence slipped over them as they sat opposite each other. A silence broken by the murmur of the other patrons of the restaurant. She searched desperately for something to say. "And how is your work going?"

Simon lifted a hand and waggled it back and forth. "Good. Making money in some places, losing it in others."

She nodded and that topic was exhausted.

Simon pushed his cup and saucer aside and took her hand in his. "This isn't working really well, is it?" he asked, his deep voice low. "I was hoping we could exchange some idle chitchat, get to know each other better. Start over on a more equal footing." He lifted his eyebrows quickly at that. "If you'll pardon the pun."

Caitlin smiled, her heart thrumming at his contact, her hand nestled in the protective warmth of his. She raised her eyes to his and once again was lost. She had never felt this way about any man before, this sense of belonging, a feeling that with Simon all in her life that was annoying and frustrating became meaningless. "So, how do we do this?"

"I don't know." Simon looked down at her hand, stroking her thumb with his. "I already know that your favorite color is blue, your favorite food is chicken. That you are a great nurse and sincere Christian." He looked up at that, his head tilted to one side. "I know that much about you."

Caitlin swallowed at the intensity of his gaze. "And I know that your favorite color is brown. You like French fries, and you don't like taking painkillers."

His slow, lazy smile wound its way around her heart, tightening it with bands of yearning.

"I know that you have a brother," she continued, striving for an even tone, determined to do this right, to confront all the issues of his life. "That you were raised in foster homes and that deep within you is a need for something more that only God can give. What I don't know is, if you've found it."

"Well, that was quite an exposé," he said, his tone dry.

"It's the truth. And if you want us to get to know each other better, then we had better start on that footing." Caitlin looked down at their joined hands, hoping and praying that she hadn't said too much, yet knowing that she was right.

"Do you want to get to know me better?" Simon

asked. Caitlin saw the smirk on his face, but heard in his voice a faint note of yearning, of wanting.

"Yes I do, Simon."

"You might not like what you discover."

"I know what I'm in for," she said quietly.

Now he sat across from her, one hand cradling hers, the other tracing her knuckles. He laughed softly, then looked up at her again. "I don't think you know what you've done to me, Caitlin. For years I've been on my own. I've done what I've wanted to do. I've made money and lost money and none of it mattered. I've never been a responsible kind of guy because I've never wanted to have something that I couldn't afford to lose. But you've made me take another look at myself." He shook his head, as if trying to understand it himself. "I didn't like what I saw. I was angry that you made me vulnerable. I've been trying all my life to be tough and strong. To be independent." He squeezed her hand, hard. "Now I've been reading the Bible, struggling with what God wants me to be. Trying to accept obligations. I don't know if I can do it."

His words alternately warmed and chilled her. "What are you trying to say, Simon?"

Simon lifted her hand up to his mouth and touched his lips to it. "I don't know," he whispered. "I just know that I care about you and that your opinion is important to me." He blew out his breath in a sigh that caressed her hand. "When I was sick, that last night you were with me in the hospital, you were reading that passage from Isaiah, something about comfort. I know what I have to do, but I'm not sure I'm ready to do it yet." He shrugged and gently lowered her hand to the table.

Caitlin smiled. "Well, then I guess I have to keep praying for you, Simon."

He smiled back and gave her hand a quick squeeze. "You do that, Caitlin Severn."

The talk had gotten heavy, yet Caitlin felt a lightness pervade the atmosphere. As if a foundation had been laid. But she could see from Simon's frown that it was time to change the subject.

"So, tell me about Oscar. How in the world did you two ever meet up?"

Simon lifted his head smiling. "That's a long story."

Caitlin shrugged, glancing at her watch. "I've got tomorrow off, so I've got time."

So he told her. The talk moved from Oscar to books they had read, places they'd been. Simon was well traveled, she discovered. He'd been to places she had only dreamed of seeing, done things she had only imagined. Scuba diving off the Tasmanian coast, trekking in Nepal, taking his chances on the Trans-Siberian Railway. She shook her head with every new adventure.

"My life sounds horribly dull," she said after he'd recounted a harrowing trip on a bus through Africa.

Simon shrugged her comment away. "Traveling can be dull, too. Planes and hotels and rented cars. It's all the same after a while, if you're on your own." He caught her eye and smiled a lazy smile. "It's more fun with someone."

Caitlin's breath caught in her throat at the suggestion in his eyes, his smile.

"Aren't there places you would love to go, Caitlin?" he asked, his voice lowering almost intimately.

"Lots. I've always wanted to see Paris and Greece.

The usual tourist travel destinations. I'm not much for adventure, I guess."

"I liked Paris. But it's not a city you should visit on your own," Simon said, leaning slightly forward, one corner of his mouth curved up in a smile. "Paris needs to be seen walking arm in arm with someone you care about." He took her hand again, playing with her fingers.

Caitlin felt her breath catch in her throat, felt her heart slow, miss a beat, then race as she understood the suggestion in his voice, his posture.

What am I going to do with this man, Lord? He confuses me, makes me afraid, makes me want to care for him. She swallowed, her hand still in his as he ran his index finger over hers again and again.

He looked up at her, his eyes intent, and Caitlin knew that if the table hadn't separated them, he would have kissed her.

And she would have let him.

The drive to Caitlin's home was done in silence, an awareness humming between them. Each time Simon glanced sidelong at Caitlin, he could see her eyes glowing in the reflected light of his car's dashboard.

He couldn't suppress the feelings of unworthiness that her gentle smile gave him. But he also knew that in spite of his feelings, he had to see her again. It was like a hollow need that only she could fill. He didn't like the hold she had over him, but he liked even less the notion of not seeing her again.

They pulled up to her house, the front window shedding light in the gathering darkness.

"Thanks for the ride," she said, reaching for the door handle. "And the coffee."

Simon watched her turn, watched as she pulled her purse close to her in readiness to get out. "Wait," he said softly, catching her arm.

She turned to face him, her eyes wide. "What?"

Simon let his eyes drift over her face, come to rest on her softly parted mouth. Ignoring the cold voice of reason, he bent over and fitted his mouth to hers. The kiss started out so gentle, so plain, but then she murmured his name, slipped her arms around him, pulled him closer.

And he was undone. He caught her close, almost crushing her, his mouth slanting over hers.

Simon was the first to draw away, his eyes seeking hers, his hand reaching up to touch her mouth in wonder.

"What are you doing to me?" he murmured, remembering his own response the last time he had kissed her. The absolute rightness of having her in his arms, the sweetness that pierced him when she spoke his name.

"Kissing you, I thought," she replied, her voice trembling.

Simon drew in a careful breath, unable to suppress the smile that threatened to crack his jaw. He stroked her hair back from her face, just because he wanted to. He didn't want to think about what was happening to him, didn't want to think that he was running the risk of making himself vulnerable to another person. This was Caitlin. She wasn't just anybody, he reasoned.

"Are you busy tomorrow?" he asked, looking down into her soft green eyes, losing himself in their warmth.

She shook her head. "Not until the evening," she whispered.

"How would you like to take a trip up-island? I have

a place I want to have a look at." Not the most romantic date he had ever taken a woman on, but he sensed with Caitlin he needed to take things slow. For his own protection as much as anything. Maybe spending some more time with her would ease the ache thinking about her created in him.

Maybe pigs could fly, he thought.

"I'd like that," she said with a soft murmur. She touched his cheek, stroking it lightly with warm fingers.

"Good," he replied turning his head to kiss her fingertips. "I'll pick you up at three."

She traced his mouth, smiling up at him. "Then I'll see you tomorrow," she said, leaning closer to press a light kiss on his lips.

Then she opened the car door, letting a blast of cold air in, jumped out and was striding up the walk to her parents' house before he had a chance to open his own door.

He got out and called to her over the hood. "You're supposed to let me walk you to the door."

She turned, walking backward, laughing at him. "Next time," she said. Then tossing a wave at him, she turned and jogged up the steps and went into the house.

Bemused, Simon got back in his car, put it in gear and drove away. He felt bamboozled by what had happened. He had gone to the hospital simply to deliver flowers and ended up with a date with Caitlin Severn tomorrow. He wondered if he knew what he was getting himself into.

Chapter Fourteen

"What do you plan to do with it?" Caitlin asked, as Simon unlocked the front door of the old Victorian house.

"It's an investment," Simon replied, standing aside to allow Caitlin to walk into the main foyer. Their footsteps echoed in the large open hallway. To one side was a set of doors, now boarded up. The other set of doors led to a large open room and a hallway flanked the large, wide stairs directly in front of them.

"Oh, look at that." Caitlin ran up the first flight of stairs, stopping at the landing. A stained-glass window shed a colored pattern of diffused light on the landing. "This doesn't look Victorian."

"I suspect one of the hippies that lived here made it." Simon came up beside her, his hands in his pockets.

They walked upstairs, inspecting each room. The heavy odor of incense hung in one of the rooms and in the other, dark paper covered a broken window. Water stains on the ceilings attested to the need for a new roof.

"It's going to be a pile of work, Simon. Are you sure

you want to even bother?" Caitlin shook her head as they walked down the hall.

Simon shrugged, reaching around her to open the door of the last room. "A person could always bulldoze it and build a new one." He had to push to open the door and when they stepped inside the room, Caitlin had to stop her surprised gasp. Windows from floor to ceiling ran along one wall and flowed in a three-quarter circle instead of a corner to the other wall. "This is beautiful," she breathed, walking farther into the room, straight to the semicircle of windows. "Wouldn't a set of chairs be just perfect here?" She stepped closer to the window, resting her fingertips lightly against it as if to touch the view.

Beyond the shoreline below them, beyond the water, she could see the mountains of the mainland with their variegated colors of blue, mauve and gray. A few gulls wheeled past them, celebrating their utter freedom punctuated by their piercing cries.

"This is just incredible." She glanced over her shoulder, disconcerted to see Simon directly behind her. His hands were safely in the pockets of his khaki pants, holding back his leather jacket, but the way he looked down at her left her with no illusions as to what was on his mind.

"It is incredible," he agreed, his hazel eyes twinkling down at her.

"I meant the view, Simon," she said breathlessly.

His lazy smile crawled across his beautiful mouth. "So did I," he replied.

Caitlin looked away, fully aware of Simon behind her, aware of the fact they stood in what was probably the master bedroom of this large, rambling house. For a brief moment she allowed herself a fantasy. Simon and her, standing together, looking out over a view they saw day after day.

It would be early morning. They would each be getting ready for work, but taking time to just be together, sharing a quiet moment before the busyness of the day separated them.

She let her eyes close as she hugged herself, unaware of the fact that she was slowly leaning back toward Simon until barely a breath separated them. Then his arms surrounded her, held her against him, his face buried in the hair that lay on her neck.

"Caitlin," he breathed, holding her closer, rocking her slightly.

It was a small movement, a mere twisting of her head, a shifting of her weight, and her cheek touched his forehead. He lifted his head and once again, their lips met in a kiss as soft as a baby's sigh.

He was the first to draw back, and Caitlin murmured her disappointment. He dropped a light kiss on her forehead and then stepped back.

Caitlin felt bereft and frustrated at the same time. She knew something important was building between them, but at the same time she didn't know if she should trust her own feelings. She cared for Simon deeply and if she were to truly examine her feelings, she would be able to say she loved him.

But she didn't dare say so, and so far he hadn't expressed how he truly felt about her. Once before she had made a mistake and wasn't eager to spend another few years of her life wondering about another relationship.

If she were to face the truth, she would realize that she was afraid to push Simon too hard. She knew enough about his life to know that Simon was afraid to tie himself down. Buying this house could be a signal that he was ready to do so, but then again, Simon was a consummate businessman. It could just be another investment.

Caitlin turned back to the view, frustrated with herself, frustrated with emotions she couldn't control. *Please, Lord,* she prayed, wrapping her arms around herself, *show me what I should do. I'm confused. I'm afraid I love him, and I'm afraid that love will go nowhere. Help me to trust You, help me to be satisfied with Your love first and foremost.*

"We should be getting back."

Simon's voice broke into her prayer, and she turned to face him, forcing a smile to her face. He only stared at her, his own expression slightly dazed. Then he abruptly turned around, the sound of his booted heels echoing in the silence of the house.

Caitlin followed him more slowly, glancing over her shoulder once more at the remarkable room with the wonderful windowed nook.

Then she relegated her own wisp of a daydream back where it belonged. Reality.

"So, what's the verdict?" Simon asked as they drove away from the property.

Caitlin craned her neck for one last look, then turned to Simon. "I think you should buy it. If nothing else, you could turn it into a bed-and-breakfast."

Simon pursed his lips, nodding at her suggestion. "Could do that." He glanced sidelong at her, then quickly away again. "I'd have to find someone to run it for me, though."

Their conversation seemed to carefully pick its way

through dangerous territory, Caitlin thought. Simon hardly dared say that he might want the house for himself and she didn't dare suggest it. To do so would give a wrong signal, create a misunderstanding.

How she hated this stage of the relationship, she thought. She had gone through it enough times with Charles, she should be good at it. The hesitation, the uncertainty. Wondering if you were presuming too much. Wondering if it was going to go beyond a few kisses, a few casual dates.

In spite of all the gains women said they had made in terms of equality over the past few years, they hadn't made many strides when it came to women being able to read men, or vice versa.

He pulled up in front of her house and Caitlin turned to him, deciding to stick her neck out a bit. "Would you like to come in? It's my mother's birthday party."

Simon shrugged, biting his lip as he looked past her to the house.

"I can't intrude on that."

"You don't intrude on families, Simon," she said quietly. "Just come in for a quick cup of coffee. Say hi to my parents, wish my mom a happy birthday."

Simon blew out his breath in a sigh, still contemplating.

Please, Lord, let him say yes, she thought. She wanted him in her home. She wanted him to meet her family. In some foolish way she felt it would show her whether she was wasting her time or not.

She didn't want to feel that way about Simon because in spite of her doubts, she knew she was falling in love with him.

"Okay," he said quietly, giving her a quick grin. "I'll do that."

Caitlin let out her breath, not even aware she was holding it. Then with a grin she couldn't suppress, she got out of the car, waiting for him to catch up to her and together they walked up the path to her home.

As soon as they opened the door, Caitlin wondered if she had made a grave mistake. She heard the unmistakable tones of Rachel's laughing voice, Jonathon's deep one and those of her grandparents.

"Got extra company," she said with forced brightness as they walked in the door. Caitlin took his coat and hung it up in the cupboard in the entrance. Then taking a breath for courage, walked through the arched entryway into the living room.

"Oh, hi, Caity," her mother said from the couch directly facing the opening. "I'm so glad you made it back. I…"

But whatever she was about to say died on her lips when she saw Simon. She glanced back at Caitlin with a puzzled look, then back at Simon.

Caitlin almost groaned. She just knew her mother was mentally comparing Simon to Charles.

"Everybody," she said, encompassing the entire room with a casual wave of her hand, forcing an overly bright smile. "I'd like you to meet Simon."

The introductions were made. Simon was gracious. He wished Caitlin's mother a happy birthday. He was witty and made Rachel laugh. Rachel tossed Caitlin a bemused look but thankfully was politeness personified when introduced.

Caitlin kissed her grandparents and listened to her grandfather's usual doctor joke. Grandma gave her a kiss and asked when she was coming over again. Her mother couldn't hide her surprise. Thankfully her father covered up by clearing the newspapers off a love seat, indicating they should sit there.

A moment of silence followed as Caitlin and Simon sat down, then...

"Do you want some birthday cake and coffee?" her mother offered both of them.

"How is work going?" Rachel asked Caitlin, with a knowing smirk.

"So what do you do?" Jonathon asked Simon at the same time.

"Where did that dog go now?" her father muttered to no one in particular.

The dog was retrieved from under the couch and sent downstairs to sulk. Her mother left to get Simon and Caitlin each a cup of coffee but not before she threw Caitlin a slightly puzzled look.

Soon the usual ebb and flow of family conversation filled the room again as Caitlin answered the "duty" questions about her work from her grandparents and asked after Rachel's health. From that the topics ranged from the traffic coming off the ferry to politics to the best way to get rid of fleas on dogs. Caitlin laughed with her sister, answered her grandparents' frequent questions and occasionally glanced sideways at Simon. He was talking to Jonathon, but would, from time to time, look at her. His expression was unreadable, and Caitlin felt a stirring of disquiet. When he smiled, it was forced. As he sat drinking his coffee, he sat on the edge of the couch, as if ready to bolt.

Simon finally finished his coffee, set down the cup and then stood up. "Mr. and Mrs. Severn, it was nice to meet you and best wishes again on your birthday," he said, his voice achingly polite. He said his farewells to the rest of the family and with a quick look at Caitlin left.

She followed him, her discomfort growing.

"What's wrong, Simon?" she asked as he pulled his jacket off the hanger in the entrance. He glanced over her shoulder at the group who she knew was watching them. She lowered her voice. "Did someone say something wrong?"

He snapped up his coat, the sounds echoing in the quiet. "Come say goodbye to me outside," he said, turning to open the door.

Caitlin hugged herself against a sudden chill as they stepped outside, closing the door quietly behind her. "What's the matter?"

He shoved his hands in his coat pocket, the overhead porch light casting his face in shadows. She couldn't read his expression, couldn't understand what precisely was happening, but her inner sense told her it wasn't good.

"Nothing's the matter. Your family didn't say anything wrong. They seem like wonderful people."

She relaxed at that, her shoulders losing their tension. "I'm glad you like them."

"I do. You're a lucky woman, Caitlin." She could see his careful smile. "No, not lucky. Blessed." He leaned closer and touched his lips to hers. A brief kiss, gentle and soft.

Then he turned and sauntered down the walk to his car, got in and drove away.

Caitlin watched his rear lights until he turned, then she leaned back against the door.

He had denied it, but she knew, deep inside, something had happened. Something very wrong.

It had been seventeen days, Caitlin figured, glancing at the calendar hanging on the wall in her parents' kitchen. Seventeen days since Simon had walked away from her standing on her parents' porch.

And he hadn't called.

How could she have been so stupid? she thought. Simon had dangled her along from the first time she met him. Back and forth, back and forth. Like she was some kind of fish on a hook. A kiss here and there, a serious conversation and then he pulled back again.

A sucker, she thought angrily, pushing her chair back and getting up, that's what she was. First Charles, now Simon. It seemed it was her fate to end up with guys who were afraid to commit.

She glanced at her watch. In an hour Danielle was going to pick her up to go Christmas shopping. And she dreaded it.

The season had sneaked up on her, she thought with a rueful shake of her head. Usually she was in the thick of preparations, helping her mother bake and putting up decorations long before it was time.

But not this year. This year it was a chore, a burden to get even the most simple of tasks done. The Christmas spirit was decidedly missing in her life.

And she knew exactly why.

She had prayed, had read her Bible, had talked to her sisters, but she couldn't seem to get around the problem of her love for Simon. Because much as she didn't like to face it, she did love him.

She wasn't able to analyze exactly why. He was exasperating, complicated, troubled.

But each time she thought of him, it was with a trembling heart and a yearning to be with him again. He made her complete, whole.

She wandered around the house, from the kitchen to the living room. A Christmas tree sat in one corner, a few presents under it already. Her mother had made up arrangements of cedar and candles and laid boughs of cedar on the mantel of the fireplace. Clusters of cedar bound with bright red ribbon hung on the wall bracketing an embroidered nativity scene her mother had done years ago.

The aroma of cedar and fir filled the house. Her sisters were on the phone every other day, making plans, gearing up for another Severn family get-together. Tony had even called, much to her parents' delight and surprise.

Caitlin wondered if anything had ever come of her phone call to Simon's brother.

And then she thought of Simon. Again.

She was tired of feeling this confused and frustrated. She walked back to the kitchen and taking a steadying breath, sat down by the phone. She knew his number by heart. Sad, really.

It rang once, then again and she wondered if he was on the road, wheeling and dealing again.

On the fourth ring, someone picked up.

Even over the sterile medium of the phone line, his deep voice could give her shivers, she thought fatuously.

"Hello, Simon. Caitlin here."

Silence hung heavy over the line.

"Hello, Caitlin."

She wished she could see his face, wished she could see his expression. But all she had to go on was his voice. And that didn't sound too welcoming.

She decided to forge ahead. "I hadn't heard from you in a while," she said. "You must be busy," she added hopefully.

"Yeah." Silence again.

"I was wondering if that was the reason I haven't heard from you."

"Well, things have been hectic with that new apartment block."

"What about the house?"

"I've decided to give it a miss. Didn't seem like a good investment."

"I see." And she did. Silly as it sounded, the house seemed to represent settling down, a desire on his part for more than a sterile apartment. Her silly fantasy had been just that. She would have gladly shared that home with him. But Simon only saw opportunities.

"Look, Caitlin. I've got to go. Oscar is coming pretty soon…"

"Am I going to see you again?"

A hesitation, then Simon cleared his throat. "Caitlin, I'm sorry." He paused and in that moment Caitlin felt her throat thickening, choking her. She swallowed and swallowed, afraid of the next words, willing them out of him, yet at the same time wanting to slam the phone on the hook so she wouldn't hear them.

"Caitlin, it just isn't going to work between us," he continued.

"Explain that please," she said abruptly. How could he say that? They had shared so much. She remembered reading Isaiah to him, talking to him, sharing. She felt more complete with him than she had with Charles, with any man she had met.

"You're a great person and you've got a lot going for you..."

"Spare me the platitudes, just give me the truth." She forced the words out, clutching the phone so hard she was surprised it was still intact.

"I have nothing to give you, Caitlin."

She forced a laugh. "Whatever do you mean, Simon? I thought you had quite a bit of money."

"I know money isn't important to you, Caitlin. But I know family is. And I can't give you that." He paused. "I'm sorry."

"Don't you dare hang up yet, you coward," she blurted, hardly believing she actually spoke the words out loud. "I don't know where you come off thinking that family is like a dowry, an endowment you bring to a relationship. I know where you come from. I know where you've been..."

"No, you don't, Caitlin." Simon's voice was hard now. "You don't know and don't presume to think you do."

"Do I need to experience precisely the same thing to be able to understand you?" She got up, pacing back and forth, trying to find some outlet for her anger, her frustration. "I have agonized over our relationship. I have wondered what I really feel for you. I've lain awake nights over you, I've watched over you. I've prayed for you, loved you. And now you so casually tell me 'it won't work' just because I have a family and you don't. I've been told by one ex-boyfriend that 'it won't work' because I don't want to move, but never because I happen to come from a loving home."

"You really don't understand, do you?" he growled. "It's over, Caitlin." He hesitated while Caitlin drew in another breath to give him another blast. "It's over." Then unbelievably, she heard a click of the phone in her ear. She looked at it, dumbfounded, then slowly hung up.

She turned around, walked upstairs to her bedroom, sank down on her bed. Then she buried her face in her hands and wept.

She cried for herself, for Simon and his confusion and for the pain she heard in his voice. She cried for all the brokenness in this cold lonely world that created people without families, without a parent's love.

When the worst of her heartache had flowed over her and dissipated, she lay back on the bed, her eyes sore from the sorrow, staring sightlessly up at the ceiling. In spite of her own sorrow, she couldn't help her prayer. *Please be with Simon*, she whispered. *Please show Him Your love and Your comfort. Help me to understand. Show me what to do.* Somehow, she knew she and Simon weren't finished yet.

Simon laid the phone down and pressed his fingers against his eyes. He sucked in a deep breath.

I've prayed for you, loved you.

Caitlin's words were spoken in anger, but he heard the absolute sincerity behind them.

He knew he had done the right thing by breaking up with her. He knew any relationship with Caitlin would go beyond casual. All the way to marriage and what kind of father would he be? What did he know of parenting, of how families worked? He came from nowhere and had nothing.

Sitting in Caitlin's house with her family had reminded Simon far too vividly of each time he was moved into a new home. Those first few weeks of uncertainty, of trying to figure out how this family worked, of wondering if this was going to be a good home or bad home. The feeling of not belonging, of being on the outside of a family that had been together long before him and would still be together after he left.

He had spent half his life outrunning responsibilities, the ties that a family like Caitlin's entailed would bind around him. He hadn't given himself time to maintain close friendships, hadn't bothered to get to know anyone other than Oscar on the most casual basis.

Somewhere in Alberta he had a brother he hadn't talked to in so long, he wouldn't even know how to begin reestablishing their long-lost relationship. There was no forgiveness for that long a silence and he knew it.

The end result of all that was he had nothing to give Caitlin.

I've prayed for you, loved you.

Her words echoed through his mind. Blowing out a sigh, he dragged his hands over his face, then looked up.

He needed to get some work done, that's what. He never spent this much time contemplating his own life before. Never gave himself enough time to do it.

He flipped on the computer and as he waited for it to boot up, picked up the estimate a contractor had sent him on renovating the apartment block in Nanaimo. Under the file folder lay a Bible.

Simon glanced at it.

He remembered a quiet voice reading to him through the delirium of his fever. *Comfort, comfort ye my people.* Words that soothed, filled, smoothed the rough places of his life. Caitlin had stayed at his side then, as well.

Simon didn't deserve her, he knew that. But he also knew that he couldn't put her out of his mind. It was sheer cowardice on his part that kept him away from her. He hadn't been able to run, but he had retreated.

But oh, how he had missed her. He knew he cared for her more deeply than he had for anyone. He knew that every time he thought of her, his heart ached. Love shouldn't hurt, he thought. Love was supposed to be a soft, gentle emotion, not these hooks that dug into his heart.

Frustrated with his own thoughts, he picked up the Bible, leaned back in his chair, crossed his legs at the ankle and started leafing through it.

He turned to Isaiah 40. "'Comfort, comfort my people, says your God.'" Caitlin had certainly followed that command, he thought with a sad smile. He read on until he came to Isaiah 41. "'I took you from the ends of the earth, from its farthest corners I called you. I said, "You are my servant;" I have chosen you and have not rejected you. So do not fear, for I am with you; do not be dismayed, for I am your God. I will strengthen you and help you; I will uphold you with my righteous right hand.'"

He laid his head on the high back of his computer chair, letting the words become a part of him. *Called, chosen.* Not *rejected.*

He had been here before, he thought. In the hospital. That last night he had been with Caitlin. He remembered his broken dreams. Words and snatches came back to him now. *My son, give me your heart,* he remembered.

He had hesitated then. To give one's heart was to open oneself up to weakness, to give someone something to hold over you.

But what was the alternative? he thought, opening his eyes and looking around his stark apartment. Keeping to yourself, making more money? Eating your heart out over a beautiful woman with a gentle smile?

His life seemed rather pathetic right now. Empty and purposeless. He closed his eyes. The Bible was still open on his lap. He knew what he had to do. He just wasn't sure exactly how to go about it. *Show me, Lord. Help me through this*, he prayed. *I can't go on like this. I love her. I know I do. I know what You want of me. I don't like being weak. I don't like letting others be in charge, but I'm hereby putting You in charge of my life.* He stopped, as if analyzing the data, then shook his head. *I'm letting go. I surrender.*

And at that moment, as he mentally pried his fingers from all the events of his life that he clung to so tightly, he felt a lightness, a peace pervade him.

He spent the next half hour paging through the Bible, remembering passages that Tom Steele used to read. He reacquainted himself with a book that had once been a part of every meal, every evening before bed.

And he slowly felt the tension leave his shoulders. He laid the Bible aside with a rueful grin. Salvation or no, he still had some work to do. And he still had to figure out how he was going to reconcile himself with Caitlin, praying he hadn't blown it.

The harsh peal of the doorbell broke his concentration on the computer. With a dazed glance he looked up. Darkness had fallen while he had worked. He wondered who it could be. For a brief moment the thought pierced him that it might be Caitlin. But common sense told him to forget that idea.

Simon got up, walked to the door, opened it and frowned.

A tall figure stood backlit by the light from the hallway. He wore a red plaid jacket over a denim shirt tucked into denim jeans. Cowboy boots completed the picture.

"Simon Steele?" the man asked.

Simon nodded, then, as the voice filtered through his memories he felt the blood drain from his face, felt his heart slow.

"Jake?"

Chapter Fifteen

❧

"Hello, Simon," Jake replied, his hands hanging at his sides, not making a move in his brother's direction.

Simon couldn't help but stare. It was Jake all right. Same dark hair with a tendency to wave, same brown eyes that looked steadily at the world from beneath level brows. Same uncompromising mouth. Same Jake, only older.

Simon forced his gaze away. "Come in," he said, stepping aside, shock making him almost incoherent.

He flicked on some lights as Jake walked into the room.

Jake stopped halfway, not sitting down, just looking at his brother. But what do you say after all those quiet years? Their last phone call had been full of anger and accusations and they hadn't spoken to each other since.

Now two grown men stared across the room at each other as the silence stretched out.

Finally Simon asked, "How did you find me?"

Jake sat down then, his elbows resting on his knees. "I got a phone call," he said slowly, clasping his hands. "From a woman named Caitlin. She called when you were still in the hospital. I would have come to visit you then, but she called in the middle of fieldwork. We were way behind so I couldn't come."

Simon sat down at that. Caitlin again. Dear, sweet, wonderful, beautiful, organizing Caitlin. "How did she find you?"

Jake lifted one shoulder, shaking his head. "Don't have a clue." He looked up at Simon. "I thought you might have told her."

"I haven't talked to you in over twelve years." Simon blew out his breath as the reality of the words settled in for both of them. He looked at his brother as he struggled to find something that would bridge the gap of time and space between him and one of the few people in his life that he had ever truly loved.

Jake looked up and for a moment their eyes held. Jake was the first to look down, pressing his thumbs together and apart. "So, what kind of work have you been doing these past years?"

Chitchat, thought Simon. A warming up, a way of circling and checking each other out from the safe distance of work and occupation. "I own a few franchises, dabble in stocks and bonds." Simon laughed shortly as he heard his job through his brother's ears. "What about you?"

Jake pursed his lips, tilted his head to one side. "I'm farming with Fred Prins. My foster father."

"So you stayed there?"

Jake nodded. "I was fortunate there."

Simon clasped his hands over his stomach, letting a silence drift up between them, full of memories. "So, you ever get married?" he asked finally.

Jake laughed shortly. "Yes. I have a little girl. My wife is dead, though."

Simon sensed a history there, but didn't pursue it, recognizing the need to keep things light for now. "Well, I didn't. Always been restless, I guess."

More silence. They both knew what the end result of that restlessness had been.

"So, how long can you stay?" Simon asked.

"I've got a couple of days off. I thought I would stay around for a while tomorrow. I have to be back the next day, though. Christmas is coming."

Simon nodded, feeling a clutch of sorrow at the mention of Christmas. He was usually gone this time of the year. However, for now his sorrow was alleviated by the reality of his brother, here. A brother who wanted to reconnect the broken thread of their mutual past. Family.

"Did you have supper?" Simon asked.

"I grabbed a burger at Blue River," Jake said.

"Then you're probably ready for something else. We could go out, but you're probably tired. I'll order in."

Half an hour later they sat across from each other at the table—a steaming pizza in a box between them. Bachelor food, thought Simon wryly. Jake paused a moment, bowing his head, and Simon realized he was asking a blessing.

Simon did the same. *I'm a little rusty at this, God*, he prayed, *I'm not exactly sure what I should be saying, but thanks.* He paused then added, *Thanks for Jake.* He lifted his head and caught Jake's surprised look. He ignored it and started eating. When they were done, they moved to the living room, settling into an awkward silence.

"Why don't you ask me the questions you want to,

Jake," Simon said after a few minutes, knowing he wanted to get things out in the open. "We can get all of this stuff from our past out of the way."

"We'll never get it *all* out of the way," Jake said, standing up and turning to face his brother. "Things don't just go away because you've decided they will."

Simon held his brother's steady gaze. "You came a long way to see me, Jake. I think you're allowed a few questions."

"Okay." Jake plowed his hand through his hair, rearranging the neat waves. "May as well get to it. Did you ever find Mom?"

"No. I would have called you if I did."

"Would you have?" Jake asked, his short laugh sounding harsh. "It would have been nice if you had anyhow. Because I didn't have the first clue where you were, Simon. In over ten years not a letter, a phone call, not even a postcard or a message sent via someone else. I thought you were dead, man. I really thought you were dead."

And as Simon listened to the pain in his brother's voice, he was forced to face the consequences of his own actions.

"I remember asking why you always ran, and you'd say you were looking for Mom. Were you really?" Jake's voice was quiet now.

Simon shrugged. "At first I was. After Dad Steele died, I hated the idea that we got moved and had no say. I missed Dad and I didn't know how to show it. So I would take off."

"The social workers would get so ticked off at you for running away all the time. I remember how flustered our foster parents would get," Jake said.

"The one, Mary Arnold, would always cry and her husband would yell."

"I think they liked us but couldn't handle the stress. So we got moved again."

"For what it's worth, Jake, I'm sorry," Simon said quietly.

"Well, we only went through one more. Then we were split up…"

"And you landed on your feet at the Prinses' home," Simon said wistfully. "I was always jealous of you, you know that?"

"You didn't like it at your last foster home, did you?"

Simon shook his head. "The Stinsons were decent people but hard. I used to hate it when she would punish me by taking away visits with you." Simon smiled. "I always enjoyed our visits together. I remember coming to visit you at the Prinses', and Mrs. Prins would always give me a big hug. It was about the only time I got one."

"Really?"

Simon held his brother's gaze. "Yeah, Jake. Really."

"You never said."

"C'mon. We were fifteen. What guy of that age is going to admit that he still likes to get a hug?" Simon shrugged off the memory. "Like I said, the Stinsons did what they were supposed to, but I didn't get a lot of affection there."

"That why you ran away?"

"Partly. I was sick of getting told what to do. I was a cocky, mixed-up sixteen-year-old who had some weird notion of finding our mother so that you and I could get back together again. You were so happy at the Prinses' home, I knew you wouldn't run away unless I gave you a good reason to."

"Tilly and Fred Prins treated me like a son. Running away to find our mother was a dead end." .

"I didn't look that hard, Jake," Simon conceded. "I didn't have the time, money or resources. And after a while, I didn't even have much of a reason."

"Do you think we might find her yet?"

"I'd like to think we might."

"If we both put our energy behind it, we could find out if she's still alive or not."

Simon had always lived under the impression that Jake wasn't interested in looking into their past. "Sounds good to me. I'd like to connect with her, be a family again. When I was in the hospital, the kid next to me would get visits from his family. And I would get jealous…"

"If I had known…"

"Doesn't matter, Jake. You're here now and for that I thank God."

They spent the rest of the evening catching up, exchanging idle chitchat, reconnecting.

The next morning Simon and Jake went to a restaurant for breakfast and Jake asked him who Caitlin was.

"A nurse at the hospital."

"But she didn't call from the hospital."

"No?" Simon was surprised. "Where did she call from?"

"Said it was her sister's place. She seems like a great person, Simon," Jake continued. "When she phoned, I wasn't exactly hospitable, but she kept at me."

"She does that well," conceded Simon with a wry grin.

"She told me that she believed God had brought her to me and told me she would be praying for us." He laughed lightly, pouring syrup over his pancakes. "Told me that you and I needed to be a family again."

"Family's pretty important to her. As is her faith." Simon fiddled with his eggs.

"I get the feeling that she's special?"

Special? The word was totally inadequate to describe the hunger that clutched him when he thought of her. The regret that he felt just now. "I think I love her, Jake," he said, unable to keep the words down, needing to talk to someone about it. Who better than his own brother?

"That's great."

Simon sighed. "I guess."

"So, what's the problem?" Jake continued.

"She's a wonderful person, just like you guessed. Her faith is so strong and so much a part of her," Simon continued, staring into the middle distance, thinking about her. "She comes from a secure, happy family. I don't know if I can give her the same. I've run away from every family I've been a part of."

"Don't underestimate what you have to offer." Jake forked up a piece of pancake. "She must care for you. Why else would she call?"

Simon hardly dared believe what his brother said. He knew he and Caitlin shared something. He knew that he loved her dearly. But for the rest of their time together, Caitlin wasn't mentioned again.

They walked back to Simon's apartment, talking, catching up. "You want to come to the farm for Christmas?" Jake asked after a moment. "I know you'll be more than welcome."

Simon shrugged, his hands in his pockets, his shoulders hunched against the cold. "I don't know. I usually spend Christmas in warmer places. I wouldn't know what to do."

"What's to do? You show up, eat, laugh. Come to church. You could meet my little girl."

Simon smiled as he opened the door of his condo for his brother. "A niece. Imagine that."

"She's a cutie, 'Uncle Simon.'" Jake nudged him. "You'd love her."

"Uncle Simon. That has a nice ring to it." Simon tried to imagine Jake with a little girl, tried to see himself as an uncle. Family.

"So are you going to come?"

Simon pulled in a deep breath and blew it out again. He had missed Caitlin more each day, wanted to be with her. *I've prayed for you, loved you.* Her words haunted him. He had told her it was over, yet he knew he would never forget her.

"No," he said suddenly, shrugging off his coat. "I think I should finish off some unfinished business first."

"Caitlin?"

Simon caught his lip between his teeth and nodded.

"I think that's wise. She sounds like a sincere, warm person. I didn't come across real well when I talked to her, but she didn't hang up on me. Thanks to her, I'm here. I'd like you to go and thank her for me."

"I haven't had to contend with so much advice since last time I saw you."

"It's good advice, you know." Jake glanced down at his watch. His grin softened into a wistful smile as he took a step closer to Simon. He held out his hand. "I'm sorry, but I've got to go. It was so good to see you again."

Simon took his brother's hand and then, grasping it tightly, pulled him closer. Their arms came around each other and Simon swallowed down a knot of emotion. His brother. His family.

Thank You, Lord, he prayed, squeezing his eyes shut.

When he pulled away, he could see Jake was as moved as he was.

"I'll walk you to your vehicle."

"That's okay. Let's just say goodbye now. I don't like goodbyes."

Simon held his brother's dark eyes as the unspoken words whispered between them as each remembered other separations, other goodbyes. "I promise this one won't be as long," Simon said, smiling, his voice thick with emotion.

Jake smiled back, and then they were hugging again, their arms tight. "Thanks for everything," Jake said, pulling back. "You make sure you come."

"I will. I just have some things to do yet. But I'll be there." He hardly dared think past the current moment, that things might work out. He only knew regardless of how Caitlin took it, he had to tell her how he felt.

"Keep me posted," Jake said, picking up the overnight bag he'd left by the front door.

"I will." Simon watched as Jake left, closing the door behind him. The visit had come and gone so quickly, but he knew he would see his brother again.

Thank You, Lord, he prayed, closing his eyes in thankfulness. *Now if You could only help me out with this next thing.*

Caitlin leaned against the wall wrapping her arms around herself as she listened to the carolers coming down the hallway of the hospital, fighting down the emotions that were so close to the surface. She blinked, staring ahead at the bright lights that someone had strung along the ward. They swam, sparkled, danced. She blinked again, and her vision cleared.

It was the season, she figured, wiping the tears from her face. Christmas was a time rife with emotions. For Caitlin it was a reminder of how alone she was this Christmas. She smiled at that thought, thinking of all the people swarming through her parents' home, filling it with laughter and noise. Hardly alone.

Her mother had been busy for weeks beforehand, cooking, baking and cleaning in preparation for the holidays. It had been a few Christmases since the three girls were together. Tony and his wife never came.

Where are you, Simon? she wondered, closing her eyes, as she dropped her head against the hard wall behind her. Another tear slid down her cheek but she let it go. Are you alone this Christmas? She swallowed a lump that filled her throat. She let herself think of him, pray for him, yearn for him.

Just a few more minutes, she thought, a few more minutes of remembering what he looked like, how his voice could lower and send shivers down her spine, what his mouth felt like on hers.

She bit her lip, clutched her waist harder, knowing she was playing a dangerous game. She was alone and in an hour she had to face her family. She wouldn't have the defenses if she kept this up.

Sucking in another steadying breath she opened her eyes, pushed herself away from the wall and blinked.

Then again.

A tall figure stood five feet away from her, his

shoulders hunched beneath a leather jacket, hands in the pockets of blue jeans. Softly waving hair the color of sand touched the collar of his jacket, piercing hazel eyes beneath level brows eyed her intently. His mouth was unsmiling.

Simon.

He's so tall, she thought. She closed her eyes and opened them again. He looks tired. Her thoughts made no sense as she stared, unable to form another coherent thought. Then he started coming nearer and she took a step backward. Immediately she hit the wall behind her, but he kept coming. Finally he was directly in front of her, his deep-set eyes pinning her against the wall.

"Hi, there," he said, his voice quiet. His lips were parted and Caitlin had to clench her fists to keep from reaching up to trace their line, to touch his cheek, to make sure he was real.

"Hi, yourself," she said past dry lips, her heart beating so hard against her chest she thought it would fly out. She had missed him so much, had prayed, had wondered. Now he stood in front of her and she didn't know what to say.

"Caitlin, I need to tell you something," he said with a short laugh.

She looked up at that and saw uncertainty in his eyes, saw two small frown lines between his eyebrows. "Okay."

"I love you," he said, his deep voice surrounding her with its reality, warming her with its sound. "I was wrong. I thought I didn't have anything to give you, but that doesn't matter, does it?"

She shook her head as sorrow and pain and loneliness were washed away by his first three words. "I love you, too," she couldn't help but say.

He closed his eyes, resting his forehead against hers, his fingers lying on her neck. "Oh, Caitlin. I can hardly believe this." His breath came out in a sigh, caressing her mouth, her cheek.

Then his arms were around her, crushing her, pressing her close, his mouth molding and shaping hers. He murmured her name again and again, kissing her cheeks, her eyes, her forehead, her mouth.

Then, he pressed his face against her neck, as he drew out a shuddering sigh.

Caitlin couldn't hold him tight enough, couldn't stop herself from repeating his words back to him. "I love you, Simon. I love you with all my heart." It seemed a weak expression of the fullness in her chest that threatened to turn into tears of happiness.

Simon was the first to draw away, his eyes traveling hungrily over her face. "I can't believe this," he whispered, shaking his head lightly. "I can't believe you said that."

She smiled so hard, she felt as if her face were going to split. She wanted to kiss him again, to throw her arms out and shout it out to the world. I love Simon. Instead she reached up and did what she had longed to do from the first time she had realized her changing feelings for him. She traced the line of his mouth, his beautiful, expressive mouth. Then she pressed her fingers against his lips as if accepting a kiss, then touched her own.

"Okay you two, break it up." A loud voice behind Simon made him whirl around, his arms still holding Caitlin.

Danielle faced them, her head tipped to one side,

grinning a crooked grin. "Just because it's Christmas doesn't mean you can flirt with the nurses, Simon."

He looked back at Caitlin, who felt her face redden in response. "I'm not flirting," he said quietly. He dropped a quick kiss on her forehead. "This is serious business." He looked down at Caitlin. "I need to talk to you later," he said, his voice full of meaning.

Caitlin looked up at him, her eyes wide at first, then as she understood, spilling over with tears. "Talk to me now," she said softly.

He glanced around the hospital ward. "No. I have a better place in mind."

"Okay, I know what you're talking about," Danielle said with a laugh. "Why don't you head home, Caitlin, and you can put this poor man out of his misery. But first, let me be the first to congratulate you." She gave her friend a quick, hard hug. "Good on you, girl," she said in her ear.

Danielle pulled away and sniffed, wiping her eyes surreptitiously. She gave Simon a quick hug as well, smiling at him as she pulled away. "You take good care of her," she said, a warning note in her voice.

"With God's help, I will," he said, his voice solemn as a vow.

Danielle nodded, then turned to Caitlin. "You're not going to be any good to me for the next half hour, Caitlin. You may as well go home."

Caitlin looked up at Simon. "You have to come with me, you know." She waited, almost holding her breath while he seemed to consider.

"I was hoping you'd ask."

Caitlin smiled up at him, her heart full.

Danielle gave her a push. "Just go already."

"Thanks, Danielle," Caitlin said to her friend. "I hope you have a blessed Christmas."

"I will and I know you will, too."

Caitlin nodded, slipped her arm around Simon and together they walked out of the hospital.

The drive back to her parents' place was quiet. Caitlin sat with her head on the headrest of the car, facing him. Simon felt the same way he had that evening sitting by his computer desk. A lightness, a lifting of burdens that had been weighing him down. He drew in a careful breath, trying to find the right words, a place to start.

"I want to thank you for Jake," he said, glancing at her quickly, then back at the road. "He came a few days back. For a visit."

"Thank the Lord," Caitlin breathed, laying a gentle hand on his arm. She squeezed lightly and it was as if her hand held his heart.

"I thank Him, too." Simon shook his head at the memory. "It was so good to see him again." He bit his lip, knowing that his next words were even more important to her. "I also want you to know that I've done a lot of discovering in the past few weeks. I've discovered a need for redemption in my life, for reconciliation with God." He laughed lightly. "It's been a long road, but I've found the way back. I know I've got a long way to go yet, but for the first time in my life I feel like I'm running toward something, instead of away." He gave her another sidelong glance. "Even though I didn't dare come any sooner than this."

"I'm glad you finally dared." Her fingers touched his cheek, lingering a moment, teasing him, and Simon made a sudden decision. They were on a quiet street and he pulled over.

He turned off the engine, unbuckled his seat belt and turned to face Caitlin. She sat up straight, her eyes gleaming in the reflected light of the dashboard. Outside, lightly falling snow ticked against the windshield, but inside they were warm, secure. Alone.

He wanted to talk to her but was unable to articulate the feelings that welled up in him. He reached out and almost reverently traced the line of her eyebrows, her cheeks. She turned her face to meet his hand and closed her eyes.

"I need to tell you something else."

She opened her eyes, her hand coming up to meet his. "So you said. You're not nervous, are you?"

"Yes, I am." He stroked her face, his fingers rough against her soft skin. Did he dare? Was he presuming too much? Maybe, but he also knew for the first time in his life he didn't want to leave, run away. He wanted to stay. Stay with Caitlin.

With shaking hands, he reached into his pocket and pulled out a small velvet box. He took a slow, deep breath and flipped it open.

The solitaire diamond nestled in the box caught the nebulous glow of the streetlights and magnified them, winking out rays of color like a promise.

"I know this is kind of sudden, but I'm scared to wait too much longer. Caitlin Severn, will you marry me?"

Caitlin bit her lip, her eyes suspiciously bright. She looked up from admiring the diamond and let her hands linger down his face, catching him around the neck. "I told you I love you, Simon. I don't know if I can say it enough. I will marry you."

He felt the tension surrounding his lungs loosen at her words. Then he leaned closer, his lips lightly touching hers, their breaths mingling in a sigh. "I want to get to know all about you," he said softly. "I want to laugh with you, to pray with you. Have children. Maybe move into that rambling house we looked at." He slipped the ring on her finger. Then he pulled her close, and then there was no more need for words.

Caitlin was the first to draw away. "We should go. My family is waiting. I want so bad for them to get to know you better."

Simon nodded, nervous again. But he started the engine and drove through the city to her home.

He came to a stop in front of the brightly lit house, festooned with Christmas lights. Caitlin was out of the car and waiting for him as he locked the doors. He came around the front of the car and took her outstretched hand, lifting it to look once more at the ring on her finger. A symbol of commitment. He raised her hand to his mouth, pressing it to his lips.

"Are you sure it'll be okay with your family?" Simon asked as Caitlin tugged on his hand, signaling her desire to go into the house.

"Of course it will be." She opened the door, glancing up at him. "Hurry up. I want my family to share this."

Simon looked past her through the large bay window, its bright light streaming out onto the lawn. Inside, by a colorfully lit tree, Rachel and her husband stood with their arms around each other. Beside them a man he didn't know slept in a recliner, his head tilted to one side, a baby resting in the crook of his arm. A child played at the feet of the embracing couple and as Simon watched, Caitlin's mother walked into the room with a tray of steaming mugs. He could faintly hear Christmas music playing and then the sound of laughter. It looked too good to be true.

"C'mon, Simon, what are you staring at?"

He watched yet another moment, wondering again what they would say when he came in with Caitlin as someone who wanted to marry her.

He felt his stomach tighten as it used to all those years ago each time he was introduced to another family, a new place.

But this was Caitlin's family and that made it even more difficult. Now, even more than then, he longed to be accepted, to be a part of that family.

"Did your leg seize up, mister?" Caitlin called out from the porch. "My family is waiting."

Simon gave himself a mental shake, drew in a deep breath and sent up a heartfelt prayer. Then he slowly walked up the steps, through the door and into light and noise and the sounds of an excited family.

"Caitlin, you're here… Caitlin's here…"

"Oh, good… Finally…what took you?" Then a moment's silence descended as the people crowding into the entranceway saw Simon and then the ring on Caitlin's hand.

Then more noise and hugs and cries of congratulation.

He greeted Caitlin's parents as Mr. and Mrs. Just like in all the foster homes, wondering what they would think of him now that Caitlin wore his ring.

"You didn't meet my sister Evelyn and her husband, Scott, from Portland." Caitlin indicated a couple he hadn't met before. He struggled to commit their names to memory.

Simon drew a deep breath, unconsciously wiping his damp palms down the sides of his blue jeans. He was hugged by Evelyn, shook hands with Scott.

Caitlin caught Simon by the arm as the family moved ahead of them into the living room. "Do you mind if I leave you for a bit? I'd like to change into other clothes."

"You look great just the way you are, Caitlin."

She glanced down at her uniform with a pained look. "Thanks, but I prefer not to look like a nurse at home."

"Go then, but hurry up."

"You'll be okay?"

Simon cupped her face in his hands and brushed a kiss over her lips. "You've got a great family, Caitlin. I think I can manage."

Caitlin pressed her hand to his. "I'll be right back."

Simon watched her run up the stairs, stop at the top, then turn and smile down at him.

He couldn't help but return her smile. Even so, as he entered the living room, he felt a slight touch of panic. This was one family he badly wanted to feel a part of.

"Sit down, Simon. If I know Caitlin, she'll be a while yet." Caitlin's father indicated the couch and Simon sat down, looking around at the family who were trying not to look too hard at him. The first time he'd met them it was only as a friend. Now, he entered their home as a future in-law.

They made small talk. Caitlin's father asked him how his work was going. Simon supposed it was a subtle way of measuring how he would be able to support Caitlin. The talk was stilted for a while and Simon could hardly wait for Caitlin to return.

"Wow, sis. That looks good."

All eyes turned to the doorway as Caitlin walked into the room.

She looks like a ray of light, Simon thought, his heart swelling with pride as she came to his side. She wore a simple red dress made of velvet, short and fitted, accented by a plain gold chain around her neck. Her hair shone, backlit by the light coming from the hallway, framing a face that radiated happiness. He stood up as she approached.

"Sorry I took so long," she said as she came to Simon's side. She brushed her hair back from her face with a casual gesture, the diamond on her finger catching the light from the Christmas tree.

"Long?" Jonathon snorted. "I've seen you take more time to change your mind."

General laughter followed that comment. Caitlin answered in kind and as Simon and Caitlin sat down again, the talk became general.

Caitlin's nephew, Scott and Evelyn's child, came and sat on her lap, her mother passed around the warm cider and noisy talk roiled around the two of them.

Simon felt the tightness in his stomach relax as family business carried on, as if it were the most normal thing in the world for a stranger to come into their Christmas celebration. Scott ended up beside him. Simon found out he had also spent time tree planting and soon they were exchanging hardship stories.

The other family members flowed around them. Evelyn interrupted them to hand Scott the baby. She rested her hand lightly on Simon's shoulder and only smiled at him. Simon felt her acceptance. Rachel gave him a quick hug from behind, Jonathon gave him a curious thumbs-up while Mr. and Mrs. Severn smiled benignly at him and Caitlin.

The Severns were a warm, loving family. The very people he had once derided. He knew he had done it out of self-protection, but now he dared accept what was freely given him.

As he looked around the pleased faces of Caitlin Severn's parents, sisters and brothers-in-law, he knew that with God's help he had discovered a family's love.

He thought of his own brother and his brother's daughter. Another family he was a part of. His heart felt full.

But the best of all was Caitlin tucked into his side, his arm around her, her fingers playing with the solitaire on her hand. He glanced down at her and as their eyes met, he felt as much as saw her slow smile.

She pulled his head closer to hers. "I love you," she whispered in his ear.

Simon felt his heart lift. Would he ever tire of hearing her say that? he wondered. He pressed a kiss to her forehead and drew her even closer.

Someday, he thought, with God's blessing, they would be a family, as well.

Epilogue

"I figured I'd find you here."

Simon's voice from the doorway made Caitlin turn her head. She still wore her nurse's uniform and had meant to change as soon as she got home from work, but she had made a cup of tea and taken it up to their bedroom.

She had paused at the bow window on her way to the cupboard and as she often did, she stopped to look out over the Strait of Georgia, to the hazy blue mountains of the mainland.

"Don't you ever get tired of that view?" Simon teased as he walked up behind her. He slipped his arms around her waist and pressed a kiss to her neck, then nuzzled her ear.

"Nope," Caitlin said, setting her teacup on the small table beside her. She wrapped her arms over his, leaning back into his embrace. With a shiver of satisfaction she laid her head back against his chest, reveling in his strength, his warmth.

"Why not," he murmured against her hair. "It doesn't change much."

"Of course it does. The morning light makes the water and the mountains look fresh and new. When it rains or storms and the water has whitecaps on it, I feel all safe and cozy in here. In the evening, like now, everything looks so soft and peaceful."

Simon looked up, rocking her lightly. "Every time I see it I think, 'oceanfront property.'"

"Oh, you do not," Caitlin chided, hugging his arms even tighter. "You just say that to get a rise out of me. I know you love this place."

Simon sighed, his chest lifting behind her, his breath teasing her hair. "You see right through me, my dear," he confessed. "I do love this place." He turned Caitlin to face him and she looped her arms around his neck. "But to me the best part of coming to this house is seeing my own dear wife standing at our bedroom window, waiting for her prince to come."

"And he always does." She brushed a kiss over his mouth and laid her head on his shoulder. "But you know the real reason I like to stand at this window and stare out of it?"

"Tell me."

"Because every time I do, you come up behind me, and put your arms around me and my day gets better."

Simon laughed, a gentle rumble beneath her cheek. "You truly are a gift from God, Caitlin Steele."

Would she ever get tired of this? she wondered, holding Simon more tightly. She knew they would have their difficulties. Any relationship came with ups and downs. They'd had their differences already, but worked through them.

But she also knew that their love was founded on

God's love. And with His help, their home would be a place of refuge and comfort.

"Let's go have supper," Simon said, drawing away from her.

Caitlin smiled and hooked her arm in his. But as they left, she glanced back over her shoulder, out of the windows to the mountains beyond, praying they might be able to show the same view to their children and, Lord willing, children's children.

Their family.

* * * * *

Dear Reader,

Our family has fostered for a number of years. Throughout that time we've seen the brokenness that can happen to children and their siblings when they are separated. We've seen some happy endings and some sad endings. Some children have stayed in touch, others we never hear from again.

As foster parents, we've had to learn to truly let go of "our" children and pray that what we've shown them of God's unfailing love will someday take root.

This book, the first of a series of three, was a way of saying "what if" with some of the stories we've been a witness to in both our and other foster parents' homes. I've portrayed some "good" homes and, in Simon's case, one that wasn't quite as good as the norm. Most of the people we have met, however, are strong, faithful stewards of what God has blessed them with. This book is for them.

Carolyne Aarsen

PS. I love to hear from my readers! Drop me a line at caarsen@xplornet.com

A MOTHER AT HEART

I have swept away your offenses like a cloud, your sins like the morning mist. Return to Me, for I have redeemed you.
—*Isaiah* 44:22

This book is for my in-laws, the Aarsen family, and the practical love they share with the many people who have passed through their homes.

Chapter One

Miriam yanked open the hood of her small, black sports car, glared down at the smoking engine, then sneezed as the harsh smell of leaking radiator fluid assaulted her nostrils.

She pushed back her short hair and dragged her hand down the back of her head, rolling her neck to ease the kink in it. She was tired, cranky and worn-out. For the past few days she'd been putting in twelve hours behind the wheel to get here. It was just her ill luck to break down only three miles from her destination.

With a sigh, she looked around. All she saw were rolling hills, and copses of poplar and spruce trees broken by fields ready for spring planting. Fields she had ridden past for most of her life on her way to school. Fields where she had ridden her horse before spring planting and after combining.

The county of Waylen. Her old home.

She hadn't been back since that horrible day, ten years ago, when she had walked down these very roads, tears blurring her eyes as she headed toward the highway, her possessions thrown together in a knapsack slung over her shoulder. She had never known why leaving abruptly was called "running away." She had walked every dreary and heartsick step on that early-summer morning, her boyfriend's words ringing in her ears. Jake didn't love her anymore.

Halfway to town her mother had caught up with her, and high drama was replaced by her mother's usual carping and nagging.

Miriam sneezed once more, yanked back to the present by the stark reality that there was still no vehicle in sight. She had no option but to start walking down a gravel road in sandals far more suited to paved city sidewalks.

She pulled out the keys to the car and threw her cell phone in her large handbag along with a bottle of water she always had on hand. She was thankful that her cotton pants were thin. If she got too warm, she could put the cardigan she wore into the bag and risk sunburning her shoulders. She just wished she had a hat.

Shouldering her bag, she took a deep breath and started walking down the road. She pushed aside her irritation, reminding herself that she was on country time now. What would be would be, and fussing wouldn't change anything.

Besides, this was supposed to be a vacation. A time to catch her breath before she went back to try to save her business the only way she knew how.

Miriam pulled a face as she skirted a small puddle in the middle of the road. The idea of going back to the hurrying and waiting that characterized most of her modeling career held little appeal.

The sun shone down on her unprotected head, and not for the first time since she'd pointed her little car west did Miriam wonder why she hadn't sold her father's farm in western Alberta from the safety of New York.

As long as her mother had been alive the farm had remained unsold. It was where Edna had been born. Even after Edna had her stroke she made it quite clear the farm was not to be sold.

Now her mother was dead. Miriam needed the money to cover part of the debt she had amassed when a creditor defaulted on a large shipment. Her fledgling clothing company had been unable to absorb the huge loss.

Miriam had also fallen back on the one thing she knew. Modeling. She found a new agent. A good man and sincere Christian. Carl Hanson. It was Carl who had suggested this break. "Drive back to your farm," he said. "Don't sell it from here. Go back to your past. Catch your breath. Take a break from your trouble."

"If Carl could only see me now," she muttered, adjusting her bag on her shoulder.

She had gone only a quarter of a mile and her feet were already sore, when a sound behind her made her turn. But she saw nothing. Heat shimmered up from the gravel road, and below her the land flowed away. Her eyes followed the brown hills, broken by groupings of poplar and spruce. The bare, lacy branches of the aspen trees held a hint of soft green that would be full when it was time for her to leave again.

Miriam eased out her breath, looked around. These rolling hills had occupied her mind many times, even in the most exotic of locales.

A yearning caught her unaware, reminding her of past events, still unresolved. Events that Carl knew occupied her mind. Events he had hinted that she should try to settle before she came back to a busy and time-consuming schedule.

Miriam stopped, her heart lifting at the sound of a vehicle coming.

She could hear it slow down by her car, then speed up again. A cloud of dust roiled behind it as it topped the rise.

The sun reflected off the glass of the cab so she couldn't see the driver. The truck skidded to a halt on the loose gravel, and the driver opened his door and got out.

She put on her most polite "I'm sorry to bother you" smile, as the man came closer and stopped in front of her, wiping his hands on his blue jeans, his white T-shirt already stained with grease and dirt.

Dark brown hair in need of a cut fell across his forehead. Heavily lashed brown eyes stared at her from beneath level brows. His full mouth was parted in a half smile. His strong jaw was dark with stubble.

Miriam acknowledged his good looks almost analytically. Her job as a model put her in the company of many good-looking men, but this man had an earthy appeal that spoke more strongly to her than did the clean, stylized looks she was used to. She was about to raise her hand to shake his when recognition dawned, and her stomach plunged.

Of all the people she would have to meet under these circumstances! Jake Steele. Next-door neighbor, one-time boyfriend and the man over whom she had shed a thousand tears.

She swallowed, her mouth suddenly dry, as she realized he didn't recognize her.

"I'm guessing that was your car parked back there. Do you need some help?" Jake said, his deep voice quiet. He looked down at her, his weight resting on one leg, his one thumb hooked on the belt loop of his jeans. The dusty white T-shirt and the faded jeans enhanced his masculine appeal. It wasn't lost on Miriam.

A girl can still lose herself in his eyes, she thought, remembering another time on this same road when she had done just that. When she and Jake had sat on the tailgate of his pickup, arms around each other, ignoring the moonlit landscape below them, lost in each other and the wonder of their love. A love Miriam had promised Jake would be his forever. A love he had quickly replaced—with her best friend.

What a fool she had been! Then came the anger. Again. She was surprised at its intensity, at the fact that after ten years she had any emotions to spare for this man. Taking a breath, she controlled herself. She hadn't come here to get even, just to find closure.

"My car broke down. I'm pretty sure it's the radiator. I was wondering if you could help me out."

Jake scratched his head, frowning, as if trying to place her. "Were you headed to my folks' place? There's no other place down this road."

Miriam swallowed down the unexpected hurt, readjusting her purse on her shoulder. "You don't know who I am, do you?"

Jake shrugged, the casual movement giving her a fresh pain. Once upon a time, years ago, she could have come up with some smart comment that would have made him smile, that would have eased away her own awkwardness. But life had been difficult the past few years, and laughter and joking didn't come as readily. Instead, she looked directly at him and simply said, "I'm Miriam."

She could tell from his expression the moment he

finally recognized her. "Miriam Spencer?" he asked, his eyes narrowing.

Miriam made herself hold his gaze without blinking. "Not too many other Miriams around," she said, forcing herself to match his own even tone.

He nodded, his hands hanging loosely at his sides as he continued to look at her.

A soft spring breeze swirled around them, and the sharp trill of a red-tailed hawk shivered down. Anticipation hovered around them.

How many times had she relived this reunion in her mind? How many times had she imagined herself coming back, full of self-confidence, preferably on the arm of an equally self-confident and attractive man? Miriam Spencer returning to the place of her humiliation.

"We've been hearing a lot about you," he finally said, his voice cool.

Miriam felt herself stiffen in reaction to his sudden reserve. She could see the condemnation in his eyes, feel the censure. She wondered which of the many false stories written about her in the tabloids he actually believed.

"I'm sure you have." She tilted her head, lifted her chin and held his gaze. "But you should know you can't believe everything you read." She turned to go, but Jake caught her by the arm, turning her back.

"I'm sorry," he said automatically, but she could see his apology lacked conviction. He was merely being polite. The way he always was. "Do you need a lift to your place?"

"That's okay. I don't want to put you out." Miriam shifted her bag, wishing she could just leave, but Jake still had his hand on her arm. Try as she might, she couldn't ignore the strength and warmth of it through her shirt. "And you can let go of my arm," she said, looking down pointedly.

Jake dropped his hand as if her arm were on fire. "Sorry," he muttered. Then he looked at her. "Look, it's a long walk back." He glanced down at the thin sandals on her feet, her loose-fitting linen pants that were already stained with dust from the road. "My truck is no limo, but it will get you to your place quicker than walking."

Miriam wished she could say no. She didn't want his help. But a three-mile walk, on the sandals he had looked at so disdainfully, wasn't appealing. Accepting his offer was the mature thing to do. And that was part of the reason for this trip, wasn't it? To show herself that she had gotten past this part of her life?

So she nodded. "Thanks for the offer," she said, and she walked around to the passenger side of the truck.

He followed, saying nothing, and just as she was about to open the door, he reached past and did it for her.

Miriam glanced at him and nodded her thanks, then climbed up into the truck and settled on the seat.

Jake climbed in without saying a word, put the truck into gear, and they were off. A song blared from the radio, but Jake reached over and switched it off. Miriam wished he hadn't. The muted roar of the truck, the faint whiff of diesel mixed with dust that permeated the cab—both combined to bring back surprisingly sharp memories.

Memories of being scrunched awkwardly into a narrow tractor cab, riding along with Jake while he plowed, cultivated, seeded, sprayed, swathed or combined, singing along with songs on the radio, as they looked into each other's eyes. It didn't matter what job he had to do on his foster father's farm, she usually managed to finagle a ride with him.

Now, Miriam couldn't help but glance over at Jake. His dark hair still curled over the back of his collar, still invited a girl to run her hands through it.

Give your head a shake, Miriam chided herself, sighing lightly. He's married, and even if he wasn't, you're not looking, remember?

She blamed her lapse on the surroundings. It was as if driving down these roads, seeing an endless sky, had immediately erased the past ten years in one quick swipe. It was as if being back here turned her from a woman, determined to keep her heart to herself, back into that young girl who gave it to the first boy she had been attracted to. Jake Steele.

Stick to the plan, she reminded herself. You're here to sell the farm, to put the past to rest. Then you go back East and keep struggling.

Miriam pushed the depressing thoughts aside and forced herself to ignore Jake, to look around. The road followed a ridge that cut alongside a hill rising above them on one side and flowing away from them on the other. Rock Lake was at the bottom of the hill, hidden by a large stand of spruce and aspen tinged with the pale green of new growth.

Ahead of them lay more fields, more bush, alternating shade and warmth as they drove along. Not much had changed since she left, she realized. The trees looked the same, the fields were the same.

It was like stepping back, and she shivered in reaction.

"Too cold?" Jake asked, finally speaking. He didn't

wait for her answer but reached over to adjust the air-conditioning.

"Thanks." She fidgeted on the seat, the silence in the cab pressing down on her. "How's the weather been?" she blurted out, and then forced herself not to groan. What a cliché question. He would think she was a total airhead.

"Good."

"Seeding done?"

"Pretty much."

"How much land do you farm now?"

Jake shrugged. "About five quarters."

"Do you still have the cows?"

"Yup."

"How many?"

"One-hundred head. Just commercial."

"Wow. You and Fred have expanded."

Jake only nodded, and Miriam turned away in exasperation. He wasn't going to make this one bit easy for her. As if he had the right to be so taciturn.

Miriam wished she had never accepted his offer of a ride. Wished she had just started walking. Sore feet and overheating would have been preferable to this heavy atmosphere.

But she was a big girl now and determined to see this through. After all, he and Paula lived half a mile from her farm; she would be seeing them over the course of her stay. Better to try to get some of that first-time awkwardness out of the way before she met Paula, her old girlfriend—Jake's wife.

"So how is Paula?" she asked, pleased at the even tone in her voice. A tone that didn't betray the hurt that gripped her even now.

Jake's hands tightened on the steering wheel, and he

threw her a quick glance, then looked away. "You've really been out of touch, haven't you?" he asked, his voice dangerously quiet.

Miriam almost pressed herself back against the seat at the anger in his voice. "I don't understand what you're talking about," she said sharply. What right did he have to use that tone with her? He was the one who had gotten married barely four months after she left. She knew she had been out of touch, but what did she have to say to either him or her old girlfriend?

Jake stared straight ahead, his expression grim. "Paula died three years ago." His words were clipped, his voice devoid of emotion.

Miriam stared at him, her hands numb, an icy cold gripping her temples as she tried to make sense of what he had said.

"What—Paula...dead?" She struggled to find the right words, to find some meaning in his words. Why didn't she know this? How come no one had told her?

The questions dropped heavily, one after the other, piling up in her mind as she tried to get her thoughts around this horrible information.

"She rolled her car on a gravel road and wasn't wearing her seat belt. The doctor told us she died right away." Jake looked up again, his lips thin. "I'm guessing this is a shock for you?"

Miriam shook her head, still struggling over what to ask, what to say, looking at him as if to find answers to the questions. "I didn't know," she said weakly. She pulled her hand over her face and then bit her lip, as disbelief fled and sadness welled up. After all, Paula had been her friend, even though Miriam had not contacted her once she found out about Paula and Jake's marriage.

Miriam swallowed the sorrow, a belated sense of guilt washing over her. "I'm so sorry, Jake. This must be so hard for you." The words were inadequate, but protocol deemed they be spoken. "I'm sure it's been hard for Fred and Tilly, as well," Miriam continued quietly.

"Mom and Dad had a really hard time with it." His words were quietly spoken, and the silence of before settled once again between them.

"And how are Fred and Tilly?"

"Okay." Jake hesitated, as if to show her she didn't deserve to hear anything about his foster parents, the same people that had been second parents to Miriam, as well. "Dad had a heart attack a month ago. The doctor said he sustained a lot of damage so he's still pretty weak."

Miriam wanted to say that she was sorry. Again. How much apologizing was she going to be doing on this trip? she wondered. "Well, I hope he gets better."

"So do I," Jake said heavily.

In those three words Miriam could hear the love that she knew Jake held for his foster parents. Though he had moved to Fred and Tilly's place as a teenager, she knew that he had become like their own son.

Miriam swallowed again, staring straight ahead, battling the envy she felt. Jake, who once had nothing, now had everything—a family of his own, parents who loved him, a direction to his life.

Whereas she, who had once had it all…

The rest of the drive continued in silence, but now other emotions had been added to the mix, creating a tension in Miriam that built with each roll of the truck's wheels.

She was thankful when she saw Fred and Tilly's

driveway, the same brightly painted horse-drawn plow at the end of it. Jake turned in.

"I'll just let Tilly and Fred know what's going on, and then I can bring you to your place," he said, his words breaking the long silence. "You may as well come in and say hello."

Miriam only nodded, clutching her purse as her own heart began to beat more quickly. It was a combination of nerves and fear and another kind of guilt at the thought of meeting Fred and Tilly again. She had spent many hours sitting at their kitchen table, had followed Fred around while he did his chores.

Miriam's father had died when she was ten and Edna had had to work. Saturdays had found Miriam either helping Tilly in the kitchen, or working alongside Fred—feeding cows, helping with the calves or helping with any of the myriad repairs required on the farm. The Prinses' home became her second home, a haven from Edna's constant criticism and "big plans" for her daughter.

Miriam had had no big plans. All she had ever wanted was to stay in Waylen. When she was fourteen, a social worker had brought Jake to Fred and Tilly's, and her plans changed to include marrying Jake.

When she first saw the dangerously good-looking teenager, she knew in her heart that she loved only him. Her mother, of course, made sure Miriam knew *her* opinion. "A foster child from who knows where." Miriam could still hear her mother. "You stay away from him, Miriam. Boy like him is nothing but trouble," Edna had said, contempt ringing in her voice.

Miriam had laughed at the notion. A girl who had

been teased most of her school years for being skinny could hardly net the attention of someone like Jake.

But to her amazement, she had. Even Paula—beautiful, blond and curvaceous Paula—could hardly believe that Jake would prefer Miriam to her.

But he had. At least at first, Miriam reminded herself.

Miriam closed her eyes at a sudden surge of pain and sorrow. Paula, her onetime friend. Dead. She could hardly bear thinking about it.

Jake parked the truck and, without giving Miriam a second glance, got out. Miriam swallowed, rubbing her damp hands over her pants. What would she say to Fred, to Tilly? she thought, hesitating. Too much time had elapsed, and she had done nothing to bridge that gap.

Well, she was here now. She had to start this homecoming sooner or later. She slung her bag over her shoulder and climbed out of the truck.

"Thanks for the ride, and the help," she said to Jake, lifting her head to look confidently up at him.

"You're welcome."

He stood back, allowing her to go first. The yard was still muddy and wet in places, and Miriam had to pick her way across. Jake stayed beside her, probably to make sure she didn't fall, she thought wryly.

They had just made it to the cement sidewalk by the house when the door burst open.

"Daddy, Daddy, you're home." A little girl, her braids flying out behind her, came running up to Jake and launched herself at him. Miriam felt a lump in her throat.

A little girl. Jake had a little girl.

Jake caught the girl, swung her around. For the first

time since Miriam had seen him, she noticed a heartfelt and sincere smile on his face.

"Hey, Pipper," he said, hugging his daughter tightly.
He straightened, holding the little girl on one arm. Her
arms were wrapped around his neck, and as they turned
to Miriam, she felt a harsh clutch of jealousy. She could
see Jake in the deep brown of the little girl's eyes, Jake
in the thick waves of her hair—but Paula in the coy
smile.

"Hi," the girl said. "My name is Taryn. What's yours?"

"This is Miriam," Jake interjected, settling Taryn on
his arm. "Her car broke down on the road, and I gave
her a ride here."

Taryn nodded, staring at Miriam as if studying her.
"Has she been here before?"

"No, Pipper, she hasn't." Jake turned to Miriam.
"Why don't you come in a minute? I'm sure Mom and
Dad would like to see you."

Miriam nodded, feeling very much the outsider.
Taryn continued to stare at her, and Miriam couldn't
keep her eyes off Jake's daughter.

She looked so much like her father, it made her heart
hurt.

Miriam followed Jake up the walk, suddenly hesitant
at the thought of meeting Tilly and Fred again. Guilt
and shame vied with one another as her steps followed
the old familiar pathway. She had skipped up this walk
as a young girl, she had run up it as a teenager. She had
always come here with a happy heart, the feeling that
someone who cared for her lived here. This had been
a home.

Jake pushed the screen door open and set Taryn

down on the floor. "Take your socks off, missy," he said. "They're all dirty."

Taryn dropped down, and, lifting her foot, yanked off the once-white sock. "I was waiting for you," she said, grinning up at him. "You didn't have supper."

Miriam dropped her bag on the chair that had always been there, without even realizing what she was doing. She had to catch herself before she kicked off her sandals and ran past Jake up the steps to sit at the kitchen table. This porch was so familiar.

But the presence of a much older Jake and his daughter showed her all too clearly how much had changed.

Taryn got up, still looking at Miriam with a puzzled expression. "Did you know my mommy?" she asked.

Jake turned to his daughter, his surprise evident. "What did you say?" he asked her.

Taryn turned to him, still frowning. "I saw her picture in my mommy's book."

"What book?"

"The one with that Miriam lady's pictures in it."

"Is that you, Jake?" Tilly called from the kitchen, interrupting the moment. She came to the door, wiping her hands on a towel, smiling at her son. "How was your day, dear?"

Miriam felt her throat tighten at the sight of Tilly. The woman's face held a few more lines; her short, straight hair was now completely gray. But she wore the same glasses she had worn ten years ago, and the soft blue eyes were the same, the smile still welcoming.

"Good," Jake said succinctly. "I brought someone back." He stepped aside, gesturing toward Miriam.

Tilly lifted her hand up to readjust her glasses, and she squinted at Miriam, who tried not to fidget. "My goodness," Tilly said as she recognized who it was, her lined face breaking out into a large smile, her arms opening. "Miriam? Little Miriam Spencer?"

Tilly walked past Jake straight to Miriam, and enfolded her in a warm embrace. Miriam inhaled the familiar scent of Tilly's perfume, pressed her cheek against the well-known softness of Tilly's cheek. She swallowed a knot of sadness mixed with nostalgia. She had missed this, she thought, this enveloping affection that welcomed you back, that showed you were missed.

She hadn't felt a mother's arms around her since she had left this place, her home.

Miriam squeezed her eyes against the sudden pain as more memories returned, and hugged Tilly as tightly as she dared.

"Oh, little girl, we sure missed you. We did." Tilly rocked her lightly, then pulled away, unabashedly wiping her eyes. "Look at you now. What a beautiful girl you've turned out to be." Tilly shook her head and reached up to wipe tears from her eyes. "You're so tall. So old."

Miriam blinked her own tears away, far too conscious of Jake watching them. It shouldn't have mattered, but she felt his disapproval as strongly as she felt Tilly's love.

She knew she had been in the wrong, keeping herself from this dear person. This dear second mother who had dried her tears and hugged her even more than her own mother had.

Miriam felt ashamed. She had known this was going to be a difficult trip. She just hadn't counted on the guilt that would come with it.

Chapter Two

❧

"You smell like dirt, Daddy."

Jake smiled down at his daughter as he washed his hands, then bent over at the waist to wash his face and neck. "I was working in lots of dirt, sweetheart," he said, drying off. "I was working on the tractor."

"Your hair is dirty, too."

Jake glanced at his reflection in the mirror, shoving his hands through his thick wavy hair. It needed to be cut. He paused, looking at himself critically, trying to see himself through Miriam's eyes. Then he wondered why he should care.

Miriam Spencer. He drew a deep, tired breath, wishing away the jolt he had felt when he had first realized the identity of the very elegant woman standing on the side of the road. Now she sat in his kitchen, chatting to Tilly and Fred, who, even though she hadn't even bothered sending them so much as a postcard, were delighted to see her.

He felt like the prodigal son in the parable. He should be glad she was back, but he just wished he knew why she had come. He doubted it was to settle on the farm to raise wheat and barley. Miriam wasn't a country girl any longer. And it wasn't hard to see. Though her clothes were casual, they had an elegance that quietly stated their cost.

High.

He remembered the first time he had seen the new Miriam. Paula had shown him a fashion magazine, and Miriam was on the front—her tip-tilted eyes gleaming with gold eye shadow, her full mouth glistening with coral lipstick. Her once unruly hair cropped and artfully tousled. Neither that person, nor the casually elegant girl now sitting in his kitchen were the Miriam he knew.

They weren't the Miriam who would sometimes wear a T-shirt backward, who wouldn't care if her jeans were ripped or patched.

The Miriam he had once loved.

"What's the matter, Daddy? You look sad."

Jake pulled himself back to the present, and, squatting down, put himself level with his daughter. "I'm just tired, Pip. And hungry for some of Grandma's supper."

"That sure is a pretty lady that is here," she said solemnly, her hands on her father's shoulders.

Jake remembered a comment Taryn had made while they were standing on the porch. "What did you mean when you said you saw that lady's picture in Mommy's book? What book?"

"Mommy's book. You know." Taryn shook her head at her father's obtuseness. "Me and Grandma found it in the attic."

"Well, you'll have to show me the book when I tuck you in." He was curious, but knew it would have to wait.

Jake gave her a quick hug, and, holding her tiny hand, walked back down the hallway.

"Your supper is on the table, son." Tilly smiled at Jake as he sat. "Taryn, you should run and get your pajamas on. It's getting late."

Taryn dropped her head, her fingers fiddling restlessly with each other, her lip beginning to curl in a classic pout. "But I wanna talk to the lady," she mumbled, lifting her eyes briefly to her father.

Jake frowned at his daughter. She got the unspoken command, and, sighing, turned and left.

Miriam was already ensconced on the bench against the wall, a cup of tea in front of her. Fred sat beside her, bringing Miriam up-to-date on what had happened in Waylen while she'd been gone.

"Here you go, son." Tilly set a plate of warmed-up food in front of him—fried chicken, creamed peas, mashed potatoes, and applesauce on the side. His mouth watered at the sight. "And here are your messages." Tilly set an assortment of papers in front of him with scribbled names and numbers. "I should charge you secretarial fees," Tilly joked. "Melissa Toews phoned three times. Said it was important."

Jake stifled a groan. Melissa could never be accused of being coy, he thought, flipping through the messages.

"Do you want the cordless phone?" Fred asked, reaching behind him to take the phone off the cradle.

"I don't feel like phoning anyone tonight." Jake set the papers aside. He often took care of his business during supper, but tonight he didn't feel like it. All of them could wait. Especially Melissa.

"Are you sure you don't want any supper, Miriam?" Tilly asked her, setting a cup of coffee in front of Jake.

"I'm fine, thanks." Miriam smiled gently at Tilly

and rested her elbows on the table, avoiding Jake's look. "This kitchen looks the same as I remember it."

He wondered why she had come. Then, pushing aside his own thoughts, he bowed his head in prayer. He pulled in a slow breath, willing the negative thoughts away. He slowly let himself be open to God, thanking him for the food, for the day. He paused a moment, his thoughts turning to the girl sitting at the same table, and he sent up a prayer for Miriam, as well.

Praying for her put everything into perspective. Praying for her changed her from an old girlfriend whom he had often thought about to just a person from his past. And as he prayed for her, he felt peace.

He opened his eyes and unconsciously sought her out. She was watching him, her soft brown eyes full of a sorrow he hadn't seen there before. But with a blink of her long eyelashes, it was gone.

"And how is your mother?" Tilly asked, leaning forward. "We haven't heard from her, either, since both of you left."

Jake stopped chewing, his own curiosity piqued by Tilly's straightforward, but softly spoken question.

Miriam looked down, running her finger along the handle of the earthenware mug in front of her. "She died six months ago in Toronto. She'd had a stroke and was just getting worse. I think death was a relief for her." Jake felt sudden empathy. He had never cared for Miriam's mother, but he knew that Miriam had loved her. He wanted to catch Miriam's gaze, to tell her he understood, but after his barely restrained hostility toward her in his truck, he felt he had no right.

"Oh, dear." Tilly reached across the table and caught Miriam's hand in her own. "I'm sorry to hear that. We never heard a thing…" Tilly let the sentence trail off. She paused, then asked, "How are you doing with it?"

Miriam reached up and carefully wiped her eyes. "It's still hard, but I think she was glad to go."

Jake heard the hint of sorrow in her voice and wondered who had comforted her when it happened. Was there someone important to her who had been with her? She was only twenty-seven years old. Old enough to be independent, yet quite young to be without either parent.

"So now you're here for a visit?"

Miriam nodded again. "I'm only here for a while, but it's nice to be back."

"And now your car is broken down." Tilly shook her head, clucking sympathetically. "Well, don't you worry. Fred and Jake will make sure it gets fixed."

"What are you going to do about Miriam's car?" Fred asked, looking up from his paper.

"It's okay where it is right now," Jake said, pushing his potatoes around on his plate. "Tomorrow we can tow it into town and bring it to Denny's Auto Parts. All it needs is a new radiator, I'm assuming."

"It was leaking already in Winnipeg," Miriam said quietly. "I think all they did was put some stop-leak stuff in it."

"Do you want me to take care of it, Jake?" Fred offered.

Jake shook his head. "You're finally out of bed. I don't think you should overdo it."

"But you'll fall behind in the field work," Fred said. "You won't have time to run around."

"Look, I can call a tow truck," Miriam interrupted. "I don't want to put anyone out."

"It's not a problem," Jake said, trying to sound nonchalant. Actually it *was* a problem. He was nicely on top of the field work, and taking Miriam's car to the garage would use up a good half day. He didn't really have the time, but knew it would look churlish not to help. People called a tow truck in the city, not in the country.

He just prayed that everything would work out.

Miriam tried once more to protest, but Fred insisted that it would be no problem.

"Do you want any dessert?" Tilly asked, when Jake was done.

"No thanks, Mom. I'm full." He smiled up at her. "It was delicious, though."

Tilly stroked his hair the way she always did, and for a moment Jake was conscious of Miriam's deep brown eyes watching them. He felt a little foolish. Not too many twenty-seven-year-old men had mothers who still stroked their hair. But he had never protested, not even as a young man.

Whenever his brother, Simon, would come for a visit from the stricter home he'd been placed in, Tilly naturally treated him exactly like Jake. Like they were both Fred and Tilly's own sons. Neither he nor Simon had received much of a mother's love growing up. Their natural mother had given them up when he was five and Simon four after their biological father had died. They never did find out where she was, although Simon was now actively looking. Simon had been looking most of his life. He had run away from his last foster home at sixteen and wanted Jake to come. But Jake knew he was in a good place with Fred and Tilly and refused to go. Simon said that Jake would never hear from him again.

And Jake hadn't. Until five months ago when Jake

got a phone call from a nurse named Caitlin Severn who had Simon as a patient.

Jake had overcome his own wounded pride at Simon's silence and traveled to Vancouver to see him. Now Simon was happily married. But he still wanted to find their mother.

Jake wasn't as interested. Each time he saw Taryn, he wondered anew how his mother could give up her own children and not even leave them with a name to track down. It was as if she wanted them swept out of her life.

"Hi, Daddy. Here I am." Taryn stood in front of him, her face shiny from washing, her hair still damp. She twirled around in her new, frilly nightgown, the ruffle on the bottom dragging on the floor.

"You look beautiful," Jake said, pulling her on his lap, tucking her under his chin.

"Not as beautiful as her—" Taryn pointed to Miriam with a giggle. Jake couldn't help but look at Miriam, who was now gazing wistfully at Taryn. He didn't acknowledge Taryn's comment—at least not out loud. And as he watched the play of emotions on Miriam's face, he wondered if she had any regrets. If the fame and fortune she had acquired satisfied her.

He turned back to his daughter, his heart full of gratitude, thankful that in spite of how things had turned out, he had this precious child.

"So, Pip, it's bedtime," he said quietly. "Kiss Grandpa and Grandma good-night, and I'll tuck you in."

"Okay," she said, lifting her shoulders in an exaggerated sigh. She slipped off his lap and walked around the table to kiss Tilly and then Fred.

For a moment Jake was afraid she was going to give

Miriam a kiss, but shyness won out. Instead, Taryn just waggled her fingers at Miriam.

"Good night, Taryn. Sweet dreams," Miriam said softly, waving back.

"Okay," Taryn said with a smile. Then she turned and flounced off through the hallways, toward the stairs, Jake right behind.

When Paula and Jake had first married, they had lived in a mobile home on the property. However, after Paula had died, Jake had brought Taryn here so often that she'd ended up getting her own room. Eventually Jake had started eating supper here, and soon the mobile home had been sold.

Now they all lived here in a house that was getting too big for Tilly to clean. But she refused to move to a smaller house in town, and Jake had to admit that it worked better for him, as well.

At the bottom of the stairs, Taryn stopped, holding up her arms for the first step in their bedtime routine.

He loved this house, he mused as he walked slowly up the broad stairs holding his little girl. As a foster child, he'd been blessed to end up here, and he knew it.

Though his mother had given Simon and Jake up, he was always thankful that they had been adopted by a single man, Tom Steele. He had given them a safe and secure home for seven years. His death had been a severe blow, and Jake knew that the loss of Tom tended to make him overprotective of Fred. He didn't want to lose another father.

"Stop, Daddy. I want to see the pictures."

Jake smiled and did as his daughter commanded. The Prinses had a veritable gallery on the wall, and Taryn always had to stop. Jake didn't mind. He was so thankful for the legacy his daughter received through Fred and Tilly that it was doubly important to him that she knew where she came from. His vague memories of his mother didn't include a father, let alone grandparents. At times he still resented that, but realized that in Tom Steele, and later in Fred and Tilly, God had made up the lack.

"There's my mommy." Taryn leaned forward, pointing out their wedding picture. Taryn always lingered the longest here, even though she barely remembered Paula. Taryn had been only two when Paula died, and unaware of the circumstances surrounding her mother's death. Paula had been an inattentive mother at best, and hadn't spent a lot of time at home. Jake often regretted his marriage, but he had never, ever regretted Taryn.

"And this is Uncle Simon and Auntie Caitlin—" Taryn pointed with a pudgy finger to a smiling couple, their arms around each other. The picture had been taken outside against a backdrop of trees. The filtered sun highlighted their features and only seemed to enhance the love that radiated from them.

"When I get bigger—" Taryn stopped as her mouth stretched open in a big yawn "—I want to be a nurse, just like Auntie Caitlin, and help her in her hospital in Na… Nomimo," she continued, snuggling into her father's neck.

"Nanaimo," Jake corrected, giving his daughter a tight hug. "That's a good thing to be, sweetie. But if you don't get your sleep, you won't grow, and then you can't be a nurse." He jogged up the stairs to miss the rest of the pictures, aware of his daughter's penchant for dawdling. And tonight he didn't feel like indulging her. Much as he disliked to acknowledge it, he wanted to be downstairs with Miriam.

A night-light shed a soft glow over Taryn's room. Jake lay Taryn down on her bed, careful not to disturb the row of stuffed animals that sat along the side, next to the wall. He tucked her in and sat beside her, his arms on either side of her shoulders.

Taryn smiled up at her father, and a wave of pure, sweet love washed over Jake. He bent over and gave her another quick kiss. "Time for your prayers."

"We have to pray for Grandpa, don't we?" Taryn said, her brown eyes shining up at him in the muted light.

"Yes, we want him to stay healthy, don't we?"

"Should we pray for Miriam?"

Jake felt his heart skip at her name. He took a quick breath, frowning down at his daughter. "What did you say?"

"I *asked*," Taryn began, putting emphasis on the last word as if to show Jake that he was being particularly obtuse, "if I should pray for Miriam."

"You barely know her. Which reminds me, what about this book you were talking about?"

Taryn sat up like a shot and, shifting around, pulled a worn scrapbook from under her pillow. She handed it to him.

"It has pictures of you in it." Taryn smiled, eager for the reprieve from sleep. "And pictures of my Mommy and pictures of the pretty lady. Miriam. I'll show you." Taryn reached for the book, and, reluctantly, Jake gave it back. He didn't like the idea of Taryn living in the past, creating fantasies about Paula. But he also knew that it wasn't fair to take what little she had away.

Taryn flipped quickly through the pages of pictures from high school—a few of them of Jake—then she stopped and tilted the book in his direction. Jake felt his heart stop as he looked directly at a picture of Miriam.

In the picture she wore a mauve silk dress held up with narrow, jeweled straps. Diamonds sparkled at her neck, her ears, her fingers, all discreetly proclaiming money. Her mouth was quirked in what he knew was her cynical smile, her head tilted back as if she were laughing at some private joke. Her dark hair framed her face, short tendrils accenting her high cheekbones, the exotic tilt of her eyes. A slickly dressed man wearing a tuxedo stood beside her, his arm resting in a proprietary manner on her shoulder.

"Why did Mommy have pictures of Miriam in her book?"

Jake blinked, pulling himself back to the present. "She used to be your mommy's best friend," Jake murmured, turning the page to find yet another color picture of Miriam. It was a makeup advertisement. Miriam's face took up the whole page, her head angled slightly downward, her eyes glancing up, her shining mouth holding the hint of a smile. Jake swallowed as he stared at the picture. It was Miriam, and yet not. How many times had he seen that look on her face—across a classroom, in the hallways of school; whenever she would tease him, flirt with him?

"I want to show Miriam the pictures, okay?" Taryn gathered up the book and made to jump out of bed, but Jake stopped her.

"No," he said firmly, taking the book away from her and setting it on the bedside table. "I'm sure Miriam has seen these pictures herself. And you need to sleep."

He pulled the blankets up around her and tucked her in. She said her prayers, and Jake said them with her.

Each evening he thanked God for the precious gift entrusted to him. And as he did most evenings, he promised he would do everything he could to make sure she would have a home as secure and loving as the one he had received through Fred and Tilly.

"...and be with Miriam, my mommy's friend." Jake felt a start at the sound of Taryn speaking Miriam's name, but he said nothing, not wanting to draw any more attention to Miriam.

He waited until she was done, then bent over and kissed her gently. He paused at the door to look once more, closed it behind him and went downstairs to face Miriam.

He heard them laughing, and stopped just behind the door, listening, remembering other times.

Like the first time he had seen Miriam.

He had been sitting on Fred and Tilly's picnic table, staring out at the view below—a young boy of fourteen, a foster child being brought to his third foster home in as many years and recently separated from his brother Simon. The social worker had been inside the house, talking to Fred and Tilly. He hadn't wanted to hear what she had to say.

So he had stayed outside, appreciating the flow of the land that stretched out below him, yet wondering how he was going to survive in a house with only two old people for company.

Then a skinny girl had ridden up on her horse and jumped off. She'd tied it to a post by the back gate and boldly walked up to him, retying the shoelace that held her ponytail in place. She'd asked who he was and what he was doing sitting at Uncle Fred and Aunt Tilly's picnic table.

When he ignored her, she just shrugged and waltzed on into the house, like she lived there. She came out a few minutes later and sat beside him on the table. She said nothing, this time. Just sat there.

Together they watched the sun going down, felt the soft chill that accompanied the fall evenings drifting onto the yard.

The social worker came out later, accompanied by Fred and Tilly. She stopped in her tracks when she saw Miriam, and spun around, asking Fred and Tilly who she was.

"Just the neighbor girl," they said. "She comes over a lot."

The social worker nodded and then stopped by Jake. Laying her hand on his shoulder, she bent down to his height—an older woman talking to an angry, young man. "This is a good place, Jake. Don't wreck things for yourself."

Jake had ignored her, staring past her at the setting sun. Social workers were always full of advice and, as far as he was concerned, misconceptions. The fact that he had been in so many homes had more to do with Simon's constant running away than with his behavior. But he didn't want to get into that. It hurt to think of Simon. It was the first time they had been separated. So he only nodded and said nothing, wondering where his brother had ended up and when he would see him again. He knew it was a waste of time to ask the social worker. She would give him some vague answer about waiting to see if they settled in. Then she left.

Fred and Tilly went back to the house.

To his surprise and dismay, Miriam stayed beside him. He had wanted to be alone, but she wouldn't leave. After a while, though, it didn't matter as much. She had been pretty quiet.

Tilly brought them a glass of orange juice and then walked back into the house.

Miriam turned to him and started talking. He had known her silence was too good to be true. She asked questions, the basic ones—What's your name? How old are you? Where did you live before?

His replies were terse. He had answered enough questions before this placement to add twenty more pages to his already thick file. Everyone knew everything about him, so the trick was to hold back as much as he could for as long as he could.

Miriam chatted about the school, the town, Tilly and Fred. She said nothing about her own mother. In fact, at first he thought she didn't even have a mother.

Miriam came to Fred and Tilly's often. She sought him out at school, introduced him to her many friends. They spent a lot of time together. She had an easy way with people, a self-deprecating wit and a love of life that he found compelling and infectious.

He ended up falling desperately in love with her. And she with him.

Miriam had filled the empty spaces that life had carved out of him. Her unconditional love had shown him that there were things worth making sacrifices for. For the first time in years he had opened himself up to another person, had made himself vulnerable. He had trusted her.

She talked easily about her faith, and shared that with

Jake. They spent hours just talking, being together, sharing dreams and plans. Jake often felt unworthy of her.

Miriam often spoke of her mother and how important it was that they keep their relationship a secret. And they did. Jake knew what he was: a foster child with an uncertain future.

But they had plans. When they turned eighteen, they would be adults, independent. They would declare their love to the world, and then leave Waylen.

The longer Jake stayed at Fred and Tilly's, however, the less he wanted to do that. While Miriam showed him that pure love can exist between two people, Fred and Tilly showed him the love of parents. They gave him a home. Jake didn't want to leave anymore. He talked of staying in Waylen, of getting a job in town.

Miriam grew frightened. Jake *had* to come with her. She was counting on him to help her get away from her mother.

It hurt to think of what they had once had. To realize that the elegant woman who was chatting in his kitchen was even further removed from him now than she was then. So much had changed in each of their lives.

He stepped into the kitchen. Fred was describing an incident he had had with a bull, many years ago.

"...And Tilly thinks I'm waving to her to come closer, and she comes roaring up with the truck and scares the bull. He takes off past me down the road and with him went all the plans for the day. We finally got him corralled at midnight." Miriam had her hand over her mouth; her eyes sparkled and her shoulders shook in time to her chuckles.

Jake stopped, unable to look away.

This was the Miriam he had fallen in love with. *This*

was the Miriam he had promised he would stay with forever. Not that overly made-up woman with the fake smile whom he had just seen in the photo. Not the defensive woman who had sat with him in the truck all the way here.

Then she glanced sidelong, her hand slowly dropped and her gaze skittered away.

He felt as if he had broken the moment.

"Taryn safely in bed?" Tilly asked, smiling up at him.

Jake nodded and sat at the table, suddenly feeling like the odd man out. He tried not to look at the clock, but couldn't help it.

Miriam caught him looking; she carefully put her spoon back in her coffee cup and folded the napkin Tilly had given her. Preparations for leaving.

"What's the rush, girl?" Fred asked, as Miriam eased herself from behind the table.

"I should go. It's been a long day of driving," she said quietly, picking up her mug. She brought it to the kitchen sink and set it down with a muted *clink*.

"Are we going to see you again?" Tilly asked as she got up herself.

Miriam turned to face Tilly and nodded. "Of course. Once I get my car fixed, that is."

"Oh, nonsense. I can come over." Tilly stopped, glancing at Jake, then back to Miriam. "What about your house? Is there any food there?"

"I bought some groceries, but unfortunately they're still in my car—"

"Don't be silly, girl, I'll give you some," Tilly interjected.

Miriam hesitated, and Jake sensed she was in a dilemma. Either she accepted charity from Tilly, or she put him out by asking him to return to her car.

"Did you have a suitcase?" he asked her, feeling foolish that he had never thought of that when he picked her up.

"It's in my car," she said, lifting her head.

"Well, it's not far down the road. I'll drive you back and you can get your other stuff."

"Thank you," she said with a gracious tilt of her head. She turned back to Tilly. "Thanks for tea." She stopped as if she couldn't say anything more.

Tilly walked over and gave Miriam another hug. "It's such a treat to see you again," she said, pulling back, cupping Miriam's young face with her old, lined hands. "I'm so glad you decided to come back."

Fred, too, walked over and gave her a hug. But Jake could see that even that small movement tired him out.

Miriam had noticed it, too. Her eyes were full of concern. "You make sure you get enough rest," she said to Fred, holding his hand between hers.

"You sound just like Tilly," he said with a shake of his head. "I'll be fine." He reached up and stroked her cheek, much the way Tilly had done to Jake.

In that moment Jake realized that, in spite of a ten-year absence, Miriam shared something special with Fred and Tilly. And for a moment he was envious.

Chapter Three

"So," Jake said vaguely as he spun the steering wheel. "What really brings you back here?"

His truck was halfway down the driveway before he asked the question Miriam knew had been burning inside of him. Miriam waited a beat, as if to establish some sort of conversational control. "I came back to sell my farm."

Jake's head snapped around and he stared at her, then looked quickly away. "This is a surprise."

Miriam didn't doubt it. Fred and Jake had rented it all these years. But all their dealings had been at arm's length through a lawyer Miriam hired to take care of her and her mother's business.

"I don't know if you're interested in buying it. I'm willing to offer you and Fred right of first refusal."

Jake blew out his breath and laughed shortly. "I would be. In a few years. Unfortunately, I can't afford to buy it now. Financially I'm stretched as far as I can go."

Miriam felt a stab of dismay. She had hoped he would buy it, had hoped he could keep farming it, that somehow something that had once belonged to her would now belong to him, creating a vague kind of connection. Though she wasn't sure why. "That's too bad," she said, threading her fingers together in her lap.

"At least we agree on that." His words were clipped, and once again Miriam sensed his anger.

But she was too tired to say anything back.

"What happens once you sell the farm?" Jake continued.

Miriam took a slow breath, willing away her fatigue. She had walked down catwalks in Milan, had modeled famous designers' fashions with aplomb and self-confidence. Surely she could handle a farmer who needed a shave. "I go back East and put Waylen behind me."

Gravel rattled against the undercarriage as they drove down the road, the oppressive silence of two people unwilling to talk to each other filling the cab.

She was thankful that it was a short trip to the car. As Jake pulled up beside it, Miriam got the keys out of her purse. She climbed out of the truck and unlocked the car's trunk.

Jake was beside her, and reached in and wordlessly pulled out her suitcase. Miriam took out a small cosmetics bag and closed the trunk.

"This is it?"

Miriam nodded and walked around the car.

"You travel pretty light."

"I've made enough airline connections with my clothes headed off to Istanbul while I was going to New York. I've learned to take everything I need with me." Miriam juggled the grocery bags in one hand while she locked the door with the other.

"I don't think this car is going anywhere," Jake said suddenly.

Miriam frowned up at him. "What do you mean?"

"This is a dead-end road. You hardly need to lock the car."

Miriam tried not to smile, but couldn't help it. It did look silly to lock up a crippled car on a deserted road. "City habits, I guess," she said, chancing a glance up at him.

Mistake. He was smiling now, his features relaxed. He looked devastating.

She forced herself to look away. "Well, that should do it." Miriam straightened her shoulders and dropped her groceries in the back of Jake's pickup, frustrated at how quickly the old feelings she had had for him returned. It was as if she had never been gone. As if she had never spent time with any man other than this tall farmer of few words.

"You might want to put your suitcase in the front. I hauled feed with this truck the other day."

"A little extra oats and soy never hurt a girl," she said quickly.

Jake dropped the suitcase in the box. When he glanced up at her, he smiled again, and Miriam's heart tripped.

Silly girl, she castigated herself. *You're wasting your time on this one.* She got in the truck, slammed the door and buckled up. The trip back to her house was as quiet as the trip to her car had been.

Dusk was gathering by the time they drove down the driveway. Miriam had so hoped to see the place in the light. But as they pulled into the yard, she caught darkened glimpses of overgrown grass, tangled shrubs and flower gardens full of weeds.

"My mother and I paid someone to keep this place up. What happened?"

"Velma Rogers? She only took care of the inside of the house. Said she wasn't paid for more. We tried to keep the outside fixed up, but we didn't have time," Jake said, his voice brusque. "We did check on the house every few months, just to make sure everything was still working. Your mother must have had the lawyer we paid to rent the land taking care of the power and gas bills."

Miriam nodded, then slowly got out of the truck, looked around. It was unkept enough in the half-light; she didn't know if she wanted to see it in the sunshine.

"Thanks for driving me here," she said, turning. Waves of exhaustion made her legs wobble. She clung to the open truck door. "Don't worry about the car. I can call a tow truck."

"That's okay," he said, turning and getting out of the truck. He pulled her suitcase out of the back. "I'll come by tomorrow, and you can help me bring it into town."

"No, really, I know how busy this time of the year is. I know the last thing you need to do is cart me around. Please." She felt a moment's warmth kindle in her heart at his thoughtfulness.

"And how are you going to call a tow truck?" Jake asked as he walked around the front of the truck. "The telephone doesn't work."

"I have a cell phone."

Jake nodded. "Of course." He strode ahead of her to the back door and stood aside so she could open it.

The sound of the door opening echoed hollowly through the house, and Miriam felt a wave of nostalgia. It was so familiar, so much a part of her youth. How many times had she opened this very door and come running in to throw her books down on the porch floor, asking if there was anything to eat?

Miriam flicked the switch by the back door, and light flooded the porch. There was a faint musty smell.

Miriam walked up the three steps into the kitchen,

stifling a cry of dismay. All the furniture was draped with white sheets; pictures had been taken off the wall and stacked in corners of the room. It all looked desolate and distinctly un-homey.

Jake walked over to the taps and turned them. "Water's still okay, although you might want to drain the hot water out of the tank. I'm sure it's pretty stale. We did it at Easter time, but that's the last time I went through this place. Velma had asked me to go over everything this fall again."

"Thanks, Jake. I'll do that." Her head was starting to buzz, and she wanted nothing more than to have a nice warm shower and crawl into bed. One look around the house, though, told her she had other things to do first.

"Do you want some help…" Jake let the sentence trail off.

"No, thanks. I'll be fine." She yearned for some time to herself, some time to gather her scattered thoughts. She wanted him gone. She wanted this cold formality between them to end, and it would only happen when he left.

Jake nodded, his one hand caught in the back pocket of his blue jeans. "I'll just walk through the house once, just to make sure everything's okay. Where do you want your suitcase?"

"Just leave it here, please."

The sound of his boots thumping through the house was muffled by the cloths draping all the furniture. Shivering, Miriam walked through the kitchen into the darkened living room, hugging herself against the chill of the house. The room here had a feeling of waiting.

With a muted rumble, the furnace started up.

Jake returned and paused in the arched doorway between the kitchen and the living room, looking around. "Well, I'll be going. Are you sure you're going to be all right?"

Miriam turned to him, nodding. "Thanks for everything. I'm sorry to be such a pain…" She let the sentence drift off as their eyes met.

The backlight from the kitchen silhouetted him, and she couldn't help but acknowledge his appeal. He was taller, broader. Not the young man she had left behind, but a man who had had his own experiences. He had buried a wife, and now had a child, ran a farm and took care of parents that looked so much older to Miriam than they had when she left. He was a stranger to her. A stranger with his own heartaches and his own responsibilities.

"I'll be by sometime tomorrow to bring your car into town." Jake scratched his head as if he wanted to say more. Then with a shrug, he turned and left.

Miriam walked to the window of the darkened room and watched through the large picture window as Jake started his truck, the headlights stabbing the darkness.

She lay her head against the cold glass, letting the emotions of the day flow over her. Then, against her will, she felt tears gather. She didn't know precisely what she cried for; she only knew that she had felt a deep sadness closing in on her since she'd first seen Jake, then Fred and Tilly. All the memories of her mother's death returned, hard and fast. Telling the Prinses had been like reliving that stark moment when she'd felt her mother's hand go limp in her own.

Once again she replayed those moments after the funeral, when all the temporary supports—the nursing home staff, the undertaker, the minister who performed the service—had slowly fallen away, and she'd realized she was all alone.

She had no one who cared. No one who mattered. The men she had met treated her like a trophy to be won

and shown. Other men treated her like a commodity—
a model, a face to sell their product.

There had been only one man in her life. Ever.

She felt another wave of sorrow thinking about Jake
and his daughter. A daughter borne by her best friend.

She cried for the loss of the dreams that both she and
Jake had spun during those innocent long-ago evenings,
and for the lives that reality had changed.

The window was cool and soothing against her hot
forehead, and slowly the tears subsided. They always
did. And as always, reality returned. She had much to
do if she wanted to sleep here tonight.

Jake turned into Miriam's driveway, the entrance
of which was barely visible in the driving rain, unable
to stop a gentle lift of his heart at the thought of seeing her again.

Yesterday, the surprise of her sudden reappearance
after ten years had put him on the defensive.

And no wonder. She had kept herself away from people who cared about her, himself included, he reminded
himself as his truck bounced through a puddle. She had
told no one what was going on in her life.

But even as Jake mentally considered a litany of her
shortcomings, he couldn't help but wonder how she had
fared last night, her first night all alone in her childhood home.

He had thought about her in this empty house during
the drive back home, then again as he lay in bed, staring up at the ceiling in his room. Surprising, how easily the memories had returned. The fun times they had
had. The excitement of the first moment of discovering
their feelings for each other. Yet Miriam had been more

than a girlfriend. She had been his closest friend. There had been nothing going on in his life, past or present, that she hadn't known about.

Jake sighed lightly as he came to a halt in front of Miriam's house. Too much had happened between them, and the only way to get past it was to talk about it.

But why bother, when she was going to sell the farm and leave again?

Jake jumped out of the truck and ran up the walk to the house, rain slicing down on his head. He huddled deeper into his jean jacket and rapped on the door. The rain was really coming down now, a typical prairie rainstorm swishing and beating against the peeling woodwork of the house.

He rapped on the door again and then pushed it open, stepping quickly inside. As he closed the door behind him, he looked up to see Miriam come to the door. She was wiping her hands on a cloth, wearing an apron over a pair of loose cargo pants that hung low on her hips and a T-shirt that barely ended above the waistband.

"Hi, there," she said, her expression neutral. "Did you want to leave right away?"

"If you don't mind." Jake slicked his damp hair back from his face, wiping the moisture from his cheeks with the shoulder of his jacket, unable to take his eyes off her. Her hair looked tousled, her feet were bare and, unlike yesterday, today she wore no makeup.

The effect was captivating. She looked younger, fresher and more approachable. More like the Miriam he had once known.

He felt his heart stir in response, felt his pulse quicken. Then she lifted her soft brown eyes to his, and in that moment they seemed connected, pulled together by an invisible cord, by memories and old feelings that had never been resolved.

He blinked and forced his gaze away, breaking the tie. "I'll be waiting in the truck for you," he said, looking past her at the wall behind her. "You might want to wear some boots if you have them."

He saw Miriam nod and take a step back. "I'll be right out," she said quietly. When she turned and walked back, he couldn't help but watch her go, noting the graceful sway of her hips.

Pull yourself together, Jake, he berated himself. She's not for you and she's not sticking around. With a shake of his head, he left the house. I need to get out more.

Trouble was, he had no desire to date again.

He had a father who wasn't feeling well, an older mother who couldn't do as much as she used to, a small daughter he never felt he spent enough time with, and a large farm to run on his own. His love life had been luckless, to put it mildly. Women were a complication he could do without. He had Taryn. She was his first responsibility. Tilly and Fred were his second, and together that was more than enough for him.

He was glad he had decided at the last minute to leave Taryn behind. The almost reverential tone she used when talking about Miriam made him uneasy. Besides, Taryn had lately taken to talking about getting a mommy, like this was an item Jake could take care of for her in a minute.

He knew Taryn, and he was afraid that her fascination would translate into simple math. Miriam was single, Jake was single. One plus one equals a mommy for Taryn. And in spite of the fancies of his own foolish heart, he couldn't imagine a more unsuitable candidate for the job than Miriam.

Jake watched as Miriam picked her way through the puddles on the driveway to the passenger side of the truck, clutching a bright red anorak tightly to her. To his surprise she had on a pair of sturdy hiking boots. He reached across the seat and opened the door. Miriam stepped in, a cloud of sweet-smelling perfume filling the cab as she shot Jake a grateful smile.

Jake twisted the key in the ignition and tried to ignore that irresistible smell that telegraphed her presence.

The only sounds in the cab were the hum of the heater fan and the slap of windshield wipers on the window. Just like yesterday, silence lay between them.

And suddenly Jake was tired of it.

"How long do you plan on staying here?"

"I figure about ten days. I was hoping to go to a real estate agent today."

"Do you think that's long enough to sell your farm?" Jake tried to inject a casual note into his voice. It made him angry that she could so easily talk of selling her farm. The idea bothered him for so many reasons.

"Probably not, but I could only spare that much time here. I have work to go back to."

"Modeling?"

"Yes."

Her quiet reply made Jake take a chance and look at her again. She was looking straight ahead, her mouth pressed into a firm line, her fingers wrapped tightly around each other.

"If you don't mind my intruding, you don't seem too eager about it."

Miriam laughed shortly, pressing her thumbs together. "It pays the bills."

Jake looked back at the road again. He was sure it did. Paula had often spoken with outright envy of how much she figured Miriam made, doing what she did.

He sighed, tapping his thumbs lightly on the steering wheel as he tried to find something to say. He felt awkward and gauche, and he didn't like it.

But she wasn't the Miriam he used to tease; she wasn't the Miriam who used to laugh at everything. In spite of his original antipathy toward her, he felt old feelings resurfacing, and through new-old eyes, he could see a sadness in her.

They turned a corner, and there was her car.

Jake stopped and frowned over a new problem. Town was west and Miriam's car was facing east.

"We'll have to tow it back to the house to get it turned around," he said, thinking out loud.

"Why don't you pull it to the next approach and turn in?" Miriam suggested.

Jake rubbed his thumb along his chin, shaking his head. "Then I won't be able to back out."

"How about pushing it around? It's just a small car."

Jake chewed on his thumbnail, considering.

"You still chew your nails?" Miriam asked, her voice tinged with laughter.

Jake jerked his head around, suddenly self-conscious. "I don't chew my nails," he said, dropping his hand.

"That's what you always said." Miriam smiled again at the shared memory, and once again their eyes met.

Why couldn't he look away? Why couldn't he just casually return the smile and turn his head? It was just mechanics—lift mouth in casual way; move neck muscles. Mission accomplished.

But other messages were ruling his head right now. Like how much narrower her face was than before, how the light caught her high cheekbones, accenting them. He suddenly noticed a delicate fan of wrinkles from her eyes, smudges of shadows beneath them. There was a weariness to her features that he hadn't noticed yesterday.

Jake took a deep breath, pulling himself back to the dilemma at hand.

"It's not a big car," she said again. "We could push it."

Jake considered this new suggestion, and then, with a shrug, said, "We can try."

Jake jumped out of the truck, shut the door and walked over to the car. Miriam was beside him.

"I could push, and you could work the steering," Jake said quickly. "The road isn't too muddy yet, so we should be okay."

"Let's try it." She pulled the keys out of her pocket and unlocked the car, then put the key in the ignition and put the car into neutral. She positioned herself, gave Jake a nod, and on his count they started pushing. The car was small, just as Miriam had said, but it was also low. Jake had to bend far down to get any kind of leverage, and going on his knees wasn't an option.

"Do they get any lower?" he grunted as he strained to move it.

"Not much," Miriam said.

"I'm surprised you didn't bottom out on these roads."

"You always—" Miriam took a breath and pushed harder "—talk this much…when…you're working?"

Keeps me from thinking, he thought.

The car was moving, slowly, but fortunately it was

turning in the right direction. The road might just be wide enough.

Jake was bent over so far that he couldn't see what was happening, so when Miriam called out "Stop, stop," he didn't know why. He looked up just in time to see her jump into the car. He was totally unprepared for the jolt as the car came to an abrupt halt. His hands slipped up the trunk of the wet car, his feet slipped on the wet gravel. The next thing he knew, he was lying flat out in a dirty puddle of water, rain dripping down his neck.

He sucked his breath in and lay there a moment as if to assimilate what had happened, embarrassment and the icy water seeping through his clothes, each vying for his attention. The water won out as he shoved himself off the ground, getting his hands dirty in the process. Amazing how quickly one could go from feeling competent and in charge to humiliated and out of control.

"Are you okay?" Miriam poked her head out of the car and quickly put on the emergency brake. She got out, and as she took a good look at him, he saw her hand fly to her mouth. Her lips were pulled in and she glanced quickly down, then up again.

"You're laughing at me," he said, pulling his wet and dirty coat away from his chest, water dripping down his face. "I'm in absolute misery here, and you're standing there laughing at me."

"Sorry," she said, her voice muffled by her hand.

He saw her shoulders shake, and then, as he looked down at his soaking wet pants and coat, he started smiling himself.

Jake wiped the dirty water off his face with the cuff of his coat. He looked over at Miriam now, and saw her eyes dancing. "You better stop laughing, Miriam Spencer, or your hair won't look so clean anymore."

"I'm not laughing," she said, dropping her hand, forcing herself to look more serious.

But then he felt a clump of mud dislodge itself from his hair and slide down his face. Jake swiped at it, but it was too late. Now Miriam was laughing out loud, her arms clutching her midsection.

"I'm sorry," she gasped, lifting one hand as if in surrender. "I'm sorry."

Jake laughed. Then, shaking his head, he walked over to the truck. "Well, you just stand there and giggle like a girl—I'm going to get the rope."

He pulled the tow rope out of the back of the truck and walked over to Miriam's car. His pants were wet anyhow, so he knelt in the gravel, staring under the car with dismay.

"Can I do anything?" she asked, squatting down beside him.

"Yeah," he said, glancing over his shoulder, forcing himself to look serious. "You can get that little body of yours under this car and hook this on."

Miriam looked taken aback. "Okay," she said quietly, wiping her hands on her coat as if in preparation.

"Kidding," he said, grinning at her.

"You rat." She gave his shoulder a push, almost knocking him over.

"Don't start anything you can't finish, Mims," he said with a mock warning tone and a wink. The nickname came easily to him and so did the wink.

Miriam's expression grew serious. "I haven't heard that in years," Miriam said, dropping her hand and straightening. Then she turned away. "Let me know if you need anything," she said quietly.

Jake looked down at the rope, shaking his head. Keep your mind on the job at hand, he reminded himself. He was surprised at how readily her old name had rolled off his tongue, surprised at her response to it. With difficulty he shrugged the memories away, and bent over to find a suitable place to hook up the rope.

"You'll need to ride in the car," he said to Miriam as he got up, pleased at how casual he managed to sound. "I'll go slow, and you'll have to brake before I do. I'll touch the brakes lightly when I need you to brake, okay? I'll give you lots of time."

"Where are we going?"

"Denny's Auto Parts. I'm sure they'll have something for you, or they'll find it. There's no dealer in town for that make of car."

She gave him a curt nod and got into the car. Jake hesitated a moment, then turned and walked back to the truck.

As he drove, Jake kept alternating between looking at the road ahead and at the car behind him, his mind on neither. He kept wondering why he had called Miriam "Mims." The name had come from a deep place he had forgotten about. He had used Mims only in times of affection.

He sighed and flicked on the radio, hoping the music would keep his mind occupied. But he couldn't forget the brief connection they'd shared when it seemed that all the ten years between them had never been.

Chapter Four

By the time they got to town, the rain had quit and the clouds above were starting to break. The weatherperson had promised blue skies and wind tomorrow. Jake hoped that would keep up, so he could be in the fields again by Monday.

When they pulled into Denny's, he got out of the truck, undid the wet and dirty rope, and coiled it up, while Miriam went inside. He threw the rope in the back of the truck.

"You're lucky," he heard Denny say as he walked into the office. "We just parted out a car with a rad that will fit yours."

The young man at the counter sported a tattoo on each hand, a bizarre haircut and a full beard. Denny was a terrific mechanic, although a trifle tough—the complete opposite of his fellow worker, Ryan, who had short hair and was clean-shaven. They both wore grease-stained overalls and, right now, foolish grins. They were unable to keep their eyes off Miriam.

It irritated Jake for a moment. He didn't like the way

they were looking at her, as if she were some exotic specimen they had never seen before.

"You done in here, Miriam?"

She glanced over her shoulder. "They said they'll have it done in a couple of hours."

"Funny. I never manage to get such quick service," Jake said, his voice laced with irony.

Denny shrugged, grinning. "You know us, Jake. We aim to please beautiful women." He leaned on the counter and glanced at Jake, his eyebrows raised at the sight of Jake's shirt and pants. "What were you doing?"

"I fell in the mud pushing Miriam's car," Jake answered tersely.

"Well, I sure appreciate the service." Miriam bestowed a polite smile on them. "Is there a place I can wait while you work on it?"

"You can sit here, or you can tell us where you will be and we can deliver it." Ryan smiled, leaning closer.

Jake resisted the urge to roll his eyes. These two were so obvious, it was sickening.

"I think I'll go to town. I have my cell phone. I'll let you know what's up." She smiled at them both and left, leaving two dazed men staring at her.

"She looks so familiar," Denny said to Jake as the door creaked closed behind her.

"She should. We used to go to school with her."

"That Miriam Spencer is 'Sticks' Spencer?" Denny's mouth almost dropped open. Jake felt an unaccountable surge of anger at the memory of that hated nickname. Miriam had always laughed it off, but he also knew how it bothered her.

"Wow, she sure became babe material," Denny continued, stroking his beard.

"She is quite attractive," Jake said, cringing at his own prim note.

Ryan threw him a knowing smirk. "Oh, very quite," he said with a laugh.

Jake caught the door handle, feigning nonchalance. "Well, gotta run. Let me know if anything changes with Miriam's car," he said.

"She gave us her cell number." Denny craned his neck as if to get another look at Miriam, who was once again sitting in Jake's truck. "But I'll call you, too, just in case." Denny gave Jake a wink, as if congratulating him. "She back for a visit?"

Jake only nodded, uncomfortable with Denny's obvious assumption—that he and Miriam were going to try again. He knew he should correct the misconception, but he figured people would know for themselves, once Miriam was gone.

When Jake got outside, Miriam wasn't in the truck. He frowned, and then he saw her walking down the road toward town.

"Miriam!" he called out. "Where are you going?"

She stopped, glancing over her shoulder. "To town."

"I'll bring you," he said, stifling his exasperation. Did she really think he would just go back to the farm, leaving her to fend for herself?

"That's okay. You don't have to."

"Come back and get in the truck," he said brusquely.

Miriam hesitated. Then, with a shrug, she turned and came back. He waited for her by the passenger side of the truck and held the door open for her.

Miriam threw him an oblique glance and got in.

Jake walked around the front and climbed awkwardly

into his truck, the wet denim of his pants clinging to his legs and constricting his movements.

"Where do you want to go?" he asked as he drove out of Denny's yard.

"Doesn't matter. Is Raylene's place still around?"

"No. She moved to Denver."

"Denver? Why there?"

"I heard some cowboy in town for a rodeo caught her fancy, and she sold the place and left."

Miriam laughed at that.

"What's so funny? Can't you see old Raylene Dansers losing her heart to some old bull rider?" Jake said with mock dismay.

"Bull riders don't get that old," Miriam said, grinning.

"Actually, he was the header half of a calf-roping team. You can do that sitting down."

Miriam laughed again, and Jake felt a lightness pervade the once-heavy atmosphere. "I'll take you to the new place in town," he said impulsively. "You can see how much Waylen has changed."

Miriam looked sideways at him and, to his surprise, smiled. "Thanks, Jake. That sounds good."

A few minutes later Jake pulled up in front of a small café that Miriam remembered as having been a bakery.

"Where did the bakery go?" Miriam asked, getting out of the truck.

"Moved into a new complex downtown." Jake got out and stared down at his dirty pants. He really looked like a hick compared to Miriam.

He glanced up to see Miriam smiling at him. "Don't worry about your pants. I don't care if you don't."

He made it to the door ahead of her and opened it for her.

"Still a gentleman," she said lightly as she stepped through the door.

"Tilly raised me right," he returned, following her in.

"Hey, Jake." Peter Thornton, a farmer who lived down the road, waved to Jake from his seat as they came in. "The rain send you to town this morning, too?"

"Yeah," Jake said briefly. He didn't want to stop, but small-town protocol deemed that he do so. "You done seeding yet?"

"Got another sixty acres to do." Peter leaned back in his chair and looked past him, then back to Jake with a grin. "How about you?"

"Pretty close to done." He glanced back at Miriam, who stood just behind him, her hands clasped in front of her. He didn't want to keep her waiting through the usual give-and-take of farming talk. Besides, he wanted her to himself for a while. "Well, take care. Talk to you later." After a casual nod, he walked across the nearly empty café to the window.

He was thankful the café was quiet this morning.

Miriam sat down at the table and looked around with a smile. "Nice place."

"They opened about a year ago. They're doing quite well," Jake said, leaning on the table.

The waitress was already at their table, a pot of coffee in her hand. "Menus?" she asked.

Jake shook his head. "Just a cup of coffee for me," he said.

Miriam looked up. "Thanks, I'll have the same."

They watched as the waitress filled their cups, then was gone again.

"You didn't used to drink coffee," Jake said, pulling his cup closer.

"I started while I was modeling. All that waiting around." She took a careful sip from her cup, avoiding his gaze. Jake wanted to ask her more, wanted to know about her world—and yet didn't. He didn't know where to start asking about the life that had taken her away from him and Waylen. Yet he had to—it was who she had become.

"So what is it like—modeling?"

Miriam looked up past his shoulder and shook her head lightly. "Busy. A lot of rushing around because there's a ton of people involved in a shoot." She laughed, but it wasn't a pleasant laugh. "The work isn't so bad. It's how you get treated after a while."

"And how is that?"

"Like a thing—a centerpiece that gets pulled on, tweaked, changed and molded. Some girls love all the attention, but I felt like an object."

Jake heard despair in her voice. Despair and the same weariness he could see in her eyes. "So why are you going back to it?"

Miriam gave a graceful shrug. "The money is good."

It wasn't hard to tell that she didn't like the work. He didn't want to accept that Miriam Spencer—a girl who never seemed to care what she wore, who used to wear her long brown hair tied back with a shoelace—had turned into this elegant woman who spoke easily of doing work she disliked merely because the money was good.

"Well, you've done it long enough—you must have quite a bit of it by now," he said sardonically.

She said nothing, only lowered her eyes—but not before Jake saw the flare of pain in them.

He felt like a heel. He had no right to judge her. Not when he himself often wished for better crops, for higher prices. Money was important to him, too.

He wondered what to say next. Wondered what he could say to bring some measure of amicability back to the conversation. Because he discovered, suddenly, that he wanted to know more about her, to find out what had happened to her.

As he watched her carefully sip her coffee, he felt a familiar stirring, an awakening of old feelings. She had been a friend—one of the first he had made here. Miriam had been the one who introduced him to other people, who included him in her circle, who made sure he was always socially comfortable. The friendship they shared had quickly changed and become more intense. Miriam was the first girl he had really loved.

And now, in spite of the complete change in her, and in spite of knowing she was going to be leaving, he was feeling attracted to her again.

Fool that he was.

He wanted to leave as if to outrun his own feelings, but there was no polite way to do so. He had invited her here.

The door opened and a woman called out a greeting to Peter, then walked over to their table.

"Hey, Jake, how are you doing?"

Jake looked up and met the smiling face of Donna Kurtz. "Doing good, Donna. How about you?"

"Busy. I just took a break from working at the church." She pulled at her paint-splattered T-shirt and flashed a crooked grin. "I thought you were going to come?"

"I'm sorry. I forgot they're painting there today." Jake felt guilty. "I'll be right over."

He turned to Miriam, who was looking up at Donna with a wistful expression on her face. "Miriam, you remember Donna, don't you?"

Donna's mouth fell open as she recognized her old friend. Then she was leaning over, hugging Miriam hard. "My goodness," she said breathlessly. "Look at you, Miriam Spencer." Donna clutched Miriam's shoulders, and shook her head in disbelief. "Have you ever changed! What are you doing back here? How come I never knew?"

"I just came back yesterday," Miriam replied.

"Really?" Donna glanced at Jake and then back at Miriam, her smile changing. "And you and Jake already met up with each other." The innuendo in her tone was unmistakable.

Jake figured he'd better dispel that notion immediately. "Miriam's car broke down not far from our place. I brought her into town to get it fixed."

Donna nodded, but her smirk showed that she didn't quite believe it. "It's just like old times, seeing you two together again."

Jake wished she would stop assuming a relationship between them. It made him yearn for something that wasn't going to happen—Miriam's next stop was a real estate agency.

He glanced at his watch. He had other things to do, other obligations. If Denny was as fast as he said he could be, Miriam didn't have much longer to wait. "I should go and help at the church," he said to Miriam, trying for a light tone. "If you need anything, you can find me there."

She nodded as her eyes met his, then looked back at Donna. He felt dismissed, and pushed his chair back.

"See you back at the church," he said, sending her a quick grin.

Donna nodded, then took his place opposite Miriam. He stopped at the till and paid for their coffees, then walked to his truck. As he got in, he could see Donna and Miriam through the window of the café. Donna was leaning forward, and Miriam's face held that same wistfulness he had seen before.

As he started the truck, he wondered what was going on behind those deep brown eyes of hers. Once he would have been able to read the slightest nuance, but now she was as unreadable as a legal document.

He sighed and pulled away. As if he didn't have enough on his mind, now he had to go and complicate his life with this woman who was so different from the one he had once loved.

"I still can't believe you're here." Donna rested her elbows on the scratched red Formica tabletop, sipping her coffee, smiling across at her old friend. "It's been years and years. Too long."

Miriam acknowledged the comment with a nod, and kept folding the napkin on the table in front of her. More guilt. "I know and I'm sorry." She lifted her eyes to Donna. "I don't think there's anything I can really say to excuse or brush it all away."

"I heard a few bits and pieces from Paula just after you left, but that's about it."

"Paula and I stayed out of touch, as well—" Miriam stopped, sorrow over their mutual friend thickening her throat. "Sorry." She looked down, blinking quickly. "I still can't get past her death."

"It happened a while ago for me, but I can imagine it's a shock for you, just finding this out now."

Miriam drew in a long breath to compose herself and then looked up at Donna. "After she got married, the relationship faded away."

"I imagine." Donna took another sip of coffee, but held Miriam's gaze. "You know, when I saw you sitting here with Jake, it seemed just like old times."

"That's all they are, Donna—old times," Miriam said sharply. Donna's words struck too close to her own yearning. It had been hard to acknowledge Jake's marriage to Paula, but it was all the harder now that Paula had passed away. If Paula were still alive, Jake wouldn't be available.

Donna looked taken aback at Miriam's harsh tone. "I know that. It's just that we used to see you guys together all the time. That's all."

"I'm sorry, Donna. It's been so strange coming back here. Everything's changed so much."

Except that it was much the same, Miriam thought as she and Donna quietly sipped their coffee. Looking at Donna somehow made her realize what she had lost when she'd left. This place where she had grown up suddenly seemed secure, unchanging. Here were people who cared. She had been hugged more in the past two days than she had been in years. More people had asked with sincerity how she was doing.

For the past few years she had been only a face, a body, an object. No one seemed to care about her soul, her heart.

"You've changed, too. I remember the first time your face showed up on the front cover of a magazine. It was the talk of the town."

"I'm sure it was."

"Oh, don't get all huffy with me. That's what Waylen is like. People are nosy, but they care." Donna grinned at her. "And now, you owe me. Big-time." Donna tilted her head, her tone full of meaning. "You don't write, you don't phone. So spill. What happened with you and

Jake? What have you been doing? What is your life like? How's your mom?"

In spite of the sorrow raised by Donna's questions, Miriam felt an easing of the tension that had gripped her since she'd come here. Easygoing, straightforward Donna never pulled any punches, never minced words. Never judged.

"My mom died six months ago." Again Miriam stopped, swallowing hard.

"Oh, Miriam. I'm so sorry."

"I can't believe this," Miriam said, her voice shaky as Donna's hand squeezed hers tightly. "It's like each time I tell someone, I relive her death." She stopped, taking in a deep breath. "It was hard, but I think she was ready. She died quite peacefully."

"I'm so sorry," Donna said, stroking her arm with her other hand. "You've sure had enough to deal with."

Silence drifted up between them as Miriam wiped a fresh rivulet of tears, but this was the companionable silence of friends reestablishing their acquaintance.

"Sorry to dump on you like this. Hardly old home week, is it?"

"I'm your friend, Miriam." Donna smiled at her. "I'm supposed to help you, to listen to you."

"Thanks." Miriam felt another twinge of guilt that Donna should offer help and support when she herself had remained so distant.

"So what is modeling like?" Donna asked, changing the subject. "How do you feel when you walk out in front of all those people?"

Miriam didn't want to talk about modeling. She had fostered a foolish hope that when she came back here, she would be able to leave the other life behind her, if only for a while. But she had forgotten how intertwined lives are in a small town. Your news is my news.

"Actually, the majority of what I do is catalog work. I haven't done much runway work lately, and, to tell you the truth, it's fairly boring."

"Boring?" Donna said in a tone of disbelief.

"Yes, Donna. Despite what you see, it's dull, plodding work." She would have preferred to talk about her clothing retail business, but it was just another failure in her life. At least for now.

"Well, you still don't seem to have trouble keeping the weight off." Donna sighed, looking at Miriam. "I could never figure out how a girl so skinny could eat so much and not put on a pound."

"Always was a poor keeper. But enough about me," Miriam said suddenly. She didn't want to reexamine her life any more than she had to. She hadn't liked what she saw out East; she liked it even less here. "What about you? Married? Kids?"

"Yeah, I'm married. My last name is now Kurtz, and my husband, Keith, is an accountant. I've got two kids. One in play school, the other in kindergarten. I'm busy with church, school. The usual." Donna smiled a self-deprecating smile. "My life must sound so dull."

Miriam shook her head, a feeling of melancholy gripping her. "It doesn't sound dull at all," she said quietly. "It sounds pretty good to me."

"Don't give me that." Donna held her gaze. "As if beneath every glamorous outfit you've ever worn beats a heart that deep down would love nothing more than to be at home baking chocolate chip cookies."

"I prefer macadamia nut, myself."

"See? A gourmet. You don't belong in this little hick town anymore."

Once Miriam might have scoffed at the idea, but as she had traveled these past few years, she had been able to look at Waylen from a distance. "Waylen isn't as bad as you might think, Donna," she said.

"You sound serious."

"I am. The fashion life reads well in short magazine articles. But a good photographer can make anything— and I mean anything—look good," Miriam said with meaning. "I haven't met many sincere people in my business. They're either putting up with you because you might be useful to them, or they're sucking up to you because you are useful to them." She gave a shrug, knowing that she had already said too much. She hadn't come back here to show everyone how unsatisfied she was with her life.

"So no one important in your life right now?"

"Nope. Footloose and fancy-free." Her wry grin belied her casual tone. "My agent, Carl, is a darling, but he's married. I've not met Mr. Right yet."

"I can't imagine that. I always thought you would be the one who would get married first," Donna said with a grin.

There it was again: the soft pain brought up by the innocent comment. The reminder of how close she and Jake had once been. How had she thought she could keep herself aloof from that?

"I'm sorry," Donna said, shaking her head. "Me and my big mouth." She sighed. "I don't know what happened between you and Jake. I don't suppose it's any of my business, but it was as much of a shock to me as anyone when he and Paula got married."

Miriam sensed the opening that Donna gave her, but decided not to seize it. She had come to set the past to rest.

"Well, that's long over, and we've both changed a lot," Miriam said lightly. "Tell me about the rest of the people here. What's Linda doing? Still hoping to write that bestseller?"

They sat for another hour, chatting, talking, laughing. Miriam found herself drifting back into life in Waylen. It was familiar, and yet, listening to her friend talk easily about children and her husband, Miriam had a feeling that she had missed out on an important part of life. Her own life seemed shallow and frivolous by comparison.

Finally, Donna had to leave. "Why don't you come with me? Sondra is there. I'd love to see the look on her face when you show up."

Miriam shook her head. She would have liked to come, but Jake was there, as well. It would be better if she kept her distance. "I have a few other things to do. Thanks, though."

"You said you're staying around awhile—we'll have to make sure to connect again. Otherwise the church is having a picnic a week from this Sunday. You should come."

Miriam paused again, considering. Memories of other fun-filled days flashed through her mind. "That sounds good."

"Great. Well, keep in touch. And we'll see you on Sunday."

They left the restaurant, each going her separate way. Miriam watched Donna stroll down the street, waving at one person, stopping briefly to chat with another. For a moment she wanted to go with Donna. She wanted to be a part of that community.

Don't be silly. You don't fit here anymore, she thought. She wondered if she should go to church on Sunday, if she wanted to risk the very stares and censure that Donna had hinted at. She had enough self-doubts; she didn't need to pile on any more.

But she remembered other times in church, other times when she had felt peace, and joy and love. She felt a yearning to experience that again, that healing, that feeling that someone did care about her, about her soul. That she was important to God.

She had strayed so far from that center of her life. She couldn't help but think of how easy it had been to drift away, to get caught up in the vacuousness of the fashion world. And she had been such a major part of it—dressing up, acting, being fussed over.

Seventeen years old, self-conscious, still smarting from Jake's defection. What girl wouldn't go a little crazy with all that attention, all those photographers telling her how beautiful she looked, all the admiration? But it was from people who saw her only as a face and figure.

Miriam spun around and strode away from the café, wishing she could as easily leave parts of her past behind.

Carl and his bright ideas, she thought. It would have been easier on her self-esteem and her conscience if she had just stayed out East and sold the farm from there. She never spent this much time moodling about might-have-beens. All her free time in the past few months had been taken up with bankers, phoning up suppliers to beg for extensions of credit, phoning up debtors to beg for payment.

When one of her biggest customers went bankrupt, it had caused her problems. She might have been okay, but for a crooked accountant. Now, thanks to him, she stood to lose her company as well, unless she could come up with a substantial influx of cash.

That accountant, Miriam thought with disgust. Another man who couldn't be trusted. Her life seemed to be a series of men who didn't want to stay with her, be loyal to her. That's why it puzzled her that Jake could still tie her up in knots. He had only been the first of many men who didn't seem to need her in the long run.

She sped up, and this time made it all the way to the real estate office. She pushed the door open and stepped inside.

Half an hour later she was back on the street. The papers were signed and the machinery had been put into place.

Now what?

Miriam sighed, looking down the street. A few trucks drove by, a couple of cars. People greeted each other as they passed on the street. Everyone belonged here. They fit.

She walked down the street until she found an empty bench and, wiping the moisture off it, sat down. She called Denny's on her cell phone and arranged for them to bring her car downtown. Then, just to make a connection, she phoned Tilly. Maybe she needed some groceries.

"That would be wonderful, Miriam. I don't dare leave Fred. He is feeling so listless, I don't want to leave him alone."

"He's still not feeling well?"

"It seems so up and down. If he doesn't get better, I'm going to have to bring him in to the doctor. But for now all is well, and God is good. We still have each other and Jake and Taryn, and for that we can be grateful, can't we?"

Yes you can, thought Miriam.

"Now, what groceries do you want?" Miriam wrote down what Tilly told her. They chatted a bit more and then Tilly said goodbye. It was like old times, Miriam thought with a smile as she closed the phone. Running errands, idle chat.

She missed it.

She was putting her phone and the list back in her purse when she saw a tall figure pausing at the traffic lights on the main street. Jake.

He was frowning. Miriam could see it from here. She swallowed down her quick response to him, frustrated with how easily old feelings came back. The light turned green and he crossed the street. He walked along the street opposite her, then looked up and saw her. His step faltered, then, after a quick glance both ways, he jogged across the street toward her.

Visiting with Donna this morning had re-created the past. Now, once again, as Jake sauntered up to her, she felt the same foolish thrill she always did when she saw him. It didn't matter that just this morning she had seen him with mud on his face and pants; he still seemed to tower above her, to dominate the area around him.

"Hello," she said evenly. "You finished at the church?"

"They didn't need me. So I had some business to do."

"I'm picking up some groceries for Tilly."

"That's not necessary," Jake said abruptly. He shifted his weight and slipped his hands in the back pockets of his blue jeans. "I can get them."

Miriam felt dismissed. Though she wanted to fight

it, she realized that putting her farm up for sale pulled her back from their lives, as well.

She busied herself looking through her purse, found the piece of paper on which she had written the list, and handed it to Jake. "Are you sure? I don't mind doing it."

"That's okay. Thanks anyhow." He forced a smile as if to compensate for his brusque attitude, but Miriam wasn't fooled. She knew what Jake's sincere smile could do. And had he bestowed one on her, she wouldn't be standing here, seething over how easily he seemed to exempt her from his life.

She had hoped to visit with Tilly for a while, but she'd have to make time for that another day.

"Well, I guess I'll see you around." She was about to turn.

"Did you want me to give you a ride to Denny's?"

"That's not necessary," she said mimicking his words of a few moments ago. "They said they would deliver the car to me."

"Okay. I'll see you around, then." And he turned on his heel and walked across the street again.

Miriam watched him go, her emotions narrowing down to anger. She felt as if she had been judged and found wanting. As if Jake Steele were above reproach, she thought angrily.

By the time Denny brought her car to town, she was tired and glad to see him.

She followed him back to the office, paid for the repairs done on her car and then drove home.

The road back was still wet from the rain of this morning and the car was difficult to handle, but that didn't stop Miriam from going too fast. She fishtailed a couple of times, and after the second time, forced herself to slow down. The last thing she wanted was for Jake to have to rescue her. Again.

By the time she got home she wasn't quite as angry as before. Instead, a peculiar hurt overlaid her earlier emotions. A painful realization that she didn't fit here anymore.

Well, it was a good thing she had realized that as soon as possible and hadn't pinned anything on this place.

She spent the rest of the day and most of the night cleaning up and making the place look a little better.

Saturday dawned warm and bright and Miriam headed outside to clean the yard. She went through the old shop on the place, a fresh wave of nostalgia washing over her at the still strong scent of diesel and oil that seemed to have soaked into the very timbers of her father's shop.

She remembered happier times when her father had helped her put the chain back on her bike, helped her with a science fair project that her mother didn't want done in the house. She remembered "helping" her father by handing him tools from the chest-high toolbox that still stood in one dark corner.

Miriam looked around her with a measure of anxiety. Yesterday, when she had signed the sales agreement, she hadn't realized the magnitude of her actions. She would have to have a farm sale to get rid of all these things.

The thought depressed her. She had been to enough farm sales as a young girl. She remembered how uncomfortable she had felt, poking and prying through other people's things, listening to disparaging comments made about some of the items offered for sale.

But imagining the contents of the house going up

for sale bothered her less than the idea of seeing her father's tools lined up and auctioned off.

She wandered through the shop, surprised to see so many tools still here. The lawn mower and garden tiller stood in their usual corner. Her father's table saw and drill press stood opposite, coated with a layer of greasy dust. Buckets and pails of bolts and nuts were lined up on shelves above the workbench. Mouse droppings were thick on the floor and an old leather carpenter pouch that had fallen off its hook had been fair game for them: it was full of holes.

For the rest, it was all intact.

With a mental shake, Miriam walked over to the lawn mower and pulled it away from the wall. She opened the gas tank and frowned. Empty, of course. And she knew there was no gas in the gas tank in the yard.

So much for mowing the lawn, she thought.

She could ride over to the Prinses' farm and borrow some gas; her father had enough jerricans she could carry it in.

But after meeting Jake in town, she was reluctant to go over there when he was around.

Monday, she could. Jake would probably be working in the fields then.

She pushed the lawn mower into its spot and walked back to the house, wondering how she was going to fill the rest of the empty evening.

Chapter Five

Miriam flipped down the visor in her car and checked her lipstick. She unconsciously ran her hand over her hair and glanced down at her clothes—black blazer over dark, narrow fitted pants. Conservative enough for church, she figured.

Yesterday she had spent half the day trying to talk herself out of coming, but when she woke up this morning, she knew she didn't feel right staying home.

She pulled the key out of the ignition and took a deep breath. Taking a walk down the country roads might have been a better idea. Standing here in the shadow of the church—the shadow of seventeen years of sermons, obligations and Sunday School lessons—she felt as if she were looking at her life with new eyes.

The parties, the late nights, the friends she had spent time with, the endless traveling from one exotic location to another, the many, many times she had thought she should visit her mother, and hadn't—all seemed so shallow. She had stopped attending church when her coworkers teased her about it.

I was just young, she appealed to a distant God who

was tied up with this church and her past. *I was finally free from obligations and a mother who never approved of anything I did.* She clutched the keys tighter, their sharp ridges cutting into her palm, as if the pain would serve as penance for what she had done.

"I don't need this," she said to no one in particular, leaning back against the seat. "I didn't have to come today."

But she had.

She had come seeking peace, but instead she was being faced with her past at every turn.

Miriam had never been a quitter, and she wasn't about to start now. She knew that people, once they found out she was back, would wonder why she hadn't come to church the way she always had when she and her mother had lived here.

So, straightening her shoulders, taking a deep breath, she stepped out of the car to finish this.

She walked slowly up the front walk to the church. A flat, wide sidewalk led to two sets of double doors.

Inside, a group of people stood in the foyer, chatting. They glanced at her, then smiled a polite smile before moving toward another set of stairs beside an elevator. Miriam didn't recognize them and was sure, from their reaction, that they didn't recognize her, either.

The doors behind her opened again, sending a shaft of light into the foyer. Miriam took a step away, making room for the people.

"Miriam," a sweet young voice called out, and Miriam spun around.

"Well, hello, Taryn." She smiled at the young girl who came running up to her. Taryn wore a yellow dress covered with an old-fashioned pinafore. Her hair was braided this time and tied up with two white ribbons. One, however, had come loose and was trailing down her front.

"You came to church." The statement was made without guile, and Miriam couldn't help but smile down at the adorable little girl. "Are you going to sit with us?"

"Maybe Miss Spencer wants to sit with someone else," Jake said to his daughter as he walked up to stand beside her.

Miriam reluctantly turned her gaze to him. His white collarless shirt was a bright contrast to his tanned complexion. His dark, wavy hair was brushed away from his face, bringing his features into stark relief.

Handsome as ever, thought Miriam with a stab of regret. His smoldering eyes, his full mouth. It was as if the man she had seen the other day, mud covering his face, his eyes sparkling—the man who had called her "Mims"—had been just a figment of her imagination.

Taryn looked up at her father, then back at Miriam, her eyes sad. "Do you want to sit with someone else?"

Miriam looked down at the little girl, her heart softening at the appeal in those eyes. Avoiding a reply, she squatted down and carefully retied the bow that hung loose. "There," she said, giving the bow an extra tug. "I made it nice and tight. It won't come loose again."

Taryn lifted the bow, tucking her chin in and almost crossing her eyes to see it. "That looks nice. Daddy can't tie these very good. He says he has farmer hands." She grinned up at Miriam. "Can you fix the other one, too?"

Miriam didn't dare look at Jake. She could sense his displeasure, yet something stubborn in her nature made her bend over and quickly tie up the other bow, then fluff it out.

"Thanks, Miriam," Taryn said, unabashedly catching Miriam's hand in her own as Miriam straightened.

Fred and Tilly were coming toward her, walking slowly to accommodate Fred, Miriam surmised.

"Hi there, Miriam." Fred walked up to her and patted her on the shoulder. "So good to see you here."

Miriam smiled at the approval on his face. At least in Fred's eyes she had gotten things right.

Tilly bustled up, greeting her with an enthusiastic hug. "I was so praying you would come today." She smiled, stroking Miriam's cheek.

Miriam felt another knot of emotion at the sincerity in Tilly's voice.

"I'm glad I came, too," she said softly, swallowing. She avoided looking at Jake, but was conscious of him watching them, fully aware of his disapproval. It shouldn't have mattered, but Miriam felt it as strongly as she felt Tilly's love.

She wished she dared confront him, to try to explain, but her own emotions over Jake were too unstable, too vulnerable. She hated it, but it was a reality she had to accept. Once she was gone, it would go away, she figured. Once she was back at work, remaking her life.

"You can come with us, Miriam. Please sit with us." Taryn caught her hand. "Can she sit with us, Grandma?"

"Of course." Tilly smiled down at her granddaughter. "Will you, Miriam?"

Once again, Miriam felt stuck. She knew Jake was not pleased, yet couldn't find it in herself to pull her hand away from Taryn, or to say no to her old neighbor.

"Sure. I guess I can."

"Goody." Taryn caught her father's hand in her other one and started pulling the two adults toward the stairs leading to the sanctuary. "C'mon, Grandma and Grandpa," she called over her shoulder. "We have to sit down."

Miriam felt the small, soft hand in hers, and something inside her melted. Suddenly she didn't care what Jake thought, didn't care what anyone else thought. This precious little girl wanted Miriam to be with them, and it felt wonderful.

She tried not to read too much into the child's actions. Taryn seemed naturally precocious, but as they walked up the stairs, two adults joined by a young girl, Miriam felt her throat thicken.

She remembered walking precisely in the same formation with her parents. Her father on one side, her mother on the other, and little Miriam safe and secure in the middle.

The memory was so vivid that she bit her lip, fighting an unexpected sorrow, the stairs wavering in her vision. Ducking her head, she quickly wiped her eyes, hoping Jake wouldn't see.

But she didn't have long hair to hide behind anymore. And as she straightened, she felt Jake's eyes on her. She couldn't stop looking at him any more than she could stop Taryn's excited bouncing.

Once again, their eyes met and held. Once again, Miriam felt as if she were drifting toward him, unable to stop herself.

But Taryn gave them both another tug, and the moment was broken.

"Daddy has to get the bulletin," she announced to Miriam, swinging her hand. "You stay with me and Grandma and Grandpa."

Miriam looked down at the crooked part in the little

girl's hair, and resisted the urge to run her hand over Taryn's head, to bend over and gather this little girl in her arms.

Instead, she blinked once more and looked ahead to the sanctuary, already three-quarters full.

She knew the instant Jake returned. Out of the corner of her eye she saw him take Taryn's other hand, almost felt his sidelong glance. She kept her eyes ahead, however, looking at the congregation, wondering where they would sit. A couple of people had already turned, then spun back around to whisper to a neighbor. This created a small ripple of movement among the people sitting in the back.

"Well, Miriam. Ready to face your past?" Jake's deep voice seemed to mock her, but when she turned to challenge him, she saw his soft mouth curved up in a hint of a smile. "You're quite notorious, you know."

"Notorious?" she repeated, trying to inject a note of humor in her voice. "Disreputable notorious or distinguished notorious?"

"Probably a bit of both," Jake said, looking away.

"Let's go sit," Taryn urged, looking up first at Jake and then at Miriam. "They're going to start singing, and then everyone will look at us."

Judging from the number of backward glances they were getting, that was going to happen anyhow, thought Miriam. She squared her shoulders and looked down the long, carpeted aisle of the church.

Just another catwalk, she thought, and a different audience. She rolled her shoulders, straightened her clothes and reminded herself not to strut.

Tilly and Fred went on ahead, followed by Jake, Taryn and Miriam. The aisle was wide enough for the three of them. She was thankful, however, that Tilly stopped halfway to the altar.

They settled in the pew—Miriam, then Taryn, then Jake; and beside him, Tilly and Fred. Fred calmly picked up the bulletin and started reading. Tilly leaned forward and started talking with the person ahead of them. Jake just crossed his arms and looked straight ahead.

Taryn sat between them, her hands folded demurely in her lap, her short legs sticking almost straight out in front of her. She tapped the toes of her shiny black shoes together, then looked up at Miriam with a huge grin. Miriam felt an answering tug of emotion. Taryn was so accepting, so open. Miriam didn't feel worthy of the obvious adoration that showed in the little girl's eyes.

The music from the organ stopped, then the organist struck the opening bars of a hymn. With a rustle and murmur, the congregation rose to sing.

Miriam took her cue from Jake and pulled a hymnal from the pew in front of her. The song sounded so familiar, but she couldn't place the title and didn't know where to find it. She tilted her head to see if the number was printed on the song board at the front of the church, but the board was no longer there.

She felt a hand on her arm, and, turning, saw Jake's book tilted toward her; he was showing her the number. She nodded, a faint blush warming her cheeks when she saw the title. It *had* been a while since she had been in church, she thought with a measure of shame as she flipped through the pages. Too long, when she couldn't even find one of her onetime favorites in the hymnal.

The words sifted down through the past ten years of her life, through all her other experiences, the multitude of Sundays she had either been working or sleeping in because of a terribly late night. They pulled up old thoughts, old memories that Miriam had slowly buried under a deluge of new experiences that at first seemed exciting, and now seemed cheap.

She stopped singing.

Once again she felt as if she were a young girl standing beside her mother. A young girl whose every action was criticized and discussed at length within her hearing.

Miriam closed the hymnal and dropped it back into the holder, ignoring Jake's quick glance and Taryn's puzzled one. Instead, she stared straight ahead, waiting for the song to finish, hoping she would make it to the end of the service. She had thought she and her mother had laid these regrets to rest. Yet how quickly the feelings came back with the sound of an old hymn.

The song finally ended, and the minister strode up to the front and greeted them, his voice encouraging and hearty. He welcomed visitors, and Miriam noticed a couple of faces glance furtively at her. She ignored them.

Then everyone sat down, and Taryn looked questioningly up at her. Miriam smiled down, then looked away. She hoped she could just get through this service without making it too obvious to the little girl beside her that she suddenly wished she were anywhere else but here.

The organ struck up the first notes of the postlude, and Jake glanced at Miriam. She stood holding the pew, looking straight ahead, her short dark hair shining under the overhead lights. She hadn't sung any of the songs and had sat through most of the service with her arms crossed tightly over her stomach, looking as if she'd sooner be anywhere else.

She turned her head and caught his eye, her expression composed. It was as if the woman who had wiped her eyes a while ago didn't even exist. He held her gaze, unable to stop his own reaction. This beautiful woman was a stranger, yet as he looked into her eyes and remembered her tears, he caught a glimpse of the girl he had once loved.

He turned away.

Taryn was chattering to Miriam behind him; Tilly was talking to someone else, signaling for him to go ahead. Jake ended up walking out alongside another farmer, chatting about the weather and the condition of the pastures. He tried not to be aware of Tilly introducing Miriam to her friends, not to listen to Miriam's calm voice replying to breathless questions.

Sunday was always a quiet day, a true day of rest. And usually he looked forward to it, but not today. He didn't know if he wanted Miriam sitting across the table from him.

"Can you walk with me to the car, son?" Fred laid his hand on Jake's shoulder to get his attention.

Jake glanced down at his father. Fred's lips were edged with a thin white line and his complexion held a faintly grayish tinge.

"You okay, Dad?" Jake asked, alarmed at how his father looked.

"Just a little out of breath."

"I'm going to take you to the hospital."

"No, Jake. Don't. The doctor told me this would happen once in a while. I want to get out of here. Fresh air is all I need."

"Okay," Jake said, taking his father's arm. But all the way to the car, he kept his eyes on the older man. It was hard not to look as if he was hovering. But by the time they reached the parking lot, Fred already looked a little better.

At the car, Jake helped his father inside. Then he got in himself. "You're sure you're okay?" Jake asked one more time.

"I'm just tired." Fred laid his head back and then rolled it sideways to face Jake. He smiled and took a slow, deep breath. "And how are you? Are you okay?"

"Yes." Jake frowned, wondering what his father was getting at.

"Doesn't bother you to see her again?"

"Her?"

"Miriam. You used to like her quite a bit, didn't you?"

Jake raised his eyebrows, surprised at how perceptive his father was. "Yes, Dad. I did."

"And now? She's still single, I gather."

"She's also come to sell her farm and then go back East."

Jake glanced at Fred again, trying to gauge his reaction.

"You going to put an offer in on it?"

"I don't know. I really don't know." Jake knew he wouldn't be able to bluff his father. Fred knew the precise financial situation of the farm.

"It would be a shame to lose it."

"But I would be doing it with your money. I'm not a risk-taker."

"The price of cereal crops will go up again," Fred reassured him. "You'll make your money on the land.

Sometimes you have to take risks, Jake…in various parts of your life."

Jake knew Fred alluded to more than just the farm, but decided to leave it be.

"You might want to consider it. Have something to maintain, to pass on."

"I don't have a son, Dad," Jake said with a smile.

"That's okay, Jake. Neither did your mother and I." Fred returned Jake's smile. "And look what happened to us. God brought us you."

Jake felt a surge of tender warmth at his father's comment. "And I'm so glad he did."

Fred only nodded and then laid his head back, closing his eyes again. Jake could tell he wanted to go home, and he got out of the car to find his mother and Taryn.

Just as he did, he saw them with Miriam, walking over to the graveyard.

Jake watched, realizing what they were up to. Tilly had Miriam's arm tucked in hers and was talking, her head bobbing. Taryn skipped ahead of them, her braids bouncing with each step, her arms held out straight from her sides.

They walked directly to Paula's grave, and Taryn bent over to trace her mother's name. Running back to Miriam, she caught her arm and pulled her along.

From his vantage point, Jake couldn't read Miriam's expression. He wondered what she was thinking. Miriam and Paula had been friends for years, yet Paula had never seemed to have the same devotion to Miriam that Miriam had held for Paula. Of course, thought Jake, Paula always took care of Paula first.

Miriam stopped in front of the stone and clasped her hands in front of her, her head bent.

Jake felt a stab of guilt at the sight. Taryn and Tilly occasionally went to Paula's grave. He never did. When Paula had died, his sorrow had been tempered by a guilty measure of relief. Paula had been difficult to live with. In the last years of their marriage, she had hardly been around. Even after Taryn was born, Paula had managed to find all kinds of reasons to be gone. It was on one of her many trips away that she was killed.

The little group stood still for a moment, and Jake was surprised to see Miriam reach up to palm her cheeks.

Taryn, never able to stay still too long, started running to other stones. Tilly and Miriam tarried a moment, moved on, then stopped again. Jake guessed they were looking at her father's grave.

Once again Miriam paused. Tilly put an arm around her shoulder, and for a moment Jake felt sorry for Miriam. He had stood beside the grave of a beloved foster father. He knew what it was like to lose a loved one. Miriam had no parents at all, now. Her father was buried here, and her mother out East.

At least he still had parents whom he loved. And somewhere on God's good earth, a biological mother whom his brother Simon was determined to find.

For a moment Jake wondered about his mother. Wondered if she was still alive, if she ever thought about them.

Then he dismissed the thought, feeling as if he were betraying Fred and Tilly. They were enough family for him.

Taryn saw him and came running over. "We saw my mommy's grave," she called out cheerfully. Tilly looked up and saw him, then said something to Miriam, who nodded and then left.

As Tilly walked across the parking lot, she waved at a few people, called out greetings to others. Then she saw that Jake and Fred were waiting, and hurried her pace.

"Sorry," she said, puffing as she opened the back door of the car for Taryn. "Miriam wanted to visit the graveyard."

"She was sad again," said Taryn, scrambling into the back seat.

"Seat belt," warned Jake as she settled in.

"That poor girl. I'm glad she agreed to come over now," Tilly said, cinching her own belt. "She can seem so strong, but inside she's hurting. She used to be so strong in her faith—I just pray she finds some peace here."

Jake started the car, his eyes on Miriam, who now walked back to her car, alone. For a moment he, too, prayed for her.

Chapter Six

"So you went to your aunt and uncle's place, and then what?" Tilly asked Miriam as they cleared the table of dishes. Jake and Taryn were playing a game on one corner of the large oak table. Fred was lying down in his bedroom.

Miriam watched Taryn for a moment, remembering the many times she had sat in the same place Taryn now did, playing a game with Fred or Tilly, and later on, Jake. The sun poured in through the same flowered curtains. On the wall above the table, ticked the same blue clock. The figurines in the window were the same as she remembered, and the sets of salt and pepper shakers still sat on the shelf that hung on one end of the wooden cupboard. It was home to her.

Miriam turned back to Tilly. "We only stayed there a couple of weeks. Then we found our own place. I finished high school and shortly after I turned eighteen I was scouted by a modeling agency."

"And what did your mother think of this?"

Miriam drew in a slow breath, reliving the roller-coaster events of her life at that time. "Mom had a debilitating stroke just before that. She was fully dependent. I knew I wouldn't be able to go to college or university. I needed to support the two of us. So I started modeling."

She declined to tell Tilly that she had also found out about Jake and Paula.

"Where did you go?"

Miriam shrugged. "The coast, California at first, then Europe," she said, deliberately ambiguous. She didn't want to admit that she couldn't remember a lot of those years. One place melded into another in her mind—planes, hotels; up early to catch good light, up late to catch the best party. Then doing it all over again the next day or week.

"My goodness, what a life for a young girl," Tilly said, gathering the rest of the pots and bringing them to the counter. "Well, I'm glad you're back here. We've missed you."

"Why did you miss her?" Taryn interrupted, looking up from her game.

"Because she was a good friend. She used to come over here all the time," Tilly replied, turning to her granddaughter.

Miriam fended off another attack of guilt. And Miriam didn't tell her mother much, either. She figured it would be better for her mother if she didn't know all the details of Miriam's life. The years she had spent traveling had left her rootless, living a life that had no adults in it to call her to account for what she had been doing. There was no voice of reason in her life, no guidance. Her mother could barely speak, let alone counsel her. She realized now how important even a quiet word of caution or chastisement would have been at that time in her life.

"What's the matter, dear? You look troubled." Tilly laid her hand on Miriam's arm.

She shook her head and curved her lips into a smile. "I'm fine."

"I win, Daddy. I win," Taryn crowed. She gathered up the pieces of the game, then leaned her elbows on the table and looked at Miriam. "You want to play with me, Miriam?"

Miriam smiled at her as she picked up the cups from the table. "I should help your grandmother with the dishes."

"Oh, nonsense. You go and play with her. It takes nothing to load up this dishwasher." Tilly took the cups from Miriam.

Jake was still sitting at the table, leaning back in his chair, watching her through lowered eyes.

"I'll be blue, you can be red," Taryn suggested, handing Miriam a playing piece. "You know how to play Snakes and Ladders?"

"I think so," Miriam said, smiling.

Taryn grinned back. "I can start, okay?"

"Fine by me." Miriam settled beside her, directly across from Jake. She chanced a glance up at him, lifting her chin as if to say, *What is your problem?* Throughout dinner she had felt as if he'd been watching, measuring. At first it had made her feel uncomfortable; now it was getting annoying. He tilted his head a bit, as if to see her from another angle, then dropped his chair with a *thunk* on the floor.

"I should go and check the cows," he said tersely to anyone who was listening.

"I have to shake the dice and then count," Taryn explained to Miriam, ignoring her father.

"Miriam, did you put that pot in the sink?" Tilly asked, looking up from the dishwasher.

Miriam felt a bit sorry for Jake. No one seemed to have heard what he said. She was about to ask him about the cows when Taryn poked her in the arm.

"Miriam, it's your turn."

"Taryn," Jake said, his tone hard. "Don't be rude."

Taryn looked down, immediately contrite. "Sorry, Daddy."

Jake looked around the kitchen, blew out a sigh and left.

Miriam watched him go, unable to keep her eyes off him. They hadn't spoken more than two words to each other since he had opened the meal with prayer. She had caught him looking at her, but had tried to act casually. It was difficult. She had thought their time spent in town might be a melting point. But she had been wrong. He sat across the table as disapprovingly as he had the first day she had come here.

She yearned to fix what hovered between them, even though, if she thought about it logically, it seemed pointless. She wouldn't be staying, and once she was gone she wouldn't be returning.

She turned back to the game and Taryn.

Twenty minutes later, with the dishwasher humming in the background, Tilly sitting at the table reading some material she had gotten from church, Miriam figured it was time she left.

"No. Stay a little longer," Taryn said. "We can play another game."

"We've already played four games," Miriam said with a smile, getting up from the table. She laid a finger on Taryn's nose and walked over to Tilly, dropping her hand on her shoulder. "Thanks for dinner. I really appreciate it."

"It was nice to have you." Tilly got up and pulled Miriam close. "It has been too long." She held Miriam by the shoulders, looking at her with her penetrating blue eyes. "You won't let that happen again, will you?"

Miriam bit her lip and shook her head. "No. I'm sorry." Apologies again, she thought. "Please give my regards to Uncle Fred for me."

"I will. I'll stop by sometime this week, when Fred's a little better. Are you going to be around?"

"For a while yet."

"Good. We'll have time to catch up." Smiling, Tilly walked with Miriam to the porch.

Miriam pulled her coat off the hanger and turned once more to Tilly, her heart softening at the sight of the older woman standing in the doorway the way she had so many times when Miriam had come over as a girl. "Thanks for having me over," she said quietly. "It meant a lot to me."

"I'm glad. You come again."

Taryn had followed them and now leaned against Tilly. Tilly absently stroked the little girl's head, and once again Miriam felt a clutch of envy. Taryn didn't know how fortunate she was, she thought—to be loved so unconditionally by so many people.

Miriam tossed them a quick wave and then, turning, left. She hurried down the sidewalk, wrapping her coat around her against the cool wind that had sprung up.

She pulled her car keys out of her purse and was about to press the remote starter when she heard her name being called.

Stopping, she lifted her head to see where the voice came from, then saw Jake come striding across the yard, his hands in the pockets of his denim jacket, collar pulled up against the chill.

Miriam watched him approach, allowed herself a moment to appreciate his height and the easy way he carried himself. Jake had always had a quiet maturity, a steadiness that had appealed to her own young, flighty nature. And once she got to know him, he had a surprising vulnerability. But the Jake Steele she'd known was but a boy compared to the man who now came toward her. This man was harder, more reserved. Each time their eyes met, it was as if he were appraising her. She never felt as if she quite measured up.

She wondered what he wanted to say to her now. Throughout the meal he had been quiet, watching her with those deep brown eyes that at one time had melted her heart, but now seemed as uncompromising as the Ten Commandments she had heard this morning.

"Out checking the cows?" she asked as he came closer. She was determined to treat him the same way she would treat any man she had just met—to be chatty and interested in what he was doing, but keep her emotions firmly intact. Ten years was long enough to move on, and it was time she did.

He stopped beside her, his shoulders hunched against the wind. "Yes. I'm moving them out to pasture tomorrow."

She was doing an admirable job of slipping back into her "country" persona. Next thing, she'd be asking him how many acres of canola he was going to plant and what kind of weed spray he was going to use.

She fiddled with her key chain, trying to think of something casual to say.

"Miriam."

Jake spoke her name quietly, almost in entreaty. Miriam couldn't stop looking up at him, couldn't stop her heart from pounding. To her shame, hearing him speak her name made her feel as breathless as a young girl in the throes of her first crush.

Which Jake had been.

He was standing quite close to her, his hands in the pockets of his coat, holding it open. Their eyes met, and Miriam forced herself to try to breathe normally at the connection. "Yes?" she asked.

"I, uh, was wondering if you…" He paused again, and Miriam felt a foolish lift of her heart. He sounded the way he had the first time he'd asked her out on a date.

Don't be utterly foolish, Miriam reminded herself. You are both older and wiser. He's a father, a widower. She forced herself to keep silent, to wait to see what he wanted.

Jake shoved his hand through his hair and held her gaze, his own steady, relentless. "I was wondering if you would mind waiting a while before you put your farm up for sale."

Funny how quickly a heart could plunge. How quickly breathless hope could be replaced with harsh reality. She slowly drew in a breath, then another. "I can't. I already went to the real estate agent on Friday and listed it."

Jake blinked, his expression unchanging. "I see."

Miriam wanted to tell him that if he wanted it, he could have it. But she couldn't give him anything. Not her heart, not her land. And she couldn't tell him how badly she needed the money to satisfy her creditors. It was too humiliating.

"How long did you say you were going to be here?" he continued.

"I was going to stay until next Monday. Then I have to leave."

He nodded again, biting his lower lip. He wanted to say something else to her, she sensed.

"I, uh, don't know how to say this," he began. "But I get a real feeling that Taryn is becoming quite attached to you."

Miriam shrugged the notion off. "I'm just someone different. That's all."

"I hope so. I don't want her to be hurt."

Miriam felt his words as much as heard them. "I understand exactly what you are getting at, Jake," she replied, her anger rising. "I can't imagine what you think I would do to her."

Jake looked down, digging the toe of his boot in the ground, then glanced back up at her. "Taryn forms attachments very quickly. I once made the mistake of taking a girlfriend home to meet her. When we split up, Taryn was more brokenhearted than either me or the girlfriend. I don't want to see that happen to her again."

"I'm hardly a girlfriend, Jake," she said, the words sounding harsh even to her.

"That's true. I'm sorry if you misunderstood me, but I have to take care of her."

Miriam unclenched her fists and forced herself to relax. "I realize that, Jake."

"Well, I better let you go then." He took a step back, turned and walked away, his head bent to the wind.

Miriam clutched her own coat closer to her, swallowing down resentment over her life situation and anger over Jake's. He was only doing what he had to. He was taking care of his family first. She couldn't blame him for that.

But it still hurt.

In Jake's life, Taryn was first.

She acknowledged the rightness of it even as she felt an alarming jealousy that this girl was now the most important person to Jake.

Even if there was a slight chance, even just a hint that Jake was interested in her, Miriam knew that she wasn't a suitable person to be Taryn's mother. Between her lifestyle and this one was a rift that couldn't be crossed. Her life was just a wasteland of broken dreams and promises. She really didn't have anything to give anyone. She wouldn't know how to be a mother, how to be a wife. The reality was that she was broke, out of work. She had a debt load that overwhelmed and frightened her anytime she thought about it. Even with the work Carl promised, it would take a long time to repay.

She was no longer an asset to a man, to someone like Jake. She would be more of a liability. In many ways.

Miriam got into her car, put it into gear and backed out of the driveway, wondering how she was going to last her allotted time here.

On Monday afternoon, Miriam pulled into Fred and Tilly's driveway. From what she could see, the big tractor Jake used for field work was gone.

Safe, she figured. She needed some gas to fill up her lawn mower, and there was none at her place. She had spent most of the day sorting through the stuff she and her mother had packed up and moved to the basement. After her "talk" with Jake, she had been so upset that she had had to keep busy, to keep her hands and mind occupied.

After about seven trips to the community landfill, she had substantially reduced the number of boxes left over. What was left could be put up for sale, and most of these she had moved to the shop.

So now the outside needed to be cleaned up. The real estate agent had said she would be coming either today or tomorrow to take a picture, and Miriam figured she might as well make it look as good as possible.

Stepping out of the car, she looked around the yard. Beyond the huge barn, she could hear cows bellowing. She wondered if something was wrong.

Curious, she walked past the barn and to the corrals beyond. Climbing up on the fence, she saw the herd of cows hanging around the two huge metal feeders— they were empty.

Cows probably need to get fed, she thought, stepping down. She walked back to the house and knocked on the door. No answer. Puzzled, she pushed open the door and put her head in.

"Hello, anybody home?"

"I'm in the living room, Miriam," Tilly called out. Miriam stepped inside, kicked her shoes off and walked in.

Tilly was sitting on the recliner, reading. She looked up when Miriam came in. "Hello, dear. So good to see you again." She put the footrest down and got up. "Come in, sit down."

"I can't stay long. I was just wondering if I could get some gas. I need to mow that lawn."

"Oh, I'm sure you can. Do you remember which tank is diesel and which one is regular?" Tilly asked with a frown. "I know I don't."

"I can probably figure it out." Miriam glanced around. "Where are Fred and Taryn?"

"Taryn is at play school, and Fred is sleeping. He

took a bad spell right after Jake left. Do you want something to drink?"

"No. I should get back to the house. It looks like there's a rain shower coming, and I want to get the lawn mowed before that. I'll probably stop by tomorrow."

"You do that, dear."

"What's wrong with the cows? They're sure making a lot of noise. Are they hungry?"

Tilly's hand flew to her mouth. "Oh, no. Fred was supposed to feed the cows this morning. Jake told him not to, that they could wait, but Fred was insistent. Now he won't be able to." She shook her head. "I guess they'll have to wait until Jake comes home. And he'll be so tired."

Miriam hesitated. It was none of her business what happened to Jake's cows. Yet, she could see how genuinely distressed Tilly was.

Tilly got up and put her book down. "I'll just have to feed them myself. I'll have to phone the school to tell them I'll be late picking up Taryn."

Miriam had to smile at the thought of Tilly sitting in a tractor, wearing her ever-present skirt and blouse.

"Don't be silly," she said suddenly. "I remember helping Jake feed the cows. I can do it."

"No, dear. You don't have to do that. You're here for a holiday."

"Feeding the cows is hardly a huge chore," Miriam said with a laugh. "It will be a nice break for me."

"Are you sure?"

Miriam could see obvious relief on Tilly's face, and nodded. "Think of it as payment for the gas I have to borrow."

"Hardly seems fair. But as long as you don't mind. It

will work out really well for me. I have to pick up Taryn in half an hour, and I know Fred can't do it. Not now."

"Then that settles it. We don't want her waiting for you." Miriam patted Tilly on the shoulder. "You just sit down and take it easy. I'll get those cows fed."

An hour later, Miriam jumped out of the gate and closed it behind her. The tractor with the bale forks had no cab, and she was still picking hay out of her hair and wiping dust out of her eyes. She figured she looked a fright, but didn't care. It was fun driving the tractor, dumping the huge round bales into the feeder and try-ing to avoid running over cows or calves. After deposit-ing the last bale, she had backed up and simply sat and watched the calves racing around, their tails up in the air, then stopping suddenly and coming back to check out who this strange person was.

She still had to smile, thinking of how clean and fresh they looked compared to the cows. She had for-gotten how cute they could be and how much fun they were to watch. For a moment she was the Miriam of old, helping Jake with his chores, hoping her mother wouldn't find out.

She walked back to the tractor and climbed on, put it in gear and then drove it to where it had originally been parked. She had to stand up to turn the wheel; the steering was tight and the front-end loader made it that much more difficult to maneuver.

But she'd done it, she thought proudly as she shut off the roaring engine.

She blinked some more and then climbed off. Before she'd fed the cows, she had filled her jerrican with gas, and Tilly had now left to pick up Taryn. Miriam could leave right away.

With a smile, she turned—and almost ran smack into Jake.

Miriam swallowed and took a step back. "Hello," she said quietly, wiping her hands on her pants. "I fed your cows for you."

"I see that," he replied, not moving. "Thanks."

"I came to get gas for my lawn mower, so I figured I would do it. Tilly seemed quite worried about them."

"I was just coming home to do it."

He sounded defensive, and Miriam felt that once again she had done the wrong thing.

"Whatever," she said, dismissing his comment. She went to walk past him, and as she did, he caught her arm.

She turned to him and unconsciously pulled her arm back.

"Sorry," he said, dropping his hand. "I just wanted to say thanks. I really appreciate the help."

Miriam sensed a discord between them that came up with each encounter. She knew it had as much to do with their past as their present, but she didn't know how to work through it.

Or even if she wanted to. What would it accomplish?

"You're welcome," she said. Then she turned and left.

Back at home Miriam threw herself back into her work. She mowed the lawn, trimmed the hedge, pruned the apple trees; and when the shower she'd talked of came, she found other things to do.

The next morning, the sun was shining and birds trilled their songs, calling her out.

She had a few other things to do, and then planned to go over to Fred and Tilly's. It was beautiful weather, so she could probably avoid Jake. Most likely, he was out in the field.

She had spent most of last night and part of this morning sorting through things, deciding what she wanted to keep and what to throw out.

She managed to put aside about two boxes' worth of keepsakes and mementos for herself—the photo albums, a few old books and records, a set of baby booties her mother had saved.

Miriam turned her head to look out the living room window, smiling at the sight of the lawn. It was a neatly clipped sweep of green, broken by a single maple tree dominating the front yard. Tall aspen trees, holding a hint of spring green, surrounded and protected it. Beyond them a double row of spruce trees stood guard, sheltering the yard on all sides from wind.

Outside had always been Miriam's sanctuary. Outside was where she went to get away from her mother and her constant demands.

Miriam pushed herself off the couch and got up. She needed to get away from the house...and the memories.

She found her jacket, zipped it up and stepped outside with the same sense of freedom she had felt as a young girl whenever she managed to get away.

Inhaling the warm scent of spring, she started walking briskly down the driveway. She didn't have any destination in mind, just a desire to get away from the cobwebs, the dust and the past.

The driveway was shielded by double rows of trees, and by the time Miriam saw the road, she felt better. As she walked down the familiar route, she felt the peace that had seemed to elude her in the house float down over her weary soul.

The land was open here, rolling and friendly. She let her eyes drift over the fields, the trees. Memories of her life in New York became overlaid with the combed-looking fields that had already been cultivated, the pastures that were already green. The soft, spring wind sifted through the trees alongside the road, and from the power line above came the sweet song of a sparrow.

Spring in the country.

Miriam felt a gentle stirring of her heart as the atmosphere surrounded her, drawing out happy memories, moments of utter abandon and freedom.

How often had she and her friends sat, hunkered over the ditches, floating sticks and leaves in the spring runoff? How often had they taken her horse and, doubling up, ridden off in whichever direction the day took them?

Paula's face came to her mind, and Miriam bit back a sudden cry. Paula, her good friend. Paula, who had listened to Miriam's adolescent complaints about her looks. Paula, who had been her confidante when Miriam had discovered her growing love for Jake Steele, the boy so many girls liked. Paula, who had ended up with the prize, after all.

Now Paula was dead. Sorrow tightened her throat, pressed on her heart.

Miriam couldn't stop the tears drifting down her cheeks, cooled by the spring breeze. She couldn't help but remember the sight of Taryn pointing out her own mother's gravestone. Seeing Paula's name etched in the granite slab had made her death so definite, so real.

She wondered if Paula and Jake had been happy for those few years they had been together. She wondered if Jake mourned her very much.

Once again Miriam felt jealousy.

Shaking her head, she tried to pull herself away from these maudlin thoughts. "Just enjoy the day," she said aloud. "Just enjoy the day."

A thicket of spruce and aspen trees beckoned, and as she walked through the moldering undergrowth, the spicy scent of freshly opened aspen leaves teased her nose. Willow branches caught at her, but she finally found the game trail that led her deeper into the bush.

And there it was, high up in the boughs of a large pine tree—the remnants of her old tree house. A few boards speckled with lichen and moss hung from a couple of nails, and the platform was still in place. On the tree beside her were nailed the single boards that provided a shaky ladder to her old retreat.

She smiled, remembering how many fantasies had been spun here. When she was older, she and Paula had come here…until Paula declared herself "too big" for games like this.

Then when she and Jake started dating, this fort had become a haven for them. Here they could sit and talk of the future, make plans, dream.

Miriam smiled lightly, then turned away. It seemed memories of her past romance with Jake would come to her no matter what she did or where she went.

She walked back the way she had come and returned to the road. Once there, she set out for nowhere in particular. She just wanted to walk and to enjoy the fact that today she had no other obligations, no concerns.

As she walked, she looked around, seeing the spread of the land, the various hues of green that told her summer was almost here. Soon the cows would be out on pasture.

"'And all the trees of the field will clap their

hands…'" The quote came to her lips as she paused, looking out over the land. She couldn't even remember where that was found—only that it came from the Bible.

She stood, looking out and smiling, and for the first time since she had come, felt peace. A soft breeze swirled around her like a benediction, rustling through the leaves of the trees above as if they were indeed clapping their hands.

There was joy in the air, and Miriam pulled it to herself and let it flow through her.

She tried to memorize each line of trees, each glade, the flow of the fields, the pastures, the farmyards she could see and the barns and grain bins that filled them. This was where she had come from. She wanted to remember this moment, this very place. In future, when she was stuck in the oppressive heat of summer in New York, when she sweltered outside or shivered in air-conditioned cool inside, she would return to this place in her mind, and know that somewhere life flowed instead of jerking and jumping around.

Miriam hadn't prayed in years, but now the words came to her lips unbidden. "Thank you, Lord," she whispered. "Thanks for this moment, for this part of the world."

She waited a moment as if to acknowledge a certain holiness to the moment.

Then she began walking again.

She had walked for about fifteen minutes when she heard a car coming up behind her. She moved to the side of the road, hoping it would slow down. The road was still wet in spots, and she stood a good chance of getting splashed.

The car slowed, all right, and then came to a complete halt, the engine running. Miriam turned to see Tilly Prins rolling down the window of her midsize car, smiling at her. Fred was on the seat beside her, Taryn in the back.

"Hello, Miriam," she called out. "Out for a walk on this beautiful day?"

"Yes, I am." Miriam couldn't hide her smile as she walked over. "How are you doing, Uncle Fred?" Yesterday he had looked a little better.

Fred opened his eyes and smiled wanly at her, and then closed them again. Tilly shook her head, her lips pursed. "He's running a high fever, so I'm bringing him in to the doctor. Fred fell when he got out of bed this morning, he was feeling so weak," Tilly added, turning back to Miriam, her head tilted up to look at her, her blue eyes looking tired. "Jake was gone. Otherwise, I would have asked him to take Taryn."

Taryn leaned forward, a frown puckering her forehead. "I can't go to play school 'cause there's not play school today."

"That's too bad," Miriam said, giving her a gentle smile. Today Taryn wore blue jeans and a pink windbreaker. Her hair was pulled back in a ponytail high up on her head, tied up with a matching pink ribbon. She looked adorable.

Tilly paused, glancing sidelong at Taryn, then back up at Miriam, beckoning to her to come closer. Tilly lowered her voice. "I know you're on a holiday, but I was wondering if you would be willing to take Taryn for the day."

"Please," Taryn pleaded, her hands curled into fists pressed under her chin. "Please let me come to your place."

"It would really help me out a lot," Tilly said.

Miriam looked down at Tilly, noting the wrinkles around her face. Yes, Tilly had grown older while Miriam had been gone. She looked tired and careworn.

She bit her lip, remembering countless times she had sat in Tilly's kitchen, eating cookies and talking. Countless times she had complained to Tilly about her mother's unfair treatment. Hugs and kisses she had received from this dear woman who was as much of a mother to her as she had been to Jake. Helping her out now would be but a drop of kindness compared to the gallons of love Tilly had given her.

"Sure," Miriam said, unsure of what she was expected to do with a little girl all day. "I'll take her."

"Thank you so much," Tilly breathed, and as Miriam saw some of the strain leave Tilly's face, she knew she had done the right thing. She would just have to take her chances with Jake.

"Oh goody, goody." With quick movements, Taryn unclipped her seat belt and jumped out of the car.

"You behave, now," Tilly said with a warning frown. Of course Taryn nodded. She turned back to Miriam. "Thanks again, my dear. You've really helped me out a lot." Tilly smiled with relief, put the car in gear, then paused. "I don't know how long I'm going to be, but if I'm not home by suppertime, can I ask another favor of you?"

"Anything, Tilly," Miriam said with heartfelt sincerity.

"Jake is going to be working your fields sometime today, and I usually bring him supper so he can keep going. If I don't come back on time, I made a casserole for him. Can you see that he gets it?"

Miriam felt her heart slow at the thought of seeing the very man she hoped to avoid.

"I'll probably be home," Tilly said, acknowledging her hesitation. "But just in case."

"If you're not around, I'll see that he gets something to eat." Miriam shrugged fatalistically. *What would be would be.*

"Thanks again, Miriam." Tilly smiled at Taryn, then back at Miriam, and with a wave, drove away, dust billowing up behind her.

Miriam and Taryn stood on the road, waving back as the cloud receded farther and farther, until it disappeared around a curve.

Miriam felt Taryn slip her hand into hers. She couldn't stop her own from tightening around the smaller one as she looked down at Jake's daughter. For a moment she indulged in a dangerous "what if."

What if…she and Jake had stayed together? What if…this precious child had been hers and Jake's?

"Do you want to keep walking?" Taryn asked, grinning up at her, swinging her hand. "I like walking."

"Then let's keep going." Miriam gently eased her hand out of Taryn's. She felt uneasy pulling back from Taryn's obvious affection, but knew it was better if she didn't allow this young child to get too attached to her.

Just as Jake had warned.

Chapter Seven

"My daddy is workin' on the tractor today and then he has to move the cows." Taryn hopped across a puddle and flashed a grin at Miriam. "He's gonna be busy, he told me. But when he's done, we're going to go to the city and buy me some pretty gloves. He promised me."

"You really love your daddy, don't you?" Miriam asked as she strolled along, hands in her pockets. She knew she shouldn't pry, but some part of her wanted to know more about Jake and his relationship with his daughter.

"I love my daddy the bestest. I love my mommy, too, but she died," Taryn stated in a matter-of-fact voice. "My friend Suzy Adams has two mommies and two daddies."

"That's a lot of mommies and daddies," Miriam said with a shake of her head, wondering how often poor Suzy Adams was shunted from place to place.

"I just want one mommy," Taryn said, as if this were the most reasonable request in the world.

Miriam instinctively knew she had to change the subject. "Do you want to make a waterwheel?" she asked, scanning the area for some cattails. She saw some on the other side of the road, their brown heads tilting slightly in the breeze.

"What's a waterwheel?"

"You make it out of two cattail stems." Grinning, Miriam walked over to the cattails and reached into her back pocket for a pocketknife.

"Oops," she said, laughing and looking sheepishly back at Taryn. "I don't have a pocketknife." Funny that she would do that, she thought. "I forgot I don't carry one anymore."

"That's okay. My daddy always has a pocketknife. It has a tweezer and a scissor. It's a red pocketknife and has J.S. on it. That means Jake Steele. He told me that. He got it as a present from someone special—not from my mommy, though." Taryn chattered on as she bent over to look at a rock, poking it with one finger.

Miriam's feet slowed, a spark kindling within her. After all these years, Jake still had the pocketknife she had given him, the one she had saved up her meager allowance for. She allowed herself a moment of wondering why.

Don't be silly, girl. Miriam pulled her thoughts up short. He's always been careful with the things he has, that's all.

"We should probably go back. It's quite some ways to walk yet," she said to Taryn, who now had three rocks clutched in her hands.

Though Miriam didn't encourage her, Taryn chattered while they walked, bringing Miriam up-to-date on what was happening in her life, her father's life and Tilly's and Fred's lives. It was a bittersweet pleasure to Miriam to hear about Jake—how much he was at home, how often he slept in the recliner in the evening, how he liked to read Taryn stories.

They had come to the top of the hill, just a few hundred feet from her driveway, when they heard the familiar growl of a tractor coming down the road. Her heart skipped. Tilly had said Jake was coming to work the fields by her house. It was probably him right now.

"My daddy," Taryn called out as soon as the tractor topped the hill. She grinned up at Miriam. "That's my daddy. Let's run and we can catch him."

Still clutching her rocks, Taryn took off, her ponytail bobbing with each step. She was heading straight for the lumbering tractor.

Miriam's heart jumped, and she sprinted after the little girl, catching her by the shoulder. "Don't, Taryn. What if he can't see you? He'll run right over you."

Taryn frowned up at Miriam. "Not my daddy. He sees everything."

As the tractor came closer, Miriam realized from Jake's glower that Taryn was right.

Jake slammed the throttle lever back, hit the clutch and braked. Why was Taryn with Miriam? And where was Tilly? He put the tractor in Park, took in a deep breath and climbed out of the cab.

"Daddy, Daddy, look at the rocks I found." Taryn came running up to him, waiting, as he had taught her, a safe distance away from the wheels of the huge tractor.

He walked closer, pointedly ignoring Miriam as he took a moment to squat down and look at the rocks in his daughter's dirty hands. "They are very nice," he said, turning one over in his hand, then handing it back to Taryn.

"And Miriam was going to make a waterwheel, but she didn't have her pocketknife." Taryn bestowed an innocent smile on him, clutching her rocks back to her chest. "I said you have one. Can we use it?"

"Sure you can," Jake said absently as he straightened, finally looking over at Miriam, who stood a distance away. A safe distance away, he thought, reaching automatically into the front pocket of his jeans to pull out his pocketknife. He walked over and handed it to her. "Taryn said you needed this?"

Miriam took it, avoiding his gaze. "We were going to make waterwheels just after Tilly met me on the road." Miriam looked down at the knife, then up at him. "Fred isn't feeling good, and Tilly had to bring him into town. She asked me to watch Taryn for her."

Jake heard Miriam's words, his heart tightening. Fred, sick again? It must be serious if Tilly was taking the time to bring him in, and Fred was letting her.

He closed his eyes briefly, sending up a quick prayer. *Please, Lord. Don't let it be serious.* He opened his eyes and caught Miriam looking at him with that same wistful expression he had seen before. He felt a sudden desire to touch her, to reassure her himself. He had to stop himself from pulling her into his arms.

"You still have this," she said quietly, holding up his pocketknife. She looked up at him again, the spring breeze lifting strands of her hair.

"Yeah. It was the first birthday present I had gotten in a few years." He shrugged, willing away the attraction he felt for her.

She smiled then, running her thumb over the worn red plastic. "I remember saving up to buy it for you."

Once again Jake suppressed the urge to touch her

hair, to curve his hand around her neck. To pull her close.

He took a step back, as if afraid he had already done so. "I better get back to work," he said abruptly. "Did Tilly say what time she would be back?"

"I'm not sure," Miriam said. "She asked if I could bring you supper if she didn't get back on time." She chanced another glance up at him, adding, "If you don't mind, that is."

Jake felt a nudge of sorrow at the uncertainty on her face. It made her look vulnerable. Not an emotion he would have associated with her at any time in her life. Not as a young girl, not as a woman. "No, that's okay." He waited as time seemed to drift away. Once again they were young and in love. Once again she smiled up at him, her eyes shining.

But he remembered the pictures in Paula's book: a girl made up and expensively dressed. He could pretend all he wanted, but this Miriam was far removed from him. He called a quick goodbye to his daughter and climbed back in the tractor.

Then he put the tractor in gear and turned into the field. Dropping the cultivator down, he adjusted the depth and half turned to look behind him.

Miriam and Taryn stood on the road, watching him.

His past and his present, side by side.

For a moment he wondered what his life would have been like had he and Miriam stayed together. Would that little girl have been theirs? Would they have had more?

"Don't be ridiculous, Jake," he said, switching on the radio. "She's in another realm now." And her leaving meant this land he now worked would be sold.

His day chugged along, punctuated by hourly news and weather reports. The songs melded one into the other, country songs usually, or classical music when he bothered to change the station. Jake worked his way up and down the quarter of land, each time on his return watching out for Miriam and his daughter. He caught sight of them once, walking down the road, heading out, he suspected, to make the waterwheel Taryn had spoken of. The sun gave off a sharp spring brightness, creating a feeling of expectation and promise, and he wished he could be with Taryn and Miriam, diking up the spring runoff, doing little family things.

He tried to concentrate on his work, but found his eyes straying to the two figures as they made their way down the road, looking for all the world like a mother and daughter.

The next time he came back to the road Miriam and Taryn were gone, and he felt as if the day had lost a measure of that brightness and expectation.

The sun moved inexorably across the sky. By five thirty, Jake once again began watching the road for Miriam. It was because he was hungry, he told himself. But when he thought of spending another mealtime with her, he felt a burst of pleasure.

"You're a strange man," he said aloud, turning the wheel of the tractor at the end of the field. "And a very stupid one." He got the tractor straightened around and lined up, then dropped the cultivator again. The roar of the tractor's engine was the only sound he heard as he worked his way down the field. He was up and over the rise when he saw a car parked on the road. His spirits lifted in spite of his previous castigation.

He could just make out Miriam's slim figure, her

hand up, shading her eyes against the lowering sun, watching him, waiting for him. It felt good to know she was there.

He parked the tractor and walked over. "Where's Taryn?" he asked as he approached.

"Playing in the ditch. We ate already. I've got your supper in the car," she said, walking over to it and opening the door. "I hope it's still warm." She pulled out a hamper.

Jake walked around the car, and when she straightened, he was there to take the hamper from her. Startled, she took a step back and almost lost her balance. Jake caught her by the shoulders, and her head came up. Once again their eyes held. Awareness arced between them. Jake didn't let go of her shoulders, and she didn't let go of the hamper.

Her eyes were the same deep brown that he remembered, fringed with silky lashes, tilted up at the corners exotically. She still had a tiny mole at one corner of her eye; her cheek still sported the barely discernible scar from the time she bumped it on his truck door. The same light freckles were sprinkled across her forehead, and her lips still held...still held... Jake couldn't keep his eyes off her mouth. The way she nervously wet her lips. The way she swallowed. The way they parted slightly as her breath quickened.

"Please, Jake," she said quietly.

Jake looked up into her eyes again, his fingers tightening, his thumbs caressing her arms through the thin material of her sweater. Then, with a deep breath, he dropped his hands. What was wrong with him? He was acting as if they were both still teenagers. Still in love.

"Sorry," he said, taking the hamper from her. There

was a moment of awkwardness as their hands meshed; she tried to let go and he tried to take hold.

"Look at what Miriam made me," Taryn trilled, skipping up to his side.

Jake put down the hamper, thankful for the diversion. "Wow. A willow whistle."

Taryn nodded. "Listen." She put it in her mouth and blew lightly. It gave a definite *tweet* and Taryn grinned her pleasure. "Miriam made it for me outa piece o' wood from the bush. She just cut it and made it. She said when the bark dries it won't work anymore. You try it now." Taryn handed it to him, and Jake dutifully blew on the willow whistle.

The spicy smell, the smooth texture of the bark and the faint bitter taste all took him back to other springs.

Other springs with Miriam. She was the only one he knew who could make these. He had asked her to teach him once, but she had played coy, telling him that it was one of her few talents and that she needed to keep some secrets.

He had never learned how to make them. He had one he had kept but as Taryn said once they got older they didn't work. He hadn't blown on one since then.

Miriam was setting up lawn chairs beside him, and he handed the whistle back to Taryn, who gave it another *tweet* and ran off back to the ditch for more treasures. Jake shifted to face Miriam.

"You still remember how to make those."

Miriam nodded. "I didn't think I'd remember, but once I started, it all came back. My dad taught me well."

Jake watched as she snapped open her chair and set it on the gravel. "I've never heard you talk about your father."

Miriam bent over the hamper again. "I don't really remember much about him. I was only ten when he died. But I do have a few good memories." She looked up at him, and ventured a half smile.

Jake felt it again—the awareness, the realization they had known each other in a different time and place, as different people.

They shared a past, memories and an intimacy that he had never really felt with anyone else, even Paula.

And for the first time since Miriam had come, he wondered if she had ever cared for anyone else. Had ever been close to another man.

He realized in the next moment that he didn't want to know.

Jake bent his head and slowly relaxed, letting his thoughts rest, settle and separate from the awareness of the girl sitting beside him.

Thank you for this day, Lord, he prayed, *for my daughter and my family. Please let Fred be okay.* He stopped, almost afraid to pray too hard for Fred, to acknowledge too deeply his own fears about Fred's health. It was as if he didn't quite trust God to take care of him. *Help me to let go, Lord. Help me to know that You love us perfectly. Help me not to build my life on my family.* He stopped again, thinking of Taryn, Tilly and even the girl sitting beside him. *I give them all to You, Lord. I give You each member of my family. Take care of them.* Then he asked for a final blessing on the food and lifted his head, a gentle peace surrounding him.

"I should tell you, Tilly phoned," Miriam said quietly.

Jake lowered his fork, almost afraid to hear what she had to say.

Miriam frowned lightly. "Fred is still running a high fever. If it doesn't go down, they're going to send him to Calgary for some more tests. He's a strong man, Jake," she said reassuringly. "I'm sure he'll be okay."

"I pray he will," Jake replied, toying with the rest of his casserole. He took a few more mouthfuls, then set it aside, his hunger gone.

"Tilly told me that Fred had a heart attack a while ago." Miriam's comment broke the silence. "I'm sure you're quite concerned about him now."

Jake leaned back in the chair, nodding. "I get afraid when I think about his health. Anything could happen." He looked out over the field, his legs stretched out in front of him.

"How old is Fred now?" Miriam asked.

"About sixty." Jake sighed lightly. "Which used to seem very old when I was younger."

"Parents aren't supposed to get old or sick."

Jake glanced sidelong at Miriam, who leaned forward on her chair, elbows on her knees, her chin resting on her hands. She was staring out over the field, but Jake suspected she was thinking of her own mother.

"I'm sorry about your mother." Jake shifted to face her, resisting the urge to touch her, to comfort her.

"It's been difficult…" Miriam stopped, her lower lip pulled between her teeth.

Jake didn't know what else to say so went back to his meal. He had never cared for Miriam's mother, but he knew that Edna had been a strong force in Miriam's life. Now Edna was dead, and what had happened was long ago.

There were questions he wanted to ask Miriam, things he wanted to know.

And what would that accomplish? he thought, turning away again. Do you want to find out how quickly she forgot you? Do you really want to know? His ego was as fragile as the next man's. Better let it sit. Once she left, and the farm was sold, he would probably never see her again.

He finished his meal and got up, setting the plates inside the hamper. "Thanks for supper."

Miriam nodded and got up, as well. She had been quiet, very unlike the Miriam he knew. Once again he wondered what had happened to her and whether he would find out while she was here.

Miriam closed the lid of the hamper and turned, just as Jake moved to pick it up. She stepped aside and watched as he put it in the car. He came back, and she turned to politely thank him, only to find him staring down at her, his expression unreadable.

"Have a good evening, Miriam," he said quietly.

His deep voice touched a memory. He towered, overpowering, his eyes delving deep into her, searching. He shifted his weight, coming closer to her. For a heart-stopping moment, Miriam thought he might kiss her, the way he would have ten years ago.

Then he stepped back, making way for her to pass. She felt an illogical twinge of disappointment, then walked past him to Taryn.

"I'll be home in about an hour," Jake said behind her. "If Tilly isn't there, do you mind waiting?"

"No," she said without turning. "I don't mind."

A beat of silence, then, "Thanks so much. For everything."

She chanced a look over her shoulder, but avoided his

eyes. "You're welcome," she returned, just loud enough for him to hear.

"Bye, Daddy. I'll see you later," Taryn called out.

By the time they got in the car, Jake was in the tractor. As they drove away, Taryn turned around to watch her father as they drove away from each other.

Tilly wasn't at the farmhouse by the time they got there, so Miriam ran the bathtub for Taryn and helped her get ready for bed, listening to the child chatter about the cows, the baby calves and how much she loved her daddy.

A few minutes later, Taryn was kneeling on her bed, pulling a scrapbook from under her pillow. "This is my mommy's book," Taryn said, eagerly holding it out to Miriam. "You want to look? There are pictures of you in it."

Miriam hesitated.

"Please look," Taryn said, pulling Miriam down onto the bed. She set the book on her lap and started turning the pages.

Miriam watched Taryn's small fingers quickly flip through until she found the place she wanted. Miriam wasn't eager to see what Paula might have put in the book, yet it held a strange fascination. Why did Paula want to know what her friend was up to? Why did she go to the bother of cutting out pictures of her husband's old girlfriend? Miriam wasn't naive enough to think that Paula kept them because of some sentimental attachment. The last phone conversation they had ever had was full of Paula's crowing over the victory she had achieved.

She had gotten Jake to take her to the prom.

"Here. They start here," Taryn said with a note of triumph.

Miriam looked down at a picture of herself on the arm of a well-known actor. She was leaning against him, clad in a shimmering sheath she had taken on a loan from a struggling designer.

Opposite it and on the next page were advertisements she had done. These were followed by more of her at a charity function escorted by a well-known fashion designer.

Miriam felt a moment of shame, thinking that Taryn, this sweet innocent child, had seen this part of her life. A part that Miriam wasn't proud of and had spent the last few years trying to live down.

"You had lots of boyfriends, too," Taryn piped up. "You still have lots of boyfriends?"

"Not friends," corrected Miriam sardonically. She closed the book and placed it on the side of the bed. "You don't need to keep this, do you?" She hated to think that Taryn had been exposed to a part of life that no girl of five should know about.

Taryn looked up at her, her expression hurt. "It was my mommy's."

Miriam felt instantly contrite. "Of course. That makes it special, doesn't it." Miriam sat on the bed beside Taryn, determined to prove herself worthy of this young child. "But you know what? Those pictures of me aren't who I am. And they aren't the kind of pictures a little girl like you should see. They are all pictures of big people doing silly things. Things you don't need to see."

"Is it a sin?" she asked, her eyes wide.

Miriam repressed the urge to laugh, yet realized she

had never considered her life in such a harsh glare before. Was it "sin"?

She wasn't sure that she was ready to categorize it so bleakly. It certainly was far removed from the life she had lived here in Waylen—that much she was willing to concede.

"It isn't a sin to look at those pictures," she said, neatly sidestepping Taryn's question. "But maybe we could take these ones of me out. Then it can be just a book about your mommy."

Taryn considered this a moment. "But I like you. And I want a picture of you."

"You know what?" Miriam said. "I have other pictures of me. I could send you some of those." She had enough comp cards—surely, she could find a recent one that made her look like a normal person instead of the party-hardy girl she used to be.

"Okay." Taryn smiled and snuggled down into her bed. "Now you have to say my prayers with me." She closed her eyes, her hands folded on her chest, and began singing.

The young voice breathlessly singing the familiar words of "Jesus Tender Shepherd" touched a chord deep in Miriam's heart. If she closed her eyes, she could remember the smell of fresh laundry, and her mother sitting beside her on the bed, singing the song that asked Jesus to stay with her through the darkness, thanking Him for His care during the day.

Miriam swallowed a lump of emotion, suddenly unable to sing along.

Taryn finished on her own and peeked up at Miriam. "You have to help me."

"I forgot the words," Miriam fibbed, sniffing lightly. "Now say the rest of your prayers."

Taryn closed her eyes and launched into a list of "please be with," and named Fred, Tilly, Jake, a few friends from play school, and then, to Miriam's surprise, Taryn asked God to be with Miriam, asked Him to make her happy and not so sad.

Miriam bit her lip, struggling against an unexpected wave of sorrow. To be prayed for, to have someone concerned about her—when had that last happened in her life?

Stop being so maudlin, she told herself.

Ah, the strong voice of reason. Miriam surreptitiously wiped her eyes, took a steadying breath and waited for Taryn to finish her petitions.

When the child was done, she grinned up at Miriam again. "I always pray for you."

"That's nice," Miriam said with a smile. "Now go to sleep."

"Are you going to kiss me good-night?"

Miriam saw a danger in that. As Jake had said, Taryn too easily became attached to people. In spite of Tilly's, Fred's and Jake's unwavering love, Miriam could see Taryn was hungry for the affection of a mother.

She knew this was her chance to let Taryn know her stay was temporary and to reinforce what Jake had asked of her. "You know what I'll do instead," she said, her heart aching at the poignancy of the moment. "I'll give you a kiss in your hand and you can use it whenever you want. Okay?" Miriam didn't wait; she lifted Taryn's small hand and carefully placed a kiss in it. Then she curled her fingers around it and laid it beside the child on the bed. "There. Now you have a kiss from me that you can use when I'm gone."

"Where are you going?"

"I don't live here. I'm only staying for a few more days. Then I have to go back to New York. That's where I live."

"But couldn't you stay? I want you to stay. I want you and my daddy…"

"Miriam doesn't live here, Pip."

Jake's deep voice from the doorway made Miriam jump. How much had he heard? She glanced up at him, unable to stop her reaction to his presence.

He stood, leaning in the doorway, his hands tucked in the pockets of his jeans, his shirtsleeves rolled up, his shirt open at the neck. The light from the hallway threw his face into silhouette. In that moment Miriam could see so clearly the difference between the young man she had loved and the man who now stood before her. His shoulders were broader, his chest deeper, even his relaxed stance showed her a level of confidence that only comes with age.

It also made him that much more appealing.

"She's only here for a little while, and then she's going back home." Jake pushed himself away from the doorway and walked over to the bed. Miriam jumped up and stepped aside. But the room wasn't very large, and they bumped into each other in the process. Jake caught Miriam by the shoulders, and their eyes met.

It was only a split second, barely measured in a heartbeat, but in that moment her awareness of him compounded. She almost stumbled but regained her balance, thankful for the subdued light in the bedroom. No one could see Miriam Spencer, onetime It Girl and cover model, blushing at the touch of a man who still smelled like the dirt he had been cultivating all day. A man whose chin was rough with whiskers.

A man who didn't really want her around.

Miriam said a quick good-night to Taryn, and then left. Once downstairs she couldn't decide whether she should leave right away, or stay. Politeness deemed that she at least say goodbye to Jake, but she didn't know if she wanted to face him.

She cleaned up the kitchen, glad to keep busy, and, before she was finished, Jake came down the stairs.

"She settled in now?"

Jake nodded and dropped wearily onto a chair, tunneling his hands through his hair. He looked tired. She was sure he was thinking of Fred.

Miriam felt a surge of protectiveness toward him, a desire to run her hands over his head, to tidy the unruly waves, to tell him that everything would be okay.

He looked up at her, his mouth curved into a wry smile. "I want to thank you for taking care of Taryn. I've had a lot on my mind."

Miriam clutched the towel closer, then walked over to the table and sat beside him, covered his hand with hers. She knew he was worried about Fred. She was, as well. "Fred is strong, Jake. I'm sure he'll be fine."

Jake took her hand between his, playing with it.

"I want to thank you for your help. I know I asked you to stay away from Taryn, but..." His voice trailed off.

She didn't want to feel a thrill at the warm touch of his hands, didn't want to look up into his eyes and feel lost again. But she did.

Her business debt seemed to hang over her head like

an imprecation. It was wise to remember that. Jake was a good father, a sincere Christian, and she knew that she wasn't the kind of person he would marry. Not anymore.

Somehow the thought hurt beyond description. She didn't want to feel unworthy. She had spent enough of her youth carrying that stigma. Her mother unwittingly reinforced every teasing comment from schoolmates by criticizing her clumsiness, her inability to meet her mother's exacting standards. Miriam had managed to ignore her fellow students and to laugh off their comments, but her mother's had buried deep into her psyche.

Until Jake.

He had been the first man she had ever loved. The first person who had considered her beautiful.

Jake continued to play with her hand, his touch sending shivers curling through her. "I don't imagine you've had much chance to be around kids, yet you certainly have a way with Taryn." He smiled carefully and tilted his head to one side, as if studying her. "What you did upstairs with her was a lesson in diplomacy and tact."

Miriam shrugged the comment away, even as it warmed her to the very fingertips Jake now held. Praise from Jake always did that to her. Silly that even now, it could move her more than any compliment from a photographer or her agent. "She's a sweet child and very intelligent. I do find I have to be careful with her."

"And you have been." He held her eyes with his, his mouth quirking up in a half smile. "Thanks again."

Miriam couldn't have looked away if she'd tried. She wanted to say something to lighten the atmosphere, to give herself some emotional edge.

Instead she leaned forward, giving in to the attraction that was building within her, hoping she could pull this off. "Thanks, yourself," she said quietly, pressing a light kiss to his forehead. But then she inhaled the earthy, farmer smell of him, her confidence wavering, her senses heightened by the contact.

Jake snaked a hand around her neck, capturing her. "Why did you do that?" he asked, his deep brown eyes delving into hers.

Miriam allowed herself a small dream, a tiny reaching toward the unattainable, and stroked his thick hair away from his face, the way she always used to do. "For old times' sake," she whispered, her voice catching.

Jake's eyes seemed to darken as tension built, almost tangibly. Then, slowly, he pulled her head down and touched his lips to hers. It was the barest of caresses, his breath warm on her mouth. Their knees were pressed against each other, preventing closer intimacy.

His warm, soft lips moved over hers, entreating, compelling. Miriam's hands went slack, then she reached up, threading her fingers through his thick hair, anchoring his head as her own mouth returned his caress.

What are you doing? The thought cut through the soft, intangible cocoon of ardor they had spun. Miriam didn't want to acknowledge it, didn't want to pull away. Jake's hand on her neck, his mouth on hers—these were so achingly familiar and so dear. His touch answered a longing that no one else had or ever would.

But…he wasn't for her. She dropped her hand and lowered her head, breaking the contact.

Miriam saw his hand clench into a fist on his knee, and she wanted to touch it, to smooth away the tension she saw there. But she had caused it, she was sure, and would not be able to offer a cure.

"Why, really, did you come back, Miriam?" he asked, his voice hoarse with repressed emotion.

Miriam felt her heart skip, wondered what she dared tell him and still keep her heart whole.

"Did you come here just to sell the farm?" Jake looked up at her. "You could have done that from out East. You say you came for a break, but I sense there's a lot of pain in your life. Was it a man?"

Miriam closed her eyes at how close he had struck with his comment, yet how far. She could tell him "yes," and she knew he would take it the wrong way. If she said "yes," he would assume she meant a man back East, and he would let go of her hand.

But their sitting here in this kitchen, his rough hand holding hers, brought back bittersweet memories. Memories of stolen kisses and whispered promises. Memories of a love that still haunted her.

And though what she had to say would make her vulnerable to him, she knew she had to finish this at this moment if she was to go back with any measure of peace.

"I guess I wanted to find out about you and Paula," she said quietly. "I had a foolish hope of reconciling with her and you. But I can't talk to her, so there's only you. I want to find out why you broke up with me. Why you married her."

Jake's head shot up and his hands tightened on hers.

As their eyes met, Miriam wondered if she had done the right thing.

Chapter Eight

Jake stared at her, trying to delve past her composed features, her shuttered gaze. "You were the one who wanted to run away," he said simply.

"Because you were talking about our giving each other space and time. And then when I was gone just a few months, I find out you loved Paula."

Jake straightened, realizing for the first time how it had looked from her side.

"Is that what you thought?" he asked.

"What else was I supposed to think?" Miriam's voice was heavy with sarcasm, and the mood in the room suddenly shifted.

"I left, and the next thing I knew you took her to the prom and married her," she continued. "What happened?"

"Why didn't you write me?" he countered.

"Are you kidding?" Miriam got up and shoved the chair back, and Jake saw a brief flash of the old Miriam. "You break up with me, and you expected *me* to write *you*?"

"I didn't break up with you, Miriam. I told you we needed to give each other some space, some time."

"So you could marry Paula."

He suddenly realized how the situation had looked to her, yet hesitated to explain.

"No," he said quietly.

"Then why?" Miriam's voice rose. "Why did you never write me. I was willing to wait. You promised you would love me forever. Why didn't you care—?" Her voice broke on that last word and her hands flew to her face, covering her shame, her pain.

Jake felt his own heart twist at the sound of her voice, the sight of her anguish. He was surprised at the strength of her emotions. Why should it matter after all this time?

He was unsure what to do. She stood, leaning against the kitchen counter, the muted sounds of her cries fastening on his soul like barbed hooks.

He got up, walked toward her and carefully, gently, took her in his arms. At first she resisted, her shoulders hunched, her hands still clutched over her face.

Then, slowly, as he continued to hold her, to stroke her back, the tension holding her in its thrall loosened, and she lay her head against his shoulder. Her slender arms slipped around him, and Jake let his eyes drift shut as she clung to him, his own arms tightening, holding her as close as he dared.

"I'm sorry, Miriam. I'm so sorry. What a mess this all turned out to be."

"Why did you want to break up with me?" she cried, her voice muffled against his shoulder. "Why did you marry Paula? Was she the one you loved?"

Jake didn't want to talk about Paula. Didn't want to

bring her between them again. For now he was content just to hold Miriam, to imagine for a moment that she was in his arms because she loved him and because this was the only place she truly wanted to be. He sighed lightly, tucking her head under his chin. And he knew he had to tell her the truth. "No, Miriam. There was another reason I married Paula."

"First tell me why you broke up with me." Miriam pulled away, looking discomfited at her outburst.

"I didn't want to. Your mother had told me that she had all these big plans for you and that I was getting in the way." Jake's chest lifted in a sigh; he carefully reached up and stroked her silky soft hair, inhaling the scent of it. *Just for now, Lord*, he prayed. *Just for now let me pretend she loves me. Just for now let me pretend that she cares for me and that she has come here because she wants to stay.* "I knew what I was, what I didn't have," he continued. "I was turning eighteen in the summer. When that happened, Fred and Tilly would no longer be responsible for me. What could I offer you? When you came up with that half-baked scheme about running away—I have to confess, for a moment, I thought of it, too." He trailed a finger behind her ear and down her neck, remembering other times, happier times, when she was in his arms. "But I also knew that running away never solved anything. It only got Simon in trouble. I knew I had to wait and see what was going to happen in my life. Your mother…" He stopped. Her mother was dead. Bringing her up was unfair and didn't solve anything.

"What about her?"

"Doesn't matter," Jake said quietly.

"Yes it does, Jake." She brushed the remnants of

the tears away from her face. "I know she had a lot to do with how my life ended up. When she was dying, I tried to ask her, but she couldn't tell me. You have to."

Jake drew in a deep breath and turned away from Miriam, his mind going back to that evening when he found out what Edna Spencer really thought of him. "She told me that I didn't deserve you, and she was right. However, she also warned me that if I continued seeing you, she would cause problems for me and social services. I was scared. I was afraid she would see to it that I was kicked out of Fred and Tilly's place, and I had no other place to go. I didn't want to talk to Fred and Tilly about it because I didn't trust them. But I also knew she was right. What she had planned for you was bigger than anything I could ever offer."

He shrugged, rubbing the back of his neck. "I thought the best thing for both of us was for me to let go of you and give you a chance at something else." He pulled his hand over his face and blew out his breath. "I thought that maybe someday, I could make something of myself and come and get you. Letting you go was one of the hardest things I ever had to do. Then you left, and I never heard anything more." He turned to face her, his eyes holding hers, his own questions demanding answers. "I guess the last thing I expected was that you would become a model."

"That happened after you married Paula. Please tell me why?" Jake heard the sorrow in her voice, and it echoed the pain in his heart.

He didn't know precisely how he was going to explain. "Paula was…aggressive."

He turned to face her. But Miriam was now pressed

back against the counter, her arms wrapped around her waist. Definitely defensive.

"You mean she came on to you, and you couldn't resist?"

"Not exactly that." Jake reached out to touch her, and Miriam flinched away. He had hoped that what he had said would ease some of the tension, but instead it increased it. "I'm not proud of those few moments in my life. I was missing you. You hadn't written. I didn't know where you were. I tried to phone and got your mother. I was lonely, and I didn't know what to do anymore. Fred and Tilly had told me they were going to send me to agricultural college and that they wanted me to stay with them after that. Fred wanted me to run the farm with him." He laughed, a bitter sound. "If he had told me that a month sooner, things would have been different for us." He carefully pulled her hand away from her waist, taking it in his own, needing to make a connection with her while he spoke. "If I had known I had a future here, security, I would have stood up to your mother."

"Why didn't you, anyway?"

"I was a foster child, and I had lived in enough foster homes to learn to keep things to myself. You don't ask about the future because no one can tell you. You have no legal rights, and your foster parents have no legal responsibilities. I had lived with Fred and Tilly for four years, yet I still hadn't learned to fully trust them." Jake stroked her fingers with his, his eyes on her hands.

"And Paula."

She was relentless. "Yes, Paula." He laughed shortly. "She asked me to the prom, and I said yes. I was lonely, and I missed you. Shortly after that we ended up at a party together. I thought you were living it up in the East, happy without me." He laughed shortly. "I thought this was the glorious future your mom had planned." He rubbed his neck, sighing. "At this party, I started drinking, and the next thing I knew I woke up in my truck. She was with me."

Miriam pulled her hand out of his, a soft cry escaping her lips.

"I know now that nothing happened," Jake said quickly, wanting to get past that part of the story and how it might look to her. "But at the time she had me convinced that we had been intimate. I had no other choice but to offer to marry her. I was young, scared and thinking I would lose my chance with Fred and Tilly. I didn't realize then that it wouldn't have, and that I'd always underestimated the power of their love for me. Always." He pulled in a deep breath. "Paula and I didn't have a great marriage. It was okay at first, but what she had done always hung between us. I tried, but I know I didn't try hard enough. She said she felt tied down by the farm. By Taryn. So she would leave. She always came back, and I would try again. It would be okay for a couple of weeks, then she'd get antsy and pretty soon she'd be gone. The last time she left I begged her to stop doing this. She got angry and stormed out the door. Two hours later the police were at the door."

"Oh, Jake. I'm so sorry."

"In spite of all of that, I have Taryn. I will always thank the Lord for her. The beauty that came out of the ashes."

Silence again. Miriam sighed lightly, her hand rubbing her forehead, back and forth, back and forth.

"What a mess," she said softly.

Jake silently agreed.

They stood in silence, Jake trying to mentally meld what he knew about Miriam's life with what he had once believed; he prayed she was doing the same.

And what was going to come of this heart-to-heart? Love might conquer all in songs, but for him and Miriam, it seemed, there was too much history to get past. He had wanted to clear the air between them, to lay old ghosts to rest. She had come to do the same.

But now, after talking with her, he wondered if they would ever have a chance.

Miriam pushed herself away from the counter and stopped a moment in front of Jake. She laid her hand on his shoulder and looked up at him.

Jake knew he should let her go, but he couldn't. He looked at Miriam, letting his eyes linger on her face, the features that were so much hers and yet older, harder.

He reached out to touch her, just once. That was all he meant to do. Then, as his hand lightly cupped her cheek, she caught his wrist, holding his hand against her. She sighed lightly, turning her head just enough to kiss the palm of his hand.

Her gesture pulled him toward her. And once again he curled his hand around her neck, once again he dared to pull her head nearer. She didn't resist, and it was his undoing. Their breaths mingled for only a moment, then he carefully touched his mouth to hers, the familiarity of it rocking him.

Then he slipped his arms around her, pulling her closer, holding her tighter, as his mouth moved against hers. She clung to him, returning his kiss, her fingers threading through his hair, capturing his head.

It wasn't enough—it was just a teasing hint of what

they had missed all those years apart. Jake kissed her again and again, his mouth on hers. Then he pulled away, ignoring Miriam's muted cry of protest, kissing her cheek, her forehead, her eyes, curving her head into his neck and holding her tightly against him.

"Oh, Miriam," he said. "I wanted to do this the first time I saw you on the road."

She said nothing, only clung to him, her movements almost desperate.

Then, suddenly, she pulled away, taking his arms and drawing them away from her. She touched his mouth with her fingers as if to capture the kiss he gave her, slowly traced the line of his lips, then, without saying another word, turned and walked out of the house.

Jake felt bereft as he watched her get in her car and drive away, dirt spinning, gravel flying out behind her. She fishtailed at the end of the driveway, then turned and drove away.

Jake took a long slow breath. *I don't know what just happened, Lord, but be with her*, he prayed quietly. *Hold her in Your hands, take care of her.* He drew in a deep breath. *Help me, as well.* He didn't know what he needed, but he knew that he had to swallow his own pride and go one step farther.

He had to talk with Miriam about the future—and that thought frightened him more than anything.

Miriam stepped on the accelerator as her car hurtled along. She drove without a destination, outrunning what lay behind her.

She felt as if her breath were still trapped in her chest, a heavy disquiet stirring deep within her. What she and Jake had shared in the past hour had completely switched and realigned her world.

All her perceptions, her ideas, had rearranged, and she had discovered one irrefutable fact.

She loved Jake Steele.

She slowed, wavering, her hand clenched to her heart. Oh, how she still loved him.

A deer, startled by her headlights, bolted in front of her. Miriam braked and swerved, narrowly missing it. She slammed on the brakes and rocked to a halt, dropping her head on the steering wheel.

She drew in a long, shuddering breath and slowly sat up. The quiet hum of the car and the glow of the dashboard lights created a safe place.

Just as it had been a haven to her as she drove to Waylen, this car was her escape now.

Miriam turned off the engine and the lights of her car. The moon was waning, a thin sliver of light in a sky scattered with crushed stars.

She stepped out and let her eyes adjust to the heavy darkness. The silence pressed in on her, broken only by the faint croaking of frogs in a marsh below her.

She was close to Rock Lake, she realized, slowly able to make out a few more landmarks. She crossed the road and scrambled through the ditch, still soggy from spring runoff. A fence blocked her way, but she climbed over it, disregarding the barbs on the wire.

Miriam walked slowly along the field, staying close to the edges, her eyes on the ground. By the time she got to the top of the hill her eyes had adjusted. The cool evening breeze was stronger here on the top of the hill, and she shivered, pulling her coat closer.

Below her yard lights winked, scattered across the

landscape, each representing a farmer's yard. There were more than when she used to come up here as a much younger girl.

Miriam pulled her coat down and slowly sat down, pulling her knees close to her, dropping her head back.

Above her hung infinite stars like crushed diamonds flung across velvet, layer upon layer going far beyond what her fragile and mortal eye could see. Her mind knew what each of those tiny pinpoints of light represented, their size, their distance a number she couldn't get her mind around. And this was only a small part of our galaxy. There were as many galaxies as there were stars. She closed her eyes a moment, growing dizzy as she tried to fathom the depth of the skies around her.

Opening her eyes again, she easily found the Big Dipper wheeling slowly around the North Star; from there the Little Dipper Ursa Minor, then to Vega, Deneb, the constellation Cassiopeia. Her favorite, Orion the hunter, was a winter constellation and no longer visible.

She remembered lying out on sleeping bags outside with a flashlight and a star book her father had bought her. When she was older, she used to impress Jake with her knowledge of the night sky. She used to wish she could be an astronaut and fly, fly away from here, away from her mother's petty restrictions, constant criticism and carping.

Miriam bit her lip, guilt stopping her memories. Her mother was dead. In the weeks before she died, Edna had tried to apologize, had tried to explain why she pushed Miriam so hard. Miriam still didn't understand, and seeing Jake—the man her mother had so feared and disliked, the man she had once loved, the man whose life her mother had threatened to destroy—made Miriam feel as if, once again, she had to forgive her mother.

Seventy-times-seven.

The formula came back from old readings of the Bible. "I've done this already," she said aloud, looking up at the sky as if speaking to God. "I've forgiven her again and again. Will it never be over? Will I never be finished with this anger, this feeling of unfinished business?"

She stopped as if waiting for an answer, her hands two tight balls of tension, her teeth pressed against each other. "I hated her so long—she took so much away," Miriam said, her voice quieter.

The silent stars wheeled slowly on, unconcerned, timeless, vast.

She was just a small speck in this cosmos, unimportant, unnecessary. She had made sacrifices for her mother, and in the process had lost the one thing she wanted.

Jake's love.

She loosened her fingers and caught her knees, resting her chin on them, as she studied the vaguely lit land below.

Closing her eyes, she resurrected the touch of Jake's lips on hers, his hand on her neck. A thrill shivered through her at the memory. It had been so easy, so familiar.

There had been no awkwardness. No hesitation. No words spoken, no promises made. Just a memory for her to hold on to…for the next ten years. The emptiness of the life that lay ahead of her became suddenly unbearable.

"What am I going to do?" she cried out. "Oh, Lord, You've got to help me."

Her cry had become a prayer and she repeated it. "Please help me. I have fought being unworthy all my life. I've struggled with feeling unwanted, feeling ugly, feeling like a failure, feeling alone. I can't do that again."

Each time she saw Jake pray, each time she saw him with his daughter and saw the absolute love he showed her, each time she saw his devotion to Tilly and Fred, it was a reminder of who he was. A man with a sincere faith, a devotion to family.

And here she was—a woman who lived a life of self-ishness, of vanity. After her mother's stroke, Miriam had visited her only rarely, using her busy schedule as an excuse. Then even these few visits had become more sporadic. She had wasted money, time and much of her earlier years thinking only of herself. Self-preservation, she had called it, and it was necessary in the cutthroat world of high fashion.

Or so she had told herself.

Her clothing business was to be her escape from that world, a chance to slow down and enjoy life, to be her own person. But even that was struggling, and all she had to show for ten years of work was a car—paid for—a year's lease on an apartment in New York—paid for—and a closet full of clothes. And thousands of dollars in bills that lay on her shoulders like the weight of the world. Bills for which she was personally responsible.

It was then that she had met Carl. Or actually, he had met her. He had heard she was looking for an agent, had found her and had convinced her to let him become her new agent. Miriam had resisted going back to modeling, going back to becoming a thing, an object—but Carl was different. Carl had spoken of a God who cared. A God who saw her as valuable and wonderful, just as she was.

Miriam had spoken to some of his other clients, had run a check on him and found out that he was not only legitimate, but well-liked and respected in the fashion industry.

So she signed on with him. He got a few jobs, and one evening, as she sat in his office, fighting tears of weariness, still grieving for her mother and lost chances of reconciliation, he had told her to go home. To catch her breath, to sell her farm, and then, when all that was done, to come back. He had a line on a big job that would help her get through this financial crisis she was in right now.

So she came. She drove because it was a way for her to relax, to see the countryside and realize that there were other things going on, other jobs getting done.

But now, after being here a few days, she felt worse off than before.

Falling in love with Jake was all wrong. She was in no position to make herself vulnerable to him again. She was in no position to give him anything. Once he had said he had nothing to give her. Now it was she who not only had nothing to give, but came with a large debt. She was all wrong for him.

What she had discovered tonight had completely changed the way she thought of him: he hadn't married Paula out of love, but because he'd been coerced.

Miriam clenched her fists in anger, pressing them against her forehead at the thought of her friend's duplicity, her mother's scheming and pressure. How could she and Jake ever hope to get past this? It seemed too big a barrier. How could God have allowed all this to happen?

She looked up, past the stars to where she figured God was, removed from the miseries of common people like her and Jake. *Please help me, Lord. I know I haven't talked to You a lot, but I don't know where else to turn.* She hadn't prayed for so long; she knew this wasn't precisely the way, but she didn't know how else to go about it. *Please help me. I don't know what to think, I don't know what to do.*

She reached out with her mind, stretching, pulling, striving, wondering if God heard or if He cared.

Chapter Nine

"I sure appreciate your taking time out to help me," Dane said to Jake. "For a while I thought I might have to feed the calves for another week or so until I found someone who could move them to pasture for me."

Jake glanced at his neighbor and shrugged. "No problem, Dane. Glad to help."

Dane Rogers was an older man who lived alone and had done so all his life. He was pushing seventy-five, yet he still farmed his own land, raised some calves and in general enjoyed his life.

"I heard Fred wasn't doing so good. How is he now?" Dane asked as they stood enjoying the sun, and the slight breeze that kept the bugs away.

Jake shook his head, watching the few stragglers pair up. "They kept him in the hospital overnight a few days back, just to keep an eye on him. He's home now, but still not great. We'll see what happens."

"Life sure keeps a man busy, don't it," Dane said. "I heard Miriam Spencer is back."

Jake gave the older man a sidelong glance. "You hear a lot for someone who doesn't get out much."

Dane grinned, hooking his thumbs in his wide suspenders. "The phone is a wonderful thing, but I sure miss the party line."

"I'm sure you do. Anything else you heard that you figure I need to know?"

"Well, I'm sure you know Miriam is still single." Dane elbowed him lightly, and Jake sighed. "She used to like you, didn't she? Surprises me that a girl that good-looking hasn't matched up with anyone. Makes you wonder, don't it?"

Actually, it hadn't made Jake wonder. Not until Dane mentioned it. He had assumed that Miriam had had boyfriends, that she had dated, but he had never wanted to speculate on why she was still single. He knew what Dane was hinting at, but since Miriam had come home, he hadn't dared let his speculation run that far.

"She's only here for a while. She wants to sell her farm and head back East to make more money." Jake couldn't keep the harshness from his voice. The other night, and the nights since, he had lain in bed, reliving every moment with Miriam, unable to come to a solution.

It seemed that too much hung between them, that the barriers were insurmountable. Yet he couldn't help but remember her response to him.

Her tears.

And the fact that she was still single, as Dane so thoughtfully pointed out. He had kept himself busy, had tried not to look too interested when Tilly talked of Miriam's visits.

"Oh, I'm sure you could talk her out of leaving. You're still a good-looking young man." Dane clapped a companionable hand on Jake's shoulder. "Give it a whirl. What have you got to lose?"

My pride, Jake thought. Yet even as that idea formed, he knew it was a small price to pay. Thinking about Miriam leaving gave him a hollow feeling that grew each day, each hour.

Jake shrugged as if to dispel the sensation. "I've got enough on my mind right now, Dane. I don't know if I have the will or energy to go courting."

"She lives just down the road. How much work could it be?" Dane chuckled. "Tell Tilly to have her over for supper. Take her for a ride in your tractor."

"And isn't that romantic," said Jake wryly, walking over to his truck.

"What I remember of you two, it used to be."

Jake smiled, remembering, too. "Right about now I've got to fix my tractor, get my crop in, check my own cows, and try to figure out how I'm going to replace the land she's selling. Seems like enough to keep me busy." He got into the truck and rolled down the window. "You let me know if you need anything else, okay?"

Dane leaned his arms on the window frame, shaking his head. "No time to court a pretty girl, but figures he has time to offer to help me. You got your priorities all mixed up, my boy."

Jake laughed lightly. "I've got to go, Dane. I'll follow you out and then shut the gate for you."

"I can do that myself, you young punk."

"Okay." Jake put the truck in gear and slowly pulled away. He swung the truck and the long fifth-wheel trailer around, then headed out the gate and down the road. He glanced in his side mirror and saw Dane pull out behind him and shut the gate.

Satisfied, he sped up. He had hoped to check his own cows this afternoon and then run back in to town for a part for his tractor. Maybe tomorrow he could get the Spencer field done. Then it would be Sunday again.

And shortly after that, Miriam was leaving.

He clutched the steering wheel, forcing himself to stay focused. They each had their own lives, he reminded himself. They each had their own responsibilities. She had been back barely a week. He must be crazy to think that just because mistakes of the past had been talked about, all was cleared away. Miriam had run away that night and stayed away. That told him, more clearly than anything she could have said, what he wanted.

She didn't fit, didn't belong.

Yet even as he thought that, he remembered how good she was with Taryn, how easily she seemed to fit in to the farm life. He remembered her feeding his cows. He still had to smile at the sight of her in her expensive clothes, manhandling that tractor around the yard; she was as tall as ever, and still had to stand up to steer.

He had felt guilty that day. Felt as if he had abrogated his responsibilities and she'd had to cover for him.

Yet it made him feel like the two of them, for a brief moment, had shared this part of his life. He felt like what he did was important to her.

Get a grip, Steele, you really are delusional, he thought, gearing down as his truck powered out on the hill.

Miriam got out of her car and looked around the yard. It looked much neater than when she had first arrived. The progress should have made her feel good, but it didn't.

This morning she had gone to Waylen to check with the real estate agent and go over some details. Then she had met up with Donna and a few old friends.

Sitting around in the café had been fun, and she hadn't laughed that hard and long in months. It had been cathartic, and Miriam regretted the moment when each of them had to return to their own responsibilities.

Miriam and Donna had lingered, and Donna had reminded her that they were going to meet again at the church picnic tomorrow. Miriam had reluctantly agreed to go. She didn't know if she wanted to sit through church again, but was eager to meet up with her old friends.

And Jake would be there. The pernicious thought clung to her subconscious, and all the way home she couldn't seem to dispel it. Since that evening when he had told her the truth about Paula, she couldn't face him, couldn't indulge in might-have-beens. The pain of regret cut too deeply.

She couldn't forget his kiss, his arms about her.

Physical attraction, that was all it was, her thoughts reminded her.

But she knew it was more. It was like coming home, like a safe place after fear.

You don't fit with him anymore, she thought. He's in a different place than you. Too much has happened that can't be changed.

Miriam tried to imagine herself with Jake again. Was it just nostalgia that made it feel so right? Would she be able to stay here, to be a wife, a mother?

It's a dream, she reminded herself. She had huge responsibilities waiting for her back East. The thought of staying here might be wonderful, but it was a luxury she had no space, no room to indulge in.

With a sigh, she walked into the house and looked around. As she dropped into her father's old recliner, her eye fell on a couple of boxes of books that she had set aside, unopened.

Miriam got up and pulled open the top of the first box. She supposed she could just have left them, but she hated the idea of unfinished jobs.

Some of the books were old storybooks of hers. She took them out, smiling at the pictures on the covers. They brought back pleasant memories of sitting on her father's lap while he read to her. Flipping through the pages she became once again that young girl who wanted to be anywhere else but where she was.

When her father died, it had gotten even worse.

Miriam quickly set the book aside and took out a few more.

In the next layer she found a Bible.

Sitting back on her heels, Miriam turned it over in her hand and then opened it. It was her parents' wedding Bible. Miriam smiled a soft, sad smile as she leafed through it. She had had such a convoluted relationship with her mother that she often wondered what kind of mother she herself would make.

She thought of Taryn's longing for a mother. For a brief moment, Miriam allowed herself to think of tucking in that dear child each night, while Jake stood in the doorway, or sat on the bed with her. Jake had said he loved her. Had never loved anyone but her.

With a soft cry, Miriam clutched the Bible to her chest, her head bent. Why had he said that to her? Why had he given her that shred of hope? She could do nothing with it.

She couldn't stay.

Miriam took a quick breath and got up. She wanted to get out of the house and away from its emptiness. This wasn't a home.

And neither is your eighteenth-floor condo, she thought, stepping outside. She had lived there for six years, often stopping only long enough to send her dirty clothes to the cleaners, sleep and then return to the airport for another flight to another destination.

Then the last two years, she had spent most of her time at her office, or running around looking for suppliers and markets for her new clothing company. When she was trying to find a way to keep her company solvent, she spent many evenings in her office as well, catching a few hours' sleep in her chair, or on the couch.

No, the condo wasn't home, either.

The only real home she had known was Fred and Tilly's. The truest love from a mother she had received was from Tilly.

Not from her own mother.

Her mother had cast a long shadow on her life, Miriam realized, settling down under the old maple tree. Her steady criticism, her constant griping about Jake, her threats to him…

Miriam's teeth clenched at the thought, and once again she wished her mother was alive so she could confront her with this.

And again Miriam struggled to forgive. Forgiveness was so difficult to grant when there was no physical person to talk to, to get angry with.

Just the memory of a broken woman who struggled to tell Miriam why she had done what she did.

Miriam laid her head against the rough bark of the tree, hearing once again her mother's halting words, reminding Miriam that even though her love as a mother was weak and impure, God's love wasn't.

But Miriam felt she had strayed so far from that love, it was no longer hers for the taking.

She flipped through the pages and found the silk ribbon at Ecclesiastes. "Generations come and generations go, but the earth remains forever," she read. Miriam looked around at the land, ready for planting. She thought of Jake working it, and knew he counted on the revenue from her own land. The land would remain forever, but it would go to different hands. She wished she could change that, wished she could give it to him. A gift.

But she needed the money. She had obligations. Debts to pay.

She wished she knew what to do and wished this Bible would show her.

But she hadn't read it in so long, she didn't even know if the promises in it were for her. Once, she could have looked at her life and said, yes, this was a life sanctified by Christ.

She could say that no longer.

The sun beat down on Jake's head as he clucked to Pinto. The horse flicked its ears, looked back, and then started walking back down the trail to the road. He slowed the horse down, reluctant to be drawn back into the rush and pressure that exemplified planting season. Fred had often told him that somehow it always got done. Seed time and harvest, the ebb and flow of the cycle, always happened. And the few times it didn't, it was often because of measures beyond their control.

Jake drew a deep breath and sent up a prayer of thanksgiving for this beautiful day. Then, he came to Miriam's driveway.

He pulled his horse to a stop, his hands resting on the pommel of the saddle, Dane's words ringing through his head. He was unable to dispel the memory of Miriam in his arms.

Courtship. He and Miriam had missed out on that when they started going out. They had had to keep their relationship a secret, and thus had never indulged in the fun stuff that came with dating.

Did he dare open himself up to her like that?

What would he gain and what would he lose?

Pinto shook her head, her bridle jangling, and snorted as Jake sifted through the reasons for and against.

It would be so much easier just to keep on going. But to what? He loved Taryn. He loved Fred and Tilly.

But he also knew that deep inside he yearned for a helpmeet. Someone who would be his partner in many senses of that word. Someone who would miss him and whom he would look forward to seeing at the end of the day. Someone who would sit with him on the couch and talk to him about her day. Listen to him talk about his.

All those roles were filled in one way or another by his daughter and his parents. Yet Tilly had Fred, and Taryn was slowly growing up and away from him. That was nature.

He was all alone in a family.

Yet, if he were to give in to the love he felt for Miriam, and she left anyway, how would he manage? He had been desolated when she left the first time. He was older and less flexible now. It would be harder this time.

Because whether he liked to admit it or not, his love this time around was deeper and stronger.

He closed his eyes, letting the memories of the other night drift around him, hold him, as Miriam's arms had held him. He knew that she cared. Something held her back, and the only way he would find out what, was to spend time with her.

Starting now, he thought, pulling Pinto's head around.

The horse trotted down the driveway. When they got to the maple tree, he stopped.

Miriam sat underneath it, a book open on her lap, her eyes shut.

Jake wondered if she was sleeping, but then he saw her shake her head. "Hey, there," he said quietly, hoping he wouldn't startle her.

Miriam looked up, her hand on her chest, her mouth and eyes wide-open. "Oh, my goodness. You scared the living daylights out of me," she said weakly.

Jake dismounted and tied Pinto to a nearby tree, walked across the lawn to her. Miriam stayed where she was, her hand still on her chest.

"I didn't even hear you coming," she said, avoiding his gaze.

"I thought at first you were sleeping."

"No. Just sitting and thinking." She moved to get up, but Jake stopped her with a hand on her shoulder. He sat down beside her, his legs crossed. He pointed to the book on her lap. "A little light reading?"

"It's the Bible. Hardly light," Miriam replied, her fingers fiddling with the pages.

Jake watched her hands' restless movement, the way

she looked as if she had pulled herself back and away from him. It was as if she didn't want him here.

He would have left, but the Bible on her lap kept him beside her.

Please, Lord, show me what to do. Give me the right words. I've never done this before. There's so much I want to tell her, but right now she needs to be shown Your love, as well.

He tried. "So what have you…" He hesitated, cleared his throat and tried again. "What have you been reading?"

"Nothing."

"What are you looking for?"

Miriam shook her head as she flicked through the pages. "I don't know," she whispered. "I used to read this more often. I remember at night, before I went to bed, I read a passage." She smiled a bittersweet smile and looked up at him. "I worked my way through the whole Bible that way. Even through all the laws and all those prophets. Now I realize they weren't just talking about Israelites. Those prophets were talking about me."

"What do you mean?"

Miriam shook her head. "Nothing. Sorry I brought it up." She made a move to get up, but Jake put a hand on her shoulder, stopping her.

"Miriam, you know I love you—"

"Don't, Jake," she said, holding out her hand to stop him. "Don't even bring that up—"

"I have to, Miriam. I don't have a lot of time with you, and you need to hear this."

"I want you to stop. You're making this too hard."

"What am I making too hard?" Jake let his hand linger on her shoulder, his fingers lightly caressing her neck. He didn't dare let go of her, but didn't dare make more than this light connection.

She drew in one shaky breath and then another. "I've fought this feeling of unworthiness many years. I don't like feeling this way, but I do. I do around you."

Jake heard her words, felt the pain pouring out of her. He didn't know what to say, or how to say it.

Gently he took the Bible from her lap and paged through it until he found what he was looking for. Romans.

"'There is no one righteous, not even one,'" he read. "'There is no one who understands, no one who seeks God. All have turned away, they have together become worthless; there is no one who does good, not even one.'"

"See what I mean?" Miriam said, pulling her knees up to her chest.

"That was written for me as well as you," Jake replied. "Let me keep going." As the soft spring wind caressed them, rustling through the leaves of the tree above, and as the sun filled the day with brightness and warmth, Jake read to her of the law, of judgment, then of Christ's intercession and love. Then he read, his own voice growing with conviction, "'For I am convinced, that neither death nor life, neither angels nor demons, neither the present nor the future, nor any powers, neither height nor depth, nor anything else in all creation will be able to separate us from the love of God that is in Christ Jesus our Lord.'"

Jake paused, letting the words diffuse through his own life, praying that Miriam would take them for herself.

"This isn't a battle you have to fight, Miriam. All

you have to do is take what is given. God is waiting for you to stop the struggle, to let Him give." He leaned forward, touching her again, praying that his weak words would be imbued with power from God. There was only so much he could do; accepting God's love, accepting his love, was up to her.

Miriam laid her head on her knees. "It sounds too easy."

Jake heard her words and fought his own disappointment. He was just a messenger, he knew that, but he had hoped that the words that had given him so much comfort would do the same for her. He loved her deeply, but he also knew that unless she accepted and believed the same thing he did, it would come to naught.

"It is easy. God made it easy for us because we can't come to Him any other way."

Miriam said nothing, gave no sign that she had heard.

Jake lay the Bible at her feet, pausing a moment as he watched her sitting at his feet. He bent over and lightly touched his lips to her exposed neck.

"I love you, Miriam," he whispered. "Always remember that. And always remember that God loves you more."

And then he left.

Chapter Ten

Miriam waited until she heard the soft footfalls of Jake's horse receding down the driveway.

Only then did she dare lift her head. Jake's words resounded in her mind. God's love. His love. The two seemed intertwined.

And she still felt as if she couldn't accept either one.

Miriam saw the Bible lying at her feet and reluctantly picked it up. She could still hear Jake reading from it, his voice resonating with conviction.

She had known God's love, had sung countless times the song "Jesus Loves Me"—one of the first songs learned by children being introduced to faith.

But it was too much for her to accept. She didn't feel worthy.

She got up, still holding the Bible, and glanced at her watch. My goodness, she had been sitting out here for a couple of hours. She wondered how long it had been since Jake had left.

Jake.

Miriam's heart plunged, then began to race at the

thought of him, at the memory of his lips touching her neck. The peace fled, replaced by confusion.

He had offered her his love. And she knew she couldn't take it. She had nothing to give him. Nothing.

She clutched her Bible closer. Then she went into the house. She wanted to talk to Tilly, but she had to make sure Jake wouldn't be there.

A quick phone call told her that Tilly was home. Jake was gone. Miriam jumped in her car and sped over. She could think of no one better to talk to than the woman who had been more than a mother to her.

Tilly was rolling out piecrusts on the kitchen counter when Miriam came into the house. Taryn was playing with scraps of leftover dough on the kitchen table— much as Miriam used to when she was younger. It looked so delightfully normal, and was a welcome contrast to the turmoil she had just felt.

"I made a duck," Taryn announced to Miriam, showing her a roll of dough. "And some snakes. They're easy."

Miriam stopped to admire the handiwork, unable to stop herself from stroking Taryn's head. She felt a connection with Jake when she spent time with his child.

Then she joined Tilly. "Need any help?"

Tilly smiled up at her. "You can get the filling ready. I'm making some lemon pies for the picnic tomorrow. Are you going to go?"

"Yes I am."

"I've got all the things ready for the filling. You can start making it for me, if you want." Tilly pointed with her chin as she formed the piecrusts.

Miriam pulled out a pot from one cupboard and a wooden spoon from the drawer. While Miriam worked,

Tilly slid the pie shells in the oven, set the timer and began cleaning up.

"My goodness, I feel like quite the domestic," Miriam said with a grin, as Tilly wiped the counter. The filling was just starting to boil, and she turned the heat off.

"You know," Tilly said, turning and leaning back against the counter, "it seems like just a short while ago the last time you were standing at that stove, helping me make pie."

"I certainly came over here a lot," Miriam said, carefully licking the warm filling off the spoon. She set the pan aside for the filling to cool.

"Can I lick the spoon?" Taryn asked, looking up from her ducks and worms.

"Oops." Miriam looked at the now-clean wooden spoon and then at Taryn's crestfallen face. She had started licking the spoon completely out of habit. Turning, she washed the spoon, stuck it in the filling again, and brought it over to Taryn. "Be careful, honey. It's still a bit warm."

"Thanks, Miriam." Taryn took the spoon from her, touched her finger to it and put it in her mouth. "I love lemon pie."

"So do I. It's still my favorite, and your grandma makes the best."

When the crusts were done, Miriam poured the filling into them, while Tilly whipped up the egg whites. Soon the counter held four tempting lemon pies.

Fred joined them then, still looking haggard.

"How are you feeling, Fred?" Miriam asked, concerned at his lack of color.

"Not great, my girl. Not great." He eased himself into

his usual chair and caught his breath. "Whew. I guess I won't be running any sack races at the church picnic tomorrow, hey, Pipper?" he asked Taryn.

"Oh, Grandpa, you're silly," Taryn said, lining up her dough ducks. She showed her grandfather what she had made, and he was suitably impressed.

Tilly had made tea, and soon they were sitting around the table, talking about all the wonderfully inconsequential things that make up a day.

Miriam felt herself relax in this comfortable home. It did that to her, she thought, taking a sip of her tea. Every time she came here, it was like coming home. She could pretend that Tilly was her mother, Fred her father.

And Taryn...

Miriam glanced sidelong at the little girl, who was busily playing with her dough animals. She resisted the urge to smooth the child's hair, to pull her close.

Jake's child.

Jake, who had told her he loved her. Told her that God loved her. And what was she supposed to do about that? What could she do? She had obligations, responsibilities.

Her debt on the business was adding up each month as the interest mounted. She needed the work Carl had lined up for her. It wouldn't get rid of all the debt, but it would be a good start. The sale of the farm would make the biggest difference. But it didn't look like that was going to happen real soon. So, she really needed the work Carl had found for her and more, which meant she needed to be thinking about going back to New York.

Not yet. Not yet, she thought.

When it was time for her to leave, it was time for her to think about all of that.

"What's the matter, Miriam?" Tilly asked. "You look troubled."

Miriam glanced up at Tilly, surprised at her perception. "I'm okay," she said evasively.

She forced her thoughts to the present. Forced herself to ask Taryn if she learned anything new in play school. Forced herself to ask Fred how the seeding was coming, hoping that maybe they would talk about Jake.

They didn't disappoint her.

She knew it was foolish to put herself through this, but she couldn't stop herself.

Eventually, the gentle chime of the grandfather clock in the living room reminded her of the time.

"Stay for supper, Miriam," Tilly said, frowning at her. "You don't have to leave right away."

But she did. Because if she stayed, she would see Jake, and right now her emotions were too fragile to deal with him.

So she got up and promised Taryn again that she would come to the picnic.

"Can you take me in your car?" Taryn asked as Miriam was putting her shoes on the porch. "I never had a ride in your car."

"Yes, you did," Miriam said, pulling on her jacket. "I gave you a ride when we brought supper to your dad."

"But can I have another ride? Please?"

Miriam was about to say no, but could really find no reason.

"Okay. I'll pick you up in the morning. You be ready, missy."

Taryn frowned. "Missy? I'm not missy. I'm Pipper. *You're* missy."

Miriam felt her throat catch at that. It was true. Fred

always called her Missy. It would be like Taryn to notice that.

"Okay, Pipper. I'll come tomorrow. On time."

"Okeydokey." Taryn flashed Miriam a grin, and Miriam couldn't help but smile back.

She stuck her head through the doorway to say goodbye to Fred—

He was lying back in his chair at the table, his eyes closed, his mouth slightly open.

"Are you okay, Fred?" Miriam asked, panic slicing through her.

"Yeah, I am. Just resting," he said, lifting his head. He gave her a smile, but it looked forced.

"You sure?"

"Yes. I'm fine."

Tilly came to the door and gave her a quick kiss. "You stop by tomorrow after the picnic, you hear?"

Miriam hesitated, unsure of what tomorrow would bring.

"You come now, Miriam."

"Okay. I will."

She could get through this. She could.

"Can my daddy have a ride in your car?" Taryn asked when Miriam came to the door on Sunday. She was sitting on a chair in the kitchen, trying to buckle up her shoes.

The thought of Jake sitting with her all the way to church was enough to make Miriam stop breathing. She tried to find a tactful way to forestall Taryn.

"I have to take my truck, Pipper," Jake said as he came into the kitchen. "I have to take some tables to the meadow."

Miriam looked up at him as he stopped by the kitchen table to take a quick sip from his coffee. His hair was still damp from his shower, shining in the lights from the ceiling. His cheeks were freshly shaven, and she caught the faint scent of his aftershave lotion. It made her stomach flip.

He caught her eye, lifted his mouth in a careful smile and walked toward her. She knew he was thinking of yesterday, of their time sitting together on her lawn, while he read to her.

She hadn't been able to get him, or the passages he read, out of her mind. Somehow, though, it all seemed too good to be true. She remembered what he had said about God making it easy to come to Him.

She wondered what she would learn in church today.

"Will I see you at the picnic, Miriam?" Jake asked, holding his mug, leaning one hip against the door to the porch.

She swallowed at his nearness and could only nod. "Yeah. I promised Taryn and Donna I would go."

"Lucky, Taryn," he said, and Miriam glanced up. She had intended to look away right away, but was unable to. Then Jake smiled again and turned to help his daughter.

"I'll see you at church, Pipper," he said, dropping a kiss on her head. "And I guess I'll see you, too," he said to Miriam.

Miriam nodded, caught Taryn's outstretched hand and walked out to her car.

Luckily for her, she didn't have to say anything on the way to church. Taryn supplied all the conversation.

They pulled up in front of the church. What a difference a week makes, she thought, slowly getting out

of the car. Last week she had come here defensive, unwilling and unready to be a part of this community.

During the week she had met up with old friends,
had reconnected with the community. Had spent time
with Fred and Tilly. Taryn.

Had found out the truth about Jake and Paula.

She glanced over her shoulder at the graveyard, wondering about Paula. Wondering how Paula had thought
she could build a marriage on a lie.

Miriam turned away from Paula and the past, and,
pulling her long skirt close to her, closed her car door.
Today was Sunday. A day of renewal and blessing. She
wasn't going to let the past and its mistakes overshadow
it.

Taryn bounced up the sidewalk, then, at the sound of
a truck engine, stopped. Miriam turned around.

Jake pulled up beside her car.

Miriam waited, feeling slightly foolish, as Taryn
went running back to her father, her cheeks flushed,
her ponytail bobbing. "You have to sit with me and
Miriam."

Jake smiled down at Taryn, then looked up at Miriam. He stood beside them, his expression enigmatic.
Then, as their eyes met, she saw his mouth lift in a
crooked smile.

And her heart did that funny little dance.

Taryn caught her hand and Jake's as they walked
toward the church.

It felt right, Miriam thought with a gentle ache. It
felt as if this was how it should be.

As they walked up the stairs, Miriam looked once
again at Jake and was unnerved by his direct gaze.

"I didn't have a chance to ask how you are doing,

Miriam," he said. His voice was quiet, but it carried a wealth of meaning. Miriam knew he alluded to yesterday, and was suddenly shy.

"I'm glad to be here," she said, looking away. Which was the truth. She was not entirely comfortable yet, but still glad to be a part of this.

Through the thin material of her shirt she felt the warm weight of his calloused hand resting on her shoulder. She swallowed at the contact, resisting the urge to lift her shoulder to hold his hand against her cheek.

"That's good," he said, squeezing ever so slightly.

"Daddy, why did you let go of my hand?" Taryn demanded.

Miriam felt her cheeks flush, and was surprised at her reaction. She hadn't felt this flustered around a man since—her heart lifted again—since she and Jake had first started dating.

"Where's Tilly and Fred?" Miriam asked, finally noticing their absence.

"Dad is really tired so Mom thought it would be better if she stayed home with him."

"I'm sorry," Miriam said, holding his gaze. She couldn't look away, couldn't break the contact.

"Miriam, good to see you." Donna breezed up beside her, and Jake drew away. Miriam tried not to feel disappointed, and turned to her friend.

Donna gave her a quick hug, smiling as she pulled away. "Hello, Jake," she said as her gaze flicked to Jake and then back to Miriam. To her credit, Donna's expression remained neutral, although when she looked back at Miriam she gave just a hint of a wink.

Donna smiled down at Taryn. "Bet your grandma made lemon pie again, didn't she."

Taryn nodded, beaming up at Donna. "We brought three. And Miriam helped make them."

"Three lemon pies? And Miriam helped make them?" Donna raised her eyebrows exaggeratedly. "My goodness. We are getting domestic, aren't we?"

Miriam laughed. The thump of many small footsteps coming up the steps behind them made Donna turn.

"Here comes my tribe, and there goes the peace. I'll talk to you later."

Miriam watched as Donna became surrounded by a noisy group of children. Donna licked her finger and smoothed down a cowlick on one, straightened the collar of another and picked up a little girl. Her husband joined her and took the girl from her. Then they all walked in to the church.

"Sort of makes you feel breathless, doesn't she?" Jake asked as they watched Donna's family walk down the aisle.

"She always had a lot of energy," Miriam said.

"I heard you had a girls' afternoon out with her."

Miriam glanced at him again. Again he was smiling.

"Yes. I had a nice afternoon catching up with old friends."

"I'm glad," he said, and Miriam wondered what he meant.

"Let's go," Taryn said, tugging on Miriam's hand.

They walked down the aisle of the church as a threesome. But this time Miriam felt less like a stranger and more like a part of things. One of her old friends glanced up as they passed and waggled her fingers at her. Another raised her eyebrows and winked.

Because the church was full, Jake ended up sitting directly beside Miriam, with Taryn on his lap.

Miriam tried to still the nervous thumping of her heart at his nearness. This was foolish, she rebuked herself. A person shouldn't be feeling this in church.

She pulled a Bible out of the pew and started to read it, trying to concentrate on the words. But Taryn kept chattering to her, and Miriam had to respond.

Then the minister came in, the worship service began, and Miriam felt as if all the loose pieces of her life were being shaken around.

She paid close attention to the songs, searching. It was as if she were on the edge of something important, earth-shattering—but she couldn't quite grasp it.

This was a good place to be, she thought, as she sang along with the hymns. She had missed so much by staying away from church all those years.

And yet, as the service progressed, she knew there should be more. This wasn't just a comfortable tradition that made people feel good. There was a sense of worship and awe, and Miriam knew she hadn't quite caught it yet. It gave her a sense of disappointment, and yet at the same time an eagerness to find out for herself what was missing.

It seemed as if the service was over too quickly.

She had managed not to concentrate too much on Jake. Taryn had fallen asleep on his shoulder, and he had held her. Once he had laid his arm along the back of the pew behind her. It had been hard to concentrate then, but she had managed.

The organ burst into the postlude, and with a gentle sigh Miriam turned.

Jake barred her way, still holding a sleeping Taryn. "Enjoy the service?"

"Yes. I did," she replied, returning his direct gaze.

He smiled and nodded, touching her arm lightly. "I'm so glad."

Then Taryn woke up, someone jostled Miriam from behind, and the moment was broken.

Somehow they got separated in the flow of people leaving the sanctuary. Miriam met up with Donna and a few of her old friends. They told her where the picnic was, and when Miriam got to her car, she noted with dismay that Jake was gone. She had been kind of hoping Taryn would want a ride to the picnic in her car.

She felt a sharp stab of disappointment, then shook it off. She had just experienced a wonderful Sunday, and she was going to enjoy the church picnic, something she hadn't attended since leaving Waylen.

And she was looking forward to being with Jake, because she also knew that once they were there, he would make sure they would spend some time together.

Her heart hitched. She didn't want to think further than this afternoon. It was a special time, a gift. The future was for another day.

"Where's Miriam, Daddy?" Taryn tugged on Jake's arm. "She has to eat her pie."

"I'm sure she's here somewhere." Jake frowned as he looked around. He had left right after church and had insisted Taryn come with him. She had pouted, but had given in.

"I wanna play with my friends," Taryn announced to Jake. He nodded, then looked around for someone to visit with.

He ended up in a group of men talking about the usual topics that take up a farmer's mind—the crops, the weather, the prices of their commodities. They stood around, a short distance from the tables being set with food, their stances identical—hands in their pockets, occasional comments punctuating the conversation.

Jake could hold his own in these situations. Once he had started farming, he knew it was the only thing he wanted to do. He loved the routine of the life, the ebb and flow of the seasons. It hadn't taken him long to establish his own position in the community. He often wished he had been able to go to school, to further his knowledge, but farmers were an independent lot, intensely involved in their own operations. There was always some seminar being offered at any given time, and Jake went to each one.

"Put any canola in this year, Jake?" one of the men asked him.

"No, Andrew. I seeded the Spencer quarter to it last year. I thought I would hold off this year."

"I heard the Spencer land is up for sale. Aren't you interested?"

Jake shrugged the comment away. "I'm stretched to the limit."

"Aw, c'mon. I know old Fred. He's got some stashed away, I'm sure." Andrew nudged Jake with an elbow, his eyebrows raised lightly as if to negate Jake's comment.

"I'm not taking any chances with money that isn't mine."

"Is it true Miriam's heading back East?" another asked him.

Jake loved this community, but privacy was a luxury not given its members.

"She has other obligations," he said casually.

"Too bad. Didn't the two of you have something going, once upon a time?"

Jake laughed lightly. "That was a long time ago, Andrew." For a relationship that was supposed to be a huge secret, a lot of people not only knew about it but also remembered it. Ten years later.

"Speaking of Miriam, there she is."

Jake tried not to turn too fast. Tried to keep his heart from jumping around like a frisky calf. He managed a semblance of nonchalance by waiting and then glancing over his shoulder.

She stood in the middle of a bunch of her old friends, talking animatedly. As she spoke, she gestured with her hands, graceful movements that emphasized her delicate bone structure. She wore a loose T-shirt and full skirt in vibrant earth colors that brought out highlights in her short brown hair, and set off the peach tone of her skin.

Her beauty made his chest tighten, and he wondered again how he could think she would even be interested in him.

An errant breeze lifted a strand of her hair and dropped it across her eyes. As she lifted her hand to brush it away, she looked up.

And straight at him.

Her gentle smile caught at him as a connection was made that excluded everyone else. There was no one around but the two of them. He saw no one but her.

We belong together, he thought, then remembered to breathe. The sound of laughter permeated the moment. Miriam's neighbor caught her arm. Andrew asked Jake another question, and the interval was swept away.

Jake felt his life shift, saw this possibility as attainable. Miriam here, with him. He knew that this moment was a hint of what could be.

He smiled as he thought of the rest of the afternoon.

Taryn would be busy. Her friends would find other people to talk to. He hoped sometime, somewhere, he could get Miriam alone.

A truck pulled up, and Jake was coerced into unloading a few more tables for more food. He caught scattered glimpses of Miriam as the tables were organized—warm dishes, still-steaming plates of soft buns, bowls of colorful salads, pans of dessert.

Then, at an unseen signal, families began gathering, parents bending over to put food on their children's plates. Small hands pointing, heads shaking their emphatic "no."

Jake looked for Taryn and then saw her. With Miriam.

He smiled, watching as Taryn made Miriam lift lids off casseroles. It wasn't difficult to tell which of the dishes met with her favor and which didn't. Miriam patiently worked her way along the table, and once glanced up at Jake. She smiled, then looked down again.

Jake waited until the families had served their children, and took his own place in the lineup. When his plate was full, he looked about for his daughter. She and Miriam had found a place under a tree and were already starting.

Jake sauntered over, nodding his greetings to people who called out to him, but not allowing himself to get waylaid.

"We prayed already, Daddy," Taryn said, looking up at him with cheeks already smeared with tomato sauce. "And I found s'getti."

"I see that." Jake pulled out his handkerchief and squatted down, trying to wipe her cheeks with one hand, balance his plate of food with the other.

"Here. I'll do that." Miriam took the handkerchief from him and wiped the worst of the sauce off, while Taryn tried to help by licking her cheeks. "There. That looks a little better."

She frowned at Taryn. "Are you feeling okay? You feel a bit warm."

Taryn shook her head. "I'm not sick."

"I didn't say you were sick, just warm. You looked flushed, too!"

"Nope, I'm good," Taryn insisted. "I have to run races."

"It is warm out," Jake said, balancing his warm plate on his lap. Then with a quick glance at Miriam, bent his head.

He thanked the Lord for the beautiful day, for having Miriam and Taryn with him. He prayed for his father and his mother. Then, almost hesitantly, he prayed that Miriam would be willing to stay. That they could rediscover what they had missed all those years ago.

With a soft sigh, he looked up. Miriam was toying with her fork, pushing around some pasta, a light frown on her face.

"What's the matter, Miriam?"

She looked up at him, her eyes wide, then shook her head. "Nothing," she replied. "Nothing at all."

Jake ate slowly, surprised to find his appetite had decreased. He managed to eat it all, but by the time he was done, Taryn was restless.

"I wanna go with my friends," she said, standing up. "I wanna go in the races."

"You didn't finish your spaghetti," Miriam said.

"I'm not hungry."

"Let's go, then," Miriam said, slowly getting up.

"We'll go together." Jake wiped his mouth, balled up the paper napkin and got up. They deposited their paper plates and plastic utensils in a garbage can and walked over to where young children were already gathering for the annual races.

Taryn pulled away from them, running over to be with her friends, leaving Jake and Miriam on the sidelines.

"I guess we'll have to cheer her on," Miriam said, glancing up at Jake with a grin.

"She expects it." Jake looked down at her, hoping he appeared nonchalant. She glanced up at him, then away, biting her lip. He wondered if she felt the same way he did.

Jake felt guilty, because much as he loved his daughter, right now he didn't want to stand beside Miriam and watch Taryn race. Right now he wanted to take Miriam to someplace private, pull her into his arms...

"You have to watch me, Daddy," Taryn called out.

Jake blinked, and shook his head to rein in his own drifting thoughts.

He looked at his daughter and couldn't help but grin. Taryn was bent over at the waist, her elbows up, fists balled at her sides, in an exaggerated runner's stance. Someone called out "Ready, set" and then "go," and Taryn was off, legs pumping, arms swinging, her face screwed up in a tight frown.

"Pretty intense, isn't she?" Miriam said, laughing.

"She stays focused."

Miriam nodded, crossing her arms over her stomach and shivering lightly.

"Cold?" Jake asked.

"No."

They were silent again, watching as Taryn came walking back to them, her head hanging.

"I didn't win, Daddy," she said with a pout. "I runned my fastest and I didn't win."

Jake crouched down and gave her a quick hug. "That's okay. I watched you run. You went real fast. You don't have to win for it to be fun."

But Taryn wasn't convinced by the platitudes. She stayed beside Jake and Miriam for the second race, complaining of a headache, but by the time they announced the sack race, she was game again.

This time she won. And this time she was all smiles. She came back with a red ribbon and a huge grin on her face.

"I wonned. I wonned." She waved the ribbon.

"Wow, that's a pretty ribbon." Donna had come up and was now crouched beside Taryn, admiring the ribbon. She glanced up at Jake with a knowing smile. "Do you mind if I take Taryn off your hands for a while? My kids are going to get their faces painted, and then we're going to do some old-fashioned apple bobbing."

Jake could have hugged her. "No. Not at all."

Donna winked at Miriam, then took Taryn's hand and walked away.

Jake felt as nervous as he had on his very first date with Miriam. He didn't quite know what to say, how to go about this whole dating thing.

"So, looks like she'll be busy for a while," he said inanely.

Miriam nodded, avoiding his gaze.

Jake tried to think of something else to say. Something that wouldn't sound fake, fatuous. Finally he decided the straightforward approach was the best.

"Let's go for a walk, Miriam. I want to talk to you."

Miriam glanced at him over her shoulder, her eyes wide. "Okay," she said.

Jake took her arm, and studiously avoided the glances of the people close by them. They walked up the hill, through the long grass, until they came to a quiet grove of trees. It was cooler in there, and Jake saw Miriam shiver again. He glanced over his shoulder, but they were still in plain sight, so they walked a little farther.

Finally, he couldn't stand it any longer. He caught her by the arm and turned her around.

"I think we're far enough now," he said quietly, pulling her into his arms as he leaned back against a convenient tree.

She came willingly, slipping her own arms around his waist, laying her head against his chest.

Jake sighed and pulled her close, resting his head on hers. He rubbed his cheek along its soft silkiness, over and over again.

"I love you, Miriam. You know that."

Her only reply was a careful nod.

"So now what?"

She didn't move, didn't reply, only held him more tightly.

Jake bent over and brushed his lips over her shoulder, then nudged her head aside with his chin. She looked up at him. Their faces were so close, he could feel her breath, could feel the warmth of her burning cheeks.

And then he kissed her.

It was like coming home after a hard day. It was like a drink of water after a long thirst.

They belonged together, and as he kissed her, it was

as if she had never left. That familiar touch, taste and feel. She felt right in his arms, as no other girl ever had.

Her lips were cool and soft, and as his mouth moved over hers, he reached up to stroke her cheek, run his fingers through her hair.

She murmured his name, her own hands caressing his shoulders.

Reluctantly he pulled away. With his forefinger he traced the exquisite line of her eyebrow, the softness of her cheek, her lips.

She closed her eyes as he touched her, her hands tightening on his waist.

"What are you doing to me, Jake?" she sighed.

"Trying to show you what you mean to me." He pulled her close again, content just to hold her. He knew she hadn't made any declaration to him, and wondered if she would. He didn't want to force anything out of her, but his own heart ached to hear something—some kind of confirmation of how she felt. He knew she felt something. She wouldn't have let him hold her, kiss her, if she didn't.

He just wished he knew what.

"Jake, tell me. Tell me in words."

He heard a yearning in her voice and wondered if she was even aware of it. "I love you more the longer you stay here." He touched her hair, his fingers playing with the soft waves. "I'm not that good with words. But when you're with me, I feel like all the things that were missing are here. I feel like holding you is what I was meant to do from the moment I was born. That this is part of my purpose in life."

She moved her face against his shirt, as if caressing him with her cheek. "Jake," she said softly. That was all. Just his name, but it held much more. She drew back, still holding him. She looked deep into his eyes; then her gaze traveled over his face, as if memorizing it. "You're the only man I ever loved. Ever."

Her words rocked through him, taking his breath away.

"I know it sounds silly," she continued, "but it's true. I had to tell you."

"Oh, Miriam. Do you know how long I've waited to hear you say those words?" He wanted to kiss her again, wanted to shout the news to the world. "Miriam, I think I've waited long enough. I have to ask you. Will you marry me?"

He felt a tremor in her arms as she clung to him. Her eyes opened wide and then slowly shut. She shook her head.

"Not that, Jake. Not that."

"What do you mean?" He felt as if all the breath had been pressed from him. He had just opened his heart to her, made himself as vulnerable as he had ever done with any woman, and now she sounded as if she hadn't wanted to hear it.

She caught him around his neck and pulled his head down to hers, kissing him hard. For a moment he let her. For a moment he pretended that she returned his feelings for her. But then, sensing her confusion, he carefully drew away.

"Miriam, what's wrong?"

She said nothing, only laid her head against his chest again. "Nothing."

He knew better, but also sensed that, for now, he didn't want to explore her reticence. She was in his arms. She had said nothing about his proposal. It still hung between them, and he didn't dare bring it up again. He felt a shiver of panic, wondering if she was still figuring on leaving tomorrow.

He didn't want to think about it. He remembered how willingly she had come into his arms. Remembered that she had told him she loved him, too.

She shivered, and Jake straightened. The moment was passed and nothing had happened. Disappointment crushed him, and he could say nothing to her as they walked back.

People were grouped together, visiting. Some were watching the little children getting their faces painted. Somehow, on their way back, Miriam drifted away from him, and Jake let her go.

He was confused and hurt and didn't know where to go from here. *Okay, Lord. I opened my heart to her, told her exactly what my intentions were. Help me to understand what is happening. Work in her heart. I know she needs to be here. I know she belongs here. Help her to see that.*

Jake wanted to leave right away, but Taryn was getting her face painted, and he knew it would look very rude if he suddenly left. So he hung around, made meaningless conversation, and all the while tried not to look out for Miriam.

Chapter Eleven

"There you are."

Miriam turned with a start to face her friend Donna.

"Taryn's not feeling well," Donna said, frowning. "She's been asking for you."

"Where's Jake?" Miriam didn't want to go. She didn't want to run the risk of seeing Jake so soon after turning down his proposal.

"I can't find him. I thought he'd be with you. Besides, it's you she wants. C'mon." Donna tugged on her arm and glancing around one more time, Miriam followed.

"But she was fine just half an hour ago." A lifetime ago, she thought.

"I wouldn't worry about it, Miriam. Goodness, you sound like a guilty mother." Donna nudged her in the side. "I know exactly what you were doing. You don't need to look so guilty."

Miriam couldn't stop the flush that warmed her cheeks. It was as if everyone here knew exactly what had happened for that short while that she and Jake had disappeared.

She felt her stomach tighten at the thought of his proposal. What was she supposed to do now? How could she go back to New York, how could she continue a life that she disliked, knowing that everything she wanted was here—but how could she stay and accept Jake's proposal? How could she make her financial problems his? She couldn't.

"What's the matter, Miriam? You look so sad."

Miriam was tempted to tell her. But she had spent too many years taking care of herself, and confession didn't come easily to her.

"I'm okay. I'm just worried about Taryn," she lied.

"Well, she's just over here, lying down." Donna brought Miriam to where Taryn lay, curled up on a blanket. She sat up when Miriam approached, and Miriam could see how flushed her cheeks were, past the bright flowers painted on them.

"What's the matter, Pipper?" Miriam asked, crouching down at the little girl's side.

"My head hurts again."

Miriam laid a hand on her forehead and was surprised to feel how hot it was. "But you seemed fine this morning," she said aloud. Then she remembered how the child had slept on Jake's lap in church. That wasn't normal for Taryn. That much Miriam knew.

"I'll go get Jake. He might want to take her home," Donna said, getting up.

Miriam sat down and drew Taryn onto her lap, cradling her warm body close. What had she done, leaving her like this, going off with Jake like some teenager? How could she be so irresponsible?

She's not my little girl, she thought. Miriam stroked Taryn's hair back from her face. It didn't matter. She shouldn't have left.

Taryn said nothing, just lay there, adding to Miriam's

guilt. Then Jake rushed to her side, falling down on one knee beside them. He also laid his hand on Taryn's forehead, and met Miriam's eyes.

"I feel terrible," Miriam said. "She just doesn't feel well."

"Let me take her. I think she'd better go home."

Taryn protested as Jake tried to take her away from Miriam's arms. "No. I want Miriam." The little girl clung to Miriam, and there was nothing she could do.

Jake helped Miriam up and tried once more, unsuccessfully, to make Taryn come to him.

"I'll bring her to your truck," Miriam said.

"I wanna go in your car. You said so." Taryn lifted her head, her expression downcast. "I wanna go in your car."

Miriam didn't know why Taryn was being so stubborn. A combination of not feeling well and just plain Taryn, she figured.

"I used my truck to bring the tables here," Jake said as they walked down to where they had parked the vehicles. "I imagine they'll need it to bring them back to the church."

"I'll get my husband to bring your truck to your place," Donna offered. "Why don't you just get Taryn home. We'll make sure your truck gets back."

Jake shot her a grateful smile and turned back to Miriam. "So we'll take your car, then, if that's okay?"

"Fine. Of course." She shifted Taryn so that the child was easier to hold.

They walked slowly down to the car, Jake beside Miriam, supporting her as they walked. She hadn't realized how heavy Taryn was. When they got to the car, Jake took the keys from her, unlocked her door and helped her in.

Then he got in on the driver's side, and they were off. They drove in silence.

Miriam couldn't look at him, but she was remembering his declaration of love. His proposal. She closed her eyes, laying her head on Taryn's, unable to think of the implications of what he had said to her.

By the time they got to Fred and Tilly's house, Taryn was asleep again, her body burning up with fever. This time, Jake took her from Miriam and carried her into the house. Miriam followed behind.

Tilly was sleeping in the recliner when they walked through the living room on their way upstairs. She sat up with a jolt when she saw them.

"What's the matter?" She got up, rubbing her eyes.

"Taryn's not feeling good," Jake said tersely as he strode up the stairs.

"She feels like she has a fever," Miriam added, waiting for Tilly to join her. Together they went upstairs.

Jake was stripping Taryn out of her clothes and putting her in her pajamas. "She's just burning up," Jake said, slipping the nightgown over her head.

"Let's take her temperature." Tilly walked to the bathroom and found a thermometer. She cleaned it, and shook it as she brought it back to the bedroom. Taryn was sitting up, her eyes looking glazed, her cheeks a vivid red.

"Here, honey, open up." Tilly put the thermometer in her mouth, and the three adults waited.

Miriam felt slightly out of place, standing here, but she didn't want to go. She felt partially responsible, even though common sense told her that Taryn had probably already been coming down with this bug last night.

Tilly took the thermometer out and tried to read it. She handed it to Jake, who read out, "One hundred and three."

"That's high," Miriam said, chewing her lip. "Shouldn't we give her something for that?"

"I have some children's medication we can give her," Tilly said, sighing lightly. "Jake, you go downstairs and get a spoon for me." When they left, Miriam sat down beside Taryn, who was fretting.

"My head is sore, Miriam. How come my head is sore?"

"You have a fever. That means there's something bad in your blood, and the good cells are fighting it. That's why you're hot."

Taryn nodded and curled up on the bed. "I'm tired."

"Your grandma is getting you something that will help take down the fever," Miriam said, stroking her hair away from her forehead. Just then Tilly came in the room with a bottle and a glass of water, and Jake came with a spoon. Miriam took the bottle and measured out the dosage according to the instructions on the bottle. "Here, open wide."

Taryn obeyed and then pulled a face. She grabbed for the glass of water and gulped it down. Then, with a sigh, she lay down again.

Miriam adjusted the blankets around her, as Jake pulled the blinds down over the window. Miriam stroked Taryn's cheek once, and then left.

Tilly brought the medicine back to the bathroom then followed Jake and Miriam down the stairs. Back in the living room, she dropped into her recliner. "Oh, Jake, Simon called. Said it was important. He'll call you again tonight."

"What did he want?"

"Didn't say."

"How's Dad?" Jake asked.

Tilly just shook her head. "Not good. I don't know what to do. I might have to take him to the doctor again, tomorrow."

"You look tired, Tilly."

"I am." She sighed and closed her eyes again.

Miriam sat down on the couch and couldn't help but glance at the clock. She was shocked to see that it was already five o'clock—almost suppertime. "What did you have for lunch, Tilly?"

"I didn't feel like making lunch."

Miriam glanced at Jake, then got up. "I'll get some supper together for you. I'm sure Fred should have something."

"He says he's not hungry."

Miriam heard the note of despair in her voice and walked to her side. She bent over and kissed Tilly lightly. "I'll see what he wants, and I'll take care of it. You just sit here."

Tilly smiled up at her and caught her hand. "Thanks, child. You are special."

Miriam doubted that, but the words warmed her heart, anyway.

Fred was awake when she peeked into his bedroom. He looked haggard and worn. When Miriam asked if he wanted anything, he said no.

"What about some soup?"

"I don't know."

"I'm going to take that as a yes. And Jake is going to make sure you eat it all," she warned before she left the room.

Back in the kitchen, Miriam wondered what she had gotten herself into. She wanted to leave, but how could she with Fred and Taryn sick? So Miriam found a recipe that she knew was Fred's favorite. It was also easy to make. Quick potato soup.

Luckily there were some leftover potatoes in the fridge, and soon Miriam had the ingredients together and was adding them one at a time to the pot on the stove.

She was just stirring the grated cheese into the soup when she saw Jake leaning on the counter beside her. She didn't want to look at him, but couldn't stop herself. How easy it was to lose herself in those eyes, to let herself drift toward him.

His hand on her arm stopped her, and she turned her attention back to the soup, stirring it as if everything important to her was in that pot.

Then he left her, and she breathed a sigh of relief. This wasn't turning out at all the way she had planned. She was supposed to be leaving tomorrow, and each encounter with Jake tested her resolve. She had no right to encourage him. But she was weak, lonely—and in love with a man she couldn't have. Shouldn't have.

Miriam swallowed, praying for strength. *This isn't fair, Lord. This just isn't fair. To give him back to me and make him so unattainable at the same time.*

Jake sat with Fred while he ate, and Tilly and Miriam sat in the kitchen. Taryn was sleeping, still fitfully. She would until the fever broke, Tilly informed Miriam.

Miriam knew absolutely nothing about childhood illnesses and was worried sick. She couldn't understand why neither Tilly nor Jake were sitting upstairs with her at this very minute.

The dishes were done, Tilly had gone to bed and the medication Taryn had taken was starting to kick in when Miriam decided to go. She tidied up the living room, delaying the inevitable, yet knowing she was playing a dangerous game. She wanted to see Jake again.

He came downstairs after checking on Taryn, and when he saw her in the living room he paused at the bottom of the stairs. "So, I guess you have to go?"

Miriam nodded, still clutching a newspaper she had found on the floor.

He shoved his hands through his hair and sighed. "I know this is going to sound terribly improper, but I have to leave early in the morning to finish seeding." He hesitated, biting his lip. "I was wondering if you would mind staying here tonight, just until Tilly gets up. I'm worried about Taryn..." He let the sentence trail off, and at that moment Miriam could see utter weariness in his eyes.

"I'll stay, Jake."

"Thanks." His eyes met hers and he slowly walked over. He was going to kiss her, she knew that.

He didn't even touch her—just bent over, his lips lightly caressing hers.

"I still love you, Miriam. I want to marry you."

She laid a finger on his lips to forestall him, her heart contracting with pain. "Please, Jake. Don't make this any harder for me than it already is."

"Don't make what harder?"

"Leaving."

She saw the stricken look on his face. She lowered her gaze as if to erase the memory, then felt his hands on her shoulders again.

"Jake." She couldn't stop herself. "I love you, I do. But I can't be what you want me to be." She felt her face twist with sorrow. "I can't be the kind of mother that Taryn needs. I thought I could, but when I saw Donna with her children I realized how little I knew. I don't fit here." She drew in a shaky breath, curled her fingers around each other. What she said was partly true. But she couldn't tell him about her debt.

"Where do you fit, Miriam?" He asked the question softly as he drew her in his arms. "If you don't fit here, why do you think you'll fit in a place that you don't want to go back to? I know you don't. I see the look on your face when you talk about your work."

Miriam bit her lip, resisting the urge to lay her head on his chest, to let him take all her problems and fix them. But it would be putting even more on his shoulders than he already carried. It wasn't fair to him, and if she truly loved him she would leave. She knew it was the only way.

Jake tightened his hold on her, caressed her head with his chin. "I won't stop loving you, Miriam. So where does that leave me?"

He took a step back, lifted her chin with his finger and laid a gentle kiss on her lips. "Think about that when you're heading back East."

Miriam swayed as he stepped back. She wrapped her arms about her waist, her chin down. She couldn't look at him. Couldn't tell him. She knew how important his family was, this farm. It was the first place he had told her that he felt he belonged. She couldn't jeopardize that. If they were to get married, her debt would become his. It was too much.

Silence again. A dark, intense silence that kept them apart.

"I'll set out some towels for you," Jake said, then turned and left.

Miriam watched him go back upstairs, his tall figure disappearing from view. He didn't look back.

Confusion tortured her thoughts. She knew she had to stay. She couldn't leave tomorrow. Not with Fred so sick, Taryn not feeling well and Tilly so exhausted. There was no way she could simply drive away and leave Jake to carry this.

But how could she stay? How could she see him every day, knowing she couldn't have him?

She dropped her head in her hands at the thought of being around Jake that long. So close and yet so far.

This isn't fair, Lord, she thought. *I can't do this to him. The only thing I can do is leave. He will think I hate him, when I'm doing it because I love him.*

She didn't know what to say, didn't know how to pray. She thought back to this morning, to the service, to yesterday and what Jake had told her.

It was too bewildering, and it was too early to go to bed. She dropped into the recliner and, glancing to the side, noticed the Bible. She needed comfort and guidance, and in these lonely hours of the night she didn't know where else to turn.

She opened it and turned to Romans, the same chapter Jake had read from. Slowly she reread the words, clinging to one love she knew she was allowed to claim.

She had lived a life close to God before. Would He take her back?

Nothing could separate her from God's love. The Bible said so. The same Bible that had brought good news to millions of people for hundreds of years. So many people before her believed it; many after her would, as well.

Miriam closed her eyes, her thoughts becoming prayers. Nothing, she thought. No present or future.

Her past, her mistakes, her mother's mistakes, the things she wished she could change—none of that would separate her from the love of God shown in Christ. He would take her no matter what she came with. His love encompassed her regardless of her debt.

She reread the words again and again, and slowly she felt power surge through her. This wasn't a battle she had to fight alone. She didn't have the strength. All she had to do was take what was given. The other night, on the hillside, she had struggled, had tried to find God, as Jake had suggested.

She had gone about it all wrong, she realized, tracing the words of the passage with her finger. God was waiting for her to stop the struggle, to let Him give.

Miriam clutched the Bible, her eyes closing as she opened her tightly held heart and gave it over to God. She felt a joy and peace flood her heart. Tears of cleansing thankfulness drifted past her closed eyelids and down her cheeks as she found herself quietly humming songs from her youth. Songs of praise.

She opened the Bible again randomly and started reading John. She stopped at John 16:24. "Until now you have not asked for anything in my name. Ask and you will receive and your joy will be complete."

I want to do something for Jake, she prayed. *That is all I ask. Something to show him I love him. Something he will remember. I know he loves me and I know that leaving will seem like betrayal, but I can't ask that of him. I can't.*

She read on, gaining strength and comfort. She knew she would need everything she could to get her through the next day—until she left.

"Thank you, Lord," she said quietly.

* * *

Everyone, except Jake, was still asleep by the time Miriam got up the next morning. She hadn't slept much. She was too aware of the fact that Jake lay only a room away from her. It made her edgy and nervous, and by the time she woke up again, she was sure she had gotten only a couple of hours' sleep. Jake's alarm woke her up. However, she waited until she heard the sound of the tractor leaving the yard before she rose.

She would have to wait until Tilly was up to run home for a fresh change of clothes.

She sat down in the recliner again and picked up the Bible. She read through some of the Psalms, again seeking and finding the comfort she had found last night. In the silence of the morning, she prayed again. Prayed for God's good and perfect will to make itself known to her.

Then, unable to sit any longer, she went upstairs and checked on Taryn. The child was still asleep, still feverish. But she didn't seem as warm as yesterday.

Miriam brushed the hair out of Taryn's face, lightly touching her cheek. Taryn sighed and turned onto her back, still sleeping.

Miriam felt a rush of tenderness for this young child, and wished she could stay, prayed she could stay. *I don't want lots of money, Lord. I don't need to be rich. If I could stay here, it would be all I'd want.*

Miriam mentally pulled herself back from these lives that she had to leave soon. Turning, she left the room.

She cleaned up what she could and then went back downstairs to set the table for breakfast and possibly make a pot of tea for Tilly.

The shrill ring of the phone broke the silence of the

house. Miriam almost ran to get it, snatched it off the hook. "Hello, Prins household," she said, breathless.

"This ain't Tilly, is it?"

"No."

"Don't tell me Jake got married without telling me?"

What a thing to say to a complete stranger! "I'm sorry. If you wish to speak to Jake, he's gone already," Miriam said, unable to keep the prim tone out of her voice.

"My goodness, you're a secretary. Since when does Jake need a secretary?" the man said with a laugh.

"May I ask who is calling?" Miriam asked.

"You may." Silence followed this comment, and then Miriam recognized the joke. And the voice.

"Hello, Simon," she said drily.

"Wow. An amazing secretary who recognizes voices of someone she has never met. Who are you?"

"Miriam Spencer."

A pause followed that, as she sensed Simon trying to place her. "Okay," he said triumphantly. "I remember. You're that old girlfriend. The high school fling."

Miriam knew she had been more to Jake than a fling, but disdained to comment on that.

"Did he get my message last night?"

"Yes. Tilly told him you called."

"Well, this is kinda sudden, but I'm leaving right away for the airport. I'll be there sometime this afternoon. Do you know if he's done seeding yet?"

Miriam was confused. "As far as I know, he should be done by today."

"Great. My timing is, as usual, impeccable. I know this is short notice, but I'm hoping to get there by about three. If Jake isn't home, then you and me can sit down, have tea, and you can remind me what a jerk I used to be."

"Okay." Miriam tried to keep her voice cool, remembering his unmerciful teasing whenever he would visit, and how Jake had always intervened, standing up for Miriam.

"Well, take care," Simon said, his voice breezy, before hanging up.

As she hung up she glanced at the clock, and, as if to force herself to stay on course, phoned Carl.

"So, you heading out today?" he asked.

"Well, something came up here. I'm probably leaving this afternoon."

"That's cutting it a bit close, but I guess you know your own limits. How are you feeling?"

In love. Confused. Scared. Forgiven. "I'm okay," she said.

"You don't sound okay."

"I'm fine. I've got to go. Talk to you later."

"Hey. Hang in there, girl. We'll untangle this financial business once you start working."

Not quick enough to make any difference here, she thought wryly. She knew she was looking at a minimum of four years of heavy payments, if she got other contracts as good as the one Carl had gotten for her. Otherwise it would be longer. "Yeah. It'll be fine."

Chapter Twelve

"Smells good in here."

Miriam turned from washing the dishes in the sink to see Tilly in the doorway, yawning. The woman had dark rings under her eyes; her skin was blotchy and puffy with fatigue. She drew her light blue bathrobe around her and blinked. Without her glasses, she looked especially vulnerable.

And old.

"Not a good night, Tilly?" Miriam asked, pulling out a chair for her. She had been busy in the kitchen, baking Fred's favorite muffins, hoping she could tempt his appetite.

"I felt like I didn't sleep, but I must have." She smiled her thanks as Miriam poured her a cup of tea from a carafe. It was still steaming.

Tilly caught the mug close to her, as if to absorb its warmth. "Jake said you have to leave today?"

"Later on. I'm driving back so I can make up the time along the way."

Tilly took a careful sip of her tea and sighed. "How's Taryn?"

"She's sleeping well now. Not restless. She's still a bit warm. I don't know if she's feverish."

"The fever must have broken, or she'd still be hot." Tilly looked around the kitchen. "Thanks for cleaning up. And for making supper last night. You're a treasure, you know."

Miriam felt a surge of warmth. She knew, but only because Tilly had been telling her that all her life. "Thanks, Tilly. I love you. I hope you know that."

"I do, dear. I do."

The thump of footsteps on the stairs made them both turn around.

Taryn. Already dressed in her blue jeans, and a big smile on her face when she saw Miriam in the kitchen. She walked around the table and sat down on the bench behind it. "I'm hungry," she announced.

Miriam glanced at Tilly, who was trying not to smile. Taryn was obviously better. Miriam felt as relieved as Tilly looked.

"How about a muffin and some juice?" Miriam asked, pulling a pitcher out of the fridge.

"Two muffins." Taryn held up two fingers, her brown eyes gleaming.

"We'll start with one, I think."

Once Taryn was done breakfast, Miriam went to see how Fred was doing. He lay, still and quiet, in his bed, and Miriam became concerned.

She came back out of the room. "I think we should take him to the hospital, Tilly," she said.

"I thought so." Tilly pulled her hand over her hair, smoothing it back with a weary gesture. "I'll go get dressed and then I can bring him."

"You're not taking him. You're way too tired. I'll bring him in."

Tilly shook her head. "No. They always ask so many questions, and you can't answer them. Besides, I don't think Taryn should go out just yet. She may look perky now, but she'll be droopy again in a couple of hours."

"Well, let me come with you, at least."

"Okay," Tilly agreed. "And thank you."

Miriam parked her car back in the driveway and glanced over at Taryn who, just as Tilly had predicted, was sleeping again.

She felt a twinge of guilt, but then realized she would have felt worse if she had let Tilly go in all by herself. Each had taken her own vehicle, but at least Miriam had been with Tilly for a while.

Now she was back at home, with nothing to do but wait for Jake.

Taryn yawned and stretched, smiling at Miriam. "I'm hungry," she announced.

"I can't get over your appetite, little girl," Miriam said, getting out of the car. She walked around and opened the door for Taryn, who already had her seat belt undone.

Once inside the house, she rummaged through the refrigerator and found some soup left over from yesterday. She heated it up, and Taryn ate it all.

"Now we need dessert."

"Not for lunch." Miriam cleared away the bowl and took it to the sink.

"Can we have a marshmallow roast? My daddy always has one with me."

Miriam knew that to be a bit of an exaggeration, but figured it was a perfect way to keep Taryn entertained for a while. She didn't know what else to do with the child, and it would probably be good for her to get outside.

Fifteen minutes later they were squatting in front of a low-burning fire, toasting marshmallows. Taryn's face was smeared with the remnants of her most recent marshmallow, and Miriam regretted not bringing out a wet facecloth for her.

"You look grubby," Miriam said, reaching across to carefully wipe off the worst of it with the cuff of her shirt.

Taryn tried to cooperate by licking her chin with her tongue and wiping her face with her hand, but only succeeded in making it worse. "I'm gonna need a bath," she said.

"Yes, you are." Miriam touched her nose lightly with her finger and smiled.

Taryn looked suddenly serious. "I heard Grandma say you're going away today. Why don't you want to stay?"

Miriam's heart sank at the sad look on the little girl's face and the plaintive note in her voice. She got up and, leading Taryn by the hand, walked over to the picnic table. They sat down together, and Miriam took a deep breath. "Remember the night I gave you a kiss on your hand?"

Taryn opened one sticky fist and looked down at it, nodding slowly, her ponytail bobbing.

"Well, that kiss was for when I'm going away." Miriam stopped as a lump in her throat cut off her speech. She waited a beat, then forced herself to continue. "I have to go back to work. I don't live here."

Taryn clenched her fist. "But I want you to stay." She looked up at Miriam, her soft brown eyes filling with tears. "Don't you want to stay with us? Daddy wants you to stay."

"I told you already, dear, I have to go back." Miriam stopped, then pulled Taryn against her, held her close.

Taryn wound her arms around Miriam in a tight hug. "But who is going to bring me to play school?" she cried, her voice muffled against Miriam's jacket.

"Your grandma will still be here. And your daddy."

Taryn sniffed loudly. "I want you to bring me."

Miriam pressed a kiss to Taryn's head, inhaling her smell. She felt a yearning toward her that she was sure had much to do with her own regrets, her own sorrow over lost opportunities.

She should have been mine, Miriam thought, closing her eyes. Remembering what Paula had written, she fought down a surge of anger, of hate over what her friend had done and the repercussions of it.

Once again she struggled to forgive her mother for taking her away, for blackmailing Jake.

Am I never going to be done with this? she prayed, rocking Taryn lightly, the hurt magnifying the more she thought of her mother, of her friend. *Dear Lord, must I go through this each time I think of them?* To forgive was difficult enough, but to forgive someone who wasn't even there seemed futile.

At the same time Miriam knew that if she was going to go back East stronger than when she arrived, this was precisely what she had to do. Forgive.

Please, Lord, help me to get through this. Help me to forgive them. I can't do any less, because I know how much You forgave me. Miriam finally realized what she was saying in her own prayer. She *had* been forgiven. The guilt she felt over past sins, her feelings of shame, had all been forgiven, thoroughly and completely. Yet she still struggled to give that same forgiveness to her mother and her best friend.

As Miriam rocked Taryn, she smiled. *Thank you, Lord, for Your love, for Your forgiveness. Please be with this little girl and help her to understand. Help her when I go, because I know she is attached to me.*

Miriam took a slow breath, and another, and then gently set Taryn away from her. "Let's go in the house and get washed up, okay?" she said quietly, wiping away a tear from Taryn's cheek with her thumb.

Taryn sniffed, nodded once and jumped off the picnic table. She stopped, her head cocked to one side. "Do you hear that?" she asked, turning back to the farm driveway. "I hear Daddy's tractor." She grinned back at Miriam and began running toward the driveway.

Moments later, Miriam realized it wasn't a tractor, and felt a surge of disappointment.

The vehicle slowed by the driveway and then turned in. It was a silver sports utility vehicle, its shiny finish coated with a thin layer of dust.

The license plates told her that it was a rented vehicle. Simon most like, she assumed as she glanced at her watch.

"Come back here, Taryn. Wait until he's turned off his truck," Miriam warned.

Taryn paused as the vehicle parked beside Miriam's. Then as it came to a stop, she jumped up and down, clapping her hands. "It's Uncle Simon!" she shrieked.

A tall man got slowly out, stopped beside the vehicle and stretched. He wore a leather jacket and blue jeans. His face was half covered with a pair of brown-tinted aviator glasses, and as he turned to look at Miriam, his mouth curved into a distinct smirk.

"Uncle Simon!" Taryn called out, running directly toward him.

"Hey, squirt," he said, bending over to grab the little girl. "How's my favorite niece? And you must be Miriam," he said, turning to Miriam. He slipped his glasses off his face and tucked them in the pocket of his coat. His smile grew broad and more sincere. He held out his hand. "Nice to meet you. I don't know if you remember me. I'm Simon."

"Yes," Miriam said quietly, returning his firm shake with an equally firm one. "I remember you. I'm sorry but I haven't had time to run out to the field and tell Jake you were coming. I thought he'd be back by now."

Simon nodded. "Oh, well. I'll just wait."

"Do you want some coffee or tea?" she asked.

Simon grinned again. "Tea. That's what we drink in this house, isn't it, Taryn." He bounced his niece once and set her down. He turned to Miriam. "So we'll have a cup of tea and then you can tell me all about what's happened in your life since the last time I saw you."

Miriam doubted that she would, so she just smiled and walked ahead of him into the house.

Jake pulled up the seed drill and glanced at the gathering clouds. Normally the thought of rain would have made him antsy, but he was done, praise the Lord.

He drove the tractor to the road and got out to secure the drill for transport. Just as he was walking back to the tractor, the first few spatters of rain hit.

He had tried not to think about Miriam while he worked. Had tried not to think of her leaving today. But he had spent most of the morning reliving what had happened yesterday. What could he have done different? How could he have convinced her to stay?

But she was adamant, and no matter what he had said, he couldn't break through the barriers she had erected. He knew she loved him. Was sure of it. She had said it herself. So why did he have the feeling he was even worse off than before?

She was holding something back from him.

So he sat in his tractor, mulling and praying and wondering if he was going crazy all at once or if it had been coming on for some time.

He reached up and turned on the radio, hoping to find something other than the usual heartbreak and honky-tonk. He settled on a classical station, which soothed him.

By the time he returned home, he felt as if his emotions were finally under control—until he pulled into his driveway and, with a lift of his heart, saw Miriam's car.

Right beside it was a rental vehicle. Probably a salesman, he thought, with a sigh of frustration. The last thing he wanted was to go over the merits of one kind of spray over another or what kind of baler he should buy. Not with Miriam still in his house and getting ready to leave.

Please give me strength to get through this, Jake prayed, leaning back against the tractor.

Then he noticed that Tilly's car was gone, and fear gripped him. There was probably a simple explanation, but he was afraid.

He looked over the yard that his father had built up all these years. Other than his time with his first father, Tom Steele, Jake had spent some of his happiest years here. *Please let everything be all right with my dad. I love him too much. I know I should let go, but I'm afraid to. I don't have the strength right now to lose another father.*

He leaned against the tractor another moment, knowing that whoever was in the house could wait. He needed to draw on the strength that only God could give him. He felt emotionally vulnerable and drained. His father was ill, and he was in love with a girl who he knew wouldn't be satisfied living here. Not after the life she had lived. He had been utterly foolish to even entertain that idea.

He turned to trudge across the yard. The rain was coming down in earnest now, so he started to run.

As he opened the porch door, the sound of a man's deep laugh greeted him. It sounded like Simon. Puzzled and apprehensive, he toed his boots off and set them aside, then walked into the kitchen.

A tall man sat with his back to Jake. Taryn sitting on the chair nearby, chattered away to him. She was looking a lot better. The man turned as Jake entered the kitchen.

"Daddy, Uncle is here," Taryn called out as soon as she saw her father.

"Simon." Jake felt surprise as his brother stood up to greet him. "What in the world are you doing here?"

Simon grabbed Jake in a most unmanly hug, then pulled away, his expression serious.

"I took a chance," he said slowly, watching Jake's face intently. "I talked to Miriam this morning, right after I got a call from Jonathon. You remember him? The Mountie?"

Jake nodded. Jonathon had been instrumental in bringing Simon and Jake together.

"You might want to sit a minute, and I'll tell you what I found out." Simon pulled out a chair and set it out for his brother. "It's about our mother."

Jake chanced a quick look at Miriam, who stood by the sink, watching him, her expression enigmatic. He looked away.

He didn't want to deal with this right now. He didn't want to think about a mother that he had never met, that he had no emotional attachment to.

Yet here he was, sitting at his own table, listening to what might be the final chapter in his brother's life-long quest.

"I found out our mother's name," Simon said quietly. He sat across from Jake, his hands folded on the table in front of him. "It's Joyce Smith."

Jake looked straight at him. "You're kidding."

Simon shook his head. "But I have an address..."

"So why don't you phone?"

"I don't want to do that. After all these years, I'd just as soon go up, see if it's true, and if it is—" he shrugged "—we'll take it from there. It's the closest we've come since I started looking."

And it had been a long search for his brother, thought Jake, remembering the number of homes Simon had run away from partly in the hope he would find his mother and partly to attain his independence. The whole point of the search was to reunite the family—Jake, Simon and their mother.

But Jake had found contentment and happiness with the Prins family, and could not be convinced the last time Simon had wanted to run away.

So Simon had left. It was only in the past half year that they had found each other again. But even now,

Jake wasn't sure he wanted to spend the time and energy that Simon did in what seemed like a fruitless search.

And his timing was atrocious.

"I can't go, Simon. Fred isn't feeling good. I've got Taryn to think of…" Jake's voice trailed off as he glanced at Miriam, unable to voice the rest of his thoughts. *I need to talk to Miriam before she leaves again.* "It's ridiculous."

"What's ridiculous about it, Jake?" Simon leaned closer. "What's so hard about wanting to finally meet your mother?"

"She's *not* my mother," Jake snapped, the tension of the past few days catching up on him. He pulled in a breath, praying again for patience and for the right words to explain to his brother. "We've never known her. She hasn't tried to contact us. She's not tried in any way to reconnect. She's out of our lives."

Even as he spoke the words, Jake thought of Miriam standing just a few feet away. Thought of her reasons for not keeping in touch, thought of the hard and difficult events of her life that had kept her away.

"I'm sorry, Simon," he added, dragging a hand over his face. "I'm tired. I've got a lot on my mind, and I just don't think I can do this right now. We don't even know if she'll be there when we get there."

"If we don't take this chance, we might lose her again, Jake." Simon leaned back in his chair, his arms crossed over his broad chest. "I'm going, whether you're coming with me or not. I just thought it would be better if we both went."

Jake understood the wisdom of that and understood Simon's unspoken request for help and support. Simon never wanted to admit when he needed help. You just had to know.

And Jake knew. Right now what Simon wanted, as much as to find their mother, was for Jake to come along with him.

"I'm sorry, Simon. I can't see my way around this."

"I can stay, if that's a problem," Miriam spoke up.

Jake swung around. "What do you mean? I thought you had to leave."

"I can put it off a few days."

Jake held her eyes with his, as if to delve into her mind. "Why would you do that?"

Miriam didn't answer, and instead turned to Simon. "Can you take Taryn for a short walk outside, please?"

Simon looked at her and then nodded.

"C'mon, squirt. You have to show me your yard."

Taryn jumped off her chair, eager to go out with her uncle.

They left, and Miriam sat at the table beside Jake.

"Where's Tilly?" Jake asked, unable to keep the brusque tone out of his voice. He disliked the vulnerable feeling she brought out in him, he disliked how he kept making himself vulnerable and she kept being evasive.

"She brought Fred into the hospital. They want to keep him in for observation. They put him on an IV because he was so dehydrated. They figure it's just a flu."

Jake felt relieved. "Now…what did you have to say that Taryn couldn't hear?"

Miriam looked down at her hands, pressed her slender fingers together. "I think you should go, Jake," she said quietly. "I think it's really important that you try to find your mother. That you and Simon do it together."

Jake caught a whiff of her perfume, watched how the

light of the window lit up her hair, placed hollows in her cheeks and the delicate bones of her shoulders. They were alone. How was he supposed to listen to her telling him to leave? How was he supposed to keep a clear head and have a sane discussion about a mother he never knew and hadn't thought much about in the past sixteen years?

How was he supposed to do that when the woman he had been thinking of all those years now sat across from him, so close and yet so distant? All he wanted to do was pull her into his arms and kiss her until she agreed to stay, until she agreed to become his wife.

But that's not what she wanted to talk about.

And he knew that was not how things were going to end for them.

He pulled his attention back to what she was saying. "Why do you want me to go?" he asked.

"Because..." Miriam bit her lip. "I guess it's because I ignored my own mother's needs so long. I got caught up in the things I wanted to do. I hated her so long for taking me away from you. I hated her because you got married. I still struggle with forgiving her." Miriam stopped, pressing her hand against her mouth and looked away.

Jake fought a manly battle to resist pulling her to him; he could tell she wasn't done.

"Yesterday after you left, I kept reading the Bible," she continued. Miriam lowered her hand into her lap, scratched at the polish on her nails. "I haven't lived the best life since I started modeling. That was my own choice. No one forced me into that. I spent a lot of time taking very good care of myself and making sure I had fun. What you read in the papers wasn't entirely true, but it wasn't too far off the mark when it came to my selfishness. I hardly visited my mother, hardly spent time with her. I thought she had to be punished for what she had done to me."

Miriam paused again.

"Your mother was a difficult woman," Jake reminded her. "It wasn't all your fault."

Miriam smiled. "Thanks for that. But I never realized what I had been holding back. My mother became a Christian in the hospital. The past few months of her life, when I was struggling with trying to keep my business afloat, I used to visit her more often. She was hard to visit with—she talked so slow. But she kept telling me that I had to lay my burdens on the Lord." Miriam laughed shortly, glancing up at Jake, then away. "It seemed too easy. I didn't think God could bail me out of my business troubles."

"What business troubles?" Jake was a little lost.

Miriam shook her head, and Jake could tell that she was hesitant to tell him.

"Please, Miriam. I won't judge you."

Miriam smiled a sad smile. "That doesn't matter. It's not important. What I wanted to tell you was that when my mother died, I still hadn't forgiven her." Miriam looked up at Jake, her eyes steady. "The other day, sitting under the maple tree in our old front yard, you showed me something. And I discovered a few things about myself. I found out that I had no right not to forgive my mother when God had forgiven me so much. I accepted that forgiveness last night."

"Oh, Miriam." Jake felt his heart overflow. If God had done that in her life, he thought, what else might lie in store for them?

"I know I'm not done," she continued. "I know I have a long way to go. But what I wish more than ever is that

I had spent more time with her. That I had taken the time to sit with her. To learn beside my mother's bed what I had to learn without her around." Miriam leaned closer, taking Jake's hand. "You have that chance. You have a chance to meet your mother, to find out why she gave you up. I'm sure you must wonder, just as I wondered why my mother did what she did to me. I still don't think it was right, but I've had to accept that she did it because, in her own way, she cared."

Jake wanted to deny what she was saying. What her mother had done was selfish. Her threats had been cruel and frightening to a young boy who was so unsure of his own place in the family he had been placed in. But he knew he had to deal with this on his own.

Had things turned out differently between him and Miriam, he might have an easier time dealing with it. But Miriam sat across from him now, urging him to leave, urging him to pursue a different part of his life even though he was sure she knew there was something building between them.

What do I do, Lord? he prayed, his head bent. He clutched Miriam's delicate hand in his own and lifted it to his face, holding it against his rough cheek. *What do You want me to do?*

He felt her fingers curl against his cheek and he turned, pressing a kiss to its soft palm, breathing out in a sigh. Then he let go of her hand and got up.

"I'll stay and help Tilly and be here for her," Miriam said. "I know you're finished seeding. You shouldn't miss out on this chance. I don't think you should do this with a phone call—I think you need to do this face-to-face."

Jake stood facing her, his hands in his pockets. "Why do you want to do this for me?" he asked, still struggling to understand why she seemed so adamant. "I thought you had to go today."

"Don't worry about my life, Jake," she said. "It's not worth the effort." She looked up at him. "But you have a chance to meet your mother. To ask her important questions. Maybe it's a way of my own mother's death making sense…if someone besides me can learn something from it."

Jake understood her need. But it didn't seem to fit with what he wanted to do. He prayed they would find a time and place where they could finally speak the truth to each other. "Okay," he said quietly. "I'll go. As long as you will be here when I come back."

"I will." She relaxed back in her chair.

"I'm pretty sure we won't be gone long. Probably two days at the most." This was not the conversation he had had in mind. He didn't quite know what he had expected. But for now, knowing she would be here when he returned was enough to cling to.

"Good" was all Miriam said. She got up, and for a heart-stopping moment Jake thought she was going to come up to him, wrap those slender arms around him, pull his head down to hers…

He forced the thought aside as she walked past him to the porch. "Where are you going?" he asked, his voice brusque with repressed emotions.

Miriam turned to him, her eyes hopeful. "I'm just going to get—"

"Taryn wants a drink." Simon's loud voice interrupted. He knocked on the open screen door. "Can we come in now?"

Miriam looked away. "Sure. We're done."

"Good." The door creaked as Simon pulled it open,

and Taryn was chattering about the calves as she came in. She bounced into the kitchen and ran straight to her father. "I need a drink, Daddy."

"What do you say?" Jake and Miriam spoke at precisely the same time. Their eyes caught and held, and Jake could see Miriam blush.

"Sorry," she murmured.

"Please can I have a drink," Taryn said with studied impatience. "Then I want to go outside again."

"I'll go with you, Taryn," Miriam offered. "I have to clean up the picnic stuff anyhow."

"Okeydokey," Taryn said, then noisily gulped down a cup of juice that Jake had poured for her. She wiped her mouth and ran outside again.

Jake watched them leave, feeling as if an opportunity had passed.

"So," Simon asked, leaning against the kitchen counter. "I'm leaving in about fifteen minutes. Are you coming?"

Jake glanced out the window at Taryn and Miriam, who were cleaning up around the fire pit. He could see Taryn was excited, and once again he was struck with a sense that this was how it should be. A family—

"Jake," Simon called out with a laugh. "I'm over here, not out there."

"Sorry." Jake averted his gaze and took a deep breath. "I've decided to come with you," he said.

Simon was quiet for a moment, as if acknowledging the difficulty of the decision. "I know this is a hard time for you to leave. But I'm scared if we wait any longer, we'll miss her. I am really praying that it will work out in the end."

"So am I," said Jake fervently, thinking not only of Fred and Tilly, but of Miriam, as well. "So am I."

* * *

"I'm glad Jake stopped by the hospital on his way out," Tilly said as she sat back in her recliner in the living room. "Otherwise I wouldn't have known anything about him going."

"How do you feel about this?" Miriam asked, curling up in one corner of the couch.

Tilly shrugged as she picked up a magazine. "I think it's a good idea. Jake has never said much about his biological mother but I know, since he had Taryn he's been curious. I know he's wondered what would make a woman give up two boys like she did. I imagine she must have been in quite a difficult position to do that."

"I pray he finds her," Miriam said simply.

"I'm glad you could stay awhile longer," Tilly said. "Otherwise Jake couldn't have gone at all. This won't make your trip back too rushed?"

Miriam shrugged the comment away. Each minute she stayed here added driving time to the trip. It would be tense, but if Jake came back when he said he would, she could make it by driving and sleeping in her car. "I'll be okay."

"And when you do go back, we are going to hear from you again, aren't we? I don't want you to feel you're all alone."

"I'm not, Tilly. I know how wrong I was to stay out of touch…" Her voice trailed off as she thought of what she had deprived herself of—Fred and Tilly and the love they had for her.

"I care for you, girl, and I sense that you are up-tight about this job you have to do. Do you want to talk about it?"

Miriam gently shook her head. "I can't. But I want

you to know that I'm not going back because I want to. I have…obligations."

"Well, I want you to remember that you can always talk to the Lord." Tilly leaned over and pulled out her Bible. She leafed through it and glanced up at Miriam. "This is a piece I like to read when I worry about the future." She adjusted her glasses and began to read from Psalm 71. "'In you, O Lord, I have taken refuge; let me never be put to shame. Rescue me and deliver me in your righteousness; turn your ear to me and save me. Be my rock of refuge, to which I can always go: give the command to save me, for you are my rock and my fortress.'"

Miriam listened to Tilly's soft voice, letting the words comfort her. Then Tilly read, "'Though you have made me see troubles, many and bitter, you will restore my life again; from the depths of the earth you will again bring me up. You will increase my honor and comfort me once again.'"

"Can you read that again?" Miriam asked, sitting up.

As she did, Miriam took a deep breath, as if to draw the very essence of the words into her. It was a promise. Did she dare cling to it? Did she dare think it would be true for her?

Tilly read on and Miriam listened, feeling strengthened and nurtured. Nothing had changed, but she felt as if she had been given a port in the storm. Somehow she had to trust.

Chapter Thirteen

"Let's stop here." Simon slowed down by the restaurant just off the main road going through town, then turned in and parked in an empty spot right beside the building. He turned off the engine and laid his head back. Neither he nor Jake said anything. They were tired and disheartened.

Jake was the first to get out. He wanted to stretch his legs. They'd spent the past two days driving, put on over a thousand miles and talked to a dozen people. Knowing they still had another two hours ahead of them before they were home made him feel exhausted. He hadn't seen this much of Alberta since he and Simon were getting shuffled around the foster care system.

"Well, that was a bust," Simon said, getting out of his side of the vehicle. "I'm sorry, Jake. I guess we should have quit at Riverview when we didn't find her, but I thought we were so close…" He let the sentence drift off.

"It's not your fault," Jake said, as they walked past the huge windows to the entrance. "Besides—" he said as he pulled the double door open "—it was a chance to spend some time together."

"A lot of time," Simon said drily, as they stepped into the restaurant.

"Are you going to stay the night when we get to the farm?" Jake asked, settling into a chair behind a table. He didn't even bother consulting the menu tucked between the sugar container and the napkin holder. He just wanted a cup of coffee and a muffin.

"Probably. If that's okay with Tilly."

"It'll be fine, and you know it."

"Will it be fine with Miriam?" Simon asked with a knowing smirk.

Jake ignored him. He didn't want to talk about Miriam with Simon. He didn't dare spend too much time even thinking about her.

"I remember a little pep talk you gave me one time," Simon continued, clasping his hands and resting them on the table, leaning forward. "I remember your telling me not to underestimate what I had to offer Caitlin. I wonder if it isn't my turn."

"What do you mean?"

"Look, I know as the big brother you're supposed to be the one who has his act together, and for most of your life, you have." Simon sat back as the waitress stopped at their table with a pot of coffee. After she'd filled their mugs and left to place their order, Simon poured sugar in his coffee and began to stir. "You've always been the one who knows where he's going."

"And your point is?"

"You don't want Miriam to go."

"I don't," Jake agreed, blowing lightly on the steam of his coffee. "I don't want her to go, but she has to. Or so she keeps saying."

"Have you asked her why?"

"I've tried to, but she puts me off, like she doesn't want to tell me." Jake shrugged and took a careful sip of the coffee. "She's hiding something, but I can't get it out of her."

"You kissed her yet?"

Jake tried not to, but could feel his neck grow warm. "Yes."

"Oh, goodness, my ever cool brother is looking a little sheepish." Simon grinned. "And?"

"And I can't believe I'm having this conversation with you, Simon. You sound like a teenager."

Simon laughed. "Caitlin always says I never really experienced childhood—that's why I won't grow up. So? Spill."

Jake sighed, knowing his brother wasn't going to quit. "I love her, Simon. Okay? I heard you say those words about Caitlin, and I remember feeling smug that I got you to admit it. So now I'm saying the same thing. I love her." He rubbed his eyebrow with his index finger and shrugged.

"And…"

"And nothing. She's lived a glamorous life, she's used to flying all over the world and making money. You saw that fancy little car of hers. Can you imagine her living in Fred and Tilly's house, getting by on a farmer's income, shopping in a little Podunk town like Derwin?"

Simon frowned as if contemplating. "You know what, Jake? I can."

Jake snorted. "You've only seen her for an hour. How in the world can you make that kind of assessment?"

Simon sat back with a self-satisfied grin. "Because I've seen the way she looks at you, big brother. That's why."

Jake heard what Simon said, his heart quickening. He thought of what Miriam had said just before he left, when she was trying to talk him into going to find his mother. How she had accepted what God had done for her. Why would she tell him that?

He clutched his coffee cup, hardly daring to imagine that it could be.

"I guess you've got things to talk to little Miriam about when you get home," Simon continued.

"I don't have much left to ask her. I've already proposed."

"Then propose again. And again. Until she accepts."

Jake heard Simon, and wondered. Simon had always been the stubborn one. Maybe his approach was better.

The waitress came with their muffins, and Jake, feeling suddenly benevolent, smiled his thanks. She paused, her brown eyes holding his, then smiled carefully back.

She set the muffins down in front of them before leaving.

"So now what do we do?" Jake asked Simon.

Simon shrugged, tapping the side of his mug with his finger. "I don't know. I could ask Jonathon, Caitlin's brother-in-law, to help. He could contact some of his fellow officers—they might find out something for us. I wouldn't know where to start looking for someone whose name is J. Smith." Simon sighed, and Jake knew how disappointed he was. He had thought they were so close. Looking back, it would probably have been wiser to phone ahead, but Simon had been so sure she would still be there.

"Well, one good thing came out of it all," Simon said with a weary smile. "We found out we have a sister. Cory Smith."

Jake returned Simon's smile. "That was a bittersweet discovery," he said. "I wonder if she's full or half."

"Does it matter?" Simon asked quickly.

Jake shook his head. "Not a bit. But it does make not finding Mom a little harder to take."

They were quiet a moment, each lost in his own thoughts. "I want to thank you for coming, Jake," Simon said quietly. "It meant a lot to me."

Jake merely nodded his acknowledgment. All the way to Riverview, he had doubted and wondered if he had done the right thing by going on this quixotic mission. But seeing the gratitude on his brother's face, and being there to find out for themselves from an old neighbor lady that they had a sister, balanced out the frustration. Somewhat.

"More coffee, sirs?" The waitress stopped by their table, holding a coffeepot in one hand.

Simon looked up and winked at her. "No, thanks, sweetie. We got a long ride ahead."

"Well, have a safe trip."

Jake felt Simon kick him under the table, and he looked up, frowning. Their waitress was looking directly at him, smiling. "Come again," she said, laying the bill on the table.

She had a throaty voice, compelling in its own way. Her cheerful smile seemed to light up a face dominated by deep brown eyes fringed with thick lashes. Her long hair, held back with a barrette, was a sandy shade of brown, curling down her back. Pretty, strikingly so.

Once she would have made him take a second look, but now she did nothing for him.

Jake returned the smile, careful not to look too welcoming. "We will," he said with false cheerfulness.

They walked out of the restaurant and into the warmth of the day, both anxious to get on their way.

The trip back to Waylen was quiet. Jake and Simon

were each lost in their thoughts. The closer they got to home, the more uptight Jake got. In spite of his brother's assurances about Miriam, Jake knew that there was a lot that couldn't just be willed away. She had other obligations and was used to a lifestyle he couldn't begin to understand. And she had a secret she wasn't telling him.

As they pulled into the driveway, Jake sat straighter, looking for Miriam's car. He felt a clench of disappointment when he saw an empty spot where it had been two days ago.

"Looks like we're too late. Again," Simon said quietly.

"She might just be back at her house," Jake said, getting out of the vehicle. He almost ran to the house, anxious to find out where Miriam was.

Tilly was sitting in her usual chair in the living room, when Jake burst into the room.

"Well, hello, Jake," she said, setting aside the book she was reading. "So you're home. And right on time like you said." She got up, carefully watching his face, probably to see if she could find any hint of what had happened. "So how did it go? You didn't say much when you phoned to tell me when you were going to be home."

"We didn't find her."

"Oh, Jake." Tilly reached out for him and drew him into her arms. For a moment Jake allowed himself the comfort, feeling a little guilty that his mind was on other things—on Miriam, rather than on the disappointment of not seeing his biological mother.

Tilly pulled back, shaking her head. "That is too bad. Did you find out anything?"

"We found out we have a sister." Jake smiled at his mother and shook his head, still unable to absorb that piece of news.

"My goodness. That's interesting." Tilly clucked in sympathy.

"How's Dad?"

"He's much better. He's coming home tomorrow. It was just a flu he couldn't get over."

Tilly was about to ask something else, but after finding out that his father was going to be okay, Jake was done with amenities.

"Where's Miriam?"

Tilly pressed her hand to her cheek and sighed. "She's gone to her house. She got a phone call from some man named Carl. He called a couple of times. Once she knew when you were coming, she made arrangements. She's only been gone a couple of minutes. I was supposed to give you a message. It's on the kitchen table."

Jake felt his heart plunge into his stomach. A goodbye note, he thought. This time it was her turn. She had said she'd wait until he came back. Leaving just minutes before his return was cowardice. Miriam was avoiding him. And he was tired of it.

He ran into the kitchen, almost knocking over his brother in the process.

"What's up, Jake?"

"I don't know."

Jake bit his lip, almost swaying with weariness. If only he and Simon hadn't stopped in that restaurant. If only they had driven straight through. If only he hadn't gone with Simon in the first place.

If, if, if.

It seemed his entire life was punctuated with those words.

But he was tired of ifs. He wanted answers, and this time he wasn't going to let her go without his finding them.

"Simon, I want you to take my truck and park it on the road. Miriam has to come by here on her way out. I don't want her going."

"Sure thing." Simon threw him a mock salute and jogged out the door.

Jake felt a measure of relief when he heard his truck start up. First line of defense in place, he thought. He turned to his mother, who handed him the folded note. "Did she say anything to you? Give you any hint why she decided to leave all of a sudden?"

Tilly nodded, a sad smile curving her mouth. "Not really. Miriam had gone for a walk, and this Carl fellow phoned. He asked where Miriam was. I told him she was outside. Then he got angry and said something about her risking this job. I asked him to explain." Tilly looked up at him, touching his shoulder lightly. "Jake, she risked losing an important job just to stay here. To help us out. Now she has to drive day and night to get there on time." Tilly shook her head. "Jake, it's a six-day drive to New York, and she has only four days to get there. It's too dangerous. Don't let her go."

Jake heard his mother's words, trying to understand, realizing that Miriam had made a huge sacrifice so he could try to find his mother. He also realized that she wasn't going to leave until she gave him the reason why.

Jake's chest lifted in a sigh. "I'm going to her house."

Tilly gave him a hug. "I'll be praying for you both, son," she said, sniffing lightly.

Jake drew back, looked down at her softly wrinkled face, her bright blue eyes that shone with tears.

Son. He hadn't found his biological mother, but he had found a mother in Tilly.

Now all he had to do was find the other woman in his life.

He ran out to his truck. Simon was leaning against it, arms crossed, looking like a modern-day highwayman. "So far so good, brother," he said, as Jake came running up to him. "Don't come back without her," Simon warned.

"I won't." He jumped in, gunned the engine, spun around and headed down the road.

Miriam dropped the last of her clothes into the suitcase and zipped it shut. She couldn't help a quick glance at her watch, fear gripping her. Could she make it? Had she cut things too close? She pressed her hand against her stomach. "Please, Lord," she prayed. "Give me strength. Let me get back safely."

It was going to be long hard driving. She would have to grab some sleep when possible.

She drew in another breath, wishing she had the nerve to stay and talk to Jake. But if she had, she might not have left. If she didn't do this job and the next and the next, her debt would keep building.

She had no choice.

Miriam thought of what Tilly had read to her while Jake was gone.

She walked out of the house and, without a second glance behind her, closed the door. The moon was out, and in its watery light she could see the maple tree. She set her suitcase down and walked over to it, touched it. While it wasn't difficult to say goodbye to the house, it was going to be hard to leave this tree. For it was here that she had first felt the healing power of forgiveness.

God's forgiveness.

She wondered if Jake could eventually forgive her.

She knew it was a cheap move, to write him a note. It couldn't begin to cover what she felt. She didn't even know what she dared tell him. It was as if she were sixteen all over again, head over heels in love with Jake and unsure of herself.

A cool spring breeze danced around her, and she shivered a moment, thinking of the dear people she would be leaving behind here. She leaned against the tree, sending out prayers. She prayed Fred's health would improve. She prayed Tilly would be able to cope with it, knowing the deep love they had for each other. She prayed Taryn would get over her leaving. When Miriam had kissed the precious child good-night and told her she was leaving, Taryn had clung to her, crying and begging her to stay.

Dear Lord, please take care of them all. Thank You for letting me come back for a while, for being able to be a part of their family. I love them all so much.

And then she thought of Jake. She didn't know how she could leave him again.

But she knew she had no choice.

I love him, Lord. I don't think I ever stopped loving him. Please take care of him. Please—

She heard the sound of a truck engine, saw the lights sweep across the field as it turned into the driveway, then bob and weave as the vehicle came tearing down the lane, spewing gravel behind.

She straightened, then felt her mouth go dry as she

recognized the truck that rocked to a halt, inches away from the back bumper of her car.

Her suitcase fell to the ground, her numb fingers unable to hold it, as Jake Steele flung the door of his truck open and strode toward her.

"Why are you going?" he demanded.

Miriam swallowed and took a step back. He was angry. She hadn't expected that.

She wanted to deflect his anger. "Did you find your mother?"

"No. And I don't want to talk about my mother. Right now, it's more important to me to find out why you keep saying you have to go without telling me exactly why. I know modeling isn't that important to you, Miriam. You said you came here to finish things off. Your farm isn't sold, and I know that you still love me. I would say there are a few unfinished things to go yet."

Miriam leaned back against the tree, watching him in the pale moonlight, unable to speak.

"Miriam…" He paused and took a step closer. "I asked you once before, and I'm going to ask you again. I love you dearly. I love you more than I've ever loved anyone. Will you marry me?"

His words laid aside all the defenses she thought she had built against him. Flimsy barriers, indeed. And for a bright moment she felt as if nothing was insurmountable.

"I told you I want to marry you," he continued, his deep voice softly caressing. "I want to take care of you. I want you to trust me. I want your problems to be my problems. I want you for better or worse, richer or poor—"

"You don't know what you're taking on," Miriam

said with a shaky cry. Once again the burden of her debt pulled her down to earth, took away her hope.

"Then tell me. Tell me what I'm taking on."

Miriam looked at him, heard the pain in his voice. He loved her. She knew that as surely as she knew of God's love. As if from another part of her mind the words of the psalm Tilly read to her came into her thoughts. "You will restore my life again; from the depths of the earth, you will bring me up." Could these words be true for her? Could she and Jake find a way around this? Would his love withstand it? There was only one way to find out.

"I'm in debt for a hundred and twenty grand." The figure, spoken aloud, sounded even larger, even more insurmountable.

Jake's silence said more than any words he could have spoken. She wanted to curl up into a ball of misery; she wanted to let her sorrow overwhelm her. But she would have to wait until he was gone.

She pressed her fingers against her mouth as if to hold back her cries until then. Her eyes were firmly shut. She had watched him leave once, she couldn't do it again.

Then warm, hard hands gently pulled her fingers away. She felt his soft, inviting lips on hers. Slowly, gently, Jake pulled her into his arms, one hand curling around her neck, the other clutching her waist.

Miriam felt a melting begin deep within her, a softening. She slipped her arms around him, her eyes still shut tight, as if she were afraid to open them to reality.

Jake's mouth moved slowly, gently over hers, and then, as her arms tightened, with more urgency.

Miriam felt the warmth of his mouth, hard on hers,

his arms holding her tightly against his chest. She kissed him back, unable to hold him close enough, unable to show him adequately what she was feeling.

He murmured her name against her mouth and kissed her over and over again, his hands caressing her back, her head, his fingers tangling in her hair.

Finally he drew away, but only to cradle her head against his, to hold her close to his pounding heart.

Miriam tried to absorb the onslaught of her own emotions as she leaned against his strength, her cheek pressed against his shirt, her arms holding him, his chin caressing her head again and again.

"Don't go, Miriam," he pleaded. "Please don't leave me again. I don't think I can go through this a second time." She felt his chest lift in a huge, shuddering sigh. "I don't care about the money, about your debt. We can figure this out. It's not too much to pay for having you with me. Nothing is."

Miriam closed her eyes, resting in this momentary haven, letting his words pull her along, beguile and captivate her. She had to trust him, had to believe him. Because if she didn't, what in life was there for her?

She lifted her face to look at him, and in the light of his truck's headlights she saw tears on his cheeks. With a trembling finger she touched them, awestruck at the sight, at the evidence of the depth of his feelings for her.

As she traced the path of his tears, she whispered his name, her own throat thickened with emotion. "I love you, too, Jake." She stopped, her voice breaking. Then the words came pouring out of her. "I don't think I ever stopped. I've never stopped thinking of you, wondering how you were, not daring to call because then I would hear your voice and start missing you all over again."

She took a quavering breath. "It hurt so much to miss you. I didn't think I could go on. And now, to know that you still love me in spite of...in spite of everything..." She couldn't continue. Laying her head against his chest, she fought for control.

"Miriam, I have prayed to hear you say that." He laid his damp cheek on her head. "Say it again," he whispered.

"I love you." The words were muffled, but strong. Then she looked up at him again, her hands cradling his beloved face. "I love you, Jake Steele. And I want to marry you more than anything."

He lifted his head and feathered a light kiss over her mouth, his gaze full of wonder, his fingers caressing her neck. "Oh, Miriam, I hardly dared hope. God has been so good."

Miriam reached up to touch his hair, her fingers reveling in its thickness. "You might not think so once you talk to your banker."

He shook his head. "I don't want to hear about that."

"But it's so much money," she couldn't help but say. "You couldn't afford to buy my land. How—?"

The rest of her words were cut off by his mouth covering hers. When he finally pulled away, he touched her lips with his finger. "I said I don't want to hear about it."

She let her head drop against his chest as he lowered his hand. "I love you so much," she whispered. "I know we can get through this."

"Because we're doing it together, that makes it much easier."

As Miriam leaned against his chest, she let her prayer of thankfulness drift up to heaven. She had come here to rest, to recoup—and to leave.

But God had had other things in mind for her.

And she was grateful.

"Let's go home, Miriam," Jake murmured, giving her another tight hug. "There are a few people who want to know what's happening."

She caught him by the arm. "Jake," she said quietly. "I don't want to do the job, but it will pay me a lot of money. And if I don't do it, I stand to lose other jobs."

"So we'll buy you a plane ticket. That still gives you a couple of days here."

Miriam felt as if a huge weight had fallen off her shoulders. "It might work out."

Jake gave her a little shake. "You're not alone, Miriam. Not anymore."

He bent over to take her suitcase, and then, his arm around her, hers wrapped around him, as if they were afraid to let each other go, they walked to his truck. Jake tossed her suitcase in the back and helped her in, then pulled her against him as, one-handed, he spun the steering wheel around, and headed home.

Then he took off down the driveway, barely slowing for the turn off onto the road, and then taking off. He pulled to a halt at his own place, held her close a moment.

"I love you. I love you," he whispered, kissing her once again.

"I'm nervous, you know," she confessed.

"About what?"

"Taryn, Tilly. Will I be able to do it?"

"You know, Miriam, I think, deep down, you're not a model. I think you're a mother at heart."

His words comforted her, and together they walked up the sidewalk. Together they stepped into the house.

Taryn looked up from the kitchen table, blinked, then grinned as she saw Jake and Miriam.

"Daddy, Miriam," she yelled, running and throwing herself at both of them. Jake caught her, Miriam caught an arm, and the three of them held each other as Miriam's tears flowed freely.

"Let me guess—you talked her into staying," Simon drawled, turning around in his chair. He got up, shook Jake's hand and gave Miriam an awkward hug. Taryn got in the way, squealing with delight.

Tilly came into the kitchen to see what the commotion was about, and smiled broadly. "My goodness," she said, pressing a hand to her mouth. She, too, joined in the celebration.

They explained to Taryn what was to happen, and the child immediately began hugging and kissing Jake and Miriam indiscriminately.

Later, when Taryn was finally settled into bed, and Simon and Tilly had gone to bed, Miriam and Jake had some time to themselves again. They sat on the couch, Jake's arms firmly around Miriam as if he didn't dare let her go.

Miriam traced circles on the soft hair of his forearm, bemused at the difference ten years had made in this man she loved so dearly. "Jake," she asked quietly.

"Miriam," he replied, his voice teasing.

"I am serious." She hesitated, but she needed one more reassurance. "I need to know, Jake—are you sure you know what you're getting into?"

Jake sighed, his breath gentle across her head. "Miriam, I'm not worried. It's only money."

"But it's so much."

"It is. I won't deny it. But if you sold that land to

someone else I would have lost it, anyway. I've been thinking I could sell one of the other quarters of land, by Rock Lake. Then I'd buy yours from you." He laid his cheek on her head. "The rest of the debt we'll have to work into the farm debt." He hugged her again. "I told you already, I'll do anything to have you stay with me."

Miriam bit back her next protest, and relaxed against Jake, reveling in his strength, in the ability to lean on someone for the first time in years. It still felt strange—wrong almost—yet liberating to put all her fears and worries into someone else's hands.

Jake nuzzled her head. "Have I told you I love you?"

"Not for about two minutes." Miriam turned her face up to him, and Jake kissed her.

"I used to dream of sitting with you on this couch," Jake said softly, tracing the line of her eyebrow, the curve of her cheek, the line of her lips.

"I did, too. I used to dream we could walk down Main Street holding hands, just like all the other lovers do."

"Well, it's taken a few years, but we can."

Then on that same couch, Miriam kissed her future husband.

And sent up a prayer of thanks. Their lives had taken some twists and turns to arrive at this destination, but they were finally here.

Together, at last.

Epilogue

"Now stay close to me, it's really busy here," Jake said to Taryn as they made their way through the throng of people in the airport. She clung to his hand.

Jake had wanted to carry her, but according to her a big girl didn't need to be carried.

From speakers overhead a voice announced the arrival of yet another flight as Jake worked his way to the arrival gate.

People wearing trench coats and suits vied with individuals in blue jeans, sweat suits and leather jackets for a spot close to the gate where the passengers from flight number 264 direct from New York were to arrive.

"Is she coming yet?" Taryn asked, clutching the bouquet of flowers Jake had picked up before coming here. "I don't want the flowers to die."

"They won't," Jake assured his daughter. "They'll still be fresh and pretty when you give them to her."

Taryn looked up at him, smiling widely. "When I get big, I want to fly on a plane, just like Mims gets to."

"That would be fun, wouldn't it?"

Taryn nodded, then buried her nose in the flowers, taking a deep sniff.

A burst of noise came from the arrival doors and Jake looked up, his expectations making his heart skip. She was coming. After a two-week absence, Miriam was coming home.

The doors swung open again and there, behind a group of laughing young kids, he saw her.

She wore a loose apricot-colored crop top over cargo pants. Casual clothing, yet Miriam managed to lend an aura of elegance and style to the simple lines.

Her hair shone under the bright lights, wisps of it accenting her face, her eyes, scanning the crowd as eagerly as Jake watched her.

She hadn't seen him yet, he realized as she paused, frowning lightly, clutching the large, oversize bag she always carried with her as hand luggage.

He noticed a few men glance her way, then stop, their faces showing their obvious admiration. One man elbowed his neighbor who looked her way, then also stared.

For a moment Jake resented their gaping, but Miriam was unaware of the minor sensation she was causing.

She stood up on tiptoe, scanning the crowd, frowning.

Then, the frown melted, her eyes widened and she began to run.

"Jake," she called out, totally unselfconscious about her reaction.

Jake's heart quickened at the sight of her rushing toward him, her arms wide, laughing.

"You're here," she said.

He let go of Taryn's hand for an instant and caught her as Miriam flung her arms around him. He swung her up, holding her close, his head buried against her soft neck.

"Oh, Miriam," he murmured, "I missed you, I missed you."

They held each other a moment, yet unable to hold each other close enough, hard enough.

He pulled back and gently lowered her to the ground. They gazed lovingly at each other, then he lowered his head and with reverence kissed her mouth.

"How are you?" he asked, drawing slightly back, as he noted each dear feature, as if looking for any changes in her.

"Better. Now." She reached up and stroked his hair back from his face. "Much better." Then, she turned to Taryn.

"Hi, sweetheart." She dropped to one knee and hugged her tightly. "I missed you, little Pip."

"I missed you, too, Mims." Taryn held out the flowers. "We got these for you."

Miriam took the flowers, sniffed them appreciatively and grinned at Taryn. "They're beautiful. We'll have to put them in water when we get home, won't we?"

Taryn nodded, then took Miriam's hand. "Daddy can take your bag," she said imperiously.

"Yes, ma'am." Jake saluted, bent over and slung the bag over his shoulder. As he straightened he noticed a few puzzled glances from the men who had been ogling Miriam, as if they were wondering how some guy in blue jeans and a twill shirt managed to snag this exotic-looking woman.

"What's the matter, Jake?" Miriam asked, as she stood, holding Taryn's hand, her flowers clutched in the other.

"I'm still trying to get used to having all these guys staring at my wife."

Miriam frowned, then looked back over her shoulder in the direction Jake was glowering. "What guys?" she asked.

The men who had been looking, quickly averted their curious gaze.

"Oh, those guys," Miriam said, glancing back at Jake with a shrug. "It doesn't mean anything."

"Maybe not. But I don't like it."

Miriam leaned against him, smiling coyly up at him. "But I'm not looking, am I?"

"I hope not."

Miriam's expression grew serious. "Jake, I would love nothing more than to stay here every day. To be wearing dirty blue jeans and a shirt smeared with flour. You know that."

Jake grinned down at her, his heart overflowing with love for the beautiful woman. "I know that. And only two more jobs and you'll be done."

Miriam sighed and nodded her head in affirmation. "Hallelujah. Goodbye to jet lag, to tight clothes, cranky photographers and temperamental clients."

"We did it, you know," he said as he slipped his arm around her. They began walking toward the exit. "It's just about done, that insurmountable debt you couldn't tell me about."

"Well, I'm really glad Simon was the one who bought the land. That way I can say I still own my old house," Miriam said, smiling lightly.

"Maybe someday we'll be able to buy it back, but for now I'm happy enough to rent it from him."

The automatic doors slid open at their approach, and Jake had to stop Taryn from wanting to go through them again.

"Miriam wants to go home," he said to her as they walked across the taxi lane toward the parking garage.

Taryn skipped beside them, still holding Miriam's hand. "I have a friend in grade one," she announced to Miriam. "She has a mommy and a daddy, too." Taryn looked up at Miriam, a slight frown creasing her forehead. "But she doesn't call her mommy, Mims. You and Daddy said I didn't have to call you Mommy, but can I? Please?"

"Oh, sweetheart." Miriam stopped, and bending over, pulled Taryn into her arms. "Of course you can."

Jake watched the two of them, both beautiful, both so very precious to him and felt a fullness wash over him at what Taryn had just asked.

Thank you, Lord, he prayed. *Thank you for my wife, my daughter. My family.*

Miriam stood and as she turned to Jake, he saw her wipe her eyes. She bit her lip and glanced up at him. "Does it get any better than this?" she asked, reaching out to him, as well.

"I doubt it," he said, pulling her close. He caught Taryn in a hug, lifted her up and, with one arm, held her, as well.

He and Miriam exchanged another quick kiss and then, arm in arm, they walked down the ramp toward Jake's truck.

A father. A daughter. A mother.

* * * * *

Dear Reader,

When he was young, Jake Steele felt he had nothing to give Miriam Spencer because he was just a foster child. But because of the love of his foster parents, his life is different when Miriam comes back into it. I wanted to show, in this book, how vulnerable foster children can feel, even in a secure home. I also wanted to show that for some children, there is indeed a happy ending. I know, we have seen it in our extended family and in other foster families.

Foster parents give much to their kids, and in many long-term situations end up adopting them or making them a permanent part of their family in other ways. The foster child/parent bond can be as strong as the natural one.

I thank the Lord for the many people who open their homes to children who are not their own, and I pray they may receive the strength they need to do their work.

Carolyne Aarsen

We hope you enjoyed reading
this special collection.

If you liked reading these stories,
then you will love **Love Inspired**® books!

You believe hearts can heal. **Love Inspired**
stories show that faith, forgiveness and hope
have the power to lift spirits and change
lives—always.

Enjoy six new stories from
Love Inspired every month!

Available wherever books and
ebooks are sold.

Love Inspired

**Uplifting romances of faith,
forgiveness and hope.**

Get 2 Free Books,
Plus 2 Free Gifts—
just for trying the Reader Service!

LI17R2

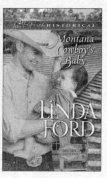

Love Inspired®

Inspirational Romance to Warm Your Heart and Soul

Join our social communities to connect with other readers who share your love!

Sign up for the Love Inspired newsletter at **www.LoveInspired.com** to be the first to find out about upcoming titles, special promotions and exclusive content.

CONNECT WITH US AT:

Harlequin.com/Community

 Facebook.com/LoveInspiredBooks

 Twitter.com/LoveInspiredBks

LISOCIAL2017

LOVE
Harlequin
romance?

Join our Harlequin community to share your thoughts and connect with other romance readers!

Be the first to find out about promotions, news, and exclusive content!

Sign up for the Harlequin e-newsletter and download a free book from any series at **www.TryHarlequin.com**

CONNECT WITH US AT:

Harlequin.com/Community

 Facebook.com/HarlequinBooks

 Twitter.com/HarlequinBooks

 Instagram.com/HarlequinBooks

 Pinterest.com/HarlequinBooks

ReaderService.com

**ROMANCE WHEN
YOU NEED IT**